The Avatar of Calderia

Book One: Awakenings

by

David M. Echeandia

ISBN 978-0-9895962-1-3

Author's Note

I want to welcome you to the first book of my epic fantasy trilogy, a tale of intrepid heroes and nefarious villains, mighty wizards and Dark sorcerers, mythical races and magical creatures, noble honor and despicable treachery, passionate love and sadistic lust, thundering armies and raging dragons—and, of course, a desperate quest that spans a continent to solve an ancient riddle, locate a mysterious talisman, and follow its path to find salvation before all is lost and evil prevails.

If these themes sound rather familiar, that's because I fully intended them to be so. After many years of reading the works of other writers, this trilogy is my personal homage to classic fantasy, my way of giving back.

I was inspired in this endeavor by another author, who introduced her first book by saying that she was a voracious fantasy reader who had grown weary of haunting the bookstores, waiting for the next sequel to be published, and so finally decided to write her own book—the kind of story that she would most like to read. I never forgot what she said. Like her, I have always hungered for more stories in my favorite genre. And, like her, I decided that, should I ever put pen to paper (or fingers to keyboard) myself, it would be to write the kind of book I most enjoy reading. So, here it is, a story fashioned with all my beloved, time-honored characters, themes and elements. If you enjoy classic fantasy, I invite you to come along on this great adventure with me.

Visit the author at:
www.avatarofcalderia.com
www.facebook.com/AvatarOfCalderia

Cover art design by Gary Val Tenuta GVTgrafix@aol.com
The World of Tiaran map by Jared Blando www.theredepic.com

Acknowledgments

To Judy, my incomparable wife and soul mate for long and long, who offered me unconditional love and support in encouraging me to live the dream and write the book; who was my first reader and my biggest fan; who slept alone so many nights while I was pecking away on the keyboard in the wee hours; and who kept after me to publish it until I finally did so at last.

To Rachel, my extremely clever techie daughter, who gifted me with her time; who offered much practical and invaluable advice about all things Internet; and who came to my rescue with her knowledge and savvy of websites, digital images, social media and numerous other arcane mysteries.

And to John L., an avid reader and fellow lover of the written word, with whom I shared many interesting discussions about books and authors we enjoyed even before ebooks existed; who offered me some timely technical assistance; and who challenged me to practice what I preach and go for it.

For Judy, my heart and my soul for as long as you will have me.

Table of Contents

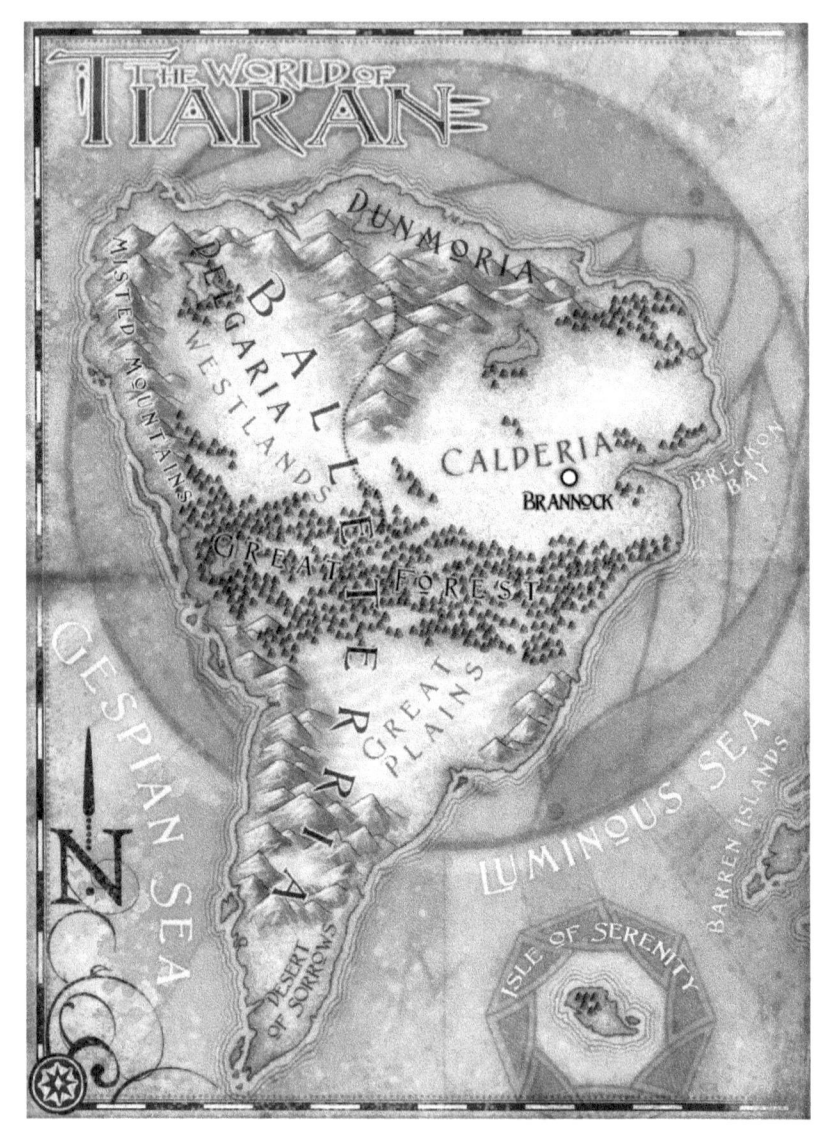

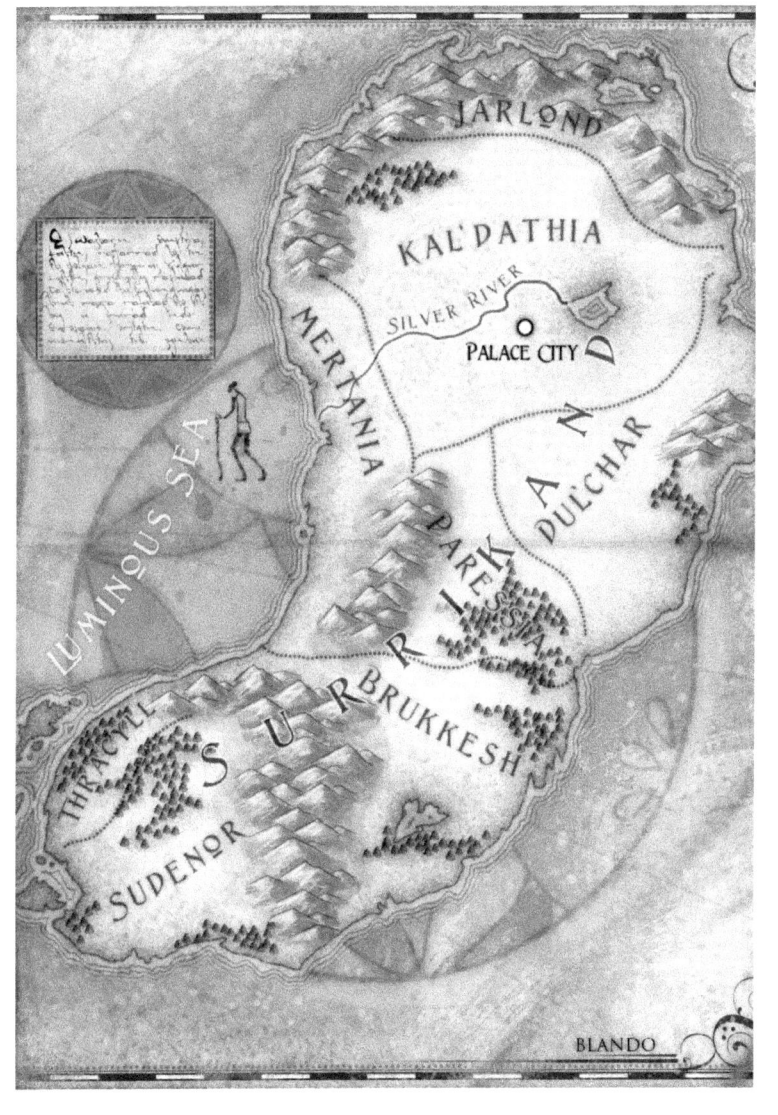

Chapter 1

The Sleeping Savior

Palace City, Kal`Dathia
Continent of Surrikand
Early Spring, 2375

The ancient graveyard lay shrouded in the cool, dark shadows of the night, but the open portal of the Sleeping Savior's Tomb was blacker and colder still. So black that the illumination from the ring of torches held aloft by the Royal Guards could not penetrate the wall of darkness lurking like a living presence inside the entrance of the newly opened mausoleum. So cold that King Nek`krod the Fourth, Esteemed Monarch of Greater Kal`Dathia, shuddered from the chill creeping out from the stone chamber, holding the warmth of the spring night at bay.

For a moment, he hesitated to cross the threshold into that ominous interior. He clutched his blue velvet robes around his thin frame as much for protection as to warm himself—though protection from what, he could not say.

Those gathered behind him sensed something untoward inside the portal as well. The seven court wizards, led by Chief Wizard Mel`kanor, waited and watched in silence. Their purple and gold robes of office, so bright and lustrous when bathed in the glow of first dawn during Temple services, were now muted and dulled in the torchlight. Nek`krod glanced at Mel`kanor briefly, wondering if that was uncertainty that he read in his old friend's eyes as they prepared to enter the Tomb.

Odd that Mel`kanor would hesitate now, for it was he who had first come to Nek`krod with news of a remarkable discovery in the dusty, decaying archives dating from the First Kingdom. He claimed to have unearthed an archaic incantation that might be used to wake the Sleeping Savior and gain his aid in delivering the land from the armies of the barbarian Dul`Chars, who had crossed over the southeastern border into Kal`Dathia, and were now threatening to overrun their defenses and put all to the sword or under the collar.

The few survivors who had escaped the Dul`Chars told grim stories of slaughter and doom, of the murder of all the grown men without exception, giving no quarter, allowing no surrender, keeping only the boys to be trained to the yoke of servitude. Even more gruesome were the reports of the barbarians raping and defiling the women, slaking their lust, then laughing as they split their victims open from throat to crotch, leaving them to bleed and die like butchered cattle while their own children watched.

And the girls...gods, the king shuddered to think of their awful fate. They were said to be kept alive as rewards for the most vicious warriors, like prized fillies to be mounted and used over and over again.

At first, when Mel`kanor had approached Nek`krod with the fantastic idea of Awakening the Sleeping Savior, the king had wondered if his oldest and most trusted counselor had gone mad, perhaps from the shame of failing to stop, or even delay, the inexorable advance of the enemy across the plains. Indeed, it had cost Mel`kanor much to admit that his own cadre of wizards was no match for the Dul`Charian shamans, evil creatures who mutilated their bodies and performed human blood sacrifices to gain power from their Dark gods. The humiliation of such an admission could have driven the old wizard to grasp at any scheme, however bizarre or addled. And yet...

And yet, everyone knew the ancient legend of Lord Rak`koth, the Sleeping Savior, a sorcerer of immeasurable power who, eight hundred years past, had served as Protector of the Crown. It was he who had done battle with the Great Monsters and their human minions when they attacked Kal`Dathia without provocation, threatening to annihilate everyone so long ago. It was he who had risen in the air and flown on the wind to the peak of Mount Kal`Dath, standing alone and defiant as he unleashed his terrible and Holy magic against his diabolical foes.

And when, in what should have been his moment of great triumph, he had suddenly been struck down and sent into the long sleep by the fell magic of the mortally wounded Shaldassamer, most evil and mighty of the enemy wizards, Rak`koth had used the last of his arcane power to send a message to all Kal`Dathians everywhere: *"Call upon me in time of great trouble, and I shall Awaken from my sleep to aid you."*

From that day on, it was known as "The Promise." It was a promise of hope, a vow imprinted on the mind of every living countryman, and passed down in lore for centuries through story and bardsong.

Nek`krod peered uncertainly into the open doorway of the Savior's Tomb, recalling the legend of how his ancestors had carefully laid Rak`koth, their fallen hero, to rest in the center of a grand burial chamber. He slept inside a finely crafted golden casket resting on a block of black marble, surrounded by other stone pedestals upon which the bodies of his fallen brother wizards had been placed to share the long sleep with their leader.

It was said that the surviving spell casters had labored for days, weaving powerful enchantments over the Savior's body to prevent decay, and binding the doorway with great spells to prevent anyone from gaining entry and desecrating his Tomb. Since that time, no one had dared to disturb Rak`koth's resting place. For eight hundred years, countless generations had come and gone, and nations had waxed and waned, while he lay entombed in his solitary slumber.

But now, Kal`Dathia itself was in mortal peril. And so, when Mel`kanor had reminded the king of "The Promise," and said, "This is surely that time of great trouble, my Liege," Nek`krod had seen no other choice but to yield to his counselor's urgent advice to attempt the Awakening.

He knew the inevitable butchery and death awaiting Kal`Dathia at her border, and saw the defeat lurking in his old friend's eyes if they did not act. With fear and hope warring in his breast, Nek`krod had nodded to his chief wizard. "Let it be done. And the gods' blessings on us all."

Mel`kanor had left immediately to begin three days of fasting, followed by two sleepless days and nights of chanting and spell casting with his other wizards, using the ancient words recorded in the faded and crumbling archives to break the magical bindings on the Tomb's entrance. This very night, he had pronounced the task complete at last, and had directed the guards to open the solid granite door, revealing the pitch-black entrance that now confronted Nek`krod.

There was some slight movement behind the king, perhaps by someone anxious to proceed. Nek`krod glanced sideways into the violet eyes of Merelda, High Priestess of the god Shalloth, supreme deity of Kal`Dathia. She stood with her group of seven sister priestesses, each of them draped in filmy gowns of blue gossamer that fluttered occasionally in the night breeze. The wind molded the light, gauzy fabric to their bodies, revealing the rounded curves of breasts and hips that had prompted many an erotic fantasy in men who watched the women move through their sacred dances in the Temple during feasting celebrations and Holy Days.

But looking, and perhaps dreaming, was all that anyone, king and commoner alike, was ever allowed to do, for each of the priestesses was a virgin, dedicated as a bride of the god Shalloth from birth, sworn to have no carnal knowledge of men from cradle to grave. The profound devotion and fervor for Great Shalloth shining in their eyes belied any imagined hint of sexual invitation tendered inadvertently by the alluring glimpses of female flesh and form.

This night, however, Nek`krod felt none of the familiar thrill of arousal to the intriguing curves and shadowed loins of the priestesses. Not even for Merelda, young for her station and endowed with voluptuousness made all the more enticing by her purity and inaccessibility. She, too, seemed oblivious to the effect of the thin fabric caressing and outlining her body as she returned his gaze.

Did she share any of his foreboding for something inexplicable awaiting them inside the chamber? If so, he saw no doubt behind those trusting eyes.

Indeed, Merelda had lent the support of her Holy Office to the Awakening—had even, after nights of prayers and fasting in the Temple, urged her king to include her and her sisters in the Rite that would see Rak`koth called back to their service and need. Now she nodded her head almost imperceptibly, as if to say that it was time.

Breathing deeply to steady his rapidly beating heart, King Nek`krod finally stirred himself to action and stepped over the threshold into the Sleeping Savior's Tomb. Immediately, the guards followed him inside, forming a phalanx around him as their torches lit the way, casting elongated shadows on the walls and vaulted ceiling of the dark granite chamber. The footsteps of the guards and wizards, and the gentle whisper of the priestesses' gowns, were the only sounds he heard, the absence of any spoken words a silent testimony to the sense of awe and trepidation they all shared.

The dust of centuries, undisturbed for the better part of a millennium, lifted up around their feet as they walked, forming small clouds that rose several inches and then drifted quietly back down to rest once more after their passing. A deeper chill sent shivers through Nek`krod and his small entourage as they passed among the lesser pedestals, which now held only small mounds of dust and bits of tarnished metal—the last vestiges of the Sleeping Savior's fellow wizards, fallen in battle, but themselves bereft of any spells invoked to preserve their own earthly remains.

At last, they stood before the golden casket resting on the marble base some four feet high. No name or inscription marred the smooth, flawless surface of the Savior's sarcophagus, but none of those gathered before it harbored any doubt about who lay at rest within. Nek`krod gestured toward the guards, and several stepped forward, dressed in ceremonial silver breastplates and greaves, holding the five heavy braziers that would be needed in the Ritual of Flame required for the Awakening.

When the braziers had been placed around the coffin, Mel`kanor waved his staff and called the flames to life. With the fire came welcomed illumination that banished the dark shadows nearest the coffin, lighting the faces of the men and women, and bringing their expressions of hushed anticipation into sharper relief.

At another sign from Mel`kanor, the seven wizards stepped to the braziers and began gesturing as they passed their hands in and out of the flames, chanting in a deep monotone the spell that would unbind Lord Rak`koth from his endless slumber. Moving as one, the seven priestesses followed Merelda down to the cold floor as she knelt and raised her hands in supplication to Shalloth, their soft feminine voices murmuring the sacred prayers in unison, calling on their beloved deity to hear their pleas for restoration of the Savior's power and glory in their time of great need.

Long, unbound feminine tresses caressed their shoulders as they lifted their heads and fixed their gazes upon the casket. The point and counterpoint of male and female, chant and orison, blended into a hypnotic harmony that reverberated throughout the chamber, lifting the king's spirit with a surge of hope and expectation.

As the vocal fusion reached a crescendo, Nek`krod heard the crack of a thunderbolt just outside the Tomb that smote their ears and left them ringing, followed by a mighty tremor in the ground, rocking the chamber to and fro, opening narrow fissures in the stone beneath his feet. It was as if some celestial force had torn the fabric of the sky and split the earth.

Guards, wizards and priestesses alike were thrown down to the floor abruptly, dazed and unable to move until the terrible rumbling ceased. Struggling to regain his footing and his dignity, Nek`krod knew in his soul that something potent had been unbound and...Awakened.

For a time, there was only silence. Gradually, the others staggered to their feet, save for the priestesses who remained kneeling, leaning forward on their hands with hips raised, their heads bowed low in obeisance. Then Nek`krod felt a new presence in the torch-lit chamber, permeating the air with the touch of something powerful, alive.

A moment later, a low, grating sound of metal sliding against metal riveted their attention in the direction of the Savior's pedestal, as the lid of the coffin began to move. It shifted sideways slowly, inching forward, then fell to the floor with a jarring crash as a single hand, its long, graceful fingers bejeweled with emerald and ruby rings, emerged from within its dark recesses to grip the side of the casket.

Someone, perhaps Merelda, gasped as the upper portion of a body rose in one fluid motion to sit erect. A black velvet robe, perfectly preserved and threaded with mystical sigils stitched in fine gold filigree, covered the chest and arms of the raised figure. The cowl, woven from the same thick, dark material, slipped back to reveal the head of a man framed by dark, curling hair that fell to his collar.

The handsome face was long and high-boned, with heavy eyebrows, a prominent nose, and full, thick lips. The eyes were closed, as if the man remained in repose. Then the eyes opened, two black irises with burning crimson centers that pierced the pall of smoke from the torches...and the world changed.

Those riveting orbs scanned the chamber slowly as the Sleeping Savior turned his head from side to side. For a moment, his eyes seemed to question everything they saw, disoriented and uncertain, as they took in the sight of the robed wizards huddling near the overturned smoking braziers, the priestesses kneeling with their flowing gowns and hair askew, and the guards, shaken and confused, their hands tightly grasping the hilts of their swords.

Then the burning eyes focused, as if a troubling riddle had been solved, bringing recognition and understanding. A smile split Rak`koth's face, a smile that soon became a booming laugh of unrestrained exultation echoing in the shadowed vault.

"Awake! Alive again!" The tone was deep and raspy, as it might sound coming from a voice left unused for ages. "So long. So cold." His head swiveled in Nek`krod's direction, and the voice, now steadier and stronger, asked, "How long?"

Stunned, Nek`krod's mouth moved, yet no sounds came forth. The Sleeping Savior, alive! It was all true, just as Mel`kanor had promised! Thoughts formed and unraveled in his mind, feelings of awe and dread jumbled together with joy and relief. He felt a desperate need to answer, if only he could remember how to speak. And again, came the question from the risen Savior, now more forceful and demanding. "How long?"

The king took a steadying breath and stepped forward, looking almost, but not fully, into those alarming crimson eyes. "Lord Rak`koth, I…I am Nek`krod…Nek`krod the Fourth, King of Kal`Dathia."

Then, with a shade more confidence: "It…It has been these eight hundred years or more since you were laid to rest here, after your mighty battle against the Monsters and their human servants, my Lord."

Amazement flickered across the features of the legendary hero's face. "Eight hundred years?" Rak`koth glanced down at his body, then rose slowly to his feet, lifting his arms and examining his hands, flexing his long fingers as if reassuring himself that the flesh was real. "Then it worked!" Another broad smile, another thundering laugh that filled the corners of the room. "My wizards…"

The king spoke quickly now. "Yes, Lord Rak`koth. Your wizards enspelled your body to preserve it against time itself. Those of your brethren who fell with you that day rest here as well." He gestured to the pedestals surrounding him, upon which could be seen the detritus of human flesh and bone that alone remained. "We…my ancestors…buried them with you, in honor of their great loyalty and sacrifice."

Rak`koth's nodded silently as his gaze quickly swept the pedestals, halting only momentarily to focus on the piles of dust before moving on and coming to rest on the priestesses kneeling before him. Their pale, upturned faces contrasted with the dark hair falling about their shoulders. A look of interest or perhaps something more...intense...in his burning eyes elicited a small sound from Merelda as his gaze lingered deliberately on her face and body.

"Yes," he breathed, as if momentarily distracted. "Yes, they died, while I live again." Turning back to Nek`krod, he continued in a sterner tone. "But why have you brought me back now, so many ages later?"

Nek`krod shivered, not expecting the tone of challenge in Rak`koth's voice. "But 'The Promise,' Lord, your vow to return to us in time of great need. The armies of the Dul`Chars are at our borders, and we are helpless before them. These savages have conquered others, using their blood magic, and now they come for us. Our own wizards have been unable to stop them. Then Mel`kanor, my Chief Wizard, found a way to perform the Awakening and bring you back to help us as you said you would." His voice trailed off to a whisper as he saw Rak`koth frown.

"Yes, of course. 'The Promise!' But eight hundred years! I was not to sleep this long! And who are these Dul`Chars, that you have need of me now?"

"They are barbarians, great Lord, murderous, evil creatures who kill or enslave all whom they conquer. Their numbers are as the blades of grass upon the plain." Nek`krod repeated the tales of slaughter, rape, and enslavement. "We have sent emissaries to inquire of their purpose, and to offer the fruit of our harvest, precious stones, even gold, should they be content to turn aside from our land." Nek`krod hesitated, fear and anger rising in his throat.

"But my messengers were taken prisoner and crucified in front of our soldiers, their blood drained and consumed by their unholy shamans for their wicked magic." He shook his head in horror at the memory. "We have no hope of stopping them. That is why we have come to you, my Lord."

Rak`koth cast his crimson eyes in the direction of the king's magic users. "Why have your brethren been unable to overcome these barbarians? Kal`Dathian wizards had great power when last I lived."

"My Lord," said Mel`kanor, speaking for the first time. "As the king has said, their shamans use blood magic—magic forbidden to us because of its evil source, the blood of human sacrifices. Against that, our powers are all too easily overcome. Already, some of our brother wizards have perished trying to halt their advance." Nek`krod heard the shame and regret in his old friend's voice as he bowed his head.

Rak`koth nodded thoughtfully, considering the meaning of these words. Then he lifted his legs over the side of the coffin and slowly slid his body down to the floor. He began to walk toward the king, but staggered, catching the edge of the marble pedestal to steady himself. Beckoning to Mel`kanor, he spoke as one brother wizard to another.

"I understand.   Your spells have brought about my Awakening. I live again. For that, I am most grateful, and you shall be rewarded. You ask for my help, and I will fulfill 'The Promise.' But my strength is sorely diminished after my long sleep. My powers are but a small spark within me. If I am to render aid, I will have need of you and your brethren."

He stumbled again as he stepped slowly, erratically, toward the Chief Wizard, reaching out his hand. "Will you lend me your staff, brother?"

Mel`kanor looked at his staff, proud of the way that he had shaped and strengthened it over many years through his own studies of the paths of power.  He felt honored that this fabled sorcerer would find it worthy of his use.  Without hesitation, he handed the finely crafted wooden shaft to Rak`koth, who leaned upon it to steady himself, then motioned one of the guards closer.

"What I am about to request can not be interrupted. Bar the door well."

As the man hastened to obey, Rak`koth addressed Mel`kanor again. "If you and your brethren will touch the staff together with me, I can use it as a focal point to gather some of your power to me. I need only a small portion of your power, just enough to rekindle and feed the weak pulse of magic within me. Then we will join together and battle these barbarians at our gates." He lifted the shaft and held it out parallel to the floor, gripping one end tightly.

Hope grew stronger in Mel`kanor's heart, even as the Sleeping Savior's request to take a portion of their power filled him with some unease. Wizards like himself used spells and incantations to gather and channel power from the ether, the mysterious, magical energy that permeated all matter in the world and the celestial firmament above. Legend had it that Rak`koth had been a supreme adept of these arcane arts, a Master of Spells.

But ancient lore also taught that Rak`koth had been more than a mighty wizard. He had been a *sorcerer*, a magician gifted with the rare ability to do something no wizard could—to draw upon the very life essence of other human beings in order to magnify the potency of his spell casting.

Mel`kanor had never known a sorcerer, and had never been asked to offer up part of his life force in this manner. Such a power would be highly dangerous in the wrong hands. Still, the chief wizard had studied the archaic writings, and knew better than any man that the Sleeping Savior had been a hero, a great warrior in the battle against evil. If uniting their powers with his would defeat the enemy, he was prepared to make some small sacrifice. He turned to his fellow wizards.

"Come, brothers. Let us do as Lord Rak`koth bids. Let us share our strength with him."

Rak`koth seemed to waver a bit where he stood, as if holding the staff up strained him. "Quickly. If you would do this thing at all, do it now!"

He waited as the wizards stepped forward, each man reaching out to the staff with his left hand. Mel`kanor led the chanting, setting the rhythm and the pace as they summoned and channeled their powers. As before, their voices blended together, the air around them charged with glowing energy. They felt the moment when Rak`koth entered the circle of power, adding his own words in harmony with theirs. Soon, they felt a part of their power being gathered into the staff...and through it, into the Savior.

As the power flowed into his body, Rak`koth waxed visibly stronger, growing taller and more erect while he absorbed their vitality. Watching this amazing transformation, his fellow wizards rejoiced in sharing this gift with this legendary sorcerer. Yet, as long moments passed, and their energy continued to flow into him and be hungrily consumed, they began to grow weakened and drained. After a time, they could hardly stand. Heartbeats grew sluggish and uneven, strength waned further, and they struggled for breath.

Then they began to cry out in panic and consternation that they could endure no more, that the depletion of their life forces was too great. But Rak`koth only laughed and drew upon their magical energies even more, sucking their essence into him, absorbing it as they screamed, until these once-powerful men withered and shrank, falling lifeless to the floor.

Mel`kanor, the strongest of them, held on the longest, his eyes filled with shock and horror as he felt his life ebb and heard the gleeful laughter. "Savior!" he cried, his last words an indictment of betrayal and pain. Then he, too, slumped down and died.

Rak`koth spread wide his arms and thrust his hands upward, his head thrown back and mouth open in a roar of triumph, his crimson eyes burning brightly as his body was bathed in the red glow of power visibly emanating from the staff. Nek`krod shrank back, astonished and disbelieving. His Royal

Guards, equally bewildered, strove to overcome their terror. Drawing upon their training as the elite protectors of their monarch, they moved to stand in front of him.

Yet, even as the hiss of steel being drawn from leather scabbards resounded in the chamber, Rak`koth spoke a phrase. Bolts of crimson fire erupted from the end of his staff, striking the silver breastplates of the warriors with such force that their bodies were hurtled backward across the chamber, stopping only when they collided with the wall.   Swords dropped from deadened hands as their mangled bodies crumpled to the floor, the pungent odor of charred flesh filling the Tomb.

Nek`krod slumped to his knees, the smell of death in his nostrils, his voice nothing more than a hoarse whisper. "My Lord. Why? 'The Promise!'"

Rak`koth turned his terrible countenance upon him and sneered with contempt. "Fools! Yes. 'The Promise!' I knew you would come to me and waken me in your need. That is *why* I made such a vow. You wanted me, now here I am! Are you not pleased with what your noble labors have wrought?" he taunted.

Devastated by awareness of the enormity of his error, Nek`krod could only stare at this...this monster who had been revered as their Sleeping Savior for so many centuries. "But, Lord," he cried, "How can this be? You...you fought the Great Monsters and their armies of men. You saved our land, our people. The stories tell of your goodness, your sacrifice…" He shook his head as if to clear it, feeling his sanity fading.

Rak`koth chuckled as he watched the king sink to the ground.   "Of course, the legends tell of my sacrifice and goodness, simpleton! I *created* those legends and sent them into the minds of your weak, spineless ancestors, even as I was falling into that infernal endless sleep."

He looked down at Nek`krod scornfully.   "Your ancestors were fools as well. I offered them a leader of power and greatness, yet they had neither the vision nor the courage to kneel to me and surrender their destiny into my hands. They hardened their hearts against me, and called upon men and beasts to do battle with me in the name of Good!"

A sneer twisted his handsome face into an ugly mask. "They used their cursed spells to banish me to this cold, forsaken Tomb! But not before I held their feeble minds in thrall, not before I altered their memories of me and implanted the legend of the Sleeping Savior and 'The Promise' in their place, knowing they would call upon their 'hero' someday and set me free. Well, I am free now, you wretched creature. Come, have a taste of how heroic I can be!"

Laughing as he reveled in his restored powers, he sent a red Bolt of light lashing out from his fingers to strike Nek'krod in the chest, forcing a scream of agony as the king's body convulsed, flopping around on the floor of the Tomb. The sorcerer sniffed with disgust at the stench of emptied bowels filling the air, then turned away from the ruined man, dismissing him like a crippled beggar lying in the street.

Chapter 2

Unholy Ordeal

Now Rak'koth fixed his burning eyes on the priestesses huddling on the floor, unable to comprehend how great Shalloth could allow this to happen. Only Merelda met his incandescent gaze, despair written clearly upon her face, with perhaps a measure of contempt as well—though whether for him or her impotent god, he did not know. He strode across the room to where she knelt in front of her sisters, her head raised slightly in a posture that suggested some remaining vestige of pride and dignity, even in the midst of the disintegration of everything in which she had ever believed or held close to her heart.

Rak'koth lifted his hand toward her slowly. When she flinched away, he spoke quiet, reassuring words, and reached out again, this time to stroke her hair gently, patiently, eyeing her with the predatory gleam of a forest cat as it pauses momentarily before pouncing upon a helpless doe. She felt his visual inspection taking in the softness of her neck, the fullness of her breasts thrust forward all the more by her rapid breathing, the curve of her hip outlined by the gown pulled tight beneath her legs.

As she moved to pull away again, as much from the fell look in his terrible glowing eyes as from the touch of his hand, he grabbed her hair and swiftly yanked her to her feet. She stood before him, her head bent backwards, her pale throat exposed, as if positioned for his teeth to pierce the skin where the warm blood pulsed. He laughed softly as his hands twisted in her hair.

"Is that pride I see, daughter of Shalloth? Or might it be contempt for your useless god? There are other things I have missed during my long sleep, my dear. Like the pleasure of warm female flesh under my hands."

Grasping her hair tightly, his other hand traced a line down the hollow of her neck and slipped inside the bodice of her thin gown to lightly stroke the curve of her soft, heavy breast with his fingertips. Her body tensed, her skin tingling under his intimate caress, even as her gasp was echoed by cries of alarm from the cringing priestesses witnessing their spiritual leader being debased by his lewd fondling.

"Oh, yes, that is right," he mocked. "You are a virgin still, are you not, High Priestess?" His disdain for the Holy title was unmistakable. "So pure. So unattainable. You have never felt a man's touch on these delicate treasures, have you, my dear?"

Suddenly, he twisted his fingers cruelly until she cried out in pain. Her anguish and shame brought a malevolent grin to his face. He laughed and released her, only to grasp the hem of her gown and yank it up to her waist, exposing her pale white thighs and the black curls between them for the first time to any man's eyes.

Frozen in horror and disbelief for a moment as his fingers caressed her, she awoke from her paralysis and began to scream, struggling futilely to free herself from his vile touch. Ignoring her struggles and cries, Rak`koth brought his lips close to her ear in a throaty whisper.

"You need not pull away from me, my dear. You have never had a man before, but you will. You will learn to obey me and please me in every way that a woman pleases a man. How fitting that the high priestess should learn to serve her new Lord. And you *will* learn to serve me!"

With no warning, he seized the top of her gown and ripped it down the front, exposing all of her. Aghast at being stripped bare in front of him, she sent a wordless, desperate prayer to Shalloth, beseeching him to forgive her for what Rak`koth was about to do, the disgusting thing that crude, lustful men did to women outside the protection of the Temple.

In truth, there had been times when, late at night in her solitary bed, she had been guilty of forbidden thoughts about the only man who had ever tempted her to break her vows of chastity and surrender to the pleasures of the flesh. She had even dreamed of what it would be like for him to steal into her room, to run his hands over her smooth skin and...But, oh, gods, no! Shalloth be merciful, never like this! She bowed her head and prepared for the worst.

The resignation and dread in her violet eyes changed to confusion when he grabbed her wrists and tied her hands together with the torn shreds of her own gown, then dragged her to the wall and fastened her bonds to a heavy torch holder bolted into the stone above her head. He leaned to brush her cheek with his fingertips.

"Oh, no, my dear. I will not use you just yet. I am going to take my time teaching you to serve me. But first, you will watch and learn."

And with that terrible promise ringing in her ears, Rak`koth kissed her mouth gently. He stroked her neck again, then walked away, leaving her hanging there, hands stretched above her head, feet barely touching the floor, naked except for ragged strips of cloth hanging down from her waist.

Rak`koth approached the other priestesses cowering before him. He gestured toward the ring of stone slabs surrounding his coffin and spoke in a low, seductive voice that carried an ominous undertone promising something very unpleasant if his command went unheeded.

"Get up on the pedestals, daughters of Shalloth. Each and every one of you. Don't concern yourselves with the sacred remains of my 'heroic,' sacrificing wizards." His tone turned contemptuous once more. "They can hardly care any longer."

The cringing priestesses remained on the floor, despite his instructions. Rak`koth shook his head slightly, as if with regret, then stepped back to Merelda and slapped her hard across the face, evoking a cry from the blow. "If you do not wish to see your beloved leader abused more harshly, you will climb onto the pedestals now!"

Eyes welling with tears, the women rose to their feet and made their way among the raised marble slabs. Moving soundlessly except for the rustle of their gowns, each of them chose one or another pedestal at random, awkwardly crawling onto the cold stone on their hands and knees.

"Now, good sisters, lie down on your backs, hands above your head," he ordered. When they hesitated once more, Rak`koth grunted impatiently, then unleashed a pair of stinging slaps to Merelda's naked flesh. As she shrieked in pain, twisting her wrists in a vain attempt to protect herself, the women cried out and quickly took the position he had dictated, shuddering at the feel of the coldness and the gritty dust of disintegrated corpses beneath them.

Rak`koth uttered a brief incantation and waved his staff. As a crimson light engulfed them, they found their wrists and ankles surrounded by bands of warm energy that anchored their hands and feet to the stone itself, leaving them spread-eagled, terrified and loath to meet each other's eyes in their shame.

Rak`koth walked among them, his burgeoning desire only enhanced by their helplessness and mortification. "You, my pets, will be granted a great honor tonight."

He stopped and looked directly at one of the younger priestesses who was arching her back as she tried to wriggle out of the magical bonds holding her fast. His hand moved to her bosom and cupped her through the filmy fabric. As she groaned, he turned back to the other captives.

"As great as I have been, and will be once again, I have need of sons...sons to command my legions and rule in places I can not be. Sons to inherit and share my powers. You, my pure, innocent virgins, have been chosen to be the vessels of my progeny. Together, we will make strong sons to become my eyes and my strong right hands wherever they go."

Then his voice turned icy cold "And this time, I will *not* be denied my rightful place!"

With a look of undisguised lust, he knelt up on the pedestal and tore the gown from the body of the trembling girl. He spared no time for gentle caresses this time, but thrust himself inside her with a force that slammed her back against the stone.

"No! Shalloth, help me!" she managed to plead, as he moved on top of her, gripping her harshly in his powerful fingers with every lunge. That she was dry and constricted, and in no way ready to receive him, gave him no pause whatsoever as he took her, his low groans of pleasure intermingled with her cries of pain.

Then, finally, he grunted once, holding still as he released his seed into her. It was the last thing she thought of before the horror of the blasphemous rape, and the thought of the abomination that might be taking hold inside of her womb, sent her mind fleeing down into the welcome depths of unconsciousness.

Even as his first victim's head rolled back in a faint, Rak`koth was climbing off her and moving toward the woman lying on the next pedestal. Her name was Saleria, had he bothered to ask. She had taken her final vows to Shalloth merely one eight-day ago, her heart filled with elation, and not a little pride, to be included in so important a ritual as the Awakening.

Now, with her joy turned to panic, she watched him come closer. As her mouth formed an "O" of surprise and fear, he looked at her and laughed. Misinterpreting the cause of her surprise—for she knew nothing of a normal man's need to wait before taking another woman so soon—he said softly, "Fear not, my dear. I have enough for you." He gazed around at all of the women lying bound before him.

"I have enough for all of you, my pets! My powers give me strength and stamina well beyond that of other men, enough to make a Paressian whore beg for mercy...as more than one has," he added, a sinister chuckle rolling from his lips as he recalled the many women, harlots and noble ladies alike, whom he had used for his pleasure all those centuries ago.

"This is the seed of my power, and I shall deny none of you the honor of receiving it," he vowed with a low laugh. Then he was mounting Saleria, his weight crushing the breath from her lungs. She felt a searing pain as he invaded her. Soon, she was crying out in anguish, but he never heard her cries, lost in his pleasure and cruel delight. Finally, his body went rigid as he spent himself inside her. In another moment, he had pulled away, leaving her sobbing as he made his way to the next pedestal.

Tormented by the sight of her sisters being ravaged, and by the numbing pain in her wrists and shoulders, Merelda began to drift in and out of consciousness as she hung against the wall. The stinging in her face and breasts was as nothing compared to the constant ache from her hands and arms being stretched taut above her for what seemed like an eternity. In truth, she had no way to reckon the passage of time in the dark chamber, except perhaps by the gradual dimming of what precious light remained as, one by one, the torches guttered and died.

From time to time, she thought she heard sounds of something heavy banging against the Tomb door from the outside, and the muffled cries of human voices. She may have only imagined that Rak`koth came to her on one or two occasions, to force a sip of water down her throat from a flame-blackened flask salvaged from the ruined body of a dead guard.

She thought she remembered the feel of her own urine flowing down her legs to puddle on the floor at her feet, as the need to relieve her bladder finally overcame her determination to spare herself one more humiliation. And still, her unholy ordeal stretched on.

In her muddled condition, she did not know when the flame from the last torch flickered out, nor did she recall the moment when she realized that a red ball of sorcerous light had formed above Rak`koth's head. She was vaguely aware of that single glowing ball moving around the chamber, and wondered about it dully—until she remembered that the monster they had Awakened was making good on his promise, going from one pedestal to the next, rutting his way through her poor, helpless sisters like an insatiable stallion covering a herd of captive mares.

She could hear the occasional screams and cries of the other women as he used each of them in turn, but their sobbing entreaties for mercy and the desperate pleas to Shalloth to deliver them from this nightmare went unanswered. She had no tears left to cry for them, or for herself, but only the desire to sleep and never wake again. She closed her eyes and slid back down into oblivion.

When next she awoke, the red glow was drawing closer. Her fear returned as she realized that Rak'koth was approaching again. The magical light hovered several inches above the staff he carried as he stopped in front of her. She could feel his burning eyes upon her, but could not lift her head to meet them. She could only wait helplessly for whatever awful fate he had in mind for her now.

She felt his hand move near her head, expecting another painful blow or another violation of her body. Instead, there was a brief sound of tearing fabric, then she was suddenly collapsing toward the floor, her arms too leaden and numbed to break her fall. Just before her head would have cracked against the stone, she felt his hands in her hair, grasping it and lifting her upward to her knees.

Now, at last, he had finally come for her. Now she would be thrown down and defiled, his last brutal assault reserved for the high priestess. But she no longer cared—or so she thought, until the sound of his malicious chuckle sparked some small remaining residue of anger inside her.

She opened her eyes to find them in a direct line with his groin as she knelt before him. Emboldened by desperation and despair, she raised her head and met his fiery gaze.

"Am I now to be next, despoiler of virgins?" she croaked, dripping venom with each word. "Have you not yet taken enough helpless women already to satisfy your filthy lusts?" She was prepared for almost anything from him— anything except the gentle touch of his hand along her cheek again and the light brush of his fingertips on the back of her neck.

"Oh, no, my dear," he whispered. "Even *my* long-denied appetites have been quenched...for the moment. I am, as you say, quite 'satisfied' for now." He laughed low in his throat. "But I have accomplished the first step in my plan. My sons! Even now, see how they grow in the wombs of your sisters."

With great effort and greater dread, she raised her head and followed his pointing finger, crying out in astonishment at the sight of the small nimbus of red light surrounding the enlarged belly of each priestess. Incredibly, each woman was beginning to swell as if she was already with child.

"Yes, quite amazing, is it not?" he laughed with evil pride. "And my sons will develop and grow much faster than an ordinary birth would allow. Such is the power of my sorcery that my sons will be born before the turn of five moons. Alas, the mothers may find it painful...and, perhaps fatal. But it matters little. They will have served their purpose."

Leaving Merelda to despair over his grim predictions of the fate of her sisters in childbed, Rak`koth moved to the motionless body of Nek`krod that lay curled up tightly on the floor. She thought the king already dead by now, for she had neither seen any movement nor heard any sound from him since early in her ordeal. Yet, when the sorcerer delivered a swift kick to the body, she heard a faint moan and saw Nek`krod stir.

"Up, oh great king," said Rak`koth mockingly, delivering another kick to the fallen monarch's side. "It is time to greet your loyal subjects and introduce their beloved Savior."

He snorted with derision as Nek`krod labored to rise to his hands and knees. Merelda saw the dark stubble on the king's chin, and a distant part of her brain registered that some time must have passed in this chamber of terror. The stain on the front of his bedraggled robe revealed that her once-proud sovereign had soiled himself. She turned away, embarrassed for him.

When Nek`krod did not stand quickly enough, Rak`koth grabbed his arm and propelled him to his feet forcefully. "Come, *Sire*," he demanded. "Our people await. Do you not hear them calling out for you to return among them? Even now, they gather outside beyond the door. We will greet them together, and we will see what can be done with our barbarian friends, the Dul`Chars. Your tales of their blood magic fascinate me."

With a sardonic gleam in his crimson eyes, Rak`koth turned back to Merelda. "As for you, I will take great pleasure in using you soon enough, when I have rested from my other...labors. But first, did I not tell you that you would be trained to please me, in all ways? We will start with a lesson in obedience." He stepped a few feet away from her and tapped the end of his staff down upon her bare hips.

"Now, let us see how well a high priestess can learn to crawl. And do try to remember that any resistance will earn…discomfort…in return, not only for you, but for all your sisters as well. Do you understand?"

Barely able to move her head, she managed to nod weakly. He stepped toward the door, his hand on the king's arm. "Good. Now, priestess, follow behind on your hands and knees. Crawl nicely for me. Oh, that is a fetching sight," he said, watching with wicked pleasure as the naked woman put one hand and knee forward and began to move as she struggled to obey.

Interlude

Somewhere else, indeed, somewhere a great distance away, a very different kind of intimacy was unfolding. The lovers lying on the silken sheets of a spacious bed inside a lavishly appointed room might have been two ordinary people anywhere, locked in an intimate dance.

Except, that is, for the bright golden glow emanating from their eyes, their flawless, shimmering skin, and the strands of hair that swam around their heads with no aid from any breeze. Except for the way the outline of their physical forms rippled and wavered, subtly changing shape and texture as they undulated together, hips and thighs meeting and withdrawing, only to meet again.

And except for the fact that the room in which they reveled floated quietly in the ether of space, far removed from any planet, drifting serenely with no visible means of support against the brilliant backdrop of a million stars.

Lying beneath her ardent lover, Morainen moaned, clutching his neck as he joined with her again. *Oh, yes! I understand now*," she breathed. *This is magnificent! I feel you so intensely inside me there. In this, alone, I could almost envy mortals.*

Shalloth nodded wordlessly as he nearly withdrew, teasing her, then moved forward again, Sending a thought into her mind as he did. *Yes. In these mortal bodies, the pleasure is so exquisitely centered in one place, every sensation converging...here!*

He felt his need for her intensify as he caressed her breasts, rolling her flesh between his fingers. His touch brought a whimper of delight from her lips, followed by an all-too-mortal giggle.

Mmm, she purred. *It seems that mortal pleasure can be centered in more than one place in this body. I do believe that mortal females may have an advantage over the males in that respect.* She laughed, willing her nipples to double in length to enhance the sensation.

He chuckled in her mind, then made himself expand and thicken inside her in response. With a squeal of pleasure, she shaped herself to accommodate his increased size, clenching and gripping him tightly. In another moment, the rapture of their shared release rolled over them and he felt his essence erupting into her.

But, unlike the mortal male whose form he had assumed, his release was not concluded in a few short spasms, but continued on and on until all of the divine energy he had fashioned into a human shape was dissolving and flowing into her, joining and blending with her—as she, in turn, abandoned the human body she had fashioned and merged with him, completely and fully. Their energies entwined in a cascade of vibrations, even as their thoughts and feelings became one.

There were no words for a time, until the exquisite pulsing finally ebbed. Then came the contented thought begun by her and ended by him: *The mortal way is pleasing...but not as pleasing as this. Mortals could never know this oneness.* As their formless entities slowly parted and floated languidly beside each other in the ether, the bed and the chamber created for their celestial tryst blinked out of existence.

They might have drifted serenely for a century or an eon, had it not been for the sudden intrusion of a powerful disruption in the Weave, a note of strident discord that destroyed their contented reverie and riveted their attention in that direction. Sharing their thoughts again, they searched their impressions and reached agreement. A disturbance in the Weave of that magnitude, still echoing in the wake of the great power manifested, could have but one source.

The world of Tiaran! The abomination has Awakened! he Sent to her angrily. *The taint carried by that disruption could come from none other than Rak`koth. Those foolish mortals have unleashed him! He walks the land again!* Shalloth's entity throbbed in disgust, while Morainen emanated waves of regret and resignation, as if to remind them both that they had expected this moment would come eventually.

Meanwhile, other entities were suddenly gathering in the ether around them, all of them emitting the same thoughts of distress and alarm over the disturbance in the harmony. Feeling their agitation, Shalloth reluctantly left Morainen's side and floated to a position in the center of the group.

Yes, we know. Rak`koth walks the world of Tiaran once more, he Sent into the minds encircling him. *We, too, have felt his return. We all remember the nearly catastrophic damage to the Weave when last he wielded his fell powers, and we know well the time and effort it took to restore the balance after he was defeated and sent into what was supposed to be an endless* *sleep. Now his black soul returns, and already his Dark powers threaten the harmony of the Weave again.*

A chorus of anxious agreement arose around him, and the thoughts of the entities coalesced into a single message directed toward him. *The time approaches to take the steps we foresaw as necessary, should this malignancy arise again. Shalloth, it is time for you to set into motion the plan that the Avatar and his chosen companion must follow, if we are to be rid of this dangerous pestilence before the damage he causes is beyond repair.*

Shalloth's entity absorbed these collective thoughts and Sent a wave of resigned acceptance back along the threads of energy connecting them all. *The present Avatar is still but a boy at this time, not yet ready to assume the burden of his destiny. We must wait a short span of years before we send a mentor to Awaken his power. But it will be done. Now you must do your parts as well.* With that, the god called on each of the other deities to offer their power as he Wove new strands into the pattern and cast them out in the direction of the mortal world.

Chapter 3

Visitations

2385 (Ten years later)

Southwest of Surrikand in the Luminous Sea lay the Isle of Serenity, so named by the small colony of scholars that comprised the island's only human inhabitants. There, a man sat beside a mountain stream swollen by the snowmelt, poring over an ancient Scroll of Healing. His brown homespun robe was belted about his waist with a length of coarse hemp, much like the braided laces of the rough-cut sandals on his feet.

The remains of his simple noon meal, a heel of a loaf of dark, crusty bread and a few scraps of hard white cheese, had been left for the hidden denizens of the tall grass to find when they gathered the courage to approach. Though only a little past his thirty-fifth name-day, his skin was weathered and darkened, the legacy of years spent outdoors beneath the bright sun tending and harvesting the rare medicinal plants and herbs that only grew on the Isle—and only in the most remote nooks and crannies, at that.

Mik`kel stroked his auburn beard unconsciously as he paused now and then to decipher some of the more obscure words scrawled in the long-dead author's archaic tongue. It was difficult work, yet he was content. He had come to this place some twelve years past, disenchanted with the destructive uses of magic and drawn by the stories of a community established solely for the study of the healing arts.

His first sight of the Isle from the deck of the ship bearing him here had been a solid wall of high, white cliffs rising from the ocean, looking like an impenetrable barrier encircling the small landmass. Yet, once inside the ring of cliffs, he had discovered a verdant valley cradled in their midst.

It was a tranquil haven hosting fresh-water streams, small groves of birch and pine, and the modest huts and cottages that housed the sixty-odd scholars and healers who had dedicated themselves to studying the peaceful paths of power. They were an isolated group, a community of knowledge seekers that had virtually no contact with the world outside their valley, but that suited him well. He was happy to devote himself to learning without distractions and interruptions.

Mik'kel was carefully unrolling the next section of the brittle vellum when he felt himself suddenly surrounded by a current of energy, like the tingling that gathers in the air before a thunderstorm. Then he felt an alien presence draw near and a deep, disembodied voice spoke inside his mind.

Mortal, attend me! A great evil has Awakened in the world. We require your aid in defeating this malignancy and restoring the balance of harmony, for the sake of mankind and the other races of Tiaran.

Magic! Yet a magic unlike any he had ever known. Mik'kel glanced around rapidly, but saw nothing except the rushing stream, the rich dark earth carpeted with blue-green grass, and a mountain goat carefully picking its way over a rocky crag in the distance. Immediately, his hands began to move in practiced gestures as he invoked a Spell of Protection, but the unseen entity had somehow rendered him helpless and his powers would not come to his call.

For the first time in his adult life, he felt himself severed from the ethereal energy that had flowed within his body since he came of age. Then the wavering outline of a face appeared before him, and Mik'kel found himself transfixed by two golden eyes.

"Who are you?" he whispered, staring in wonder. "Who are you, to come and lay this wyrd upon me, unasked and unwelcome?" For a moment, he heard only the splashing of the brook over well-worn rocks and the cry of an eagle circling high above him, scanning the ground for telltale movements of prey. Then the voice resumed.

I am Shalloth, god of your people. Be at peace, wizard. Your spells are of no use against me nor are they needed. You have been chosen because your strand in the Weave is strong and vibrant, and because you are wise in the ways of mortal magic. Now, question me no further, but listen closely.

Unable to do otherwise, and intrigued by this mysterious intrusion in spite of his fear, Mik'kel swallowed his questions and did as he was bade.

Know that your homeland, Kal'Dathia, is lost. Ten years past, King Nek'krod foolishly revived a Dark sorcerer called Rak'koth, who usurped the throne of Kal'Dathia and then conquered every nation on the continent of Surrikand— Dul'Char, Paressia, Brukkesh, Mertania and the others— crushing all resistance and establishing himself as Emperor over the whole land through ruthless enslavement, subjugation and *death. He did so by allying his fell powers with the foul blood magic of the Dul`Charian shamans he had subdued, and by creating great armies from each nation that he had vanquished. And now he sets his covetous eyes on greater conquest beyond his shores.*

Mik`kel could not credit the words he was hearing. "My homeland lost? Conquered by Rak`koth? But Rak`koth is the Sleeping Savior, an ancient hero who has slumbered for these past eight centuries!"

So Nek`krod believed as well, when he invoked 'The Promise' and called this so-called Savior from the long sleep, thinking he was summoning a champion to their cause. Alas, that ignorance spelled his doom, for Rak`koth was never a hero—and he sleeps no longer.

Awash in confusion and disbelief, Mik`kel listened while the god recounted Rak`koth's rise to power and the horrors visited upon his people in its wake as the sorcerer carved out an empire in blood and brutality. As the awful tale unfolded, his dismay grew until he felt compelled to ask, "But what of the king? Could Nek`krod do nothing to stop this sorcerer?"

Silence for a heartbeat. Then: *Your father is dead. Rak`koth slew him shortly before he took the throne.*

Now Mik`kel slumped forward onto his hands, his head bowed. He had fled from his father's kingdom, turning his back on the future his sire had planned for him. Indeed, he had scarcely thought of Nek`krod in all his years on the Isle. But to hear of his father dead at the hands of some treacherous usurper brought pain and sorrow that he had not expected.

When Mik`kel raised his head again, his eyes were reddened and narrowed, and his voice tight with anger. "Why come to me *now*, after ten years have passed and my father so long in the grave? Why was I not told sooner, if you would seek my help?"

Because there was naught you could have done when Rak`koth was Awakened. Had you gone against him then, you would have surely been defeated, for the time was not right. The Avatar was not yet grown to manhood, and would have been of little use.

Avatar? As Mik`kel stirred to question the god once again, Shalloth's glowing eyes fixed him with a stare that brooked no further interruption.

All will be explained in time. For now, know this: You must leave this sanctuary and travel northward on the Luminous

Sea to the Kingdom of Calderia, on the continent of Balleterria, where you will find the Avatar. Your destiny is entwined with his. You will set his feet upon the paths of power. To accomplish your task, you will have need of this.

Without warning, a beautifully engraved silver pendant set with a sparkling blue sapphire in the center materialized in Mik`kel's hand. Transfixed by the exquisite gem, he held it up by the silver chain to examine it more closely in the light of the sun. The stone appeared to grow warm and pulse brightly as it turned slowly before his eyes.

This talisman will guide you. Those you seek will know you by this sign. Do not tarry, for time grows short. Now, here is what must be done...

Mik`kel listened in silence for some time, the afternoon shadows walking slowly across the floor of the valley as the god spoke. Then, at last, the presence faded from his head, and he felt the power of his own magic coursing through his body again.

He shook his head, perhaps as a last gesture of resistance, sending his hair whipping around his shoulders with the movement. The fear had vanished with the god's abrupt departure, but a residue of wonder remained.

He wanted to ask more about why *he* had been chosen, why *he* should be burdened with this fate now, after the years of solitary study that he had embraced since leaving the palace. But he heard only the rustle of the breeze in the trees, and the wind offered no reply.

Collecting his scroll and his leather satchel, Mik`kel rose with the aid of his staff and began walking toward the small, simple cottage nestled comfortably amid the white birch trees, the cottage he had built with his own hands, without the use of magic. A wistful smile of pride crossed his face as he looked upon the modest structure, thinking of the hand hewn logs and shingles, and the few pieces of furniture shaped and crafted by adze and honest sweat, all providing shelter and comfort in the long winter months.

He entered the dwelling, leaving the door open behind him. Sounds of drawers being opened and closed, and objects rattling against each other, could be heard, though only the birds flitting about in the trees above took notice. After a time, he emerged from his home, shouldering his pouch and carrying his staff of power. He set off down the shallow path to tell his brother scholars of his departure, wondering if he would ever again see this gentle valley that he had come to love.

††††††

Across the Luminous Sea from Surrikand, in the kingdom of Calderia, King Gavan peered up at the host of stars crowding the cloudless sky as he paced the shadowy battlements of Brannock Castle, making his final rounds before retiring to his chambers. The nightly tour was a ritual begun when sleep would not come easily, after a day filled with casualty reports from the battle front, dispatches from his field commanders, orders awaiting his Royal Seal, and the steady stream of minutia attached to governing a kingdom in the midst of a war—in this case, a war with its hated enemies, the Elves of the Great Forest. The fact that he kept the ritual with such regularity now was testament enough that sleep had become a very elusive companion of late.

His tour finished, he left the battlements and made his way down the stone stairs and along the darkened hallway to his chamber. As he entered the room and closed the door behind him, he heard a rustle of sheets and the soft, sleepy voice of Briana, his queen.

"It is late, Gavan. Come to bed, my love."

Crossing to the bed, he lowered himself down, sinking into the feathered mattress as he leaned over to kiss her cheek tenderly. Briana turned her head to meet his lips as her arm went round his neck, her scented skin radiating an inviting warmth that called to him more than any spoken word.

Reluctant to leave her embrace even for the brief moments needed to shed his boots and outer clothing, he finally broke the kiss and began to unbuckle his sword belt. It was then that he heard a gasp from his wife, and turned to see her staring at a faint light that hovered like a will-o'-the-wisp at the foot of the bed. As they watched in stunned silence, the luminescence expanded and took shape until the spectral face of a beautiful woman with glowing golden eyes could be discerned.

"Morainen!" whispered Briana reverently, speaking the name of the goddess worshiped in great Temples and humble shrines across the length and breadth of Calderia. "Morainen," echoed Gavan in astonishment, though the voice that formed her name held a harder edge.

The goddess smiled benevolently and spoke as if from across a great distance. *Yes, mortal king and queen. Please, do not be afraid. I have come to you this eve to tender my help in a matter of great importance.*

Puzzled by Morainen's words, Briana made to rise from the bed and offer full obeisance. But, as she began to sink to her knees, Gavan gripped her arm and held her firmly, preventing her from kneeling.

"*Help? You would offer help?*" growled Gavan, with a vehemence so lacking in reverence that it shocked his queen. "If you are, indeed, Morainen, then you may recall that I prayed to you for help in avenging my brother when he died, cut down by an Elfin assassin. I also begged for succor when the Scourge took so many of my people in slow and painful death. Where was your help *then,* goddess?" he demanded, his eyes flashing.

Morainen's gaze lost some of its warmth as her voice grew firmer. *Heed me, mortal. Even the gods do not have unlimited freedom to meddle in the course of mortal events, no matter the fervor of your pleas or the justness of your cause.* Her tone softened. *And has it not occurred to you that the Elves also pray to their own god? Would you have great Sallamarian take their side and grant their prayers at your expense?*

Gavan said nothing in response, though his eyes burned with accusations of betrayal. It was left to Briana to temper her husband's anger with greater deference as she asked, "Please tell us why you have appeared now, my Lady."

I come to tell you that your people, and all the peoples of this land, face a grave and dire threat. An infamous and wicked sorcerer, a mortal man bound in immortal sleep for eight hundred of your years, has arisen again. Across the sea in old Kal'Dathia, misguided men broke the bonds meant to hold him for eternity, and loosed this plague upon the peoples of the world.

Briana heard the deep disquiet behind Morainen's words, and it came to her that such a man must be terrible, indeed, to provoke unrest among the gods themselves. She listened as Morainen continued.

This sorcerer, called Rak'koth, has conquered all the nations of Surrikand with his Dark magic. Now, when he holds that entire continent in thrall, he looks across the sea to Balleterria—to Calderia and all the lands around it. In a short time, perhaps less than a year, he will bring his Dark armies here.

Briana sat speechless, but Gavan chose that moment to break his brooding silence. "And now you deign to intervene at last, when it suits your purpose. Tell me, goddess, what is this 'help' you offer?"

The image of Morainen faded for a moment, then grew clear once more. *Mortal king, your eldest child has been chosen by the gods to perform a formidable task. He is destined to unite the races of this land, and to seek out another of great power and wisdom who can aid in defeating this abomination.*

Daunted by the mention of their son's name, Briana was finally driven to offer some protest of her own. "Our son Killian? But he is not yet even a man. What role could a boy play in this great destiny?"

Before the goddess could offer any reply, Gavan shook his head in disgust. "Surely, you have not forgotten that we are in the midst of a war with one of these 'races' as we speak. I can foresee no circumstance, however dire, that would lead me to seek alliance with those cursed Elves."

For that very reason, there must be an end to the fighting, a peace that must be sealed with your son's betrothal to an Elfin maid, to bind humans and Elves with ties of blood.

Gavan's explosion of rage could have been heard in the deepest dungeons of the castle. "A marriage to that Forest scum, that band of murderers? Have you no ears for the treachery we have endured? I would sooner die than let my son play the sacrificial calf for the sake of your precious peace!"

Morainen's face grew solemn. *Take care for the words you speak, mortal, lest you bring down the very fate you would avoid upon yourself, and on all around you. Now, heed me closely. One will come, a man of learning who bears a blue stone, a token of the favor that the gods have bestowed upon him, and a sign of the geas he must fulfill. It is he who will set your son on the path of great power. Harken to his words and abide by his counsel, if you would save your land and all that you hold dear.*

Then, before Gavan could offer further angry protest, the glowing eyes dimmed and the image of the goddess vanished, her voice echoing in the thoughts of king and queen as they stared at each other in astonishment and fear.

✝✝✝✝✝

Deep within the Great Forest to the south, high above the ground in the Elfin Tree Palace, King Rillandariel sat in evening council with his royal advisors, listening to reports on the number of warriors lost this day in the war against the humans of Calderia. The fighting had worn on for three years since the war's beginning, with no clear victor thus far.

The Council had been meeting for several candlemarks, and Rillandariel found himself angered and disheartened by the latest accounts of foul depredations suffered at the hands of the accursed enemy. At the moment, General Trillafarien was holding forth on a familiar theme, the melodious voice that had charmed many an Elfin maid now hard with bitterness.

"It was not enough that they invaded our sacred Forest, encroaching upon our land and stealing the leaves of our Thalesi trees to make their mind-eating drug. Each day, more of our warriors are slain defending our birthright. We must not rest until the fields flow with human blood, until we have avenged our deaths and our enemies have learned the folly of their avarice." Trillafarien pounded his fist upon the table for emphasis and glared around the room, challenging any to dispute him.

No one there, certainly not the king, could argue the truth of his words. Scarcely three months earlier, Rillandariel had lost his only son to a Calderian arrow that pierced the boy's strong young heart. They had brought the lad's body to his father, draped in his Forest cloak of greens and browns, the gold insignia of his royal blood woven on the breast of his tunic. Rillandariel had taken one look at the lifeless face of his beloved first-born and collapsed on the throne.

No, the king would scarcely gainsay any charge brought against these wretched humans, nor would he seek to temper the calls for revenge from others when the very same bloodlust coursed through his own veins. My son! Even now, the pain of his loss threatened to overwhelm and shame him in the Council.

Then, in the midst of a vociferous call for more extreme retaliation from several council members, Rillandariel felt himself grow strangely detached and distant from the meeting, as if a curtain had fallen between him and the others. An urge to be alone, to seek the coolness of the night air, came upon him suddenly.

He rose gracefully to his feet and waved a hand, dismissing everyone with no explanation. Cut off in mid-speech, the advisor holding the floor noted the king's drawn face and narrowed eyes. He respectfully bowed himself out of the royal presence as the others took their leave in similar fashion.

Rillandariel stepped out onto the balcony of the palace, drawn into the shadows of the night by some impulse he could not own. It was then that he saw the apparition materialize before him, an amorphous outline of a man's face with riveting golden eyes, and heard the voice inside his mind. *Rillandariel, hear my words.*

Fearful, the king peered closely at the ghostly visage. "Who are you? Do you come to haunt me, specter?"

The reply came quickly, with a hint of amusement: *You do not need to fear me. Your people know me as Sallamarian.*

Then Rillandariel, King of the Forest folk, fierce warrior and stern monarch, fell to his knees in awe. Sallamarian! Father god of the Elfin race! Guiding spirit of his people for millennia who had last appeared to his forefathers centuries ago, or so he had been told. He bowed his head humbly and raised a hand in supplication.

"What would you have of me, Lord?"

Listen, my son, for there is much you should know. In a land beyond the Luminous Sea, a dreadful power has Awakened...

As evening darkened into night, Rillandariel listened with deepening foreboding as Sallamarian spoke the grim tidings he had come to share. When the tale had been told, the ghostly figure drifted closer to the Elfin king.

This is no time for the peoples of Balleterria to war among themselves. No nation, no people, can stand alone against the coming threat. You must set aside your anger and make a peace with the Calderian king.

"But Lord, how can this be?" cried Rillandariel. "Humans have raped your Forest and slain your children. Lord, they have taken my *son* from me!" His voice broke, as the image of his dead child lying before him, of all the beautiful sons and daughters murdered by the barbaric humans, choked his soul with visceral hate.

Nevertheless, intoned Sallamarian sternly, though not without sympathy, *a peace must be made. In time, a man skilled in the arcane arts will visit Gavan, the human king. He will come to Awaken the king's son to the power of the gods seeded within him. When this has been accomplished, the human king will come to you, seeking to mend the wounds of this war with the offer of a pact between men and Elves—a pact that must be forged with a promise of marriage between his son, Killian, and an Elfin maid.*

This betrothal will help to unite the royal houses and the peoples of both races, so that you can put an end to this useless hatred. And, when they have sworn their oaths to each other in the Handfasting ritual, they will join in a quest to find that which can prevail against the Dark powers. You must give them all possible aid.

Only the presence of his deity before him prevented Rillandariel from raging aloud at the unthinkable demand echoing in his head. Still, his voice trembled with anguish. "But, Lord! One of our own, Handfasted to a...cursed human?"

Sallamarian's apparition drew closer. *This must be done. The lives of all your people—my people—will depend on it.*

Rillandariel struggled not to grasp the god's full meaning, hoping desperately that he had misunderstood. "And this Elfin maid?"

A pause. Then: *Yes, mortal king. Your daughter, Princess Ellianthia.*

As the words of this pronouncement faded, not even the gods could have silenced the cry of outrage and dismay that erupted from the king's throat to shatter the quiet of the Great Forest.

Chapter 4

Warnings Unheeded

He was old. Very old. The few stray wisps of hair
ringing the crown of his aged head were as gray as winter fog,
and did little to conceal the brown liver spots visible on his scalp
when the cowl of his plain, mud-brown robe fell away from his
face. His unruly beard, as gray as his hair, grew halfway down
his chest in an untidy mass, and the hands gripping the carved
walking staff were gnarled and spotted as well.

The soiled hem of the coarse outer garment tied around
his spare body bore witness to a lengthy journey along the dusty
roads of the countryside, a trek familiar to any villager who had
traveled those same byways. And the weariness in his face, also
streaked with dirt and grim, gave silent testimony to the strain
imposed upon his aged body by the long trek.

Walking slowly through the streets of Brannock Village,
his thin shoulders slightly stooped, the old man might have been
mistaken for a venerable monk in the Holy Order of St. Senorix,
an ascetic brotherhood that dwelt on Penitents' Isle off the
eastern coast of Calderia, and sent its members on annual
pilgrimages to the mainland to minister to the spiritual needs of
common men. Or rather, he might have been mistaken for one
of the Holy brethren until a poor soul driving a creaking cart
piled high with wheat and barley had the temerity to
inadvertently block his path.

While the driver tried to urge his mules around the
plodding brace of oxen pulling a wagon laden with iron from the
castle foundry, a stream of scathing invectives and angry
mutterings issued forth from the old man's withered lips,
revealing guttural tones that marked him as an outlander to any
local resident—and making it abundantly clear that, unlike the
soft-spoken, gentle-natured monks he resembled, this one did not
suffer fools gladly.

In truth, the driver could hardly be blamed for the chaos
of traffic and congestion that slowed travel through the village to
a walk. The signs of a kingdom at war, a protracted war at that,
were everywhere visible. Companies of soldiers marched in
formation through the village streets, crowding aside any citizens
not quick enough to vacate their path. Colorfully clad Royal
Lancers, pennons streaming smartly from their lance tips, yelled,

"Make way!" as the iron shod hooves of their campaign horses clattered over the cobblestones in the village square.

Then there was the steady flow of supply wagons going up or coming down from Brannock Castle. The gray granite fortress rose high and wide on a small hill above the settlement that had grown up beneath its southern walls, and from which the village took its name.

The old man did not yet know the causes of the conflict between the humans and the Elves dwelling in this land. Still, he had seen evidence of war throughout the countryside from the moment that he had wobbled down the gangplank of the Flying Seahorse when the vessel docked in Breckon Bay.

Disembarking had not come a moment too soon for him, as his stomach had never really adjusted to the days of roiling seas and turbulent storms he had had to endure on the voyage. The soldier manning the dockside guard post had eyeballed him with mild suspicion as he disembarked.

"What be yer name, granther, and what business have ye in Calderia?" he had asked gruffly.

The old man had lifted a worn leather satchel and replied, "I am called Morgander. I have some small skills as an apothecary."

"Then mayhap they will have need of ye in the village or the castle itself. Move along," the guard grunted, waving him on his way.

During the long walk to Brannock Castle, seat of the Calderian monarchy, Morgander had seen the movement of soldiers heading southward toward a place they called the Great Forest, or simply the Woods, a thick, dense expanse of trees that was home to the Elves. Oftentimes, the old man had had to step off the dusty, winding road to make way for military forces moving toward the battlefront.

He had passed groups of King's Knights trotting in the vanguard, armored with steel plate and wearing knee-length hauberks beneath sleeved red and black tunics, carrying burnished silver shields decorated with Calderia's Royal Crest of opposing black Gryphons rampant on a red field

Soon after, he had been forced aside by ranks of infantry, their pointed, silver-colored helmets and breastplates glinting in the bright afternoon sun. They marched with their leather-covered wooden shields slung across their backs, gripping the hilts of the swords belted on their hips to steady them.

Behind the infantry had walked smaller squads of archers wearing boiled leather vests and caps over brown tunics and leggings. Some walked with unstrung long bows in hand, others carried curved crossbows—and all were equipped with quivers bristling with arrows and slung over one shoulder.

Finally had come the heavily-laden carts and drays heaped with all manner of supplies and equipment: canvas tents; wooden posts; great iron cauldrons for cooking and heating water to scour pots and pans; thick haunches of beef and venison; enormous baskets of grain and flour; crates of salted pork; large tuns of wine and barrels of water; and piles of spare armor and weapons to replace those lost or broken in battle.

But there had been traffic going the opposite way along the road as well, traffic that gave evidence of the grievous toll taken by the war. Covered wagons passed by carrying the wounded, their heads and bodies wrapped in blood-encrusted, foul-smelling bandages. These gory wrappings barely staunched the flow of precious life blood from ugly sword-inflicted gashes or jagged holes pierced by the deadly blue and green fletched Elfin war arrows, some a yard or more in length—arrows that the Forest fighters favored as their primary weapon, and which they launched in lethal barrages from the relative safety of the shadowy, and often impassable, Woods.

The stench emanating from these wounds, some open and festering, had assaulted the old man's senses as he walked past the wagons, hearing the groans and cries for surcease from the pain. Still, as grim as that was, the reek of death from the bodies laid out in wide flatbed carts, staring up with vacant eyes while flies buzzed around their open mouths, had been cause enough to make him turn away and wretch into the earth churned to ankle-deep dust by the steady passage of iron-rimmed wheels, marching feet and hooves.

Those haunting images were still lingering in the old man's mind as the driver of the stalled cart finally managed to move it a few feet forward, allowing him to continue on his way along the village street. He looked longingly at the inns and taverns he passed, yearning for a clean, soft bed and a goblet or three of wine to wash the miles of road dust from his throat. Yet, the bed must needs wait until he had gained audience with the king, and said what he had come to say.

However, he did allow himself the small luxury of a short delay for a mug of cool red ale, which he purchased for two cesters from an enterprising wench with a friendly smile and an inviting bosom who stood outside a tavern doorway selling drinks to passersby. He sipped the liquid slowly while sitting on a hard wooden bench carved with the names of other travelers who had whiled away an afternoon with a tankard while resting their feet. By the time he rose wearily and resumed walking, the sun had set and the air had cooled.

Now the gray stone walls of Brannock Castle loomed in front of him, imposing and dark, save for the flickering yellow lights from torches set high upon the battlements where guards patrolled, occasionally visible in silhouette as they paused at the embrasures to look out over the village and countryside—and save for the torches flaring more brightly beside the raised portcullis across the short drawbridge spanning the castle moat.

Two of the King's Elite stepped forward as the old man crossed the bridge, his staff tapping on the wooden planks. The older of the two men, an officer judging from his air of authority and the gold trim on his jacket sleeves, leaned his head forward and looked the stranger up and down, from his straggly hair to his traveled stained-sandals, then confronted him in a brusque, though not unfriendly manner.

"What be your business here, granther, and so late at that? Monks and beggars find such charity as they can in the village."

The younger man standing in the background snickered, which brought a stern look from his superior. Ignoring the rudeness, the old man addressed his response to the officer. "I am called Morgander. I have business with the king. I have traveled far to find him and the need is urgent."

The officer dismissed his request with a shake of his head. "No one enters the castle at night, sirrah. Leastways, nae without orders posted to the Commander of the Watch, which be me. Return in the morn."

Hearing the curt dismissal, the old man gave a sigh of impatience and made a small, barely seen circular gesture with his left hand, speaking in a low, firm voice and looking directly into the other man's eyes. *I have urgent business with the king. He is expecting me. You will take me to him now. All will be well.*

The officer's eyes opened wide, then stared straight ahead with a glazed expression. After a long pause, he nodded slowly and repeated in a monotone, "You have urgent business with the king. He is expecting you. I will take you to him now. All will be well." With that, the man turned and led the way past the other guard and through the gate, ignoring his companion's surprised expression.

The inside walls of the castle towered above them, cold and silent, as the captain walked rapidly across the courtyard and approached the massive oaken doors of the aging fortress. Braced with iron and steel, and measuring the height of two men, the great doors dwarfed even the tallest of the King's Elite who stood before them, halberds crossed, barring unwarranted access to those who dwelled within—the royal family, ranking nobles and those courtiers high enough in the king's favor to be granted residence, especially in time of war.

As he grew even with the posted guards, the captain brushed the crossed halberds apart with a wave of his hand. Accustomed to obeying an officer's orders without question, the King's Elite nearest the great doors pulled on the handles and stood aside.

Inside the doors, a short arched hallway opened onto a great hall, dominated by a wide, sweeping stone staircase in the center of the room. Its steps were carpeted with broad red runners trimmed with black borders, as if guiding the way to upper floors cast in shadow from the fire burning in the large, open hearth off to the left side.

The old man's gaze traveled up the walls that were easily two stories high, and hung with long, colorful tapestries reaching from ceiling to floor. Offering some protection against the chill drafts that plagued all stone fortresses in any season, the woven hangings depicted noble lords and ladies, ferocious beasts, and scenes of conquests and heroic deeds that were thoroughly unknown to him.

Without pausing, the officer lead the way up the staircase, his back held erect and rigid, the heavy thud of his hobnailed boots muffled by the runners. Climbing at a slower pace, the old man took note of the sturdy, finely carved wooden balustrade that ringed the stairwell on the second floor. A lengthy walk down a narrow, carpeted hall lined with sculptured busts of noble faces and hanging banners embroidered with the Royal Crest brought them to a pair of dark, polished doors, set with gold-plated handles.

The officer knocked firmly on the right door, then immediately pulled it open and stepped aside to allow the old man entrance. A minor gesture from Morgander's hand released the officer, who closed the door behind him and took up guard outside the chamber.

He stood inside a small throne room, of the type used for private ceremonies or to receive important visitors with personal business to conduct with the Crown. The king's throne, a highly polished affair carved from a single block of blond oak and elevated on a granite riser, and a somewhat smaller throne fashioned from the same oak, were placed side by side against a windowless wall covered by a large tapestry recording the crowning of a monarch.

At present, the larger throne was occupied by a broad-shouldered, lean-hipped figure dressed in a red military jacket and black trousers that disappeared into knee-high black leather boots. Handsome in a rugged way, with high cheeks and an aquiline nose, his hair was a mass of bright red curls falling to his shoulders, held in place by a small, plain band of gold circling his forehead.

Regal and poised in his bearing, he looked to be a man in his prime, though his face revealed signs of strain and discontent. The haggard, weary look in his blue eyes spoke of too many difficult decisions, and the pallor to his cheeks was evidence of too few nights of peaceful sleep.

King Gavan of Calderia looked down from his throne at the old man. His face was expressionless, without any hint of surprise or offense from this uninvited intrusion on the royal personage, as if Morgander had been expected this very night. This was confirmed when the king turned his head to the side and asked quietly, "Is this the one you foresaw in your auguries, Aisleen?"

With a whisper of cloth against carpet, a woman stepped out of the shadowed corner. She was clothed in a deep blue satin gown, her hair long, straight and black, save for the first streaks of gray showing along her temples. Her dark eyes and full, red lips contrasted with her pale, smooth complexion. Taller than most women of the land, her figure slim and lithe, though amply bosomed, the seeress stood with a calm, centered bearing usually seen in those who possessed great inner strength and confidence.

The old man could feel the aura of quiet power emanating from one gifted with magic by the gods—a different kind of magic than his own, but strong and deeply rooted all the same. Beyond that, she was easily among the most beautiful women he had ever seen.

When she spoke, her voice was soft and steady. "He is the one, Your Majesty, of that I am sure, although he did not appear nearly so...ancient...when first I Scryed him. Perhaps our guest would deign to gift us with his true countenance?" Her mouth turned up slightly in amusement as she looked at him expectantly.

Morgander smiled ruefully and inclined his head in her direction, acknowledging her powers as a seeress. Then he released the glamour that had served as his disguise over the long journey to this land. The air around him shimmered, a bright blue light surrounded him, and the old man was gone.

In his place stood a man of middle years with a full head of wavy auburn hair and a short beard of the same hue, each showing early signs of graying. He now appeared tall and strong, unbent by age or infirmity, though leaner than the king.

"Permit me to introduce myself, Your Majesty," he said, touching his heart with his hand as he bowed from the waist. "My name is Mik`kel."

The king inclined his head in return, but said nothing. Mik`kel took that as an invitation to continue. "I am a wizard and a prince of Kal`Dathia, though my father, the king, is no more. I have been sent to you by the gods to…"

Now Gavan raised his hand to interrupt him, his voice edged with hardness. "I *know* why you are here, mage. The gods have seen fit to visit me as well. I have known of your coming for some time." He gestured to the woman standing on his left. "My seeress followed your journey and foretold of your arrival this night."

Aisleen nodded, and, after a moment of hesitation, asked, "May I inquire why you came to us wearing the glamour, my Lord?"

Mik`kel spread his hands. "A small conceit, my Lady. I have reason to believe that…others…might have taken note of my arrival, had I appeared in my true form."

"Others?" she asked, arching a delicate, perfectly curved eyebrow.

"Yes, my Lady," he replied. "People from my native homeland of Kal`Dathia, agents of Emperor Rak`koth sent here as spies to gather information. I have worn the glamour to disguise myself since first I left the Isle of Serenity, making use of my humble powers."

A wry look crossed Aisleen's face at his use of the word "humble." Hardly that, she thought to herself, but kept her own counsel, continuing to take her measure of him with those captivating eyes that seemed to see everything.

"Then, too, I am the last living heir to the throne of my country, since my father had no other children."

King Gavan shifted impatiently on his throne. "Your father?" he echoed in a gravelly voice.

"Yes, Your Majesty. My father was King Nek`krod the Fourth, ruler of Kal`Dathia, though I had not seen him for some years since leaving his royal court."

"And why was that, mage?" Gavan leaned forward, peering more closely at him.

Mik`kel bore the king's gaze calmly. "Your Majesty, my royal father and I did not agree on questions of my...future. He was grooming me for the throne to become, in his words, 'the first Wizard-King of Kal`Dathia in hundreds of years.' He wished me to join with the other magic users in honing my powers for use in battle. I preferred my studies in healing, and found in myself no bent or inclination to assume the governance of my country. Yet I bowed to his will as a dutiful son and learned the Spells of Destruction, growing strong in the power. But that was not all I was nor all I longed to be.

"For that, and other...personal...reasons, I left my father's court and Kal`Dathia at last. I traveled to neighboring lands and studied with healers and other wizards for a time. Eventually, I made my way to a small center of great learning, the Isle of Serenity, far from my homeland. In truth, I would still be there, content amid my books and scrolls, living in the company of other scholars and seekers of knowledge, were it not for the return of the sorcerer who has enslaved my people...and the wyrd placed upon me by the gods to seek the Avatar."

The king sat upright and slammed his hand upon the rounded arm of the throne. "The Avatar!" he spat, with an intensity that took Mik`kel aback. The wizard glanced surreptitiously at the seeress, but observed no measure of surprise in her eyes. Gavan stood erect in one fluid movement.

"You mean my son, my Killian, the heir to *my* throne! The boy that the gods would sacrifice to some divine design to undo their own folly! The boy they would see betrothed to some gods-damned Elfin bitch to make a peace with the bastards who murdered my own brother!"

The haggard look was gone from the king's face, replaced by fire crackling in his blue eyes. "And did your gods also bother to mention that Rillandariel, the Elfin king, denied us the cure for the Scourge last year, while hundreds of my people were taken by that terrible plague? The gods be damned! Where were they when I was forced to sit here helpless and watch my people perish from that cursed pestilence?"

Gavan slumped back down onto the throne and sighed deeply. As quickly as the anger had flared, it was gone, replaced by a weariness and sadness palpable in the small chamber. Surprised by the depth of rage and despair fueling the monarch's outburst, Mik`kel fell silent. Nothing he could say would assuage the waves of raw pain and loss that radiated from the man on the throne, threatening to flood his own magically heightened senses.

Mik`kel looked sideways to the seeress and saw the same pain mirrored in her eyes. He did not wish to belittle their obvious suffering. Then he thought of the persecution befalling his homeland far across the sea, the tales of torture and death visited on his own countrymen by Rak`koth—perhaps even in his father's name—and he steeled himself to speak again.

"Your Majesty," he said softly, "I know little of the war that rages here in your land, nor are the causes clear to me. I grieve for your brother, and for all the people lost so tragically to sickness and battle." Now his voice hardened with resolve.

"But I have knowledge of the devastation and horror that Rak`koth and his foul creatures of the Dark magic have unleashed upon *my* people. You speak of a plague that killed hundreds. Well, his black sorcery is a virulent plague upon the *world*, and his victims already number in the thousands, nay, the tens of thousands!"

He stopped and met Gavan's eyes directly. "Know this also, my Lord King. One kingdom, one continent is not enough for this man. Even now, while he holds my country and all Surrikand in his cruel grasp, his greed for power is not sated. He is coming, great King. He is coming here! The gods have foretold this; and, however else they may have failed us, they do not lie."

He pointed to the floor before the throne, as if naming the very spot upon which Rak`koth would stand. "And when he comes here, bringing his blood magic and his Dark armies to your shores, and finds your peoples disunited and estranged, fighting among yourselves, he will overwhelm you—humans, Elves and all the other races of this land. He will grind your towns and villages into dust and lay waste to all nations, do you not put aside your anger and make common cause."

Mik`kel paused, for he knew that this was the hardest part for Gavan to hear. "Though you do not wish it thus, great

King, your son has been selected by the gods to play a role of great import in this cause, a necessary part upon which hinges all hope for success."

The king sat motionless, staring through him, saying nothing, his refusal to relent writ large upon his face. The silence lengthened, until Aisleen broke the spell with a soft query. "Lord Mik'kel, how is it that the gods look to the king's son to shoulder this weighty burden? And why Calderia, so far from Surrikand's shores?"

Mik'kel spread his hands, as if helpless to explain the minds of the divine. "I know only that he was chosen at birth, against the time when Rak'koth might return to walk this world. He is not the first such chosen. Over the centuries, once in every generation, a child has been selected by the gods, gifted with powers seeded within him but lying dormant, unAwakened, unless the need arose. Countless others have lived out their span of years and died without being called to power and to duty. But now, in this era, Rak'koth has arisen, and Prince Killian, the Avatar chosen in our time, must answer the call."

"But, my Lord Mage," said the seeress, "the king's son is only now approaching his eighteenth name-day. He is barely a man, hardly ready to wed an Elfin princess, much less carry the burden of making peace and uniting all the peoples of Balleterria."

Mik'kel nodded, understanding well her confusion, for his own doubts weighed heavily on his heart. "It is sufficient for now that only a promise of marriage, a betrothal, be arranged, as a symbol to both peoples that the war must end. I will need time, precious time, in which to call upon my arts to Awaken his dormant power and train him in its use."

"Yet," Aisleen persisted, "I have seen no signs of any such power. To be sure, he is a bright boy and quick to learn. He is his father's son, after all, and has been gifted with many strengths. But I have detected no magical gift or potential—not in his aura, not in my auguries."

Mik'kel gave a slight shrug. "Lady Aisleen, I believe the gods have seen fit to hide the power of the Avatar from mortal eyes unless, and until such time as, it is needed. But there can be little doubt that this *is* the place, this *is* the time, and that the prince *is* the one."

He reached into his robe and brought out the blue sapphire hung around his neck. It sparkled in the torchlight as he held it aloft. "I have followed the path directed by this stone. It has drawn me like a siren's call to this kingdom, and to this very castle."

He heard sounds of movement from the throne, and knew that the king was staring at the talisman he held. "The task of the Avatar goes far beyond a marriage of state alone. What more he will be called upon to do remains a mystery to me. Perhaps when his power has been…"

"Enough!" Gavan's voice echoed loudly in the quiet chamber. "I will hear no more talk of my son's power and his duty to the gods this night or any night! Killian is not a tool to be used and discarded at the whim of deities who scorn my prayers for aid, who allow my people to die in agony. And I will not go crawling to that treacherous Forest snake to beg for peace and offer Killian up in the bargain, on the threat that this 'Dark sorcerer' might cross a wide sea and march against me in my own kingdom some time hence!"

The king stood, glaring at Mik`kel, his hand resting on the gilded pommel of the knife in his belt. "You will stay away from my home and my son! I will make my own 'peace' with those murderers, in my own way. And if this Rak`koth comes, I have my own magic users as well! Aisleen, be good enough to show Lord Mik`kel out." He pivoted sharply on one foot and strode from the chamber, leaving mage and seeress staring at his back.

Chapter 5

Seeds of Hatred

They walked in silence for a time down the long hall, until the seeress slowed her steps and touched the sleeve of Mik`kel's robe. "He has not always been like this. He is a good man and a good king. He has not always been so..." She hesitated.

"Bitter? Stubborn?" Mik`kel asked, giving voice to the inescapable impression that had formed early on in his discourse with Gavan.

Aisleen glanced at him, then away. "I was going to say 'driven,' but perhaps you have the right of it after all." She sighed, competing emotions flickering across her face. He thought she might be gathering her resolve to do something unpleasant by the way she pressed her soft, full lips together in a thin, straight line. She must have made her decision, for she stopped walking and gestured with her slim, delicate fingers toward a nearby alcove located midway down the long passage.

When he had seated himself at her wordless request, she lowered her body gracefully to the marble bench beside him and smoothed the satiny fabric of her gown with her hands. She sat framed by the casement set into the niche in the stone wall behind her, against the backdrop of the dark night sky visible through the slitted shutters. The toes of the blue satin slippers peeking from beneath the folds of her skirt were set close together, feet flat on the floor, marking her composure as did the way she folded her hands neatly in her lap before beginning again.

"Perhaps some history of the war and how our peoples came to hate each other will help you to understand the king's strong...convictions."

"I would be indebted to you for anything you can tell me, my Lady."

Aisleen inclined her head. "Two hundred years ago, our people crossed the Gespian Sea and came to settle in what we now call Calderia, seeking a better life. But we were not the first arrivals to this land. The Dwarves had long claimed the Misted Mountains in the west of Balleterria as their home, for it is there that they had burrowed deep within the rock to build their steading and mine the precious ores and gems they hold so dear."

"Who are these Dwarves?"

"The Dwarves are a secretive race, guarding the location of their stronghold closely. When we came, they were willing enough to undertake some limited trade with humans, and do so to this day, though they come down from their mountains but twice a year. They have offered commerce, if not friendship, and we get along well enough. But, though the Dwarves favor us with their trade, they remain apart from the conflict between our people and the Forest dwellers."

Mik`kel had seen no sign of these Dwarves thus far, but held his curiosity in abeyance, content to let the seeress continue her history unimpeded.

"Like the Dwarves, the Elfin people had been living here in their Great Forest for centuries before us. The Forest folk that our ancestors first encountered spoke of abiding in harmony with all nature among their Woods, the tall trees south of us that stretch in an unbroken line across our continent from end to end. Few of our people have traveled into their Forest, and none have gone beyond its southern borders where, we are told, dwell other peoples of whom little is known."

Aisleen shifted slightly, though her back remained poised and slightly arched in a manner that unconsciously emphasized the smooth, elegant line of her neck and the fullness of her bosom. Mik`kel allowed his gaze to linger momentarily on her body, wondering briefly whether her air of quiet serenity masked stronger passions. Then she coughed lightly, and he lifted his eyes to meet hers again. She made no comment on the focus of his interest as she resumed.

"We have not journeyed deep into the Great Forest because we have never been invited to do so. Like the Dwarves, the Elfin people have always been an isolated folk, mostly preferring to keep their own company within their Woods, and venturing only rarely onto the open plains. My ancestors sought them out when they arrived, but found the Forest folk aloof from trade or exchange—at least at first."

Here, she shrugged slightly. "Still, the Elves were not openly hostile. They seemed to tolerate us, and watched from a distance as we built our first homes and tilled the fields for our first harvests. Their life spans are said to extend far beyond that of humans. We have been told that they observe our busy, short-lived endeavors with some amusement and fascination."

"How did the war with the Elves begin?" Mik`kel asked.

The seeress paused, collecting her thoughts. "Our people build with stone quarried from the mountains, and with oak and pine cut from the smaller forests to the north. Brannock Castle was the first fortress raised. It is said to have been modeled on the castles from the old world. The Elves seemed to have no quarrel with our using timber from our own domain, but made it very clear that they considered their Great Forest to be sacred, and would allow no encroachment by anyone with designs on their trees."

Mik`kel stroked the sides of his beard absent-mindedly, feeling the fatigue of his journey warring with his curiosity. The latter got the better of him, and he asked, "So humans and Elves remained apart?"

"No, not entirely. Over the years, a limited trust developed, encouraged by the gradual realization that each people might have something of value to offer the other after all. We looked with longing at the tall trees of the Great Forest that offered excellent timber, resistant to decay and insect destruction.

And we had heard of a plant, the Thalesi bush, whose leaves, when crushed and boiled, were said to offer a cure for many ailments. We hoped it might be proof against The Scourge that Gavan spoke of, a deadly plague that has decimated whole towns and villages every two or three generations since our arrival.

"But we learned that these curative plants grew only inside the Great Forest, so we approached the Elves to bargain for lumber and Thalesi leaves. At first, they disdained our offer of trade, until they saw the beautifully wrought gold jewelry and gems worn by our envoys—gold and jewels bartered from the Dwarves in return for our cloth and finely spun silks."

Aisleen stood and began to pace slowly back and forth with small, precise steps, as if seeking to discharge some internal distress. The hem of her gown lightly brushed the floor as she moved, underscoring the first signs of agitation in her soft, cool voice that Mik`kel had heard since meeting her.

"The Elves agreed to trade the wood from fallen trees— and only from fallen trees—and a yearly supply of Thalesi leaves, in return for the gold and gems we could offer, along with some of our finer cloth. And, for some years, this arrangement prospered. That is, until five years ago, when a long drought brought countless brush fires and a root disease that destroyed vast numbers of our oak and pine trees in the north and west. Without wood, we could not build or expand our towns and villages.

Our supplies largely exhausted, King Gavan sent to the Elves to treat for more timber. But they refused, saying that they could not increase our supply of wood without cutting down live trees, which would be a sacrilege. They claimed that they 'shared consciousness' with the living trees in some way we could never comprehend, and would never abjure their sacred trust as Guardians of the Forest."

Aisleen bowed her head as if saddened. Mik`kel had an urge to offer comfort with a touch, but recalled his hand before it could span the small space between them, just as the seeress resumed.

"King Gavan was deeply disappointed, but accepted their decision, proclaiming the need for honor and keeping faith with the Elves. But other, less honorable, men did not agree. The building guilds and the merchants who had thrived on commerce in lumber protested the lack of materials for their trade, when a ready supply lay only miles away in the Great Forest."

"So this conflict began over a shortage of wood?"

The seeress shook her head. "No, it was more than just the wood. The Thalesi traders had discovered that, when administered in larger amounts, the curative tea of the plant produced a...sensual...euphoria, temporary in duration, but apparently quite powerful in its effect."

"Sensual?"

At his question, Aisleen averted her eyes shyly. "It is said that larger doses of the Thalesi tea can heighten the senses and stir the physical passions. That it will make a woman more willing, more ready to...receive...a man." Mik`kel saw a blush suffuse the seeress' cheeks, which did not lessen as she continued. "And it is said to make a man more potent and better able to sustain his...arousal...when taking his pleasure."

Sensing that any further discussion in this vein must proceed with some delicacy, Mik`kel said mildly, "This would doubtless put such a 'curative' in great demand."

The embarrassment on her face gave way to deep concern. "Yes. All too great a demand, I fear. You see, we also discovered that the tea in high concentrations was quite addictive when used repeatedly. Too late, we learned that the cravings it engendered required larger and larger amounts of the Thalesi leaves as the needs of the users grew apace, for when withheld after lengthy usage, those addicted to the tea fell stricken with great tremors and sickness, some even unto death."

Aisleen stopped pacing entirely, her voice taking on a bitter tone. "The black irony was that these desperate addictions also created even greater profits for the Thalesi traders, who seemed to care nothing for the tragic fate of the victims. Indeed, they even urged the Elfin king to *increase* the yearly allotment! But he refused, as he had refused the requests of the building guilds for greater access to the trees. Then the traders and builders formally petitioned King Gavan to insist that the Elves meet our demands."

Mik`kel smiled ruefully. "Having 'petitioned' the king myself this very eve, I can scarce imagine him bowing to the insistence of anyone, gods or men alike."

Aisleen nodded, and he saw her pride in a king who would not be easily compelled. "Indeed, they could not prevail upon the king to change his mind or go back on his word to the Elves, though he himself was vexed by the attitude of their king, Rillandariel. But, when King Gavan refused their demand, the greediest of the builders secretly underwrote clandestine ventures with loggers and woodsmen to steal from the Elves what they could not obtain by honest means.

"So, too, the Thalesi traders sent men into the forest to thieve the coveted leaves they could not win through trade. The Elves, who detect the smallest disturbance in their Forest—and who even claim to communicate with the animals within—captured the woodsmen and the traders, and sent them back in fetters to the king, with a warning that further incursion would be met with harsher measures."

Mik`kel pursed his lips, seeing the direction in which her tale was going. "I gather that was not the end of the matter," he observed.

"No, sadly, it was not. King Gavan punished the interlopers and vowed to enforce the agreement. But his soldiers could not patrol all the borders of the vast Forest, and the traders sent woodsmen to secretly 'harvest' the trees again, this time with deadly consequences. The Elves attacked and slew every woodsman they found inside the Great Forest, then dumped the bodies, bristling with arrows and slashed open with knives or swords, out onto the open meadows. Among the bodies was that of a well-known Thalesi trader, with a message written in his own blood and pinned to his chest, saying that all trade was ended."

Looking drained, Aisleen sat down on the bench again. "The country was outraged. The embers of longstanding resentment among many of our people for the aloof and alien Forest dwellers were kindled into open flame, and a great cry arose to reciprocate against the 'murderers' who would 'hoard' the wood and medicine that Calderia needed so badly—and to which we were 'entitled' by the greatness of that need."

"Was King Gavan swayed by this outcry?" he asked gently, seeing her need to defend her sire.

She shrugged her shoulders and looked away, her face beautiful in profile, though she now appeared older and tired, as if wearied by the tale she told. Something in the way she reacted to Gavan's name hinted that this beautiful woman might harbor secret feelings for her king, emotions about which she could not speak concerning a sitting monarch with a queen and a family.

The memory of his own forbidden passions for someone unattainable brought a twinge of old pain to Mik`kel's chest. He wondered if Aisleen had found a modicum of comfort and release with lovers; or whether this lovely woman, gifted with the Sight and with wisdom by the gods, went to her bed alone, as he had for years.

Aisleen's reply brought him out of his musings. "Gavan could not help but be affected by the loss of his countrymen, however wrongful their activities, and by the cries for vengeance raised in his own court. Yet he tried to behave with reason and honor. He instructed his own beloved brother, Prince Orrin, to travel to the Elves under flag of truce, with instructions to negotiate in good faith to end the crisis."

Here, her voice took on a grimmer tone. "But, even as Orrin prepared to journey to the Great Forest to sue for peace, a small band of Elves caught outside the safety of their Woods was attacked and killed by relatives and friends of the slain woodsmen. They mutilated the bodies of the slaughtered Forest folk and nailed them to the very trees they called friends."

The seeress looked at Mik`kel, her eyes glistening with unshed tears. "When Prince Orrin arrived at the Forest border for the peace talks, he was met by enraged Elves who bitterly demanded the immediate execution of the slayers of their Forest kin. While Orrin pleaded for calm and reason with the Elfin leaders, tempers flared like sparks to dry grass between the other Elves and a few of the men in the prince's party who were suspected of the killings. Fighting broke out between both sides. The soldiers escorting the prince acted to protect their countrymen, a melee ensued, and, in the confusion, the king's brother was stabbed to death."

Mik'kel heard a catch in the seeress' voice, and felt the sorrow behind her words. "Were the killers ever brought to justice?" he asked quietly.

"No, for no one knew exactly who killed Orrin. But when King Gavan learned of his brother's murder, he wept and raged. He buried Orrin in the Royal Crypt below the castle, then emerged from the tomb with a look in his eyes I had never seen, a hard and terrible stare. He ordered his army to the field, and we have been at war with the Elves ever since."

She hesitated, as if debating to tell him something more, something grave by the look of it. "The saddest part was that, on the morn of the meeting between Prince Orrin and the Elves, I had a vision—a vision of a great Gryphon mortally wounded, falling from the sky. I rushed to tell Gavan, to warn him of some danger to Orrin, for a Gryphon could only mean royalty, and all the other members of the royal family were safe here in the castle. Gavan believed the warning and sent a rider to call Orrin back. But it was too late. He was already lying dead on the ground when the rider arrived."

Mik'kel wondered if Aisleen held some part of herself to blame for the death of the king's brother, though he could not fathom how that could be so. But he did not know her well enough to broach the question, and then she had moved beyond it.

"I have heard that the Elfin king, Rillandariel, lost his own son in one of the more recent battles. I think of both kings, each lost in grief and anger, and I can not see an end to this war until all lie dead, save for the smallest hope that something might heal the grievous wounds between them."

With that, her composure crumbled, and she wept silently, her hands over her eyes. Mik'kel gave in to the impulse to console her, and reached out to draw her head to his chest. She tensed briefly at his touch, then surrendered herself to the comfort of his embrace.

They sat together like that for long moments, saying nothing, she leaning against him, him feeling her body's warmth through her satin gown. The scent of lilac from her hair and skin filled his nostrils, and he felt the dampness from her tears upon his chest.

He found himself reluctant to move, to disturb this first intimate contact with a woman of any kind since leaving his father's court and the love he had never fully forgotten. And when, after a time, she lifted her head and moved away from him, her face flushed with embarrassment, he felt a small sense of loss.

Later, after she had thanked him for his comfort and promised to speak to the king again on his behalf, Aisleen walked him to the door of the castle and touched his hand in farewell. The feel of her hand on his, and the fragrance of her perfume, lingered with him all the way back to the village, where he roused a sleepy innkeeper, paid his coin for a tiny room and collapsed upon the narrow pallet.

On the morrow, he would have to see about making arrangements for more permanent lodging and some means to support himself while he waited for events to unfold. He prayed that the king did not wait too long to heed his warnings, but the matter was out of his hands for now. He slipped into a dreamless sleep, his last waking thoughts centered on the sad, beautiful lady in the great castle on the hill.

Chapter 6

Man in the Shadows

The man calling himself Morgander was not the only stranger to arrive in Brannock Village that season, nor was he the only one wishing to conceal his true purpose for being there. But, while Mik`kel employed a glamour spell to hide his identity, the man who called himself Faram used no magical artifice or trickery, relying only on the guise of a man skilled in the art of looking so ordinary and unremarkable that he could go virtually unnoticed by anyone who happened to glance his way—and then be just as easily forgotten.

Indeed, his nondescript appearance and ability to blend into the background was as much a key to success in his line of work as any other stratagem devised by his cunning mind. To this end, he had taken a commoner's name and, entering the village, he looked every inch the common man, from his dark, rough-cut hair and weathered skin to the muted colors of his humble clothing. He was clad in a homespun shirt, well-worn leather breeches and sturdy, mud-stained boots, as would befit someone of modest birth who labored with his hands to earn his bread.

He was neither especially short nor tall, with a plain face lacking any particularly distinguishing features. He had learned to speak the language well enough, affecting a slight country drawl that might place him as coming from a farm or town to the west, perhaps even the Westlands.

His small belt pouch contained a few coins of the realm, mostly cesters and copper pennies, sufficient to buy several mugs of ale or simple food and lodging for a few nights, but hardly enough even to tempt any self-respecting cutpurse. His real cache of money, which included gold and silver crowns needed for the expenses of his work, was hidden in a flat narrow belt worn around his waist beneath his undershirt.

Like Mik`kel, this visitor had seen the signs of a country at war all around him, ever since disembarking from the ship at Breckon Bay. In the sprawling "village" of Brannock that was actually, he thought, closer in size to a city than its name suggested, knights and lancers rode through the streets in tight formation. Whether they were going to or coming from the battlefront could be determined from a casual glance at the state of their weapons and armor—clean and polished or dirty, dented and stained with mud and body fluids.

As he continued on, he saw off-duty swordsmen, pikemen and bowmen walked the streets alone or in small groups, some headed for their barracks to sleep, others stopping to frequent the taverns, ale houses and brothels that catered to weary men given leave to enjoy a brief respite from the fighting.

Since the king and queen frowned on ladies of the evening plying their trade openly on the streets, most women in that oldest of professions provided their services under the auspices of an established house of pleasure, often advertising their charms by leaning over balconies clad in low-cut bodices and nearly transparent gowns that revealed more than they concealed. They called out as he passed by, promising various inventive bed sports and pleasures, but their bold displays and verbal enticements held little appeal for him.

Instead, he was more interested in the conversations to be overheard in taverns and alehouses patronized by soldiers, where useful information might flow more freely after a few rounds of strong drink. And so, he followed a pair of burly swordsmen into a well-lit tavern called the Crowing Cock, as indicated by a sign over the door depicting a large rooster leering with a predatory gleam at a well-endowed, half-naked wench.

Slipping inside quietly, he made his way carefully through the raucous crowd of patrons to an empty table in a corner. There he settled in, several feet away from the place where the swordsmen had settled down to commence some serious drinking.

Soon, they were joined by two more friends, a bowman and another swordsman, both of whom had already been enjoying a few mugs, judging by their slurred speech and loud laughter. He ordered dark ale from a harried serving girl in a fetching blouse and short skirt who somehow managed to maneuver in and out of the narrow spaces between the tables, holding her tray aloft while trying to avoid the clumsy hands that groped at her swaying hips as she brushed by. Then he sank back into the shadows unnoticed and nursed his drink for a candlemark or two while he listened.

Filtering out the din of voices, the noisy clatter of dishes and the discordant strains of drunken singing, he paid close attention when the soldiers' talk turned from debating where the best ale and easiest women could be had to a more sobering discussion about the most recent battle between the king's army and their Elfin enemies. He took note of the number of men and Elves mentioned, the type of forces employed by both sides—in this instance, an array of knights, lancers, Elfin skirmishers, swordsmen and bowmen—and the number of casualties inflicted, both wounded and dead.

He listened to their bitter stories of companions killed in the fight with the "Elfin scum," and heard the grim satisfaction in their voices as they spoke of butchering their foes with their blades or riddling the flesh of "those Forest bastards" with their spears and arrows. There was no mistaking the deep hatred harbored for the Elves, and their determination to exact bloody revenge for the deaths of their fallen comrades.

When the time grew late, the crowd thinned out as the patrons drained their mugs and went to seek their beds. In keeping with his rule of remaining unnoticed by never being the first to arrive at a gathering or the last to leave, he rose and made a quiet exit into the night.

Had anyone been asked, they would have been hard pressed to describe him or even recall that he had been there. He found a modest inn, and took a small room in the back of the establishment where he was less likely to encounter any of the other residents on a regular basis.

After an uneventful night's sleep, Faram awakened and left the inn, finding his way to the main market place. He wandered through the crowded square, attracting little attention from the buyers and sellers, and those just browsing or enjoying the street musicians and performers ensconced on nearly every available corner. He noted the wide variety of goods and wares of every sort on display in the stalls, and the range of services offer by tradesmen and craftsmen.

Even with the throngs of people and the hubbub in which business was conducted, most of the citizens were peaceful and relatively well behaved, no doubt due, in part, to the visible presence of uniformed guardsmen who walked the streets in pairs, keeping an eye out for any untoward behavior. He took special care to avoid attracting interest from that quarter, blending in easily with the other folk.

Despite the apparent prosperity and civility in evidence around him, his exploration revealed a city enduring the heavy burdens of a lengthy war. Not only was there evidence of the toll taken in human life, as seen by the wagons carrying the wounded and dead encountered on his journey to the village, but there were also other signs of the strains and deprivations that affected the people in a host of other ways—like the shortages of certain commodities and resources that drove their prices up, when they were to be had at all.

Purchasing a steaming meat pie to break his fast, he learned that beef was harder to come by because many of the cattle were either being stolen by the Elves in bold raids or being requisitioned to feed the Calderian army. When he paused for a cup of cheap wine to wash his plain meal down, the vendor bemoaned the fact that the smaller merchants could not compete with the high prices paid by the taverns and inns to insure a steady supply of beer, ale and other potables.

From what he heard, it seemed that even steel used for making tools, knives and personal utensils was in short supply, as was leather for belts and harnesses. So, too, were the healing herbs and powders used for medicinal purposes, for these were sorely needed at the battlefront.

That evening, he sat quietly in the corner of the Broken Plough, a tavern that catered to a different clientele than the Crowing Cock. Here, most of the patrons were not military men, but rather local farmers, tradesmen, laborers and the odd merchant or two. Men dressed like him in plain clothing, from humble backgrounds and living simple lives, wanting only to earn their living and provide for their families.

More than one story overheard from men sharing a mug after a day's work revealed sadness and loss in their lives or the lives of friends and neighbors. They spoke of sons, fathers and brothers who were hale and hearty when they joined up to fight, only to return crippled and broken; of loved ones killed or gone missing, never to return at all; and of women left to raise children without a husband or father.

The visitor was no stranger to tales of woe, for they were common enough in the recent history of his own homeland, where so many thousands had lost their lives or their loved ones in the wars. What he was not accustomed to hearing were the angry mutterings openly directed at the king by a few of the patrons, blaming him for his policies or his failure to win the war.

While most seemed loyal to the Crown, one father who had lost a son spoke loudly of feeling betrayed, and the need to make his grievances known. In the visitor's homeland, such sedition voiced in public would be answered with an immediate, painful death.

Yet he felt no sympathy for the father, and only disdain for a nation who could not support a leader with the strength to enforce order. These Calderians were a weak people, he thought, divided among themselves and ripe for conquest. And this king was a weak leader if he allowed open treason from his subjects to go unpunished. But he kept these opinions to himself, content to remain in the background and observe.

In the days that followed, he continued his careful pattern of watching and listening, gathering information where he might in other taverns and eateries, market squares, and merchant shops where he lingered, pretending to examine the goods for sale. Much of what he overheard was trivial and of little value; but, when it came to acquiring knowledge, long experience had taught him that sifting through the dross often uncovered little kernels of gold.

He learned about the private lives of the royal family from castle servants and staff who gossiped as they shopped for goods and materials or ran other errands in the village. From them, he gained insight into the devastating blow that King Gavan had suffered when his brother, Orrin, was murdered while meeting under a flag of truce with the Elves; and how that heinous betrayal had fueled an undying thirst for revenge in both the king and the eldest son, Prince Killian, who would soon be going into battle.

Seeking more sensitive information of a military nature, he even sought temporary employment at the Gryphon's Roost, a tavern just outside the walls of the castle where knights, lancers, general staff officers and some members of the King's Elite could often be found of an evening. He approached the owner with a woeful tale about coming to Brannock to find his son, a young man who had left the drudgery of the farm to seek his fortunes in the army.

Playing on the owner's sympathy, and taking advantage of the shortage of good workers after years of war, he soon found himself earning a small salary unloading delivery wagons, sweeping floors and waiting tables. Cloaked in the near invisibility of a lowly servant, he hovered nearby unobtrusively while officers and commanders openly discussed troop movements, logistical problems and battle plans over expensive dinners and numerous glasses of fine wine.

Within an eight-day, he had made a rough tally of the various fighting forces at the king's disposal, their strengths and weaknesses, available reserves and the like, as well as similar estimates concerning their Elfin enemies, all of which the officers unwittingly revealed to him when reviewing battle accounts and intelligence reports as he served their food and drink.

Based on what he had learned, any idiot could see that both sides were at a stalemate. The king's heavily armored knights and lancers could not penetrate far into the Woods with their massive warhorses, and swords and pikes were poorly matched against hidden Elfin bowmen firing their deadly arrows from the trees and undergrowth of the dense Forest.

Conversely, the Elfin bowmen and lightly armored horsemen could not hope to stand against the sheer brute force of the knights and lancers thundering down upon them on an open field. It was a war that neither side could truly win, yet the fools fought on.

From time to time, his clandestine activities also included pre-arranged, highly secret meetings with his cadre of agents, other faceless men and women he had personally trained and assigned the task of gathering information from different parts of the continent. Well before his arrival, they had been dispatched to travel across Calderia, posing as tinkers, itinerant blacksmiths, hostlers or merchants, visiting the towns and villages, chatting up homewives, innkeepers and other tradesmen while quietly noting the presence of soldiers and assessing local defenses.

Some of the women had been prostitutes whom he recruited for their special "skills." He had sent them to work in the brothels, providing intelligence gained from fighting men and other paying customers who were inclined to talk more freely when relaxing in bed after being pleasured.

Some of his men had journeyed as far as the Westlands, through baronies and duchies nominally loyal to the king, but far removed and apparently disinclined to involve their forces in the war with the Elves. He heard stories of age-old hostilities with another kingdom called Dunmoria located in the mountains northwest of Calderia; and tales of a reclusive race of Dwarves who closely guarded the plentiful deposits of precious stones, minerals and ores that they mined in the Misted Mountains to the far northwest.

His people reported little success thus far in penetrating the Great Forest, due to the uncanny ability of the Elves to detect any intruders, and their proclivity for killing outright any humans found trespassing inside their homelands. Still, talking to those living in villages and homesteads close to the Forest had yielded some useful information to add to what he had already acquired by himself.

It was widely known that the deep hatred and distrust felt by the humans for the Forest dwellers was matched in equal measure by the loathing and contempt that the Elves felt for them, especially since the death of the Elfin king's only son at the hands of a Calderian bowman. The king was said to sit brooding in his Tree Palace deep in the Woods, while ordering his warriors to extract deadly vengeance in reprisal for his terrible loss.

Of the lands south of the Great Forest, little was yet known, except for some mention of primitive tribes of nomads who herded cattle on the plains and fought among themselves with some regularity. Apparently, like the Dwarves, they kept themselves apart from others, save for some occasional barter with the Elves along their northern border, though their rumored propensity for attacking with little provocation made trade a rather dicey proposition.

Finally, satisfied that he had seen the lay of the land for himself and learned much of what he needed to know about Balleterria, the man who called himself Faram decided it was time to make his way home. He knew all too well that his master would be growing impatient for his return, and would not look kindly on anyone who kept him waiting.

And so, he paid his people and instructed them to continue their efforts without fail, all of them knowing the consequences of displeasing the great one they served. Then he gathered his notes together, collected his few belongings from the inn and set out to book passage on a ship sailing from Breckon Bay, careful to ensure that no one took any more notice of his departure than they had of his arrival.

After the long voyage, he landed in the port of Mertania and hired a horse to take him to Palace City, changing mounts along the way and riding into the night to speed his journey. Upon arriving at the palace, he hurried down the long corridor, passing huge, brutish guards wearing the ebony armor and horned helms of the Black Legion. He could not see their eyes, but he was certain that they followed him with their stony stares as he entered the throne room. There, he presented himself to the ominous figure in a black velvet robe who sat upon the throne, toying roughly with the slave who knelt before him.

"You have returned at last," said Rak`koth, looking up from his pet, his crimson eyes burning like red coals as he beckoned him forward. "It has been some time. I trust you have learned something of value that will justify keeping your position...and your head."

"Yes, my Emperor," said the Spymaster, bowing deeply and trying to keep his voice steady. "I have much to report..."

Chapter 7

The Rose and Thistle

Crown Prince Killian, heir to the throne of Calderia and various other lesser titles, was spending the eve of his eighteenth name-day in a tavern in Brannock Village, getting pleasantly drunk. His two closest friends, Lord Colum and Lord Gilmore, sat at the table on either side of him, co-conspirators in some mysterious plot to celebrate his name-day "in a style befitting of a fuzz-faced youth about to be named a man, despite all evidence to the contrary"—or so they had announced as they descended upon his room in the castle just after dinner and spirited him away to the private upstairs room of the Inn of the Rose and Thistle.

Tomorrow, he would officially become an adult in the eyes of the law and Calderian society. He would stand before King and Court and drink from the ritual Cup of Reason, borne to his hands by his mother, the queen, and said to wash away the folly of youth and grant him maturity and wisdom. But that was tomorrow.

Tonight, Colum and Gilmore had promised him a special coming-of-age ritual of another sort entirely. Apparently, as they saw things, achieving the ripe old age of eighteen several months before him qualified them as seasoned adults, entitled to assume the mantle of mentors in guiding him through the hazardous shoals as he entered manhood. Killian grinned at them with affection, enduring their ribald jibes and endless slaps on the back, knowing them to be true friends, even through the warm glow of wine that, in sufficient quantities, could turn virtual strangers into boon companions.

Each lord was dressed in a fashion similar to his own, a sleeveless velvet tunic worn over a white, open-neck silk shirt with full collar and bloused sleeves, snug doeskin breeches, and ankle-high leather boots. But there the resemblance ended.

It was not only his crimson tunic trimmed with black and embroidered with the Royal Crest upon his left breast that set him apart from them. Though slightly younger, he had already surpassed them in breadth of shoulder and chest. He could outwrestle and outfight them in hand combat and swordplay with embarrassing ease. At six feet two inches tall, with the fiery red hair and crystal blue eyes he had inherited, he was clearly his father's son to all who knew the king.

Colum leaned over and refilled his wine cup. "Drink up, my fine lad," he urged. "The night has just begun."

Killian already had a fairly good idea that their mysterious "manhood ritual" would consist mainly of getting besotted on wine and enjoying the company of the trio of willing serving girls who hovered nearby. He also knew that too much of the former could seriously interfere with accomplishing the latter, especially if he had a mind to explore what tender treasures lay beneath those fetching skirts and blouses. And that, undoubtedly, was a substantial part of the master plan devised by his mentors, since they had already informed him in less than subtle terms that they had rented the inn's suite of upstairs rooms and engaged the "services" of the girls for the night.

As Killian was not entirely a stranger to intimate adventures with girls, he wondered what the "special treat" his friends had mentioned might be. Since they were uncharacteristically steadfast in their refusal to say more, he was left to mull over the possibilities as he sipped his wine, feeling the strain in his shoulders from a long afternoon spent in sword practice.

They used wooden swords, for Armsmaster Doughal knew better than to risk injury or worse to his noble charges by allowing the royal scion and the young lords to have at each other with naked steel. Still, the old man did not spare them their daily ration of bruises and cuts inflicted by the heavy practice swords, wooden or not; and more than one lad of noble lineage, including himself, had suffered a broken nose or a cracked rib as Doughal hovered behind the panting boy, practically jumping up and down as he screamed in his ear.

"Fight like a man, damn it, laddie!" the Armsmaster would yell. "I do nae see boobies sprouting from yer chest! So fight like you have a wee bit of something down there between your legs! You got your noble nose bloodied because you did nae take the fight to him. Do nae hang back, waiting for him to come to you, dainty as you please. Parry and thrust! Parry and thrust! Watch his eyes, boy. By the Four Hells, how can you expect to lead men in battle if you will nae set an example?"

Then, having vented his spleen at the boy's lack of progress, the grizzled instructor would shake his head disdainfully, throw up his hands and look to the sky, as if beseeching the gods to take this impossible task away from him, before turning away to seek out the next hapless victim of his righteous wrath.

But, after his eighteenth name-day ritual, things would be different, thought Killian, smiling from the warmth of the wine in his belly. He comforted himself with that thought, only half hearing Gilmore's latest appraisal of the blonde wench's bosom. After this night, Doughal might still be yelling in his ear, but he would finally be sparring with real swords and real armor.

Men did not play with toy swords, he thought. Men went off to battle, sooner or later, though he doubted it would be sooner, because he had overheard his father tell his mother that he wasn't going to "sacrifice" his son like he did his own brother. The king's voice had broken a little, and Killian had slipped away unseen.

Yet, he had mourned the loss of his uncle, Orrin, too. Men got to avenge the deaths of people they loved, people who should never have died...people like Orrin, like Jenny. The thought of their loss left him staring into space, and brought a downward turn to the corners of his mouth.

Something cold and wet drenched his head. Sputtering and blinded, Killian leapt to his feet, amid a chorus of laughter from his friends and stifled giggles from the serving girls. Wiping his eyes, he cast a murderous glare at Colum, who still held the drained goblet in one hand while he bent over almost double, struggling to control his mirth. As Killian took a step toward him, intent on terrible revenge, he felt a restraining hand on his shoulder and turned to see Gilmore, grinning and cackling like a hen.

"Now, laddie, there will be no woolgathering in my classroom, or ye will feel the crack of my staff on your royal noggin," Gilmore croaked, in a fair imitation of old Parlan, the ancient schoolmaster who tutored them in reading, writing and history; and who was known for administering a sharp rap on the head when a student drifted off during one of his rambling discourses on the intricacies of ancient heraldry or the esoteric lineage of noble bloodlines.

Killian's face twitched as he tried to restrain his own laughter, but it bubbled up despite his efforts to remain stern. Gilmore's "Parlan" was just too good, and besides, they were right. This was not a night for gloom and melancholy. On the morrow he would be a man!

He took only token revenge on Colum with a playful jab of his elbow to his friend's side, then called for a fresh cup of wine with a wicked gleam in his eye that sent both of his companions edging away in mock fright. But all thoughts of further retaliation quickly evaporated when he saw the blonde wench approaching with his wine, balancing the serving tray on one raised hand and moving toward him with a roll in her hips that left him wondering how she could walk that way without spilling all that she held.

Getting a close look at her for the first time, Killian quickly concluded that Gilmore's praise for her breasts had scarcely done them justice. Large and deeply rounded, they spilled up over the edge of her low neckline in a wave of soft, pale flesh that threatened to burst the three small buttons that held them captive within the tightly-stretched bodice, should she breathe too deeply.

Below her waist, her short skirt flashed long expanses of white thigh with each step. She stopped in front of his table; then, one hand still holding the tray aloft, she smiled at him and deliberately took that deep breath. The buttons on the bodice held, but only just. He grunted with equal measures of relief and disappointment as she winked at him boldly, her eyes sparkling with amusement.

Just as deliberately, she laid the tray down, placed both palms flat upon the table, looked him directly in the eye, and leaned toward him. His groin tightened as his eyes followed her deepening cleavage. He felt himself begin to press against the soft fabric of his breeches as she bent forward slowly, letting her neckline slip down inch by tantalizingly inch until she was nearly fully exposed.

Her eyes dropped down to her chest, then back up to meet his, and she laughed shamelessly, enjoying her effect on him. "My name is Catriona, my Lord, though men who know me…well…call me Catty," she said, her voice low and throaty. "I am here to serve you. Is there anything else I can offer you?"

As she said this, she gave a small shake to her shoulders in a manner so brazen that Killian could only gape. Meanwhile, the Lords Colum and Gilmore erupted with raucous hoots of laughter and exaggerated groans.

Killian just kept staring. It was not as if he had never seen breasts before. More than one young chambermaid or noble's daughter had been willing to unlace her bodice or lift her skirts for the young prince's pleasure. Yet, they had been girls his age or slightly younger, not overly experienced themselves, though quite eager to please him.

But Catty was no giggling girl. He could see that she was, most assuredly, a full-grown woman, easily four or five years older than he, with the ripe body and the look of an experienced female who understood lust and knew how to take pleasure for herself as well. As she was doing now, enjoying the hunger in his eyes, laughing with delight in a way that did even more fascinating things to her ample bosom. And, when she leaned forward to whisper lewdly in his ear, it was all he could do not to bury his face in her flesh then and there.

Then she was around the table and settling down snugly into his lap, with a calculated wiggle of her rounded hips that brushed the length of his groin and drew an audible groan from Killian. Colum and Gilmore, already well into their cups, laughed uproariously and slammed their hands down on the table, congratulating themselves on their choice of his name-day "gift" with looks that were positively smug.

But he hardly noticed when his friends staggered up from the table and led the other wenches away to private rooms, calling out obscene suggestions that produced a new round of giggles from the girls. He was much too occupied with the way Catty was ruffling the thick red hair on the back of his neck with one hand, while she opened her blouse with the other, slowly, one button at a time. At last, she pulled her bodice completely away, releasing smooth, white mounds tinged with light blue veins, her nipples pink and large.

"Do you like what you see, my Lord?" she asked. Then she was pressing down gently on his head and bringing her breast up to his lips, saying, "Please, my Lord, let me help you."

Killian groaned, wondering if he was asleep in his bed and only dreaming this. Then he was kissing her smooth skin while she worked a hand down between their bodies and traced the outline of his manhood through his breeches.

"My Lord," she purred, "Your breeches seem to have grown too tight. You must not do yourself an injury." Unlacing them deftly with her fingers, she freed him and began teasing him, until his eyes nearly glazed over and he thought he must explode from desire and need.

But before he embarrassed himself, Catty released him and stood up slowly. "Oh, my Lord," she said, raising her hand to her mouth with a look of feigned innocence. "It is a good thing that you warm me so. The room has a chill, and I fear that I am wearing naught underneath."

Killian's eyes widened as she turned her back to him and leaned forward across the table, reaching behind to grasp the hem of her skirt which was already riding high above the back of her knees. "Perhaps my Lord would care to see for himself," she said with a wicked smile. Then, before his lips could form the only possible response, she was lifting her skirt to her waist and parting her naked thighs.

Killian needed no further encouragement. He lurched to his feet, grasped her hips with both hands and entered her in one quick thrust. She gasped, then quickly threw her hips backward to meet him. Matching her rhythm to his, she reached behind her again and brought his hands forward to her bosom as she squirmed beneath him.

For long moments, the only sounds heard in the chamber were the crackling of the fire, the rocking of the table, and their ragged, intermingled moans and cries as he buried himself in her again and again. Then she was crying out with pleasure and clenching him tightly.

Enveloped in her tender vise, he erupted in short, explosive spasms that left him spent and weak—and utterly exhilarated. Long moments passed before he found the strength to pull away from her and slump down in his chair with a contented sigh.

†††††

Someone was battering inside his head with a Dwarven war hammer while a voice screamed in his ear. Killian flailed out with his arm until his hand connected with something soft and he heard a low curse. He struggled to rise up, but fell down dizzily, then settled for lifting his head and opening his eyes to face his tormentor. This turned out to be a mistake of major proportions when a dazzling light speared his eyes, leaving him blinded.

He groaned and rolled over, trying to escape the brilliance, but something hooked his arm and rolled him back again. When he cracked his eyes open this time, he could barely make out Gilmore's face, contorted with exasperation and sporting a fresh red mark on his cheek.

"Wake up! Wake up, you dunderhead," Gilmore called through the fuzziness in his ears. "You are going to miss your own gods-be-damned name-day ceremony, do you not drag your arse out of that bed!"

Killian groaned again and tried to retreat under the bed covers. That war hammer was still pounding inside his head, landing blows on his temples with a precision clearly intended to inflict permanent damage. His mouth tasted like the bottom of an old wine vat, and the mid-morning sun streaking through the open casement was still dazzling enough to make him flinch. Gods, where was he? Then it all came back in a dizzying tangle of images. Last night. His friends. The wine. Lots of wine. And Catty.

Suddenly, he sat straight up and turned around in the bed. No, it had not been a dream, because here she was, lying beside him, every beautiful, curvaceous female inch of her. She stirred in her sleep and made little noises, her long blonde hair flared across the pillow carelessly, one perfect plump breast exposed where he had pulled the cover away in his random thrashings.

The memories of last night flooded back…images of mounting her over the table and burying himself inside her, and then being taken by the hand and led willingly to bed, where she had coaxed him back to readiness and mounted him in return. Then more wine. He wondered if he remembered a third time and smiled at the thought, though it hurt his face to do so. By the gods, the little vixen was insatiable.

He glanced again at her uncovered body, feeling a familiar tightness growing in his groin, and briefly imagined slipping behind her and pressing himself against her warm inviting skin. Indeed, he might have done so, had not Gilmore seen the speculative look in his eyes and grabbed his arm.

"Oh, no, my randy Prince. You have exactly one candlemark to get back to the castle and dress for your name-day ceremony. And your dear parents, you do remember them, the king and queen? They will have my guts for garters if I get you there late." With that melodramatic pronouncement, he heaved a rumpled bundle of clothing at Killian and stomped off indignantly to call for their horses.

By the time Killian had struggled into his wine-stained garments and stumbled down the stairs, Gilmore was leading the horses around from the stable. His dappled stallion, Sutherland, nuzzled him as he sagged against the saddle for support.

"It will do no good holding up the horse, Killy boy. Get your royal behind in the saddle and ride, fuzz-face, before the king has my head for hash," Gilmore demanded, mounting his bay stallion and starting to trot briskly toward the castle, leaving his prince to follow.

Finding the stirrup with his foot after several futile tries, Killian swung up and lurched the horse forward, ignoring the jarring ache in his head. "Hey," he called out, flashing a half-grin as he drew abreast of the other horse, even though the small smile cost him pain. "What is this about having your head for hash? I thought it was your guts that were in peril."

Gilmore laughed ruefully. "Laddie, your royal father will have every piece of my precious anatomy on a plate, do we not hurry." They stared at each other solemnly, then broke out laughing and spurred their mounts forward.

The most direct route to the castle lay directly through the village square, past the open market where local vendors and traveling merchants stood sheltered from the sun beneath the brightly colored awnings of their stalls, hawking their individual wares in a cacophony of loud cries and earnest promises. Despite the shortages imposed by the war, there was still a great deal of food on display.

Farmers touted the merits of locally grown fruits and vegetables, next to booths exhibiting more exotic fare, such as melons, oranges and lemons imported from the Duchy of Delgaria to the west. Live chickens and fat pigeons screeched and squawked in wood and withe cages, while the less fortunate fresh-killed geese and turkeys hung upside down from hooks, attended by flies drawn to the warm blood still dripping from severed necks.

Rotund butchers with thick fingers offered strings of sausages, quarters of beef, smoked hams and strips of venison, while bakers positioned their hot pigeon pies and honeyed rolls steamed on open racks to tantalize passersby. Here and there, serving lads and wenches tempted the thirsty with cool mugs of beer and ale dipped from lidded casks.

Stalls catering to other needs were scattered throughout the market as well. There were copper-bottomed pots and pans; used clothing in various states of wear or disrepair, depending on the fatness of one's purse; and snow-white sabercat pelts from the northernmost mountains or cured leather hides from the stinking tanneries on the edge of town.

A short distance away, blacksmiths displayed sturdy swords and axes made of Dwarven steel, flashing in the sun.

Traders from distant towns hovered over baskets of exotic spices and tinted bottles of perfumes.

Local women spread bolts of sturdy tan cloth made from flax and other hardy materials intended for sewing garments worn by those who toiled at physical labor. Further down the lane, delicate silks in a rainbow of brighter hues and shades tempted the eyes of servants sent down from the castle by noble ladies to bargain with the foreign merchants come to the kingdom from Gallardy in the west, across the Gespian Sea.

The prince and his anxious friend guided their horses through the crowded market at a walk. Gilmore growled in frustration, occasionally glancing up at sun to hazard a guess as to how much time was left before his doom was upon him and the most tender parts of his anatomy were forfeit. Then they were away from the market and racing past buildings that housed expensive inns catering to a wealthier clientele; indoor shops where finer jewelry or delicate glassware were sold.

Here, too, were discreet storefronts where herbalists and apothecaries dispensed remedies and potions to commoners and nobles alike, all "guaranteed" anonymity for a price. Soon, these commercial enterprises gave way to two and three storied homes inhabited by minor nobility, courtiers, richer merchants, and wealthy landholders with outlying estates who thought it more convenient to keep a home in town, nearer the center of power.

Finally, they were trotting across the drawbridge and under the portcullis of the castle, waved through by guards who drew the obvious conclusions from their Lordship's rumpled clothing and bleary eyes. "That good, was she, Milord?" they called after him. Despite his deteriorated condition, Killian took some pride in their approval and sat a bit straighter in his saddle, at least until he and Gilmore reached the castle doors.

Then they were sliding off their horses, tossing the reins to the waiting grooms, and dashing inside, taking the stairs two at a time in a race to win the safety of their chambers before some family member cast a baleful eye on their tardy disarray. They reached Killian's room bent over and fairly gasping for air. Gilmore caught a pungent whiff of his prince in passing and wrinkled his nose in disgust.

"Morainen's tits, laddie, you smell like you spent the night on the floor of a dockside bar. Better wash off some o' that stink of wine. And, while you are about it, better wash off the smell of Catty as well." He leered evilly. "Her scent is a wonderful aroma for a man to carry with him, but I doubt your queen mother would appreciate its fine bouquet."

Killian snorted, making a point of sniffing the air in Gilmore's direction. "Well, oh ancient one, best you heed your own advice. Standing downwind from you is no walk in a spring meadow, either."

Ducking the lazy swing of his friend's fist, he laughed and closed his door. Once alone, he stripped and tossed the pungent bundle into a corner, then submerged his face in the washbasin, raking handfuls of the cool clean water back through his disheveled hair.

Mindful of Gilmore's warning, he soaked a towel in the basin and gave himself a hasty bath, shivering briefly as the cold cloth met his warm groin. That made him think of Catty again. Pulling on the clean small clothes and stockings laid out by his page in anticipation of his last-minute arrival, he wondered if she had awakened by now, and whether he would cross her mind as well.

Chapter 8

Name-Day

Killian stood outside the door of the larger castle throne room, resplendent in his red belted dress tunic and black velvet breeches, his fiery hair brushed and smoothed, looking every inch a crown prince come of age, with all traces of the bedraggled, odiferous pub denizen now vanished. Beside him, Gilmore blinked his slightly bloodshot eyes while Colum fidgeted with the stiff collar of his own tunic, which seemed intent on cutting into his neck, despite his best efforts.

"Damn this cursed thing!" he exclaimed, tugging it away from his neck yet again. "And I will not be hearing any more about getting fat!" He glared back and forth between his two best friends, daring them to slander his trim frame.

Killian rolled his eyes and said nothing. Gilmore raised his hands in mock innocence, then returned to pressing his ear against the door, listening for some cue that the ceremony was about to begin. This was unfortunate timing, because, at that very moment, the door suddenly opened and Gilmore found himself nearly falling into the lord seneschal, who stood there wearing the disdainful frown that elders of all stripes and stations seem to reserve for the foolishness of youth.

Lord Nigel, the seneschal of the castle for the past ten years, looked drawn and aged since the loss of his daughter, Jenny, to the Scourge. It was said that his wife, Lady Sara, had not yet finished mourning, and remained cloistered in her darkened rooms where any trace of sunlight was forbidden. Killian doubted that Nigel knew how deeply the girl's death had affected his prince as well.

As Gilmore struggled to regain his feet and his dignity, the older man cleared his throat. The solemn moment at hand, Killian suppressed a grin and straightened his shoulders. Preceded by Nigel, and flanked by his loyal companions, he took a deep breath and stepped forward into the throne room.

Judging from the number of people turning to greet his entrance, it seemed as though the whole castle had congregated to celebrate his name-day. The room was crowded with lords and ladies dressed in their fall finery: rich brocades or velvet tunics for the men, flowing silk or satin gowns for the women, a number of them displaying the intriguingly deep cleavage that had spawned many a fantasy with increasing frequency as Killian passed through puberty and into young manhood.

Killian looked longingly at the glasses of wine being offered by servants clad in colorful livery who circulated through the room, replenishing their guests' supply as needed. He saw side tables laden with sliced meats, breads, fruits, sweetmeats and other delicacies prepared for the occasion by a proud but harried castle cook.

Killian would have been unnerved by so many people, save that he had known most of them for as long as he could remember. Indeed, many of those present had helped to raise him in one way or another. There was Lord Randal, tall and balding, and thin as a rapier, holding the arm of the Lady Kylia, his wife of thirty years, whose thickened waistline and fleshy jowls did nothing to offset the warmth of her heart and the sparkle in her eyes. Randal bred the most prized horses in the kingdom, pure of bloodline, and strong in stamina and speed. Killian had passed several summers at their estate, leaning to ride under Randal's patient tutelage, while Kylia fussed over him and fed him until he had nearly burst.

Off to his left stood Baron Glendannon, a stocky, powerful man with a great mane of white hair and bushy eyebrows that ran across his forehead without a gap. The baron, who raised many of the cattle in great demand for provisioning the army, was a close friend of the king.

Since Gavan had thought it important for his heir to know something about such a vital part of the kingdom's food supply, Killian had spent more than one tedious afternoon in Glendannon's company, inspecting livestock while the elder man held forth on the merits of corn-fed beef and the reason for the axiom that an army marches on its belly.

Hovering on the edge of the crowd was old Parlan, Killian's much-maligned but fondly regarded aged tutor, leaning on his cane and peering around the room with rheumy eyes that seemed to reflect a perpetual look of faint surprise. Killian's lips quirked at the memory of Gilmore's rendition of the old man on the previous eve.

A few feet away stood Kennith, the King's Bard, who had sometimes sat with the young prince late at night before a dying fire, teaching him a ballad or two "because a future king must feel the music in his soul, does he wish to know men's hearts. And besides," he would add with a sly wink, "it will not hurt your chances with the ladies."

There was Armsmaster Doughal, fearless in battle, though looking rather stiff and out of place among the gentry. Beside him stood General Brurik, Commander of the Royal Army, gruff and terrible to behold when crossed, yet who more than once had found the time to lift an excited four-year old princeling up across the withers of his fierce black charger and set off at a gallop on the meadow, laughing as the wind whipped their hair behind them.

Hovering somewhere to his right was Father Venutius, the well-fed cleric who had served as the royal family's spiritual guide for longer than Killian had been alive, and who had always been ready with a word of cheer and guidance in difficult times. He felt a sense of gratitude as he recalled the generous spirit that the clergyman had always shown to him.

Standing in the background was Lady Muireann, his mother's near-sister, to whom he had gone in private to cry his tears of loss and pain when his Uncle Orrin died, because he could not cry before the queen. Truly, if a man could count as kin those beyond blood alone, then all these gathered here were his family, too.

The crowd parted before the seneschal as he advanced, his prince and escort in tow, until they reached the dais upon which the dual thrones rested. King Gavan and Queen Briana were, as always, seated side by side, their hands clasped as they watched their eldest son approach.

The queen, her slender figure gowned in forest green that complimented her emerald eyes and amber curls, graced him with a warm, loving smile and leaned to whisper something to her husband. The king nodded and squeezed her hand gently, gazing upon Killian with an unmistakable look of fatherly pride.

Behind the king and slightly to his right stood Aisleen, the seeress, her air of quiet detachment belied by a curious expression of unspoken concern as their eyes met. To the queen's left sat the other royal progeny in smaller chairs: Aaron, Killian's twelve-year old brother, who favored his mother in his fair, delicate features and quiet, serious manner; and Rowena, his four year-old sister, a small, red-headed frenetic bundle of energy, who, at this moment, was striving dutifully to sit still and obey her mother's earlier admonishment to "act like a little lady."

The girl had been doing fairly well until the moment when she saw her big brother dressed up all fancy and playing at being grown-up, then her ladylike demeanor gave way to giggles. Killian smiled at his sister with brotherly fondness, then winked broadly, as if acknowledging that she alone had seen through his pretense.

He continued to smile until his eyes strayed to the black wreath of mourning hanging on the wall above the king's right shoulder. There was only one person missing from his name-day ceremony, the man who, had he lived, would have been charged with the duty and the pleasure of sponsoring Killian to those assembled, publicly vouching for his right to henceforth claim his place in the kingdom as a man.

By tradition, the closest male relative of a boy's father stood for him on the day of his manhood ritual. But Prince Orrin—Uncle Orrin—lay dead in a cold grave these long months, slain by Elfin treachery.

Killian found himself struggling to fight off unexpected tears that welled up, even now, after others had done their mourning and moved on. But others had not loved his uncle as he had—loved him for his hearty laugh, his smell of horses and leather and steel, and his willingness to be silly and undignified in games of hide-and-pounce with a young unruly nephew.

It was Orrin who had given him his first "sword," a wooden stick with a wrapped leather handle, after swearing him to "Holy secrecy" because his mother would not approve. He still kept the treasured weapon in his chamber.

It was Orrin who had interceded in his behalf when punishment was due for minor—and not so minor—escapades; Orrin who had counseled him in the mysteries of the opposite sex; who had been a friend...a second father; and Orrin whose life had been wasted so cruelly on that trampled meadow in the shadow of the Great Forest.

The sharp rap of the seneschal's staff on the floor recaptured his attention as King Gavan rose from his throne to speak. "It is the custom among our people to welcome our sons and daughters to the rights and responsibilities of adulthood on their eighteenth name-day. Over the years, it has been my privilege to share in the joy of many gathered here as I watched their children achieve this momentous milestone. Today, it is now my pleasure to welcome my own son and heir to the company of adults." His look of affection gave no one there cause to doubt the sincerity of that pleasure.

"By tradition, my brother, Prince Orrin, would have stood before you to serve as sponsor to my son." Here, the king glanced briefly at the mourning wreath, his eyes momentarily darkening with anger and the pain of unhealed wounds. Then his features softened. "But today, it falls to me to rise in his stead, a duty I take on gladly."

He gestured for Killian to come forward to the edge of the dais, then laid a large, strong hand on his shoulder and turned him to face the room.   Killian felt a warm flush of embarrassment at the sight of so many eyes upon him, but the king's hand closed firmly to steady him.

"This is my son, Killian. Most of you have known him since my beloved wife brought him forth into the world eighteen years ago. He came to us a feisty, squalling child who gave my Briana no little difficulty at his birth." The queen nodded with a rueful smile, and the crowd smiled with her. "Nor has he been a complete stranger to trouble from that day to this," Gavan added wryly, giving his son a look of mock sternness before a grin split his face and those gathered there joined in his laughter.

"But I have seen him grow from stripling to manhood. I have looked into my son's heart, and I know that it beats strong and true. He has been a dutiful and obedient child in all things important to his parents, and to the realm that he will rule someday. He has shown courage, and the will to endure in training at arms, and has won the respect of his peers and teachers." Gavan's gaze touched Doughal and Parlan, whose answering nods of assent brought a glow of pride to Killian's heart.

"His ability to inspire loyalty is affirmed by the fine friends who stand with him this day." At his mention of them, Colum and Gilmore stood straighter and nodded once in unison. "That loyalty and trust will serve him well when he is called upon to lead men in battle and, the gods willing, in the time of peace we all pray will come."

The king turned and held out his hand. Doughal stepped forward and placed a sheathed blade into his open palm. Gavan beckoned Killian to mount the dais. "This is the sword my father, Nicholas, passed to me on my eighteenth name-day. I wore it with pride until the day I ascended the throne upon my father's death. May you wear it with the same pride, my son."

Gavan reached around his son's waist to belt the scabbard on, then gripped his son's shoulders with both hands and kissed him once upon each cheek. Killian saw a stray tear escape his father's eye, and felt a corresponding moistness in his own. His right hand went to the hilt of the blade and, for the first time, he felt the true meaning of the rite of passage. Then the king stepped back amid loud applause and cast his glance upon the queen.

Briana rose gracefully and turned to Aisleen, who had moved to her side and now placed a jeweled silver chalice in the queen's outstretched hands. She walked forward slowly, regally, her skirts susurrating across the carpeted dais. She stopped in front of Killian, her hands holding the finely worked goblet close to her breast.

"My son," she began, her soft voice quavering slightly, then growing steady and firm. "The king, your father, has spoken of your courage, strength and loyalty. All of these you have in abundance. But a mother sees her son through different eyes. I have loved you, and I have felt your capacity to love in return, love for myself, for our family and others. You have shown compassion and a caring heart. These strengths you will also need in the years to come. May they serve you well all the days of your life."

Then, tears flowing freely down her face, she held the chalice up. "On this day of your majority, I offer you the Cup of Wisdom. It signifies a putting away of the ways of childhood and embracing the wisdom and maturity of manhood. Let impulse be tempered with restraint, anger be moderated with understanding, and passion be melded with judgment. Drink deeply, my son, and know that my love will abide."

Killian reached up to take the cup from his mother's hands, then brought it to his lips and swallowed the fine rare wine, its rich, fruity aroma filling his head. When the cup was empty, a loud cheer erupted in the room. The formal ritual now completed, his family moved to offer hugs and laughter.

Aaron approached him, a look of awe and longing on his young face, breaking out in a shy, boyish grin when Killian pulled him close in a tight hug. Rowena tugged on his tunic, reaching up with her small hands in an open demand to be held. He scooped her up and bit her ear playfully, which triggered a round of sisterly squeals and giggles.

Then he was being surrounded by well-wishers offering congratulations, pithy bits of advice, and invitations to visit. There were also the occasional vulgar suggestions—mostly from Colum, Gilmore and his other male peers—about where they might go this night to "help you sheathe your sword."

Among those pressing close were several noble matrons who whispered invitations to dinners where their daughters of marriageable age might by happenstance be found in attendance as well.   One bold lady even hinted at an opportunity for an uninterrupted dalliance with her daughter, to "get to know each other better without others fussing around, you know, my Lord."

Killian smiled and nodded politely, heartily wishing himself away from the crowd and mounted astride Sutherland with his friends riding beside him.   He paused a moment to wonder if there was time this eve for a quick sojourn to the comforts of the Rose and Thistle.

With all the commotion, the portly, middle-aged man garbed in servant's livery went all but unnoticed as he lingered on the fringe of the throng, examining the prince with shrewd, piercing eyes. If the seeress, also standing apart, saw something more familiar about him than the casual observer might perceive, she made no sign or mention, but only watched with a private smile as the disguised Kal`Dathian mage met her eyes briefly and winked, then took his leave and melted quietly away.

Chapter 9

Rain of Fire

Captain Farris raised his hand to signal a halt to the stealthy progress of the other scouts moving quietly through a patch of undergrowth deep in the Great Forest. He crouched low to the ground, leaning forward on one hand as he scanned the trees ahead for any movement, any sign, that might reveal an Elfin bowman lurking in the dense foliage and branches above or hidden behind the massive tree themselves—some with trunks so wide that it would take six men standing with arms spread apart and hands joined to encircle the base completely.

Seeing nothing of the enemy, he closed his eyes and listened intently for any sound that presaged danger, beyond the raucous cawing of blackbirds and the muted rustle of the wind through the canopy of the trees looming high above his head. Very little sunlight found its way down to the forest floor, preventing the growth of smaller trees or bushes that might have served as cover for the men as they moved carefully through the alien Woods.

Still, even without sheltering cover, Farris had managed to infiltrate his scouts into the Forest without alerting a single enemy warrior. After two days of travelling and eluding Elfin patrols, and one night spent huddled beneath their camouflaged forest cloaks in a cold, fireless camp, they were within a half-day's journey from the Thalesi grove—if they could believe the sketchy map drawn by an old man who had claimed to know the location of the hidden site.

The captain made a beckoning gesture with his hand, and his men crept forward to form a rough semi-circle around him. Lydell and Damon, his two veteran lieutenants, and as good at their work as any in the kingdom, squatted to either side, while the others leaned forward to listen for his muted directions.

There were nine scouts in all, plus a tenth man, less gifted at stealth and hardly a woodsman, but perhaps the single most important person along on their mission. That was Niocal, a senior mage in the king's service, to whom they owed their success in escaping detection thus far.

When Commander Haggan had first broached the plan to send a patrol of elite Royal Scouts into the Great Forest to bring back a new supply of the much-needed Thalesi leaves, he had met with considerable resistance from experienced officers who pointed to the futile, and usually fatal, attempts to penetrate the Woods in the past. Commander Lennox had arisen to flatly dismiss the notion out of hand as foolhardy and ill fated.

"They will know the minute you cross the boundary into the trees. It is said that the plants and animals listen for intruders and alert the enemy. Be that fact or myth, the Elves have arrived without fail to repel our scouts and traders, always with dire results." With that, Lennox had taken his seat, prepared to move on to other matters.

Commander Haggan had then revealed the second part of the plan. He intended to employ the powers of a skilled mage to provide a magical shield that would hide the scouts from surveillance and discovery by all inhabitants of the Forest—plant, animal and Elves alike.

"The number of men shielded, and the length of time that shield could be maintained, would be limited, of course," said Haggan. "But I believe it can work...and must be risked, for we all know that our need for the curative powers of the plant is great."

Lennox and some others had scoffed at the idea that anyone, mage or not, could disguise himself so effectively for so long. Their derision had ceased when Haggan spoke the word "Now," and Mage Niocal suddenly materialized in their midst, having been present and undetected behind his shields for the length of a candlemark. After that, further resistance to the plan had evaporated, King Gavan had given his cautious approval, and the mission had begun.

Farris looked over at Niocal, who was taking advantage of the temporary halt to rest. Maintaining Spells of Undetection around the party constantly was a draining process, even for a mage of his experience and power. Moreover, Niocal was no scout, accustomed to running for long periods without stopping when necessary, eating only trail rations, and drinking water on the move. Their rigorous, sometimes brutal, training fostered all manner of necessary skills.

Each scout learned archery and close-in fighting, long range border patrol, silent tracking, clandestine spying on enemy positions to gauge numbers and weak points, and carrying messages through hostile territory—in all weather and terrain, often in circumstances of great physical deprivation requiring stamina and endurance well beyond ordinary men. By design, this training culled the weak of heart and body alike, and those surviving long enough to win the Royal Scout badge wore it with pride.

Still, despite the need to rest more often than the hardy scouts, Niocal had matched their pace and gradually won their respect. Now, feeling the leader's gaze upon him, the mage nodded once, a sign that he was ready to go on. Farris signaled for his men to check their gear once more to ensure that no weapon rattled or clanked, and that no metal surface reflected what little sunlight they encountered.

Satisfied that all was in readiness, he stood and began moving forward again, the others following with similar caution. Farris hoped to reach the Thalesi grove by midday. Allowing time to gather all the leaves available, they could be miles away on the trail heading back to Calderia by sunset. He imagined arriving home in two days, where a chilled mug of ale and the warm arms of his wife, Kaitlina, would be waiting to welcome him.

He was smiling at the thought of her embrace when he heard the thunk! of the war arrow as it struck Damon, just as the yard-long shaft pierced his lieutenant's neck and emerged from his shoulder in a spray of blood. While Damon was still falling, two more thunks! resounded and two more Elfin shafts sprouted from his body. All at once, the trees seemed alive with Elfin bowmen, firing with a speed and accuracy that Farris would not have credited, had he not seen it for himself.

He saw at least two more scouts go down in that first deadly hail of arrows, and another two fall as he darted for cover. The few remaining scouts had managed to take refuge behind nearby trees, and were now attempting to return fire with their own bows. He thought he heard a muffled yell off to his right as Lydell fought back, loosing a short barrage of steel-tipped missiles into the surrounding trees.

Suddenly, scathing fire erupted from behind him in an angry stream of red flame that whooshed over his head in the direction of a line of trees concealing some of the Elfin archers, and he knew that Niocal had entered the fray. Hearing the screams of the enemy, Farris notched an arrow to his bowstring and glanced around desperately for a target, any target, hoping to slow the terrible onslaught enough to gather his surviving scouts and find a more defensible position.

He knew that retreat would not be likely. He could only pray to Morainen that he and his men would kill as many of the enemy as possible before they died. There! A glimpse of golden hair and a feathered hat appeared among the lower branches of a tree some fifty feet in front of him.

Quickly, he unleashed his arrow, watching it speed toward its mark, only to miss the Elf by a hand span and sink into the branch behind him. Now the enemy archer, alerted to his position, took aim at him, forcing him to drop his bow and throw himself into a roll to escape certain injury.

He managed to avoid the first shaft as it sliced into the earth in the very spot where he had been crouching a moment before. The second arrow took him in the chest, slamming him to the ground with such force that the impact left him breathless.

Searing pain assaulted him as his hot lifeblood pumped from his chest and soaked the soil beside him. His vision blurred, but his hearing remained acute enough to hear the death cries of his remaining men as the enemy circled around their position and picked them off with cruel precision.

A coldness began to spread throughout his body, bringing with it a strange lassitude and an unexpected sense of calm. He turned his eyes back to the tree in which his assailant had been kneeling, and watched with odd detachment as the archer aimed another arrow in his direction.

Just then, another plume of fire raked the trees where some of the remaining archers crouched. This time, the heat was so intense that the trees instantly burst into flames and exploded, Niocal's fiery storm incinerating everything in its path. Farris heard a few anguished cries, but most of the Elves caught in the blaze died without a sound. Their charred, twisted bodies toppled and crashed to the ground like dead branches amputated by a high wind.

He thought he saw the golden-haired bowman dive from his perch just before the fire spread to engulf that tree as well, but the wall of flame obscured the warrior's fate. Then Farris lost the will to care anymore. He closed his eyes and surrendered to the darkness enveloping him. His last thoughts before his heart stopped were of Kaitlina's warm lips on his.

Ten feet away, Niocal slumped against a tree. The Rain of Fire Spells had drained him to the core, leaving him dazed and trembling. He looked around him in disbelief at the wave of devastation he had wrought. He had never thrown such fire against the enemy before.

By consensus, he and his fellow mages had used only minor offensive spells in battle, relying more often on spells of defense—creating confusion and fear, or warding the king's soldiers from arrows and other missiles with Spells of Deflection and Disintegration—but never unleashing massive Fire or Bolt attacks against the Elves or the trees that harbored them. His brethren had deemed such wholesale destruction to be a barbaric misuse of their gods-given power, and had refused to do so in the past.

But this time, shortly before the Elves' attack had begun, his shields had faltered when a gnarled tree root suddenly rose above the Forest floor and wrapped around his feet, disrupting his concentration as it nearly pulled him down. It was as if the root was sentient, for it seemed to act with purpose and intent as it ensnared and dragged him to the ground.

By the time he had kicked himself free of the grasping root and regained his balance, Farris and many of the scouts had been cut down and lay dead or dying. Panicked and desperate to stop the enemy from killing them all, he had spoken the Rain of Fire incantation, and the fiery wall of devastation had twice flowed from his hands.

Niocal stood erect and looked around again, then slowly made his way over to Farris, who lay impaled by the war arrow that had taken his life. The scout captain had accepted him, befriended him...trusted him. Shamed by his failure to protect the life of this brave and dedicated captain, and the lives of all the courageous men given into his care, Niocal lowered his head and silently begged their forgiveness.

Then he moved on, treading softly past the bodies of the other scouts sprawled or slumped where they died, his eyes and throat burning from the acrid odor of cooked meat that grew stronger as he approached the blackened Elfin bodies. He counted ten or eleven corpses, some only charred skeletons where the blazing holocaust had melted the flesh from their bones.

Appalled by the carnage around him, he was turning away in despair when he heard a low moan coming from behind the scorched trunk of an enormous tree up ahead. A few stumbling steps brought him to a body of an Elfin fighter lying trapped beneath a fallen branch that had shielded him from certain death.

He looked to be a younger warrior, judging from the lean, muscular build and the youthful, almost delicate facial features barely visible beneath a black layer of ash and soot. His yellow curls had been singed to brittleness that broke off in

Niocal's hands as he knelt to turn the head toward him, looking for further sign of life.

Another soft moan prompted him to shoulder the heavy branch aside and drag the Elf free from underneath it, where its weight had been pressing on his chest and slowly smothering him. Enemy or not, he could not bring himself to be a party to another death this day, not after the destruction he had already loosed upon the living.

The Elf was clad in a loose green tunic and snugly fitting brown leggings that still smoldered in several places, and the skin on his arms and neck was red and blistered. His chest was covered by some kind of armor—not chain or plate, but rather the hardened hide that the Forest dwellers were wont to wear into battle.

The Elf seemed to be gasping for air, so Niocal hastened to loosen the laces of the armor and push it aside to allow freer breathing. As he opened the tunic underneath, he was startled to find soft, mounded flesh where he had been expecting lean muscle. A closer look revealed firm, well-developed breasts tipped with large brown nipples.

By the gods, it was an Elfin maid! A maid who chose that moment to open her hazel eyes and stare at him with fear and confusion. Her gaze flickered down to her exposed breasts, then back up to his human face. After a moment of bewilderment, her look of sudden understanding was followed by one of unadulterated hate and a feeble attempt to struggle out of his grasp.

"Be still, my Lady," he said softly, pressing her shoulders back down to the ground and closing her tunic. "I mean you no harm. You were trapped beneath the bough. I only meant to see you safe."

Her eyes followed his pointing hand, taking in the sight of the narrow furrows her heels had made in the soft earth as he had dragged her free. She stared at him, perplexed by this inexplicable kindness at the hands of a cursed human, her despised enemy. Then he gestured at her chest.

"I meant no disrespect. I have never before encountered an Elfin maid in battle."

His mention of the battle brought back the horrific image of her entire company perishing in the inferno she had barely escaped, and the hatred returned to her eyes. But even as her hand reached for the knife sheathed on her hip, he was up and moving away, listening to the sounds of something approaching through the trees. He caught a glimpse of movement in the distance and turned to her, speaking quickly.

"Someone comes, perhaps your kin. I must go. You will be safe now." Even through her rage, she sensed profound regret and sadness, as unexpected as his kindness. Then she watched in amazement as he gathered his last shred of power to him, spoke the Spell of Translocation, and vanished before her eyes.

†††††

The Elfin patrol that found her struggling to rise on shaky legs immediately dispatched three warriors to carry her back to the Tree Palace on a stretcher made from wooden poles and woven cloth strung together with sinew. The rest of the warriors remained to bury the dead—though when she left them, they were standing motionless, gazing around the killing field in stunned silence at the burned corpses of their comrades, and at the unspeakable damage done to the trees.

She had briefly protested being carried, but secretly welcomed the help, for she felt too weak and numb to attempt putting one foot in front of the other. The injury to her body was relatively minor, but the wounds to her spirit ran deep and raw.

She had been their leader. She had known most of them all her life, and Elves measured their lives in centuries, rather than years. She had laughed and joked and trained with them, bickered and competed with them, shared cold mornings and warm evening campfires together, fought and bled at their side. On occasion, she had even taken one of them to her leafy bed, sharing her warmth and her passion beneath the tall, majestic trees that watched over them through the long nights and sighed their blessings on the wind.

She hadn't loved Darillian enough to Handfast with him, though he had hinted at it once or twice. But she had loved his strength, his wit and tenderness. Now he lay dead, reduced to a grotesque lump of cinders, along with all the rest of her patrol. Gods, they had been her responsibility. She had been so proud when they had cast their votes in secret, and come to her carrying the silver-fletched arrow that named her their leader.

And now...now, she could not imagine how she would ever find the strength to face their families and friends, and all the others with whom their lives had been interwoven in the closely-knit fabric of their Forest community.

By the time her bearers reached the towering canopy of the Tree Palace that spread its limbs out across the sky, dozens of people had gathered in the clearing surrounding it. The tree housing the palace measured over one hundred paces around the base, and soared nearly two hundred feet into the air. The king and his royal family made their home in rooms created from covered platforms cradled in giant boughs that arched some fifty feet above the ground.

Other platforms nestled among the higher branches, serving as lookout posts and storage areas for food and weapons. These platforms were connected by a web of ladders and walkways equipped with safety guide ropes, although the nimble-footed Elves scarcely had need for them, save for the very young and the very old.

She watched the faces of her Forest kin as the escort carried her past them on the litter. Although Elves valued strength and courage, and were not given to revealing the depths of their emotions in public, she could see the fear and anxiety growing as they saw her blistered skin, took notice of her scorched hair and clothing, and realized that she alone had returned from the patrol. One of the warriors took his leave and went to speak to those present, his words drawing cries of disbelief and grief from those close enough to hear his grim news.

Then her bearers reached the base of the palace. She twisted out of the litter and began climbing slowly up the ladder, her hands tender as she gripped the rungs, her legs unusually weak and unsteady from the exertion. She felt ashamed at her sense of relief to be nearing the refuge of her private chamber, longing only to shed her ruined clothing, wash the grime from her skin and sink into sleep.

She waved the waiting servants away, their eyes wide at her appearance, and stepped into her room. She had scarcely begun to wash her face when she heard the rapping on her door. She turned, steeling herself for whatever was to be, and said, "Come."

The king entered, filling the doorway with his tall, slender frame, his blonde hair falling past his shoulders. He lowered his head slightly to enter and walked several feet into the room, where he stood for a moment, saying nothing, only looking at her with a mixture of relief and concern. Shaken by her appearance, perhaps most of all by the loss of her thick, sunlit hair, Rillandariel spread his arms open and said simply, "Ellianthia."

She dropped the cloth and fell into his embrace. "Father," she cried. Then, for the first time since she was a child, she began to sob in his arms.

†††††

Sometime later, when she had cried herself out, Ellianthia sat beside her father on the bed and told him everything, beginning from the time that the trees had alerted her patrol to the presence of intruders deep in the center of the Forest. She still could not explain how they had penetrated so far in without detection, save that the tree she had climbed sent her an image of magical power surrounding one of the men.

"Darillian thought the trees were finally able to sense a trace of the power he was using to hide them when they drew close to the heart of the Forest, where the tree magic is strongest," she said, shrugging her shoulders despondently. The king heard the catch in her voice when she mentioned the warrior's name, but said nothing, only hugging her again.

After a moment, she continued, in a muted, detached tone. She told him of their race to get ahead of the humans before they reached the Thalesi grove, and how she had chosen the spot for the ambush with care, stationing her warriors in what she believed to be "good" cover.

She described how the patrol had known the enemy scouts were approaching, but could see nothing until a tree willed its root to rise up against the human mage. With the spell broken, the invaders had suddenly shimmered into view directly in front of them, and the Elves had launched their attack.

"We cut them down where they stood, Father, as they deserved. I took down their leader myself...Then the fire exploded, killing everyone." Her voice broke and she looked up at the king with haunted eyes. "I heard them scream, Father. I heard the trees screaming in my mind as they died."

Rillandariel pulled his daughter closer to his chest as the sobs began anew. "I would give anything to have spared you that, my beloved," he said softly, rocking her gently and stroking the back of her neck beneath the scorched ruins of her hair.

He wondered when it was that she had grown too old to come to him and lean her head against him like this, sharing her small triumphs and failures with him, her innocent joys and disappointments—before that unknown day, unmarked on any calendar and scarcely noted at the time, when she had ceased to seek him out that way, when she had grown "too old" to run to him and spill out all her tears and dreams.

In his mind's eye, she was five years old again, laughing with delight as she touched the mind of a Forest deer for the first time. "I did it, Father!" she had cried happily. "I heard his thoughts in my head. I think he is hungry. Let us gather some tender shoots for him."

Rillandariel had smiled with pride and pleasure at hearing that, for she was clearly gifted in Linking, and the appearance of the ability at so early an age foretold of a strong talent indeed. But the person he held in his arms now was his little girl no longer. She was all grown up, strong and brave and...Oh, gods, he had almost lost her today. An instant too slow in escaping the fire, and he would be preparing to bury her, as he had buried his son.

The thought of her brush with death, made so real at this moment, shattered the last of his control. The arms encircling her began to tremble, and tears filled his eyes as well, as he imagined life without her.

Ellianthia looked up at him with surprise, alarmed and frightened by the sight of her stalwart father weeping. She had only seen him cry twice, once at the death of her mother and, again, when her brother passed the veil. Misreading the cause of his tears, she swallowed her own desolation and gripped his arm in reassurance.

"Oh, Father, do not be discouraged," she pleaded. "The deaths of our brave warriors will not go unavenged. We will make the cursed humans pay with their lives for their treachery and their greed." She gathered her anger around her like a cloak, her voice hard and determined.

"I will personally lead a raid that will destroy their homes, as they destroyed the trees we are sworn to protect. I will make them pay. Only...only do not despair, Father."

Rillandariel rubbed the palms of his hands across his reddened eyes, then shook his head in weary resignation. "Yes. We will make them pay. As we have always made them pay." His shoulders sagged under the weight of his words.

"We will go on fighting this war, avenging our losses. But revenge begets revenge, after all. So, we will go on killing them, and they will go on killing us in return. Perhaps until we all lie dead, humans and Elves alike, their villages and towns in ruin, our Forest ablaze." He stood and walked to the doorway, resting his hands on the lintel above him and gazing out at the beauty of the Woods he loved so well.

"But Father," she said, with an urgency born of alarm at his despondent tone and fear that she would be denied her revenge for the fiery death of her patrol. "We can not surrender to them! We can not give in!"

His broken voice carried back to her as he continued to look away. "My love, I have already lost a son to this gods-forsaken war. Today, I nearly lost my only daughter as well. Perhaps the next great battle, or the next, will bring the news that you lie slain and lifeless on the ground, staring at the sky through sightless eyes. And where will my victory be then?"

He pounded his hand on the lintel, then turned back to her. "No, my daughter, we can not surrender. But I begin to wonder if our only choice is victory or death."

Chapter 10

Dark Conquest

Across the Luminous Sea in the Palace City of Kal`Dathia, Emperor Rak`koth leaned back on his gem-encrusted golden throne, idly running his long, graceful fingers through the thick black hair of the naked slave kneeling beside him as he looked out over the cavernous, torch-lit throne room and his subjects gathered there. The slave held her voluptuous body carefully in the position of attendance, watching him surreptitiously from the corner of her soft violet eyes.

She could see his angular, handsome face in profile, his strong nose and cruel, sensuous lips, his curling black hair as dark as the night on which he had been Awakened. Fervently, she hoped he would deign to look down upon his obedient pet, to offer some small sign that he found her desirable and worthy of his attention, cruel though it might be.

On another night, he might have permitted her a little clothing in public, usually a few wisps of sheer gauze stretched tightly over her breasts and a narrow panel of cloth between her legs, held in place by a thin, diamond-studded belt fastened around her slim waist. But she had annoyed him last evening when she was pleasuring him.

So, this night she knelt naked beside him, hands clasped behind her in the position purposely intended to display her lush body, to remind her that she was his property to do with as he pleased. In this position, the gold collar around her neck was clearly visible, as were the golden rings that pierced her body as symbols of his ownership—one ring dangling from each delicate ear, and one from each nipple.

The slave knew that it amused him to make her display herself like this, on exhibition as his pleasure slave. She also knew that she was only one of many women who served as playthings in his palace harem. But she did not care how many other women he used to satisfy his sadistic lusts. He was her one true master, the center of her existence. All that mattered was that he keep *her* by his side, giving her the privilege of his attention and discipline that she had learned to crave over the ten years that he had owned her.

Rak`koth knew full well her desperate need to be with him, to feel the pleasure and the pain of serving him. Indeed, he had trained her to that need, as he had promised that he would so long ago. But this night, he did not trouble himself to favor her with a glance or a word that would ease her mind. Instead, he left her to wonder about her fate while he turned his crimson gaze on the vassals that had been summoned from all corners of the continent to attend him.

It had taken years to conquer Surrikand, to subjugate all its peoples through a series of ruthless and vicious campaigns, using his Dark sorcery and callously expending the lives of his soldiers to kill thousands more of his enemies—never relenting until the vanquished learned to kneel before him or feel the weight of his boot crushing their necks.

It had taken more years to consolidate his rule, working with the regional commanders and governors he had installed, those who could be trusted to oversee the conquered lands exactly as he directed. Years spent establishing a common Imperial currency, placing wizards in every major city and principality to keep him informed, and building new roads linking all the major centers of power to Palace City, the hub of the Empire.

Countless slaves and outlaws—meaning anyone who resisted his rule—had died under the lash while building those roads, forced to labor in sweltering heat and icy, immobilizing cold, allowed no respite from their endless ordeal but the final release of death. And when they died at last, emaciated and broken, their blood and bones had been ground up by other slaves and mixed in with the mortar that held the paving stones together.

Some called these new highways the Emperor's Death Roads. Rak`koth did little to dissuade them from using that name, for it served as a reminder to all who traveled them of the fate that awaited any one who would not submit to his will and his vision of a Surrikand united under his heel.

But ruling all of Surrikand was not the end of his dream. Nay, it was but the beginning. Now the commanders and leaders from all across the continent—those who had proven their loyalty and strength by surviving his merciless purges—had answered the summons to his palace on this dark night.

He had gathered them to hear of his plans for conquest beyond the shores of the Empire, and to learn what he expected of them in undertaking his grand scheme. They had traveled from Jarlond to the north, Dul`Char to the east, Mertania to the west, Paressia and Brukkesh to the south, and even the smaller, more remote lands such as Thracyll and Sudenor to the far south.

Rak`koth peered down at his subjects through the murkiness of the throne room, the only illumination provided by the burning torches that hung along the side walls of the vast chamber and cast long shadows from the marble columns spaced every twenty feet to support the heavy domed ceiling. Some might have expected the resurrected sorcerer to hold court in brightly-lit venues with sunlight streaming through open windows, after being sealed away in the total blackness of a closed sarcophagus for eight hundred years. But he found that he often preferred the gloomy pall of night, and the dark, hazy atmosphere, as if it matched the Darkness in his soul.

As they waited for Emperor Rak`koth to convene the gathering, his vassals stood in the shadows beneath the dome, talking quietly in small groups, while beautiful slaves wearing only gold collars and jeweled ankle bracelets passed among them carrying silver trays laden with goblets of wine and small tumblers of kokesh, a potent liquor made from Brukkeshan grain. Under Rak`koth's rule, it was understood that a naked palace slave could be used for pleasure at any time—and in any way—by the guests they served.

Even now, many of the vassals were amusing themselves by casually fondling the women who offered them drink, the slaves accepting the groping without complaint. When sufficiently stimulated by the flesh on display, some guests would casually gesture for a slave to kneel before them and satisfy their lust, while they carried on mundane conversations with other vassals that were interrupted only by the occasional crude grunts of achieving release.

Rak`koth observed this and gave silent approval. He cared little for how his people pleasured themselves with the women he provided for their use, as long as they attended him closely when he spoke.

At that moment, his sensitive ears were taking in the chittering sound of Chu`tek, Chief Shaman of the Dul`Chars, speaking in his strange, clicking tongue to several of his fellow shamans. He glanced at the small group of little brown men who were gathered around one of the columns. Without seeing them, Rak`koth would have known that these vile practitioners of the blood magic were lurking nearby.

The acrid, coppery tang of human blood pervaded the air around them, permeating their meager clothing, their matted, tangled hair, and the pores of their filthy, unwashed skin. Even their teeth were stained brown from their daily ritual of drinking the precious life fluid that they caught in hand-held bowls as it spurted hot and red from the slitted throats of human sacrifices, their hearts still pumping it out through their jugulars as they died.

Rak'koth eschewed the drinking of blood himself, for he had no need of that revolting magic. His sorcerous powers were mighty and terrible in their own right. But he tolerated the ghoulish rituals of the Dul'Charian shamans, allowing them a steady supply of fresh victims for their gleeful slaughter, because he employed their magic to augment his own in battle when he did not wish to drain himself while smashing the resistance of any enemy foolish enough to stand against him.

From time to time during his converse with his foul brethren, the chief shaman glanced up at the throne. Though Chu'tek always wore an obsequious smile and adopted a servile posture in the emperor's presence, Rak'koth knew that the little brown creature's eyes masked a mixture of fear and hatred for the man who had conquered him, and pressed him and his barbarian horde into the Empire's service.

Chu'tek was not even his right name. His full name, when spoken in his clicking tongue, sounded something like Chukkutekkuth; but Rak'koth could not be bothered to learn to say it when addressing him. So he had arbitrarily taken to calling him Chu'tek, which was yet another cause for the shaman's hatred of his Kal'Dathian master, though he took pains not to display any overt sign of protest over this casual and intentional humiliation.

A wicked grin split Rak'koth's face as he savored the memory of the day that he had met Chu'tek for the first time...

2375 (Ten years ago)

Three days after his Awakening, Rak'koth rode out at the head of the Kal'Dathian army, having won the support of the awe-filled soldiers and their commanders who were eager to believe their Sleeping Savior's promise of a great victory over the enemy. He arrived at the place where thousands of jeering Dul'Charian tribesmen had spread out over the trampled plain. They were lanky, bearded men clad in rough animal hides and coarsely woven cloths, their brown faces smeared with bright yellow and orange ochres, carrying long, barbed spears and powerful curved bows.

In the distance behind them, he could see a host of domed, hide-covered yurts, populated by barbarian women and children gathered around cooking fires. He saw few cattle or other livestock, which prompted him to wonder just what those women expected to be cooking up in their steaming stew pots.

Rak`koth gazed out at these painted warriors, recalling the abject terror which had filled that fool Nek`krod's voice in describing the threat from this enemy. In truth, they did look fierce enough, and they clearly outnumbered the Kal`Dathian army. Still, they seemed more confident of victory, and more openly disdainful of the mounted cavalry and foot soldiers at his back, than he might have expected—until he noticed the little clutches of small brown men, five to each group, that were scattered among the horde of tribesmen.

Then he remembered what Nek`krod had said about their shamans using blood magic to defeat Mel`kanor's wizards, and he knew the reason for their confidence and disdain. A malicious smile quirked his lips, for these stupid savages had no idea of the power that had arisen from the sleeping death to confront them now.

Just then, amid much jeering and shaking of spears from the tribesmen, one small cohort of the scrawny shamans began murmuring something unintelligible. A wizened little man who appeared to be a spokesman or leader of some kind stepped away from them and approached Rak`koth, insisting in broken Kal`Dathian that his people only wanted to dwell on a portion of his land, and promising peace if given leave to do so.

But, Rak`koth noticed that, while the leader was pleading so sincerely for peace, his little group was now chanting something over and over again. Having long ago perfected the art of trickery and deceit himself, he recognized their crude attempt to distract him while they gathered an attack spell.

As the intensity of the chant increased, signaling the imminent release of the magic, Rak`koth unobtrusively called power from his staff and placed his own Spell of Protection and Deflection around himself and those within a radius of ten feet. A moment later, the chanting ceased and the shamans' attack came, erupting toward him in the form of a Bolt Spell that smashed against his magical shield with a crackling force.

It might have shattered the defenses of other spell casters, but Rak`koth was no ordinary wizard. He was a sorcerer who had battled his country's strongest magic users eight hundred years ago, and would have won, had it not been for the untimely interference of that bastard Shaldassamer and his lackeys at the last.

Though the violent impact of the shamans' attack was formidable, it could not penetrate Rak`koth's more powerful defense. Instead, their Bolt Spell deflected off his shield and hurtled back to strike the shamanic circle itself, immediately blasting them to the ground, leaving their bodies twisted and smoking. The expressions of the chief shaman and his barbarian warriors quickly turned from confident contempt to surprise and dismay, as they saw their magic users destroyed so quickly and horribly with their own spell.

Still, the shamans were not so easily cowed, and several groups began chanting their own battle spells. This time, Rak`koth did not wait to be attacked, but focused the power stored in his staff and launched a FireBall Spell directly at the nearest group of small brown men. Within seconds, they too were slain, burned to ashes and bones. A third group was just about to unleash their attack when they were demolished by a sizzling Lightning Spell that shot from his hands and sliced through the air to explode them like a thunderbolt.

Soon after, the air was filled with death as Rak`koth ordered his fellow Kal`Dathian wizards to join their new master in unleashing Bolt and Fire Spells against the enemy. In moments, waves of this deadly magic were unleashed, raining flame and lightning down on tribesmen and shamans alike.

Seeing their magical attacks thwarted and their men beginning to panic, the shaman leader screamed with rage and ordered their warriors to an all-out attack. Thousands of barbarians roared their battle cries and ran forward, brandishing their barbed spears and loosing their arrows against the Kal`Dathian army and their wizards. But, without their shamans to protect them, the rag-tag horde of Dul`Charian fighters were no match for the armored cavalry who, on Rak`koth's command, called the charge and thundered through their ranks, skewering the invaders on the points of their lances and crushing them beneath the hooves of their warhorses.

Following in their wake, the Kal`Dathian foot soldiers ripped into the dazed enemy, stabbing and slicing with sword and pike until the trampled field became a mire of mud and blood. The Dul'Charians cried out in terror and turned to flee, but nowhere was safe from the onslaught of the wizards' deadly magic and the army's steel.

Then, just as the Kal'Dathian cavalry was regrouping to mount another lethal charge, the chief shaman cried out to his warriors to abandon the fight and surrender. The call was taken up by others across the battlefield and, within moments, thousands of barbarians heeded their leader and laid their weapons down. Rak'koth signaled his commanders to delay pressing the attack as the little brown man approached, holding up his hands and bending forward in what passed for an awkward bow.

In a whiny, plaintive tone, he began to explain in butchered Kal'Dathian that the Dul'Chars had not come as invaders but as "friends," that this was all a "terrible misunderstanding," and that his people only sought to find a new home after being driven from their own land by a prolonged drought and famine.

Snorting with disdain, Rak'koth called a temporary halt to hostilities. His decision to refrain from continuing the bloody slaughter had nothing whatever to do with feeling any shred of mercy or compassion for a defeated enemy, and everything to do with the notion forming in his mind that these barbarians might be of some use to him if left alive to serve him. But first, he would dispense with these pathetic lies and show them their proper place.

He began by loudly naming the Dul'Charians for what they were—the phrases "lying scum" and "vermin spawned in a refuse heap" figuring prominently in his declarations—and told them in no uncertain terms that he would use his power to slaughter them to a man if they did not bend a knee and swear fealty to him as their new king.

Chu'tek blanched visibly, which was no small feat for a brown-skinned man, and chattered to his fellows in that rapid, clicking tongue. When he turned back to the sorcerer, his eyes were filled with that expression of hate and fear that would amuse Rak'koth for years to come.

He doubted not that Chu'tek would have happily cut out his heart and gorged on his blood if he had dared. But the defeat of his most powerful shamans and the rout of his fierce warriors left the grimy little man no choice, did he not wish to be among the next victims.

So, with a barely concealed desire for revenge burning in his eyes, Chu`tek gave the command for his tribesmen to fall to their knees. They did as they were told, their eyes filled with equal parts of shame and fear.

Not yet satisfied, Rak`koth announced that surrender was hardly enough, demanding the lives of twenty Dul`Chars for each of the five royal emissaries that had been crucified and drained of their blood. He also commanded that the wives and children of the sacrifices be brought to watch the executions of their husbands and fathers, so that the price of killing Kal`Dathians would be indelibly burned into their minds and hearts.

Chu`tek raised no protest but simply called for one hundred men and their families to come forward. Such was his power that, when he spoke, the warriors did so without voicing any complaint, accepting the fate in store for them as they stood with heads bowed.

Then, with the cheers of his own soldiers and the anguished cries of the enemy's women and children pleasantly filling his ears, Rak`koth borrowed a sword from one of his generals and walked down the row of tribesmen. One by one, he disemboweled them by his own hand, thrusting and twisting the blade with relish until the blood and gore from their gutted bodies drenched his black robes.

And so, within days of Awakening from centuries of sleep, Rak`koth made his first conquest and won the adulation of his people, who acclaimed his return to the Palace City with great relief and joy. Only later would many Kal`Dathians come to curse the day when the Sleeping Savior had risen anew, after he began to impose his brutal and despotic rule over them as well. But for now, he was their hero, and the clamor for his favor surpassed that for their own king, who seemed to have suddenly withdrawn from public appearances.

Rak`koth ordered Chu`tek to remain encamped with his people until further notice, under the watchful eyes of Kal`Dathian forces and a coterie of wizards. After conferring with his military commanders and advisors, Rak`koth devised what was to become an established plan for his conquest of the continent—the use of one conquered people to vanquish another.

He directed Chu`tek to march his ragged barbarian army north to Jarlond, a kingdom that lay along the border of Kal`Dathia. The Jarlonders were a tall, fair race of rugged men and women whose mountainous lands held rich deposits of coal, iron, copper and other ores and minerals used to produce high quality steel. Such steel could be shaped into a wide array of weapons and armor that would be needed to equip the large armies that Rak`koth intended to create.

Kal`Dathia, poor in mineral deposits, had long coveted these natural resources, but her northern neighbor had restricted trade and charged a dear price for the limited amount of ores they did offer. Rak`koth, who had once controlled Kal`Dathia when the Jarlonders were little more than highland savages rooting in the earth for roots and mushrooms, had neither the ready gold nor the inclination to bargain for larger amounts of the minerals that he foresaw himself needing.

So he sent an envoy north with a letter demanding that King Olev, the Jarlond monarch, agree to provide these resources freely or face his wrath. Knowing that Olev, a crafty old highlander, considered himself safe in his mountain reaches and would never agree to these terms, Rak`koth then crossed into Jarlond at the head of the combined armies of Kal`Dathia and Dul`Char to enforce his demands.

At first, Olev refused to engage Rak`koth's larger forces, preferring instead to withdraw further into his mountain keeps where any fighting would favor the defenders. But Rak`koth would have his way, no matter the cost in lives and sorrow to those who had the temerity to defy his will. So he set Chu`tek's barbarians the task of laying waste to any inhabited towns and villages they found, a task they performed with bloodthirsty glee.

Over a short period of time, entire Jarlonder villages were brutally decimated, the men butchered for their hot blood, the women raped and mutilated with such wanton savagery that Olev was finally forced to come down from his sanctuary and meet Rak`koth in open battle.

The Jarlonders were huge, fierce fighters who wielded great steel broadswords and axes made from the very ore deposits that Rak`koth was so intent on possessing. The Jarlonder women often fought beside their men—tall, full-breasted, powerfully-thewed females with long, golden braids who expected no quarter because of their gender and gave none in return.

Men and women alike fought in the berserker style, working themselves up into a frenzy with strong ale and ritualistic, highly-sexualized dancing, then charging into battle naked but for a little armor, so crazed with battle lust that they could fight with incredible strength and sustain terrible wounds without falling to their enemies.

But battle lust was not all that consumed their passions in war. The men often went into combat sexually aroused from the combination of heightened aggression and the sight of their females' naked bodies churning beside them as they ran together to meet the enemy. Equally as lusty, the women raced to war excited by the anticipation of bloody fighting and the sight of their aroused men.

Indeed, it was not uncommon for a Jarlonder man to celebrate victory in battle by throwing the nearest Jarlonder female down on the ground and taking her right there amid the blood and the screams of the wounded and dying. He would lie atop her while she encircled his waist with her muscular legs and raked his broad back with her sharp fingernails, urging him on until they both collapsed from sated lust and the waning of the berserker frenzy.

Unfortunately, however, for all their prowess and stamina in battle, the Jarlonders had few magic wielders and little in the way of battle spells to stand against the combined power of Rak`koth's wizards and the Dul`Charian shamans. When they met in battle, Rak`koth and his minions let loose a withering barrage of Lightning, Blaze and Quake Spells that slew hundreds of charging berserker warriors before they even reached his lines.

Then he sent his cavalry to flank the defenders and cut off retreat, while his foot soldiers joined the Dul`Charian horde in surrounding them and herding them into a circle. Working together, Kal`Dathian swords and barbarian spears steadily hacked the beleaguered enemy down, inflicting grievous losses.

Witnessing his countrymen being destroyed so mercilessly, Olev saw the futility of further resistance and threw down his battle-axe in surrender. Rak`koth had the proud highlander king brought before him in chains and made to kneel at his feet, where he pronounced the sentence of death—not by his hand, but by the hand of the king's own son.

"Either your son comes forward to execute you or I will level every remaining town and village in your land," he said, with a tone of indifference that suggested he almost hoped the Jarlonder king would refuse his command.

So Olev the Younger, eldest son of the mountain king, was brought forth and handed his father's own axe. With tears of horror and anguish in his eyes, the tall, brawny youth kissed his sire's cheek and whispered his love, then raised the shining blade and sliced through the gristle and bone of his father's neck in one strong stroke. Even as King Olev's severed head lay on the ground, his fresh blood spurting from the gory neck of the headless body nearby, Rak'koth made the son fall to his knees and lead all the Jarlonders in a pledge of fealty and obedience to their new king.

Thus Rak'koth's plans for an empire took shape, following this strategy of conquering and absorbing the defeated foe into his army and under his heel. When he struck next against the Kingdom of Paressia on his southern border, bent on plundering their thick forests for the timber to build a mighty fleet of ships for his Imperial Navy, the Jarlonders marched into battle beside the Kal'Dathians and the Dul'Chars. And when he invaded the coastal Kingdom of Mertania, to gain access to their deep-water port where he would build and launch the navy, the swarthy, stocky swordsmen and bowmen of the defeated Paressian army fought under his banner as well.

Over the next few years, Rak'koth methodically attacked and subjugated Brukkesh and the other remaining nations on the continent of Surrikand, the ranks and might of his armies growing with each annexation. He even penetrated into the desolate hills inhabited by the Gruks, a non-human race of eight-foot tall, brutish, fur-covered beasts, in order to take control of the rich veins of gold and silver virtually lining the walls of the caverns where the fearsome creatures made their homes.

The Gruks cared little for the metal ores, but took rather strident exception to having their foul-smelling, vermin-infested caves raided by strange humans seeking access to the treasure within. Yet the brute strength and primitive weapons of these club-swinging creatures were no match for the overwhelming power of Rak'koth's forces. Though ferocious in battle, the beasts were superstitious and stupid, and easily frightened by even minor displays of magic.

They soon came to look upon Rak'koth as the closest thing to a god they had ever seen—especially since no real god would admit to even being associated with them or encouraging their worship. It was not long before the sorcerer's coffers were filled with captured gold and silver, while a contingent of Gruks was herded back to Kal'Dathia to be trained to fight with some rudimentary discipline and skill.

Much of this conquest would not have been possible without the creation of the Black Legion, one of Rak'koth's pet projects in building his Empire. Conceived as both an elite fighting force against foreign enemies and a ruthless, efficient means of enforcing his laws and commands at home, the Legion had been formed by recruiting the biggest, strongest and most brutal men from every land under his dominion.

Nearly four thousand men answered his initial call, the greatest collection of hard-drinking, unscrupulous, merciless bastards and killers ever gathered in one place. Rak'koth promised that those who won the right to join his new Black Legion could look forward to being well-paid and highly feared for exercising their natural inclinations for murder and mayhem in his service. They would be a power unto themselves, answerable only to him.

Then he took them all to a large green valley, which he sealed off at both ends with his soldiers. He armed the recruits with weapons of their own choosing, and told them that only half of the men gathered there would be admitted to the ranks of the Legion—the half still left *alive* at the end of the day.

After that, Rak'koth sat back to enjoy the spectacle as, for the next several candlemarks, the ringing clash of steel against steel, the ripping sound of blades slicing into living flesh, and the screams of the wounded and slain were heard up and down the length and breadth of that valley.

At sunset, two thousand survivors were led away to begin Legion training in earnest, while nearly as many corpses were hauled away like so much refuse and thrown into blazing pyres that climbed thirty feet into the air. The burning bodies left behind a sickening stench of charred and roasted flesh that lingered in the surrounding countryside for several eight-days.

After similar "culling days" were held several times in the following months, the surviving Legion members were then subjected to a rigorous and deadly training program designed to increase their killing efficiency as a fighting unit, using spear, sword, morning star and axe. Many died during the training, their bodies hauled away and tossed into a nameless grave without service or ceremony.

Those merely crippled and broken were discarded by the Legion like so much refuse. Shunned by their former comrades, they were left to beg on the streets or make their way home in poverty and disgrace.

Within a year, the ten thousand strong Black Legion were ready to be deployed throughout the Empire. The Kal'Dathian people lined the streets of Palace City to cheer the parade of row upon row of these enormous, fearsome warriors clad in black uniforms and shiny black leather boots, and armored in black horned helms, cuirasses and greaves, as they marched off to take up stations across the continent. Seeing them on display, men flocked to join their ranks, while women offered themselves freely to these ebony gladiators.

But the citizens of Kal`Dathia found less to cheer about when some of the hardened veterans of the Legion were ordered to become the enforcers of the new laws and decrees that began issuing forth from the palace—laws that controlled commerce, imposed heavy taxes to pay for Rak`koth's empire building, required youth to apprentice in trades and skills deemed necessary by the emperor, and allowed ordinary people to be involuntarily pressed into service for extended periods.

He even regulated marriages, requiring prospective brides in nearby regions to present themselves at the palace for examination. Many of the young women summoned by decree did not return home in the same state of innocence as when they left. Others did not return at all, never to be seen again by their families and would-be grooms, whose protests were met with silence or threats.

Soon, every major town and village was patrolled by Black Legionnaires who compelled obedience to laws and meted out cruel justice for any infraction, real or contrived. These towering, stone-faced hulks became widely feared, as men were beaten or killed in the streets, women taken in their homes, and shops and domiciles smashed or burned at will. And when, eventually, some desperate civilians and isolated units of the old Kal`Dathian army rose in rebellion against these draconian practices, their doomed uprisings were crushed pitilessly under the hobnailed boots of the Black Legion.

Often, the men who did not die outright on the edge of spear and sword were executed by public crucifixion on wooden crosses or impalement on barbed pikes, as warnings against future resistance. Others were taken to slave camps and forced to build the Death Roads.

The surviving women fared little better. The old and infirm were sent to work in the fields under brutal conditions, while most of the younger females were consigned to army brothels to service the lusts of the regular soldiers.

The largest and sturdiest of these captured women found themselves trapped in the living hell of the Legion breeding pits. Rak`koth had foreseen that breeding the biggest and mightiest men in the Empire with the hardiest, most able-bodied females available would yield a new generation of Black Legionnaires that were even stronger and tougher than their predecessors.

With this in mind, stone barracks filled with small rooms were constructed inside the Legion camps, then stocked with specially selected specimens of womanhood whose sole purpose was to conceive and bear the children that would become this next superior generation. If the women protested, they were bound naked on wooden frames, and offered to Legionnaires who were encouraged to take their pleasure with these more recalcitrant "breeders" in particularly brutal ways.

Most women, seeing the fate of those who resisted, made themselves available to all comers. In truth, many welcomed having a child gotten on them by some Legionnaire. The women knew that becoming visibly pregnant meant being removed from the breeding pits for a period of time, and taken to another locale to await delivery of their babies—albeit by stern, unsympathetic midwives who often came to them covered in the birthing blood of other women whom they had just attended.

Unfortunately, this brief respite from routine rape was short-lived, for they were soon returned to the pits to resume their duties until they quickened again. By the end of a decade of Rak`koth's rule, some women had borne seven or eight children, babes whom they never saw again and had no chance to name or nurture.

The female babies were sent off to become servants and slaves, while the male offspring were taken away to special children's quarters, bereft of any further contact with a natural parent, to be raised by harsh teachers who instilled in them the canon that the Black Legion was their only mother and father. They soon learned that they owed their entire existence and their unstinting loyalty to the emperor, first and foremost, for he held their lives in his hands...

Chapter 11

Visions of Destiny

2385 (Present)

A harsh, deep-throated growl interrupted Rak`koth's pleasant reverie of his conquests and triumphs during the past decade. On the floor in front of his throne, the most feared animal in all the Empire—a Sudenorian war hound—had stirred from its doze, when a terrified slave made the nearly fatal mistake of walking too close to the creature on her way back from pleasuring the Paressian governor. Part-canine and part-dire wolf, the monstrous war hounds were three hundred pounds of vicious russet fury when ordered to the attack.

Over eight feet long and standing as tall at the shoulders as a pony, with a massive head and slavering jaws that could snap the neck of a full-grown horse, the Hells-spawned beasts had been loosed against Rak`koth's soldiers when his armies invaded Sudenor to acquire their diamond and emerald mines. Impressed by the way his men had been savaged and ripped apart by the fiendish creatures, Rak`koth now bred them for battle himself.

Most of the people in the room, even Olev the Younger, the tall, brawny Jarlonder king, cast nervous glances when the war hound raised its head and growled. However, there was one man present who showed no sign of concern. It was Val`mak, general of Rak`koth's elite Black Legion. Seven feet tall and weighing twenty stone, the hulking, powerfully built general had risen to his current position by the only means of promotion possible—fighting his way up through the ranks, challenging and killing his superiors in single combat.

It was known that Val`mak had sent twelve men to their deaths to get where he was, and had relished every one of the kills. Now he commanded some fifteen thousand Legionnaires, ruling them with an iron hand and a complete disregard for human life—traits that had won the favor of the emperor when he approved Val`mak's final promotion.

Val`mak glared at the war hound with disdain, as if daring the animal to attack. Rak`koth chuckled at the general's response and called out to him.

"You do not care for my pet, General?" he asked wryly.

"Gods-be-damned beast," growled Val`mak in his hoarse, grating voice, the result of a blow to his throat from the officer he had killed to achieve the rank of colonel some years back. "That overgrown cur will eat my steel if he comes at me," he said matter-of-factly, gripping the hilt of his well-used blade.

Rak`koth briefly considered pitting his commander against the ferocious animal in a fight to the death, intrigued by the thought of such a spectacle. But Val`mak was too valuable to him, and too necessary to his current plans, to risk injuring him at the moment. He needed a strong leader at the head of his elite Legion for what he had in mind. Maybe sometime in the future, he mused, when the man was more expendable.

Rak`koth turned away from Val`mak as a muted stir signaled the arrival of the only other person he knew who would not cringe from even so deadly a beast as a Sudenorian war hound. The emperor noted with amusement how his vassals moved aside for the pale, gaunt man dressed all in gray who strode through the darkened chamber toward the throne, his long cape flowing behind him. But then, Dek`ker, Commander of the Imperial Dread Riders, always seemed to stand alone, even in a crowded room, as if an invisible barrier forestalled all others from getting too close.

All others, save for the Dul`Charian shamans. Chu`tek and his foul-smelling brethren had no qualms about approaching Dek`ker or any of the three thousand Dread Riders he commanded. After all, they had "created" him and his followers with their fell blood magic, as much as if they had given birth to them. The Dread Riders drank fresh human blood every day, supplied by the shamans who fed them goblets of the hot, red elixir obtained from scores of human slaves and "outlaws" in gory ritual sacrifices performed each morn on the stained altars in the House of the Doomed.

Imbued with evil shamanic magic, the blood they drank made the Dread Riders nearly invincible in battle, endowing them with superhuman strength and rendering them almost impossible to kill with ordinary weapons, for they did not bleed, not when stabbed with a sword or impaled on a lance, not even when their limbs were severed from their bodies. They rode to battle in eerie silence, slashing and hacking about them while uttering no sound, inspiring terror and panic for the gray men who seemingly would not die.

They ate little and slept even less, relying mostly on their daily ration of blood for sustenance and life—if they could truly be said to be alive, these men who looked out at the world through sunken, lifeless eyes, rarely spoke, showed no human emotion, sought no carnal pleasure from women, and claimed no kith or kin.   In return for gaining invincibility, they had surrendered their souls.

Dek`ker approached, his dark, expressionless eyes flickering dispassionately over the war hound and the naked, kneeling slave before he bowed his head to Rak`koth, then straightened to attention.

"At your command, Your Majesty," he said in a monotone, staring straight ahead, prepared to stand motionless on that spot until directed to do otherwise.

Rak`koth nodded slightly, then gestured with his hand. Suddenly, the torches on the walls blazed incandescently, illuminating the chamber and all those gathered with stark white light that banished the shadows. Rising to his feet, he gripped his staff and called up his power, willing a red aura to limn his body. Then he spoke.

"Ten years ago, I arose from a sleep of eight centuries to find that many things had changed. The kings and princes who ruled the world of Tiaran in my time had long since passed into obscurity, their bodies moldering to dust, forgotten and alone in their royal vaults and sepulchers. Nations had come and gone, their boundaries drawn and redrawn by petty wars. The courses of rivers had been altered, and tall mountain peaks eroded by time and the elements. Even the spoken language of Kal`Dathia was not entirely the same."

Now Rak`koth's voice rose in volume and intensity, the crimson centers of his eyes flaring. "But no matter the passage of time, some things *never* change. The call to power has not changed. The right of the strong to command the weak has not changed. People have ever needed a ruler with the determination and the might to lead them to greatness, to shape the world to his vision, and to take what is rightfully his—and *that* has not changed!"

With a wave of his staff, a brilliant crimson light appeared and hovered in the air. Astonished, his subjects gaped and stared as the image took shape and form, transforming into an outline of the continent of Surrikand floating before their eyes.   The vision was recognizable as a landmass roughly resembling a crescent, complete with lines demarcating the boundaries of each vassal country and region, each major mountain range and forest.

"In ten short years," Rak`koth continued with pride, "I have built an Empire that spans the continent, encompassing every nation and land of import from east to west and north to south." As he spoke, the lines defining the separate countries of the continent disappeared.

"The Empire has united every nation of Surrikand, and every people dwelling therein. Is there any one here who can say he has not prospered, that the land has not prospered, under my rule?" He peered across the chamber, as if daring any present to dispute him.

The chorus of "No, Your Magnificence" and "Long live the Empire!" that reached his ears was expected, but gratifying all the same. If the memory of being forced to behead his own father with an axe to save his people made the Jarlonder king's affirmation a little less enthusiastic than it might have been, Rak`koth chose not to notice. And if some of the vassals in attendance privately pondered the question of whether peace under the iron hand of a despot and murderer was truly peace at all, no one seemed inclined to voice those dangerously traitorous thoughts aloud.

"Yes, we have prospered and grown. But Surrikand is only the beginning!" Rak`koth exclaimed. "For it is my destiny to create an Empire that will reach beyond our shores, across the seas to the far corners of the earth." With that, his staff released another pulse of crimson light, and a second image began to form in the air beside the first.

"Behold the continent of Balleterria, the soon-to-be Empire in the West!"

The vassals gaped and stared again as the emperor's vision revealed the outline of the continent to the west across the Luminous Sea. Balleterria was roughly equal to Surrikand in size, but with a more elongated shape, broader at the top and tapering down to a point near the bottom. Mountain ranges bordered the sea on the north and northwest part of the continent. A wide band of forest stretched across the middle portion of Balleterria from coast to coast. Below the forest lay a large expanse of plains, enclosed by mountains on each side and another mountain range to the south. The southern tip of continent appeared to be unmarked wastelands.

Rak`koth's voice was laced with malevolent excitement and naked greed as he pointed his staff at the magical image for emphasis. "My closest commanders already know of my great plan for this continent. Now the rest of you will learn of your

Emperor's vision. It is my birthright and my destiny to bring this foreign land under my dominion…and a rich prize it will be.

My agents tell me that Balleterria has great timber forests, ample deposits of gold and silver, precious gems and minerals, large herds of cattle, sheep and horses, fertile farmlands, vast prairies—and an abundant supply of 'workers' who will have the privilege of helping to build and expand my Empire."

The emperor chuckled as he watched Chu`tek's face light up with a malicious grin at the mention of new slaves. Then he beckoned to a plain, nondescript man dressed in muted colors standing off to the side, the kind of man few would notice unless someone pointed him out. And, in fact, no one had taken note of him until Rak`koth did so.

"This is Spymaster Ek`kron, who has been gathering the information necessary to prepare for the acquisition of Balleterria. Share what you have learned with my vassals."

The man who had called himself Faram stepped forward, bowed low to Rak`koth, then cleared his throat and raised his hand to point at the image floating in the air.

"This is the human Kingdom of Calderia," he said, indicating a large area extending from the eastern coast across a wide swath of farmlands, open prairie and grasslands for many miles west. "Northwest of Calderia lies another, smaller kingdom called Dunmoria, bordered by several minor baronies and duchies that are hostile to the Dunmorians, who themselves were at war with Calderia for well over a hundred years. At present, there appears to be an uneasy truce, but my agents speak of bitter feelings and lingering hatreds on both sides that could flare up into war again at a moment's notice."

Ek`kron looked at Rak`koth, who gestured impatiently for him to continue. "These mountains to the far west are inhabited by Dwarves, a race of miners and delvers who dig the gems and ores they use for making weapons and for trade, though they hold themselves in isolation, except for occasional barter with the humans. Some of the mountains reaches on the continent are also home to Ogres, wild creatures similar to our Gruks."

The Spymaster pointed to a thick band of woodlands to the south. "This area, called the Great Forest, is inhabited by Elves, a longer-lived race of people who rarely venture out from beneath their trees, save to do battle with the Calderians, with whom they also have been at war for some years. Many have died on both sides fighting what is essentially an unwinnable campaign, yet no one that my people spoke to there foresee any end to it soon."

He then gestured toward the area south of the Great Forest. "Little is known about the people who live below the Forest, though we have had word of some nomadic tribes of cattle herders who are described as hostile and prone to warring. They, too, remain isolated from the other lands of Balleterria." Ek`kron hesitated here, cringing a little as he glanced at Rak`koth from the corner of his eyes.

"As for what lies beyond the southern mountains...My agents have not *yet* been able to penetrate that far south. But I hope to have that information soon," he added hurriedly. "Still, I believe there is nothing of consequence beyond that point." With another timorous gaze in the direction of the throne, he bowed and melted back into the shadows once more.

Rak`koth raised his staff again, sending the translucent map into a slow rotation that brought new looks of wonder from his subjects. He *did* love a spectacle, after all, and he never overlooked an opportunity to inspire awe and fear.

"As you have heard, the lands of Balleterria are ruled by weak and foolish leaders who squabble among themselves. They have involved their peoples in petty wars with each other that have depleted their armies and their resources, and left them vulnerable to conquest. Most of them remain aloof from each other, wallowing in their own self-interests and showing no capacity for cooperation—another advantage for a ruler with the vision and strength to seize the opportunity. I see no evidence that these pathetic creatures have the will or the capacity to offer any real resistance to the might of the Surrikand Empire."

"Sire, if I may inquire?" The reedy voice belonged to an older, graying man with a beaked nose and shrewd eyes. It was Luk`kod, Chief Imperial Wizard, clad in the robes of his office and leaning on a bejeweled staff.

"Yes, Wizard Luk`kod. You wish to ask a question?"

"Well, Sire, if I my say...That is, my brethren and I were wondering if you have gathered any further information about the spells casters that we might encounter in Balleterria. Do they have wizards like ourselves?"

Rak`koth fixed the chief wizard with a disdainful stare. "You are worried about their magic?"

"Not worried, Sire. We were merely wondering..." His voice trailed off as he dropped his gaze.

The emperor uttered a mocking laugh. "I am informed that the Elves and Dwarves do not practice battle magic, at least not as we know it. The humans do have some wizards— they call themselves 'mages'— but they are not known to use any but the simplest battle spells, and those mostly of a defensive nature. Indeed, though these mages are said to possess some power, I am told that they have rarely employed major Spells of Destruction, not even in their bitter war with the Elves." Rak`koth shook his head dismissively.

"But, no matter what magic they can bring against us, powerful or not, they will be no match for *my* powers or those of my wizards and shamans. Or have you forgotten what I am capable of, Chief Wizard? Perhaps you need a reminder."

"No, my Emperor, I have not forgotten," a chastened Luk`kod replied hastily, blanching at the threat of suffering his master's wrath. "I have no doubt whatsoever that we will prevail."

Rak`koth briefly considered drowning Luk`kod in his own body fluids then and there; but, like Val`mak, the chief wizard might have his uses in the future. So he settled for cutting off the man's air for a few seconds with a flick of his wrist. Then, enjoying the sound of choking gasps, he turned to his Black Legion general.

"I trust, Val`mak, that you do not doubt that whatever military forces they may muster will fall before the might of my armies, my Legionnaires and my Dread Riders."

"Certainly not, Sire," came the confident reply from the rugged commander who had remained ramrod stiff in a position of attention throughout Rak`koth's demonstration.

Rak`koth struck his staff upon the floor with a crack! that echoed across the chamber, his burning eyes piercing into the soul of every person in the room. "It is my *destiny* to rule this new land as I rule Surrikand. Once before, my vision was thwarted by misbegotten creatures that meddled in my affairs when they had no right to do so. But they have long since vanished from this world, lost and forgotten in the shadows of ancient history. There is no one who can stand against me now. This time, I will *not* be denied. This time I *will* fulfill that destiny."

Then his voice dropped. "And each one of you here tonight will play a part in my design. Do not fail me," he added softly, his tone all the more ominous because it left the dire consequences of such failure to burrow deep into their imaginations like a cancer.

While the others waited apprehensively to learn their assigned roles in the emperor's grand plan, he saw Val`mak eyeing the distance between the floating map images. Rak`koth watched him closely, and was not surprised when his Black Legion general turned to ask the question he had been expecting.

"My Lord Emperor," rasped Val`mak in his ruined voice, "As we have discussed before, such an undertaking will require transportation of many men, many horses and much equipment on a long voyage across the sea, as well as weapons, stores and supplies sufficient to sustain our warriors in the field when we arrive. Then, too, there are certain…special elements…of our forces to be considered," he added, glancing pointedly at the Dread Rider commander and the painted shamans, the latter whom he could smell from across the room.

"I would ask what progress has been made on building a fleet that will be sufficient to the task?"

Rak`koth nodded his approval and settled back down onto his throne, his right hand reaching down to fondle the beautiful slave gently, almost lovingly, until she felt pleasure— then cruelly twisting the gold rings piercing her tender flesh until she gasped aloud, as he responded to his general's inquiry.

"A reasonable question, Val`mak. As you know, when I first envisioned the conquest of Balleterria, our navy lacked the number and type of ships required to launch an invasion of this magnitude. For that reason, Master Shipwright Suk`kar has been working for quite some time, overseeing the construction of more ships to expand our fleet.

"I have charged him with completing his task at all possible speed, for I am determined to land our soldiers in Balleterria by summer next, before the sea storms begin. I have Suk`kar's assurances that all will be in readiness by that time. I trust that he will not disappoint me," he concluded, in that same silky voice.

Val`mak clicked his heels and bowed from his waist sharply. "The Legion will be ready, as will the rest of our forces, my Lord Emperor," he said, proud that any invasion on such a large scale would necessarily involve the Empire's most elite warriors. "And the number of Legionnaires you will require, my Lord?" he asked.

"Patience, General," Rak`koth replied, enjoying the look of painful need in the slave's eyes as he continued to torture her with his long, powerful fingers. "I will meet with you and Commander Dek`ker shortly to continue our discussions."

He turned to look around the room at the leaders of his vassal states. "For the rest of you, there will be a levy of men and supplies from each of the lands you govern at my pleasure," he announced. "You will all be notified of the particulars, so that you can begin making your preparations accordingly. Any one who fails me in this can expect to find himself missing a head, as will all the members of his family. Is that clear?"

Once again, the chorus of "Yes, Your Magnificence!" filled the chamber, for all there had witnessed the fate of those who earned their emperor's displeasure.

"Good. I believe we understand each other. Now, you are dismissed for the night. Enjoy the feast awaiting you, and avail yourselves of the services provided by my servants and slaves, but stand ready to attend me again on the morrow."

As those assembled bowed to his command, Rak`koth stood, releasing his hold on his slave's bruised flesh, amused by the expression of loss in her violet eyes as he withdrew his attention. "Wait for me in my chambers, my pet. I may wish to use you later." He flicked his hand, dismissing the visions hovering in the air without a sound.

Then he snapped his fingers and the war hound rose up on all fours. "Val`mak. Dek`ker. Attend me now," he called after him, striding from the room with the beast trotting meekly at his side. The naked woman was left to crawl down from the dais and hasten to her master's chambers, where she would await his pleasure with equal parts of fear and anticipation.

Chapter 12

A Tale of Two Princes

Having been banned from Brannock Castle in no uncertain terms some time ago, the old man who called himself Morgander had found himself a small building with a tiny bedroom in the back for a modest rent. There, he had hung a neatly drawn "Apothecary & Physic Shoppe" sign above the doorway to help make ends meet, and settled in to await the opportunity for another audience with the king, having tried in vain several times to gain access to King Gavan's presence. Now he could do naught but trust in the gods that the chance to change the Calderian monarch's mind would not come too late.

In truth, the cantankerous persona Mik`kel had adopted as a disguise of sorts had done little at the outset to attract potential customers to his doorstep. Yet, after one or two neighbors had turned to him as a last resort, in moments when another healer was not to be found nearby, his skills with herbs and healing had won their grudging trust.

Gradually, through word of mouth, other villagers had begun to bring their ailing children, wives or husbands to his door, seeking his healing skills to soothe their fevers or mend their broken limbs. Less often, they came to bargain for love philters to win the heart of one they desired or for hexes to be cast on business rivals or hated in-laws—neither of which the old man would countenance, sending them on their way with a dose of the rough side of his tongue.

Yet, when they came with true illness or injury, the old man never turned anyone away, even when they knocked on his door in the dead of night. He would grumble and take on the look of a long-suffering soul much abused by gods great and small to be roused so cruelly from his sleep; but, for all of that, he would crawl out of his solitary bed and open the door, peering into the night.

Motioning the visitors to enter, he would issue dire warnings of untoward consequences if they failed to duck their heads to avoid disturbing the carefully collected baskets of herbs hanging from the rafters. Then he would step closer to stare at the patient intently and begin probing and prodding, lifting eyelids or touching pulse points, asking but a few pointed questions.

After a short time, he would nod to himself and turn to the cupboards and shelves laden with packets of dried herbs, vials full of colored powders, and sundry other concoctions of mysterious origin. Squinting at the contents of one bottle, tasting a pinch of another, he would finally grunt with satisfaction and go to his cluttered table to mix the ingredients for a healing tisane or a warm poultice.

Soon, he would return to the patient to administer the remedy, often accompanied by sotto voce mutterings and the laying on of hands. Despite his brusque manner, he could be surprisingly gentle, especially with children and women, offering a calming caress or an encouraging word when he saw pain and fear in their eyes. Most often, the patient improved, leaving the family grateful and relieved. More often than not, they were inclined to tell others of the old man's success.

So, for all his harsh imprecations uttered in moments of high dudgeon, Morgander had come to be respected and valued well enough by the villagers in the time since his arrival. Eventually, word of his healing talents spread throughout several quarters of Brannock Village. The widow Bairre told other homewives of finally getting merciful relief for her arthritis, after suffering in pain for years. Peadar the wheelwright would sit in his favorite tavern of an evening, swallowing dark ale and lifting his hand to show all assembled how he could again wiggle the fingers that had been crushed when the miller's wagon collapsed on him.

His reputation grew even more when Mayor Oweyn told of how his beloved daughter, Cara, had been brought back from death's door during childbirth by the efforts of the old man. With praise from the mayor of Brannock Village himself, it was inevitable that word of the old healer's skills would reach all the way up to Brannock Castle itself.

Thus it was that Aisleen came to hear the name of Morgander mentioned with respect within the castle proper. She had sent him a note or two from time to time, informing him that her efforts to influence the king in his cause continued, though to little avail thus far. But, while she had often thought of the words they had shared the night of his arrival, and the unexpected pleasure of his strong, comforting arms around her, she had never journeyed down from the castle to see to him.

Not, that is, until one afternoon, some time after the prince's manhood ceremony. The old man answered a soft knock on his shop door to find her standing there, as beautiful as he remembered, wrapped in a dark sable robe against the late autumn chill.

After a brief, awkward silence, he overcame his surprise and ushered her into his cluttered shop, clearing off a seat by the small fire and offering to take her robe. Aisleen settled into the chair, her long black hair falling to either side of her smooth pale neck.

"I must confess that I prefer you in your...younger form," she said, with more than a hint of amusement in her soft, dark eyes. "You look positively decrepit in this guise. I fear that a strong breeze might be your undoing."

He grinned somewhat sheepishly and held a finger to his lips, then turned to lock the door and close the casement shutters. A brief gesture with his hand and his image wavered. Then, returned to his natural state, Mik`kel smiled and bowed with a courtly flourish, provoking a small chuckle from his audience of one.

"Do you still fear discovery if you show your true self?" she asked, her face solemn again.

Mik`kel shrugged as he busied himself making fresh herbal tea. "The Dark powers of the sorcerer and his tame Dul`Charian shamans are formidable. Were their agents to spot a Kal`Dathian wizard here, consorting with the very king whose land Rak`koth covets, they might dispatch their magic users to seek me out. And, do they come here and find the Avatar when he has fully Awakened—for his signature of power will be unmistakable to any who walk the paths of magic—they will know him for their sworn nemesis, and he will be sorely imperiled as well."

Outside, the loud clopping of a host of iron hooves echoed off the pavement, by the sound of it a large company of armored knights or lancers passing close enough to rattle his shutters. As they waited for the racket to fade, he raised an eyebrow.

"Has this kingdom always felt itself sufficiently threatened by the Elves to maintain so sizable an army, even before the war?"

Aisleen shook her head with some embarrassment. "No, my Lord Mage, I am afraid that we have kept such a force at the ready to fight among ourselves."

"Among yourselves?" asked Mik`kel, with little clue to her meaning.

"Yes, in a manner of speaking. You see, when our people came to this land, we were united under one king, one royal house. And it remained thus for more than one hundred years, until the king on the throne at that time, Connall the Just, suddenly took ill and died. Some said he died of a wasting fever, though others suspected that less natural causes hastened his passing.

"In any event, at his death he left behind twin sons, Steafan and Dunmore, each of whom felt that he alone was fit to rule. Each prince gathered his faction of noble supporters who saw power and riches to be gained by casting their lot with the heir whom they believed would ascend the throne."

Mik`kel nodded, knowing all too well the lengths to which nobles in his own father's court had intrigued and maneuvered to gain favor and influence with the king.

Aisleen sighed as she continued. "Eventually, civil war broke out between the factions vying for the throne. After several years of bloody conflict, Prince Steafan gained the advantage and defeated his brother's army decisively in battle. When he emerged the victor, Steafan demanded that Dunmore accept him as king and swear fealty to him, but the vanquished prince hated his brother bitterly and could not bring himself to bend his knee."

"I am guessing that this Dunmore was too proud to humble himself thusly," said Mik`kel.

"Indeed," replied the seeress. "And when Dunmore refused, he was banished from the kingdom. He and a large contingent of his followers, nobles and commoners alike, traveled to the west, and there established their own separate kingdom in the mountains, in what is now known as Dunmoria. They vowed to fight on against the 'usurper,' as they called the victorious prince, and continued to come down out of their mountain hold and attack Steafan's lands whenever they could gather enough forces to do so.

"The war went on for generations, long after Prince Dunmore and all of his original followers had died. The bitterness, and the sense of being robbed of their rightful place while forced into a harsh life in the mountains, went on and on as well, passed down from father to son to son, even when there was no longer anyone alive who could remember the truth of what had occurred so many years ago."

"Are Calderia and Dunmore still at war?" asked Mik`kel, unable to fathom why the descendants would continue fighting for generations for a cause no longer understood by either side.

"Well, the last serious battle with the Dunmorians happened twenty years ago. Since then, there have been skirmishes along the borders of the two kingdoms, but no open warfare. Still, the relationship between both countries remains highly acrimonious and strained. MacRae, their current king, still nurtures the seeds of hatred sown by his ancestors and will not relent, though Gavan has let it be known that he would see an end to hostilities. We do not trade nor even exchange envoys."

"And the Elves took no part in this internecine conflict?"

"None," she replied. "They preferred to remain aloof from what they undoubtedly regarded as the petty struggles of humanity."

Mik`kel poured the steaming tea into one of the two cups he possessed and brought it to her. She smiled her appreciation and sipped it slowly, content to sit quietly as the hot brew and the welcomed fire warmed her body. He found himself enjoying her companionable silence just as it was, and it came to him that he had been looking forward to seeing her again. He was loath to disturb the mood, but his curiosity about her visit won out over patience.

"My Lady, I am honored and pleased to see you anew. Might I inquire as to what brought you here to me today? Is there any news?"

Aisleen placed the cup down on the table. "I came because...well, because I have reason to believe that the king's resolve to continue this war might be weakening."

The mage looked up, feeling a quickening in his pulse, but maintaining an even expression with some effort. "How so, my Lady?"

She paused, reluctant to repeat the sad news. "We, and perhaps the Elfin king as well, have suffered a grievous loss. Not long ago, the king sent a patrol of his scouts into the Great Forest, to find and retrieve a supply of Thalesi leaves—only for their curative power, and against another outbreak of the Scourge."

He saw her chin lift in defense of her king; then she relaxed and sighed again. "Because the Elves can sense the slightest intrusion into their Woods, this time the scouts were accompanied by a senior mage, in hopes that he might shield them from detection."

"It would take a powerful mage indeed to maintain that large a shield," said Mik`kel, calculating the strength required even as he gazed at her.

Aisleen nodded. "I know the man. Niocal is very strong in the power. And perhaps his spells worked, for a while at least, because the party penetrated deeper into the Forest than ever before. Or perhaps the Elves preferred to set a better trap. In any event, the scouts were discovered and ambushed a short distance from the Thalesi grove, slaughtered to a man...save for the mage, who said the trees themselves attacked him. Stunned by the deaths of his men, Niocal retaliated with fire, killing all but one of the Elves in range of his flames and igniting the trees in which they had been hiding. Only he escaped to tell the gruesome tale."

"Such fools, all of them." Mik`kel shook his head in disbelief. "And for a mage to loose such a killing fire..."

Aisleen looked at him thoughtfully, heartened by his disdain for so flagrant an abuse of gods-sent gifts. "King Gavan took the loss of his men very hard. He felt responsible for their deaths, since he had approved their mission. And, at first, he raged against the Elves, as did many others, especially the kin of the slain. But later, he spoke to the queen in my presence about the uselessness of all the deaths, men and Elves alike, and the unintended damage to the trees. I believe this latest tragedy has brought him to a deeper sense of futility about the war itself."

"Enough for him to sue for peace?" Mik`kel asked, with a glimmer of hope.

Aisleen shrugged and spread her hands apart. "Perhaps that time is approaching. Gavan is headstrong and slow to forgive, but he has never lacked in intelligence." Mik`kel saw the flicker of pride in her lovely eyes, and felt a twinge of envy for the man who commanded her loyalty, and perhaps her love, though he said nothing of this as she continued.

"I believe that he struggles between his mind and his heart, between that awful knowledge of futility and the terrible anger and sense of betrayal that still lives within him. He is a proud man, as well; and, like many proud men, unable to easily reverse his course once set in motion without sufficient cause to swallow that pride and let reason prevail o'er rage."

"I have seen that pride and rage firsthand," Mik`kel said, "strong enough to defy the wishes of the gods themselves. Perhaps, with this tragedy, the gods have shown him the need to stay the anger in his heart and make an end to this senseless war."

At this, Aisleen looked up sharply. "My Lord, are you telling me that the gods would have deliberately caused this reckless tragedy to further their own ends?"

Mik`kel held up a forestalling hand. "No, my Lady, I do not suggest that they themselves set this calamity in motion. For reasons unclear to me, I believe that they preclude themselves—or are precluded—from taking a direct hand in controlling the will of mortal beings. Elsewise, both Gavan and Rillandariel would have long since struck a peace at their command, and my work here would be nearer to completion."

He lowered his hand and sank into the chair beside her. "But the gods have warned both kings that it is folly to pursue this war, when the celestial harmony has already been so profoundly threatened by Rak`koth's return. It may be that their refusal to heed the gods and join together only further widens the rift in the Weave, so that every reckless act of anger and hatred they commit sows the seeds of their own destruction. The kings, and all the peoples of this land, must come to see this, else all are surely doomed."

Aisleen nodded grimly, knowing all too well the bitter harvest already reaped in the fighting on both sides. "Then we can only hope that somehow the kings will be moved to see that, and put an end to that folly, before the doom you speak of is upon us. I do not know what will tip the scales in that direction, but I pray it happens soon."

They fell silent again, and Aisleen eventually rose to take her leave, though, in truth, she did not wish to go. Mik`kel walked her to the door and watched as she stepped into her carriage and rode away, then turned back into the room that suddenly felt a little emptier.

Chapter 13

Night Ride

The sky was bathed in the purple shadows of dusk when the golden-haired Elfin warrior led her mounted patrol of twenty riders out of the Forest and onto the cold grassy plains of western Calderia. She had chosen this time because the waning light helped to conceal their passage as they made their way northward into human territory. She had chosen this place because these open, wind-swept lands were home to the largest herds of cattle bred and raised by the enemy—cattle they had come to steal.

Ellianthia was not leading cattle raids because the Forest dwellers needed the meat. Elves relied more heavily on grains, fruits and vegetables in their daily diets, along with trout, salmon and other fish that teemed in their Forest streams and ponds or swam in the waters of the West River flowing down from the northern mountains. When they did eat meat, they usually preferred the flesh of deer, elk or even the occasional bear, along with fowl such as pheasant, goose and wild turkey.

Still, some Elves had developed a taste for beef, so the stolen meat would be butchered and roasted or dried into strips for jerky. The hides would be cured and used to make leather goods and clothing, even the kind of hardened leather armor that she wore this evening.

But this raid was not a hunt for food or hides. It was an act of war, intended to strike a blow at the heart of the cattle-dependent humans, who regarded their herds as a form of wealth. Stealing that wealth from under their noses inflicted damage by reducing their food supply, and demoralized them by undermining their sense of security and control.

Indeed, although the Calderians still had vast herds at their disposal, Elfin leaders were convinced that the numerous raids carried out thus far had already taken a toll on the enemy, making a mainstay of their diet scarcer and requiring King Gavan to move some of his forces away from the front lines to protect against the repeated thefts in the west.

It was these enemy forces that the Elfin rustlers were taking pains to avoid. Ellianthia was under strict orders from her father to avoid unnecessary loss of life—particularly *her* life—in conducting these raids. It was the condition he set for allowing her to take command, saying that no amount of enemy cattle was worth losing his only remaining child. Fully aware of this, she and her patrol exercised due caution as they approached a herd of several hundred cattle that had gathered beside one of the shallow branches of the West River.

Their black and white coloring identified these longhorns as belonging to Baron Glendannon, the largest cattle owner in Calderia. Some were drinking from the stream, their tails lashing back and forth to drive away the insects that buzzed around in the evening air. A few had knelt down near a small copse of trees that grew along the water. But most were still standing, grazing or chewing their cuds, which was fortunate because it was far easier to get the animals moving before they had bedded down for the night.

Ellianthia held up her hand to call a halt while she examined the surrounding area closely, using her excellent night vision. She saw no campfires or other signs of herders near the stream or in the trees, and heard no sounds except the rustling of the wind and the deep lowing of the animals as they called out to each other. Still, she waited for some minutes longer, wanting to be certain that nothing was amiss. But it appeared that all was well. They seemed to be alone with the cattle on the chilly open plain.

She was just about to signal her riders to begin circling the herd and getting into position to drive them south when she heard a faint noise. What was that? It sounded like...like a horse snorting. It might have come from the direction of the trees, though she could not be sure. She gave the hand signal for silence to her riders, her senses now on highest alert. Again, nothing. She was thinking that perhaps her imagination was getting the best of her wh...Wait! There was a muffled clinking noise.

Was that the sound of metal jingling, perhaps a horse's reins? Yet there were no horses but their own in sight. Not any in sight, but...Oh! The gods be damned! The hairs on her neck stood up sharply, screaming a silent alarm as the pieces fell into place.

"Ware! Ambush!" she yelled, just before a chorus of angry shouts erupted and a large force of mounted men suddenly burst out of the copse of trees, their swords and spears raised as they thundered directly toward the startled Elves. Gods-cursed humans! At a glance, she estimated that the enemy outnumbered her patrol by at least two to one, perhaps more, and looked to be more heavily armed and armored. Too many to fight out here without risking a bloodbath.

"Break off and ride for the Forest!" she cried, urging her patrol to flee, all interest in the cattle abandoned as the most immediate goal became escaping the disaster that was about to unfold if the enemy caught them in the open. As much as her blood burned to engage the human bastards in combat and feed them her steel, she knew that, if they turned and stood their ground, her lightly armored riders would be no match for more than twice as many warriors wearing plate and barreling down on them on their heavy warhorses. If they were outflanked and surrounded, they would be slaughtered.

Cursing the gods for having to turn tail and run, she wheeled her mount around toward the south and galloped away, hoping that the lighter, faster Elfin horses would open up a lead as they fled. And, indeed, luck seemed to be on their side when the cattle took a hand in the unfolding drama, milling wildly around in fear and bellowing loudly in protest over being disturbed. Many of the enemy horsemen found their path to the Elves blocked by the herd, forced to lose time working their way through the panicked animals before they could take up the chase.

Better still, several mounts reared and threw their riders off after an enraged bull took umbrage at his harem of cows being harassed so rudely, and proceeded to make his point by sticking his horns into any exposed horse flesh in his vicinity. A malicious grin crossed Ellianthia's face as she watched them topple their owners onto their arses, the bull's angry roars and the wounded horses' squeals only adding to the chaos and confusion.

It was obvious now that the humans had been lying in wait in the trees, in anticipation of another raid. Whether it was simply bad luck that Glendannon's men happened to be watching this herd, or whether the enemy had taken to guarding all of their cattle in this manner, it was clear that raiding had just become a much more dangerous undertaking.

But that was a concern for another day. At the moment, all that mattered was getting her people home alive, back to the safety of the trees off in the distance.

She could hear the hoof beats of a few enemy horses behind her, snorting and blowing as their riders drove them on, yelling insults and threats as they came. But by now, the Elves had distanced themselves from their remaining pursuers as the difference in weight and speed began to tell. Most of the enemy who had managed to get around the herd had already fallen behind, unable to maintain the breakneck pace. The few spears they managed to hurl fell short, leaving them no recourse but to shake their mailed fists and shout curses as they demanded that the "Forest scum" stand and fight.

She laughed and raised her hand in an obscene gesture, taunting them as it became apparent that she and her patrol were no longer in real danger. She would have much to report about the enemy's change in tactics when she met with her father to recount the tale of the failed raid. She turned her back and spurred her horse toward the Forest.

But she had not reckoned with the enemy archer. She heard a whizzing sound as an arrow sped by her ear, barely missing her. Unfortunately, it did not miss the Elf who was riding just to the right of her. She heard a dull thunk! as the speeding shaft hit Corlendrial, a close friend, slicing through his leather armor and lodging in his back.

"No!" she cried, as he moaned and slumped forward in his saddle. She turned to see a human bowman, dismounted and down on one knee some distance away, nocking another arrow and aiming at the wounded Elf who was now an easy target. "No!" she swore again, determined not to lose another friend to the hated enemy. Kicking her mount forward, she reached his side and positioned her body between him and the archer as she leaned over to stop him from falling.

She was pleading with her friend to hold on to life and ride when, a moment later, the second arrow intended for him struck her instead, driving deep into her right arm just below her shoulder. Stunned from the impact of the barbed steel point ripping through her flesh, and reeling from the agony of the pain shooting up and down her arm, she was knocked back and almost driven from her saddle.

Gritting her teeth to stifle a cry, she somehow managed to right herself and grab the reins of Corlendrial's horse with her left hand. Then she Sent both mounts a desperate plea to break into a gallop again, guiding her horse with the pressure of her thighs alone, and praying to the gods she had so recently cursed that they could both keep riding long enough to outdistance another arrow.

Fortunately, one of the other Elfin riders had seen what happened and turned back to help, reaching over to brace Corlendrial in the saddle as they continued to race to safety.

Another rider offered his support to the warrior princess but she waved him off, pointing to the Woods that they were fast approaching.

She cared nothing for her own injury, although she was barely holding on to consciousness. All she could think of was saving the life of her friend, and how it would feel if she had to look into the eyes of his family and tell them of his death—a death that had occurred on her watch, and for which she felt responsible because she had not been more vigilant in protecting her own.

She did not want to think about what her father would do when he learned that she had been wounded again. The king had nearly forbidden her to fight again after she had barely escaped being burned alive by the human mage some time ago.

Only her threat to leave the Tree Palace and strike out on her own to do battle had moved him to allow her participation in the less dangerous business of cattle raids, though even then, his fear and anguish was etched on his face every time he watched her leave. She could only imagine what he would say now.

Grimacing from the pain and weakened by the loss of blood, it took every remaining bit of strength and determination she had to stay on her horse until she and her patrol reached the Forest at last. She watched through heavy-lidded eyes as all of her patrol passed safely into the Woods. Then, beneath the sheltering canopy of her beloved trees once more, she collapsed and pitched forward, her world going black even before she hit the ground.

Chapter 14

Turning Point

Whether it was fate that finally took a hand in tipping the scales or just the natural consequence of iron meeting ice, the turning point in the relentless prosecution of the protracted war between men and Elves came unheralded early one winter morn on a training field lying just north of Brannock Castle.

The day began uneventfully enough when Killian rose at dawn, shivering as he stepped into the garderobe to relieve his morning bladder. That pressing problem solved, he donned his riding clothes and headed for the kitchen, where Bethia, the harried head cook, greeted him with a preoccupied smile as she rushed to rescue a new batch of loaves from the smoking oven before they blackened. He crammed a hasty breakfast of warm bread and soft yellow cheese into his mouth, washed it down with watered wine, and hurried to the stable, on his way to morning practice with the King's Light.

The King's Light Cavalry was an innovation forced upon Calderian military commanders by the nature of the combat most often waged between men and Elves. The strategic importance of this lightly-armored, more highly mobile mounted force lay in the fact that the Elves did not field a conventional army as such, arrayed across a battlefield in standard formations of foot and pike and mounted knights. Thus, the Calderian heavy horse and Royal Lancers were of limited use in a battle where the Forest dwellers rarely exposed themselves en masse to any large attack on the open plain.

For their part, the Elves had quickly discovered in the early stages of the war that they were simply no match in the open for the Calderian knights. These heavily armored humans, mounted on their massive destriers and wielding axe or mace or lance, would rumble down upon them like a bristling wave of shining steel, shaking the very earth and smashing through their vulnerable ranks like so much dry kindling.

Instead, the slimmer, lighter Elves had learned to rely upon their inherent strengths of speed and mobility, and the deadly accuracy of bow and javelin. They rarely ranged far from the shelter of their trees, save for lightning raids conducted against nearby towns and villages under cover of darkness. In fact, some had taken to calling it the "Skirmish War," because great pitched battles were less frequent than briefer clashes.

The Elfin light cavalry were accomplished riders who fought in small mounted groups, darting out from the Forest on lighter, fleeter horses and firing their war arrows from a gallop, then fading back into the Woods behind rows of deadly Elfin archers positioned at the tree line. They liked nothing better than to lure the humans into the trees in hot pursuit, where mounted charges were impossible, lance and pike quickly became tangled in branches and undergrowth, and the weight of heavy armor became a liability against quicker and more agile fighters.

To counter these mounted Elfin skirmishers, the King's Light also employed smaller, faster horses, and trained their riders to engage the enemy on their own terms, dashing out at great speed to meet the Elfin horsemen, launching arrows and javelins from a distance, then using sword and axe if they were swift enough—and fortune smiled—to catch the enemy at close range. But these nimble tactics required learning skills that did not come easily to the human riders accustomed to simply pointing their huge, powerful warhorses at the enemy and charging.

The opportunity for training in light horse combat caught the interest of many young men, among them Crown Prince Killian. His size and prowess as an armored knight-in-training had already earned him a reputation as a fierce and awesome foe on the practice field. Yet, he found himself drawn to training with the King's Light as well, in part because he delighted in racing across the plains, air streaming by him, unencumbered by the weight and restriction of heavy steel plate.

The other reason was that this cavalry troop was likely to see action against the enemy sooner than the heavy horse units, which meant less delay in getting his first chance to inflict revenge on the Elves for Orrin and all the others whose deaths could be laid at their feet. Like other young men his age, he had been watching older men ride out to battle long enough, and was anxious to see some "real fighting," as he called it, for himself.

The queen had deep misgivings about her son's desire to go to war just months after celebrating his eighteenth name-day and barely reaching manhood. The king, having been a soldier, and understanding a young man's need to prove himself, swallowed his own fears and gave his son permission to practice with the King's Light, hoping it would help satisfy his youthful appetites for "fighting" while keeping him out of harm's way, at least for the nonce.

And so, on this cold, clear winter morning, Killian was en route to the training field. His red woolen cloak flapped around his shoulders, held aloft by the gusting northerly wind as his black riding boots crunched through the thin layer of ice left from last night's chilling rain. As he rounded the corner, he met Colum and Gilmore, already mounted and holding the reins of a sprightly little sorrel that the stable boy had just led out of the stall.

"Look at him, Gilly," Colum said with a condescending snort. "All dressed up real pretty like that, you could almost think him a man, 'cept I heard from the chambermaids that he still pees his bed of a night."

"Truly, Col?" Gilmore asked, craning his neck around for an exaggerated look at the back of Killian's leather breeches. "He does nae look to be wearing a diaper, but then those things are hard to tell."

Killian made a show of studied indifference to what passed for brilliant repartee between his comrades, mounting the sorrel and turning the horse toward the courtyard gate before pausing to remark, "At least I still have something to piss with. I heard Col's fell off from one too many nights with Poxy Bernice over at The Twisted Pizzle."

His reference to a particularly tawdry brothel in Beggar's Alley, notorious for sending its customers on their way with a case of "the itch," brought howls of laughter and gestures of mock surrender from the others. Having thus tendered morning greetings in their usual friendly fashion, the three companions rode through the gate and headed toward the practice field.

"We have not seen much of you lately, fuzz-face," Gilmore commented amiably as they trotted along. "Catty's been asking after you down at the Rose and Thistle. It is all I can do to keep her...occupied...so she does nae pine her heart away for you," he chuckled, with a leer that left little doubt about the form of "comfort" he was offering the wench.

At the mention of her name, Killian felt a grin creep over his face. Closing his mind to the image of Catty's magnificent breasts, he grunted and shook his head. "My father has decided that, since my manhood name-day is behind me, I should be spending part of my time being privy to council meetings and watching him hold audience with the daily round of petitioners, 'as befits the heir to the Crown,'" he intoned solemnly, in a fair imitation of the king's official voice.

"Between that, and daily practice with Doughal, I hardly have time to piss, much less to while my time away 'consoling' needy women like you idle layabouts."

They were all still laughing at his sad plight as they arrived at the field, somewhat warmed by the brisk ride. There, they found Captain Rodric, formerly of the Royal Lancers and now attached to the King's Light, sitting astride his roan mare, barking orders to his troop of horsemen in the chill morning air. "Mornin', your Highness," said the Captain, before resuming his instruction.

Killian nodded, watching Rodric's breath leave his mouth in small, white clouds as he explained the nature of the exercise at hand. Colum and Gilmore sat to either side of him, trying to suppress yawns, but doing a poor job of it.

"The task is fairly straightforward, men," said Rodric, pointing across the fields to a row of posts adorned with straw-filled effigies of Elfin warriors. "You are to ride at full gallop toward the posts until you are in javelin range. Then you are to rein in, throw the javelins at the targets, turn and hightail your arses back to your lines before the enemy can return fire."

Even as he spoke, a group of five riders spurred their horses forward from a dead stop and raced down the field toward the dummy targets a hundred yards in the distance. Three of the men managed to rein in properly and launch their javelins in the general direction of the stationary Elfin "warriors," while the other two were still yelling "Whoa! Whoa!" as their horses thundered past the posts.

Rodric shook his head in disgust as Killian and his friends nearly fell out of their saddles laughing. The captain turned a glaring eye on the three mirthful youths.

"Think you can do better, lads? Then grab a spear and we will see who be laughing next. And mind the ice!" he called after them. "The ground is still slick enough from last night's frost."

By the time he finished the warning, Killian and his two comrades had already grabbed javelins from the stack and were prodding their mounts to a gallop. Holding the short spears aloft, they laughed with delight and screamed dire threats as they closed upon the "enemy." When they had brought their horses up short some thirty feet from the effigies, they whipped their javelins forward and watched them sail through the morning air.

Killian's weapon pierced the foot of his dummy, while those thrown by Colum and Gilmore went wide of the targets. The prince gave a triumphal shout, laughing at the red faces of his friends as he reined the sorrel in a tight half-circle to race back up the length of the field for another javelin.

He was still chuckling as his mount's ironshod hooves hit a narrow patch of ice hidden in a deep furrow carved out by some wagon wheel when the ground was soft and muddy. The horse scrambled furiously to regain its footing, but the iron shoes could find little purchase against the slick frozen surface. Killian could feel the sorrel going down, and fought to kick his foot out of the stirrup, but his boot heel caught in the leather triangle and would not come free.

Then the panicked animal was crashing to the ground and rolling over on his left flank, crushing the prince beneath hundreds of pounds of squirming horseflesh. Killian felt something snap in his spine, just before his boot finally disentangled from the stirrup. The horse continued to roll until it came to rest on its right side.

Killian felt a strange numbness spreading throughout his body as he struggled to breathe. He was trying unsuccessfully to rise when the horse kicked him in the back of his head as it fought to right itself, driving the edge of the metal shoe into his skull. An exploding pain was the last thing he felt before blackness overwhelmed him.

Gaping in horror, Colum was the first to reach the fallen prince. He slid down from his saddle and fell to his knees beside the unmoving body, while Gilmore quieted the nervous sorrel and led it some distance away. Killian lay flat on his back, his eyes closed, his fiery mane brown and muddied.

Dreading what he knew he must find, Colum took his friend's head in his hands and gently rolled it to one side, seeing the blood flowing and pooling behind his skull. A stark emptiness descended over the young noble as he looked down at his boyhood friend, wondering what words he could possibly find to tell the king that his eldest son and heir was lost.

†††††

They brought Killian back to the castle in a wagon, escorted by Colum and Gilmore, who refused to leave their prince's side during the agonizing trip home. A rider had been sent ahead to bear the dreadful news, so the king and queen were waiting in the courtyard when their son arrived, lying unconscious on the wagon bed and wrapped in a blanket, the back of his head an ugly mass of blood and slivered bone.

Briana nearly collapsed at the sight, but steadied herself with the help of Gavan's hand as Killian was gently carried to his room. All those present at the castle, noble and commoner, lord and servant, were stunned to silence as word of the prince's grave injury and imminent death spread throughout the halls and chambers of the gray stone fortress.

The king and queen hovered near Killian's bedside with tears and trepidation, while their other children, Prince Aaron and Princess Rowena, waited anxiously in a nearby chamber, knowing only that something very serious had happened to their beloved older brother. Agonizing moments passed as the court physicians examined their son at some length, probing his spine and carefully wiping away the dried blood to expose the extent of damage to his skull.

Within minutes, their eyes met over the body and reached a terrible consensus without the need for words. It was left to Bartholomew, the chief physician, to render their grim opinion. His face ashen, he straightened and turned to the anguished parents.

"Your Majesties, I fear that you must prepare for the worst."

Briana gasped, having hoped against hope that the learned healers might offer some small encouragement. Gavan fought to keep his voice steady and calm as he asked, "Is there no hope, Bartholomew?"

The aging healer read the unspoken plea in his sire's eyes but could not grant his wish, though he would have given all he had to do so. "Majesty, the prince's spine is sorely damaged. That alone could be enough to cause his death or leave him crippled in his bed for life, though my healing arts might offer some small repair. But the injury to his skull is terrible indeed, and far beyond my humble skills. As it is, I fear he will not last the day. In truth, I marvel that he lives at all."

Briana turned her face into her husband's chest, sobbing. Gavan thought of Father Venutius, who might employ his clerical powers to heal the prince; but the rotund cleric had been called away to attend the investiture of the new bishop in Leinster, several days ride to the north. The king fixed his gaze upon the man who had helped to bring his son into the world, and now seemed the only one who might save his life.

"You must try, Bartholomew. My Killian would not give up without a fight, and neither must we. For his sake, though all hope be gone, you must try."

The healer bowed in acquiescence. "Of course, Your Majesty. But..." He shook his head unconsciously and turned away to gather the other physicians about him, for what must be a tragically futile effort in the service of his king.

"There is one healer who might be able to save the prince."

All heads turned at the sound of the seeress' voice as she entered the bedchamber, lifting the hem of her robe above the floor. Briana raised her head from Gavan's chest, scarcely able to see Aisleen's face through her tears.

"A healer? There is someone who can heal my son? Tell me who!" she demanded, a hint of the hope so recently quashed creeping back into her voice.

"He calls himself Morgander. He is said to be a most powerful healer." She watched the king's face as the mention of that name brought a look of hope joined with fear to his eyes.

"Morgander?" the queen repeated. "I have heard his name. One of my maids spoke highly of his skills." She turned back to her husband, her excitement rising. "Oh, Gavan, let us send for him at once!"

The king's reply was lost when Bartholomew stepped forward to offer protest. "But, my Queen, I know of no trained physician by that name. You can not think to trust the prince's life to a stranger, an untrained charlatan fit only for treating cold sores and cases of the flux."

Disheartened by this stern pronouncement from an old and trusted friend, Briana looked at Aisleen, who was staring at Gavan with a strange intensity. Then the seeress turned back to Briana.

"I have knowledge of this man's healing skills. And," she continued, her eyes never leaving Gavan's face, "I believe the king has knowledge of him as well."

Briana looked up at Gavan with surprise and some confusion. "You know of him, my Lord husband?"

The king said nothing for a time, his face impassive and unreadable. Then he turned to Bartholomew and said, "Please excuse us for a time, my friend. I would speak to the queen in private."

The court physician began to object, then thought better of it and gestured for his fellow healers to withdraw. When all but Aisleen had departed, Gavan took Briana's hand.

"Yes, my Lady wife, Aisleen speaks the truth. I have met this man who calls himself Morgander. But perhaps you will know him better as Mik`kel of Kal`Dathia."

The queen blinked, momentarily at a loss. Then her green eyes widened. "Mik`kel? You mean the mage who came for our Killian? He is a healer?"

Gavan gave a short nod of his head. He had told his wife of Mik`kel's visit, and of the mage's insistence that he be permitted to Awaken their son's dormant power; but, in his great rage and fear, the king had neglected to mention the alter ego Mik`kel had assumed as a healer in the village after Gavan's refusal.

Briana stared at her son lying helpless and broken on the bed, his red blood staining the sheets even now. Then she gripped her husband's arms and, with a piercing, pleading look, spoke directly from her heart to his.

"My love, I know this man's terrible purpose for coming here; and I, too, fear the fate that he would lay before Killian. But the gods themselves have spoken for him. We must send for him, if there is *any* hope that he can save our son."

Knowing she was right, he asked, "And if the price of Mik`kel's aid is our acceptance of that very fate the gods would impose?"

She hugged him then and spoke the words they both knew to be true. "My Lord husband, Killian must *live*, is he to have any fate at all."

Chapter 15

A Promise Given

And thus it was that the king sent for the man called Morgander, moved by the pleas of his queen and driven by his own desperation. The old man learned of the summons when a quartet of the King's Elite entered his shop just after dusk and announced that they had been sent to escort him to the castle "forthwith." Informed of Killian's dire condition, he paused only to gather up some essentials into his old leather bag before setting out with them at once.

Flanking him on either side, the guards set a vigorous pace through the village. The small entourage hurried through the square, now nearly empty of the daily crowds of jostling market goers. The merchant stalls were vacant, save for a few that catered to stragglers stopping to buy dinner on their way home or pausing for a cup of wine before heading for the taverns, gaming houses and brothels just now beginning to welcome the evening custom.

Even as they crossed the drawbridge and entered the castle courtyard, the heavy oaken doors swung open, and the king himself appeared just inside the entrance. He said only "Come!" by way of greeting, and led the old man up the wide staircase and down the hallway to the prince's chamber. Gavan stopped at the door and turned to Mik`kel, his face drawn and pale, his eyes filled with sorrow and despair.

"Mage, my son lies dying behind that door. My most learned physicians tell me they can do nothing to save him, that his death is already written. Aisleen reminded me of your healing arts when I had forgotten, and spoke highly of your skills. My queen beseeched me to send for you, and I would not say her nay, for I, too, would give all to save our boy—no matter the cost."

The king's eyes showed firm resolve as he gripped Mik`kel's arm tightly. "Save my son if you can, mage, and I vow that I will accept your plan for his destiny."

Knowing what that pledge had cost the king, Mik`kel shook his head slightly and placed his hand over Gavan's. "My Lord King, it is not *my* plan. It was the gods who chose his destiny. I am but a tool in their service. And I will not force a bargain for my aid. I will do all I can to save him for his sake, and because I believe him to be the key to the future of us all. But if I succeed in healing him, you will owe me nothing. The choice of what to do will still be yours."

Gavan stared in silence at the mage for a moment, then turned around and opened the door to the room where Killian lay pale and unmoving, attended only by the queen and the seeress. Briana looked up with some confusion at the frail old man following behind her husband. She leaned over to whisper something to Aisleen, who nodded, then spoke aloud.

"Welcome, my Lord Mage. Your presence fills me with hope. But, perhaps the glamour is not needed here?"

Mik`kel glanced around the chamber. "Of course, my Lady." As the queen looked on in surprise, Mik`kel gestured and released his Transformation Spell, shedding decades and untold infirmities as he did. Gavan led the now hale and vibrant mage to Killian's bedside.

The youth laying in repose might have been dead, save for the shallow rise and fall of his chest. Some of the blood and mud had been wiped from his face and hair, though the back of his skull remained a clotted, ugly mess.

"And the cause of these injuries?" Mik`kel asked, bending over to carefully examine the prince's head.

"A training accident, while riding across an icy field," the king replied. "His horse went down on top of him, then kicked his head. My physicians say he should be dead already from so grievous a wound."

The mage looked up at the king. "Perhaps an Avatar is not so easy to kill," he said softly. Then he opened his well-worn leather satchel and laid out a small collection of herbs and powders on the table beside the bed.

"Send for some boiling water, if you will. I would brew a tisane to give him strength. He will need it for what I must do."

As Briana rushed to call for the water, Mik`kel asked for silence, then closed his eyes and focused inward, sending his senses flowing down into Killian's still form. For long minutes, he traced the pathways of nerve and muscle, probing the wreckage of blood and bone, searching for the core, the inner essence of this youth who clung so tenuously, yet so tenaciously, to life.

There, deep within! A faint spark of life, a minute glowing kernel of energy that pulsed and flickered weakly. He sent a small surge of his own life force to nurture that golden essence until the healing could begin, then withdrew.

When he opened his eyes, he found a pot of steaming water on the table, and three pairs of eyes staring at him expectantly. "The damage is great, indeed. His aura is dangerously weak, and yet he holds to life where others would have given up. But there is little time to spare." Mik`kel quickly poured a crystalline powder into the pot and stirred until the water darkened. "Try to get some of this into him, if you can."

The king looked on with muted hope as queen and seeress strove together to coax precious drops of the concoction down Killian's throat. Mik`kel paced around the bed, chanting softly and halting to scribe a sigil of power in white chalk at each of the four corners. Finally, he motioned Briana and Aisleen to step away.

The queen went to the circle of her husband's arms, while the seeress stood close to them, holding herself with arms crossed below her breasts. For a moment, Mik`kel imagined his arms enfolding her again, offering comfort, as they had on the eve of their first meeting. Then he wiped the image from his mind.

"It is time, gods grant me strength," he said earnestly.

Mik`kel stood beside the bed and pulled the covers away, gently rolling Killian on his side. He was naked from the waist up, his skin cold and clammy as the mage traced a sigil of power above his back and head. Then, taking up his heavy polished staff, he knelt beside the prince and closed his eyes. His breathing slowed and deepened as he prayed to Lurendal, goddess of Healing, and drew upon the power of the ether everywhere around him.

Moments later, a blue-white light flared brightly in the chamber, banishing the shadows from every niche and corner, as if the sun had risen inside the room. As Gavan and the others stared in awe, Mik`kel channeled the power through his staff and down into Killian's body, until the light suffused the prince and lit him with a strange cerulean glow.

Slowly, painstakingly, Matthew guided the healing light along the length of Killian's spine, willing the severed nerves to reform and be whole again, the broken vertebrae to knit and mend. Then, more slowly, more carefully, he began the arduous and delicate work of reconstructing the shattered skull bones and fusing them together, then repairing and reforming the soft tissue of the brain.

Down, down he went into the labyrinth of tiny capillaries and myriad nerve endings. There, he labored long and hard to regenerate flesh and redirect the flow of blood to ease the swelling, reviving neural pathways that crossed and looped in patterns far too complicated for the eye to see.

Evening passed into night as Mik`kel toiled at his intricate task, the candles burning low in their silver holders. While the queen entered the next chamber to hold her children tightly and offer them a measure of hope and assurance, a small repast of meat, bread, and cheese was brought to the door by worried servants and passed inside to Aisleen. It lay untouched on a side table.

The queen returned, exhausted by the grief, fear and unrelenting angst that she had striven mightily to keep hidden from her younger son and daughter. She leaned against the shoulder of her husband, dozing fitfully as he held her close.

From time to time, she would startle to fearful alertness, until Gavan whispered some calming words and stroked her hair to help her rest again. Now and then, he would glance over at Aisleen, who could see the fatigue and fear in his face, although he remained awake to keep silent watch over his elder son.

For her part, Aisleen was transfixed with wonder, and something else she could not define, at the sight of this mighty mage, whose power and dedication transcended anything she had ever encountered in a healer. Midnight had come and gone, and still Mik`kel worked diligently to save the young prince, calling on his magic and all the skills and knowledge learned in his long sojourn among the gentle brethren of the Isle. She watched him, unable to turn her eyes away.

Finally, the blue glow encompassing Killian's body began to fade. Then Mik`kel released his power and it was finished. Wearied and drained, he rose slowly, using his staff for support as he stood. The king straightened his shoulders, which brought the queen awake again, this time to find the mage smiling and nodding his head.

"It is done," he said. "He will live, though he will require some time to fully recover from the shock and the loss of blood. He will sleep for a while now but, the gods willing, he will be whole and well again before too long."

At that glorious news, the king and queen hugged each other tightly, their eyes streaming with tears of joy and relief. Briana finally released her husband to grasp Mik`kel's hand tightly between her own as she sobbed her gratitude.  Clutching his wife close to him, Gavan reached across the space between them to touch Mik`kel's shoulder.

"My Lord Mage, you have done a great service to the kingdom, and to two desperate parents. When you first came to me, I sent you away in anger and in pain, because I could not bring myself to sacrifice my son to make a peace with so hated a foe; and because I feared for the future course that the gods would have my son undertake."

Keeping his eyes fixed on Mik`kel's, Gavan continued in earnest. "I still hate the enemy for what they have done. And I still fear for that future. But our people grow weary of killing and death, and the loss of sons and husbands who will never return to hearth and home. Today, my son nearly died while training for that war, a war that will surely place his life in danger again when he recovers, unless we find a way to make a peace."

He dropped his hand and looked down at his queen, who nodded her agreement with what he had said, and with what he was about to say. Resolved to his decision, Gavan straightened and gripped Mik`kel's arm once again.

"Mage, you are a man of honor and strength. Though you refused to force a bargain when it was within your power to do so, I repeat my vow, given freely, that we will place Killian's fate in your hands. We will trust to you and the gods, and may they grant wisdom as you guide him. Come to me when you have rested, and tell me what must be done."

As Mik`kel's heart filled with relief, Gavan began to turn away, then stopped and looked again upon the mage with a rueful expression. "The last time you were here, I banned you from the castle. A most inhospitable host, indeed. Please accept my invitation to come and live with us within our walls as an honored guest."

Mik`kel bowed his acceptance as both monarchs went to stand and gaze with love and hope upon the son whom they had given up for dead. He smiled with weary satisfaction to see them thus, joined arm in arm, oblivious to all but the sight of the prince resting quietly.

He had begun to gather the contents of his satchel when he felt a light touch on his arm. He knew her by the sweet scent of her lavender before she spoke.

"My Lord Mage," she said, her lovely eyes brimming with tears of happiness. "You have done a wondrous thing this day. I have never seen...I could not have believed...You were..." Then she was throwing her arms around him and hugging him fast against her as she sobbed.

Though taken by surprise, he did not resist her embrace, raising his arms to gently draw her closer, inhaling the sweet smell of her soft, black hair and feeling her breasts press into his chest. Despite his great weariness, he felt a stirring of something inside him that he had not felt for years, a yearning that he had thought long dead, perhaps irrevocably so, until now.

He wondered if she felt something as well, something more than gratitude alone, from the way she clung to him, as if reluctant to relinquish her hold and move apart. And indeed, could he have heard her private thoughts, he would have known that, beyond her deep respect and soaring admiration for him, there was something wakening inside her that she, too, had thought sealed away tightly in the closet of her heart.

Finally, she released him and stepped back to meet his eyes. "Forgive me, my Lord," she said shyly, with a rising blush that he found quite appealing. "I did not mean to smother you so. It is only that I am so grateful for Killian's life, for his sake and for his fath...his parents. Truly, the gods have gifted you with great power and skill. I am honored to know you, Lord Mage." She bowed her head in respect.

"Please," he replied, touching her hand with his and allowing it to linger there when she did not immediately withdraw hers. "I am flattered that you thought highly enough of me to speak to the king. And I am grateful for your support in ways great and small since my arrival."

Her full red lips curved up in a smile. "Please come and visit me when you have settled in?" she asked, returning his touch with a small squeeze of her own before turning and gliding from the chamber.

Chapter 16

A Promise Honored

Within an eight-day after Killian's healing, the king sent for Lucas, his personal scribe. While he waited, he stood in front of the fireplace in his smaller throne room, poking at the flaming logs that fought to keep the drafty chill of a blustery afternoon at bay. His promise to Mik'kel weighed heavily upon him, though his relief at making the decision had brought him restful sleep for the first time in months. It is a momentous thing to make a peace, he thought, to seek a way past the anger and pain that had been his constant companions for so long.

He recalled how his son had awakened after several days of quiet sleep with no memory of the fall or the healing that had brought him back from certain death. Killian had pronounced himself fit to stand, until he tried and fell back on the bed when his legs betrayed him. Mik'kel had prescribed more rest and regular doses of the healing powders he had left in the queen's hands, saying that it would be some little while before the young man recovered fully.

Gavan wondered what Killian would think when he heard of his father's decision to sue for peace with the race he held responsible for the murder of his uncle, and all the others who lay buried beneath the frozen winter soil. He wondered what his son would say when he learned of his forced betrothal to, gods, an Elfin maid, as the price of that peace.

Would he see unspoken accusations of cowardice and weakness in Killian's eyes that echoed his own doubts and fears? Or would Killian understand that the mantle of leadership weighed most heavily on a king when he must put aside his own feelings, even those of his loved ones, to serve the greater good?

He had not yet found an answer to these vexing questions when Lucas' arrival brought an end to his internal colloquy. The scribe entered quietly, carrying the slim, rectangular writing box that contained his finely sharpened feathered quills, assorted shades of ink, and the sheaf of precious vellum reserved for royal correspondence and proclamations.

"Your Majesty sent for me?" asked the slender, balding man, bowing formally to the king.

Gavan dropped the poker back into the wrought iron basket by the fireplace and turned to face him, nodding. "I would have a letter drafted, Lucas, an official letter drawn in your best hand."

"Of course, Your Majesty." Lucas bowed again and placed the gleaming lacquered oak box on the side table, opening the gold clasp with ink-stained fingers that were as much his badge of office as the calluses on a carpenter's hands or the scars on the arms of a veteran swordsman.

He spread the sheet of vellum out before him with great care, dipped his stylus in his best black ink, and poised his hand expectantly above the cream-colored parchment. Seeing that the scribe was ready, Gavan began to pace before the fireplace as he spoke.

"Begin the letter thusly: *'To Rillandariel, King of the Elves and Guardian of...'*"

He stopped his pacing when he heard a small snapping sound and looked to see Lucas staring up at him in amazement, a broken quill point lying amid droplets of dark ink pooling on the ruined vellum sheet.

"I believe you will need a new quill and paper, my friend," he observed mildly with a wry smile, thinking that he had never seen his scribe so much as smudge a letter in all his years of service. He waited patiently while Lucas retrieved fresh quill and parchment from his box.

"Shall we begin again? Very well. *'To Rillandariel, King of the Elves and Guardian of the Great Forest, from Gavan, King of Calderia. I give you greetings...'*"

†††††

The following morn, a squad of Elves charged with patrolling their section of the Forest perimeter looked out at the barricades and fortified encampments constructed by the enemy just beyond the tree line. What their eyes beheld was something they had not seen since the war began: unmanned barricades and empty encampments, devoid of any sign of human soldiers.

No smoke from breakfast campfires, no soldiers mustering for morning duty, no rows of horses staked along the picket lines. Nothing. Sometime in the night, with no warning and for no apparent reason, the Calderians had withdrawn from fixed positions occupied for more than three years.

Even as word of this perplexing news was being dispatched to the Tree Palace, a lone rider appeared in the distance, approaching under flag of truce. He walked his horse forward to the edge of the trees and lifted his hands to show that he bore no weapons. He was met by Mellarion, leader of the patrol, who strode out from the Forest cautiously, alert for enemy treachery.

"What do you want, human?" Mellarion asked, his eyes full of suspicion and disdain.

"I am Aral, Herald to the King of Calderia," the rider said in clear, measured tones. He reached into his leather pouch and withdrew a rolled parchment imprinted with the Royal Seal. "I bear a message from His Majesty for your great king."

†††††

"He asks for a meeting to consider terms for peace!" Rillandariel looked up in amazement from the parchment scroll in his hand and glanced around at the War Council called in haste. His advisors seemed as startled and bemused by this unexpected news as he was.

"Terms for peace? He offers to surrender?" That from Amarillia, a seasoned battle captain much valued for her brilliance in strategy and tactics.

The Elfin king shook his head. "He says nothing of surrender. He speaks of the benefits to both our peoples of finding a 'resolution to this tragic and useless conflict,' and offers to meet me face-to-face to speak of 'mutual redress and an end to the fighting.'"

Rillandariel watched the reactions of those gathered around him as he read these words aloud, and saw that their faces mirrored the very same emotions that churned within his own heart and mind: confusion, curiosity, skepticism, disbelief, anger and...hope.

"A trick! A ruse to lure you to your death!" cried Trillafarien angrily, rising to his feet. "These humans must think us fools. I suppose he invites you to visit him in his gray fortress behind his walls of stone, where he is in his power—and where you would be helpless against his steel or his foul poisons."

Rillandariel held up his hand. "Hear me, General," he commanded, his voice soft but firm. Trillafarien knew that tone well and subsided for the moment, though the angry flare of his nostrils made it clear that he would not remain silenced for long. The Elfin king nodded and continued.

"Gavan proposes that we meet in the open, the two of us alone, unarmed, in full view of both sides. Each would be equally vulnerable, and thus, equally protected."

"But why does he seek peace now, after so long?" Trillafarien persisted. "Perhaps the humans are weakened and fear defeat," he sneered.

"The fire storm they unleashed against Ellianthia's patrol some time back did not taste of weakness to me." The speaker was Mellisandria, Keeper of the Secret Grove, a wise and ancient Elf whose waist-length silvery hair and finely wrinkled skin had not diminished the reverence and esteem in which she was held as the greatest living wielder of the sacred tree magic.

"The human mages practice powers different from our own. In friendlier times, I sought knowledge of their magics, and I will tell you that they have Spells of Destruction that are terrible and mighty indeed. Why they have not brought them to bear against us in battle until now is more than I can fathom. But I do not think they fear defeat."

Rillandariel listened as different members of the Council rose to speak their mind. Trillafarien led the faction that argued against any negotiation with "murderers and thieves," while others voiced their willingness to listen to the human king's terms. Though few were ready to admit it openly, Rillandariel knew the toll that the war had taken on his people, just as he knew that many of his Forest folk would be willing to accept a way out of this conflict if it would not dishonor those who had sacrificed their lives to defend kin and home.

But could *any* peace be honorable if the dead were not fully avenged? He thought of his son, lost forever to an enemy arrow, and his hatred rose like bitter bile in his throat.

Just then, he heard Ellianthia's strident voice joining those urging the Council to reject any peace proposal from the "human murderers," and to continue the war until the enemy had "paid the just price." He looked at his beloved daughter, standing there so beautiful and strong in her anger and proud defiance, the child whom he had nearly lost twice in the past few months.

She had tried to avoid him for a time while recovering from the wound suffered in the cattle raid, clearly wanting to pretend that nothing had happened, that she had not been sorely injured—as if the healers who attended her were not reporting every detail to their distraught king. Her wound was largely healed now, but the injury to her father's heart was not so easily repaired, nor would it ever be as long as he was still in danger of losing her for the sake of hatred and the never-ending thirst for revenge.

Haunted by that thought, it came to him that there was really very little choice after all. He cleared his throat and waited until the Council quieted and gave him full attention.

"We are a brave people, a strong people. We have never shrunk from defending ourselves or the land we hold dear in our hearts. We have fought with honor and with courage, and have shown the enemy that we will never be defeated. We will continue to fight when fight we must. But it is not weakness to seek an honorable end to a war that serves no purpose, when the enemy is willing to talk of peace. It is not weakness to do all that we can to save the lives of those whom we love, if it can be done safely."

He glanced again at his daughter as he said these words. Seeing the dismay in her eyes as she grasped his intent, he steeled himself for the bitter protest that was sure to follow, then squared his shoulders and met the eyes of all gathered there.

"As your leader, I must do what is best for our people. I will meet with this human king and learn what is in his heart."

†††††

Mik'kel was walking down the castle hall on the way to his room, contemplating the Ritual of Awakening that the gods had instructed him to perform when Killian was wholly recovered, when he heard his named called and turned to see Aisleen hurrying toward him. From the way she was smiling, looking positively jubilant, he knew that something good had happened.

"He has done it!" she announced as she grasped his hands tightly, forgoing all formality in her excitement. "Gavan received a reply from the Elfin king. Rillandariel has agreed to meet and talk about making peace!"

A great feeling of relief came over the mage as the meaning of her words sank in. Gavan had kept his word. The king had promised to open negotiations with the Elfin king, and now he had fulfilled his oath to do so, somehow convincing Rillandariel to meet with him. Aisleen's joy was contagious, and he found himself grinning widely as he ushered her over to a seat in an alcove and sat down beside her. He could still feel the warmth in his hands where she had held them tightly while delivering the good news.

"When did this happen?" he asked, staring into her lovely eyes.

"Rillandariel's written acceptance of the proposal to talk was delivered to the King's Herald, who had been waiting outside the Forest for a reply. Aral brought the letter just this evening. Oh, Mik'kel, it is going to happen! We have a chance for peace!"

The mage had the impulse to grab Aisleen up in a hug, but he settled for squeezing her hand and pressing her for more details. She explained that, from what Gavan had told her, it would take some time for the details of the meeting to be worked out, for all necessary precautions for security to be taken on both sides, and for determination of the proper protocol required for a meeting of two heads of state.

"But Gavan is hoping to expedite the matter. Now that he has finally set his mind on making peace, I believe he will move as quickly as possible. Killian's near miss with death, and his miraculous recovery at your hands, inspired him greatly, and Briana has given him her full support. It will happen soon."

"Not a moment too soon," he replied, "with all the time that has been wasted. There is much to be done. But I am greatly relieved that the first steps have been taken."

They spoke for a while about the changes they hoped to see forthcoming from the peace, and what it could mean for finally beginning to prepare for the coming threat from across the sea. As they talked, Mik'kel could not help but be acutely conscious of the beautiful woman sitting so near to him.

They seemed to enjoy each other's company, and to feel comfortable together. He thought about inviting her to his room for some tea or some wine to celebrate the good tidings, but decided that she might not be comfortable in his bedchamber.

Still, she *had* invited him to come see her when he had settled in. He was thinking of a way to take her up on that invitation to visit when he heard her say his name, and realized that she had asked him a question.

"Mik'kel? You seem lost in thought. Or perhaps you would rather not answer so personal a question."

"I am sorry, my Lady. No, please, what were you asking me?"

Aisleen regarded him thoughtfully, hoping that he would be willing to satisfy her curiosity, though she would never insist that he do so. Looking into his gentle eyes, she found the courage to begin again.

"Mik'kel," she said softly, "there is something I would ask you, if you feel free to tell me."

"My Lady, if it is within my power to tell you, I shall."

Aisleen pressed on. "You once told me that there were other 'personal' reasons why you left your father's court in Kal'Dathia, besides the need to escape from his plans to make you a Wizard-King. I have been…curious…to know. Did these personal reasons involve someone else?"

Caught somewhat off guard by her insight, Mik'kel was silent for a moment, gazing away as if considering something. Then he smiled.

"What makes you smile so?" she asked hesitantly, suddenly a little less certain that she cared to hear the reason.

"Yes, Aisleen, my personal reasons for leaving did involve someone else. But I am smiling because I just realized that I have not thought of her seriously for a long time."

Strangely relieved, Aisleen settled back into her seat. "Would you mind telling me of her?"

Mik'kel shook his head. "Not at all." He gazed away again, as if to marshal his thoughts, then began.

"In Kal'Dathia, magic and religion are more closely aligned than here in Calderia. When I was at my royal father's court, it was the common practice for the wizards—whom you here call mages—to attend the services held at the Temple of Shalloth, our supreme deity, during Holy Days and feast days.

"The Temple services were led by the high priestess, with assistance from her other sister priestesses, all of whom were sworn to remain virginal and pure, completely dedicated to their worship of Shalloth from birth—and expressly forbidden any sexual...that is, any intimate contact with men for life."

"How...unfortunate   for   them," Aisleen   remarked sympathetically.

Mik'kel's lips quirked upward. "My fellow wizards and I thought it was unfortunate for us as well, especially when we would watch them dance on Holy Days and during celebrations. They would move and twirl in a most beguiling manner, clothed only in their flimsy..." He broke off and looked at her with some chagrin, expecting to find disapproval for his admission of lust for the devout women, but saw only an expression of mild amusement.

"Do not be embarrassed, my Lord Mage. I understand the ways of men," she said, with a small smile on her lips.

He laughed. "Yes, well...When the dancing for each service was finished, the priestesses would sit next to the wizards in the Temple, separated only by a narrow aisle, while the high priestess read from the Holy Scriptures. By coincidence, on several occasions, one particular young priestess sat close to me. She was very beautiful, though also quite pristine and aloof. I began to look forward to seeing her, intrigued by her beauty and her inaccessibility."

The mage offered a rueful grin. "Perhaps she felt my gaze on her from time to time, but she gave no hint of interest. If our eyes did meet, I would smile but she would always look away. Until one day when, instead of averting her gaze, she smiled back at me. And I knew, without her saying a word, that my interest was returned." He stopped, continuing to look into the distance.

"Please, go on," Aisleen prompted, though she found herself feeling uneasy about his description of this woman's beauty and his strong interest in her.

Encouraged by her request, Mik`kel proceeded. "I continued to see her on Holy Days. We would sit near each other, never touching, but exchanging furtive glances and secretive smiles. Then one day, the chief wizard had business at the Temple with the high priestess, and bade me go along with him. He was rather aged and, though he would not admit it, he needed someone to lean upon to mount the long stairs leading to the Temple doors."

Mik`kel chuckled softly as he thought of the old wizard. "While he met with the high priestess, I was shown into a small garden to wait there for him. As it happened, the young priestess was there, tending the flowers. She looked up, startled to see me, or any man, in that cloistered setting."

He smiled faintly at the memory. "We were not alone, of course. The older priestesses would never have permitted that. But I managed to start up a banal conversation about the cultivation of dahlias or some such nonsense, all the while speaking silently with my eyes, telling her of my desire. As we chattered innocently about the perils of insect damage and root rot, her eyes spoke back to me of her own need, and my heart was lost."

He hesitated for a moment. "As the king's son, I had...known...many other women. But I had watched this pure, unattainable beauty from afar for months; and, after meeting her in the garden, I thought I could not live without her. Such is the passion of youth," he added wryly.

"From that day forward, I would volunteer to accompany the chief wizard whenever I could without arousing suspicion. She would always know of his coming, and somehow arrange to be in the garden when I arrived. Finally, on one such occasion, I could hold myself back no longer, and I whispered my need to see her alone. She said nothing, as if she had not heard me. But when she rose to leave, she dropped a scrap of parchment on the ground."

It was Aisleen's turn to laugh softly. "Love will find a way," she said kindly. "And the note?"

"The note. Yes. It said simply, 'Temple Hill at dusk.' She meant the small hill behind the Temple grounds. I came back at the time she suggested, hardly believing she would be there. Yet, somehow, she had managed to slip away from the others just after the evening repast. We met on that hill, knowing how forbidden it was. But soon we were embracing and confessing how often we had thought of each other and how we yearned to be together."

"But that was forbidden," said Aisleen, sympathizing with the would-be lovers' dilemma.

"Yes, we both knew that breaking her vows of chastity would mean dismissal from the Temple, or worse, for her, and charges of blasphemy against me. In that brief time, we shared but a few kisses and caresses. Then she had to hurry back before she was discovered missing, but not before she had agreed to meet me again the following night."

"And the next night?" Aisleen asked softly.

Mik'kel's face took on a dark expression. "The next night, as I left my chambers to steal away to our tryst, I was met by a squad of the King's Guards and the chief wizard himself. They marched me off to my father's throne room, where he informed me that I had been seen alone on the hill with a priestess. He raged at me for bringing dishonor on his family, and asked me if I cared at all about my future, which I took to mean the future he had already chosen *for* me."

Aisleen heard his voice grow cold with anger. "When I told him I did not care a whit about his plans for me, and suggested that he consider my feelings instead, he rose up in fury and demanded to know the name of the priestess. When I realized that she had not been recognized, I refused to reveal her name. He sent me back to my chambers under guard, with orders that I was not to leave until I repented my sin and told him what he wished to know."

He sighed, letting his anger die away, to be replaced with sadness. Perhaps, thought Aisleen, it was sadness for the loss of the girl, or for the rift with his father that could never be mended now, or both.

"In his rage, my father overlooked the extent of my powers. Seeing this as the final stroke against my dreams and desires, I resolved to leave my home that very night. I knew I dared not see the girl again to tell her of my plans, lest I risk exposing her. So, I used my magic to escape the king's palace, and left the land of my birth behind. That was the last time I saw her or my father."

"And now?" asked Aisleen quietly, reaching over to touch his hand lightly. "Do you miss her still?"

Mik`kel put his hand over hers. "I missed her for the first years. During the time that I lived on the Isle of Serenity, the pain faded, leaving only a kind of emptiness. I feared I would never feel close to anyone like that again, until I..."

He paused, with a rather curious look in his eyes as he gazed at her. "Well, since leaving the Isle, I have come to think that perhaps that I am still too young to wither away for a love lost so long ago."

Feeling oddly pleased by his words, Aisleen thanked him for allowing her a glimpse into his past life. She stood to go, then turned and posed the last question she ever intended to ask on the subject. "This priestess. Would you tell me her name?"

"Of course, my Lady," he replied. "Her name was Merelda."

Chapter 17

Acts of Defiance

Across the sea in Kal`Dathia, the slave hurried along the corridor of the palace that led to Lord Rak`koth's private chambers, anxious to prepare herself for his arrival. Her bare feet padded noiselessly over the thick black carpet running down the center of the long Hall of Kings, where magnificent life-size portraits of past monarchs and leaders who had ruled Kal`Dathia over the past millennium—many of them faded and cracked from the passage of centuries—lined the walls to either side.

The light from the flickering torches cast a soft red glow over her pale skin and black hair, yet offered no real warmth for her unclad body as the coolness of the night invaded the palace passageways, sending shivers rippling down her back. Yet, the chill of the night air was not all that Merelda, former high priestess, had to endure as she moved quickly down the hall.

The palace guards stationed at regular intervals along the way leered at her, making lewd comments about her anatomy and the various ways that they would enjoy using her. Not that any mere guard would actually dare to take her without Rak`koth's permission.

Naked or not, she was still the emperor's personal slave, and they would do well to remember that if they valued keeping their anatomy intact. Still, that did not stop one or two of them from reaching out to fondle her crudely as she passed by.

Having no right to protect herself from these groping hands, she made no protest but continued in silence until, at last, she reached the safety of Rak`koth's rooms and shut the door behind her with a sigh of relief. Even after ten years of being subjected to more pain and humiliation by her master than she could have possibly imagined, she still shrank from the thought of any man besides her beloved Lord touching her body in the places that belonged to him, and him alone.

She banished the thought of those other men from her mind and stepped into the emperor's privy, where she squatted over the opening—she was never permitted to actually sit down on the seat—and emptied a bladder grown painfully full during the long evening. She had held her water without complaint as she knelt beside her master's throne this night because she knew that, had she mentioned her need, he would have ordered her to relieve herself into a bowl as all the court looked on. The vivid memory of having to do exactly that had taught her to wait, no matter how uncomfortably, until the royal audience was completed.

Merelda wiped herself carefully with a damp, rose-scented cloth to insure that she came to him clean and pleasing to his senses, as he always required. Nude until he allowed her clothing again, she brushed her long, luxuriant hair, applied a touch of rouge to various places, and settled down in front of the door to wait patiently for as long as it took him to return.

As she knelt, silent and unmoving, her thoughts returned to the day ten years ago when her master had been Awakened from his long sleep, a day that had changed her life forever. More than once, it had occurred to her that, with his return, she had experienced an Awakening of her own, a kindling of the need to surrender herself completely and irrevocably to the exquisite pain and pleasure of serving him, and to the passion and fulfillment of his terrible, cruel affection. She scarcely recognized the person who had crawled out of the Sleeping Savior's Tomb at his heels so long ago...

2375 (Ten years ago)

When Merelda and Rak'koth emerged from the Tomb, the restless crowd of guards and citizens who had gathered outside the mausoleum roared their happiness and relief to see the legendary hero emerge alive and hale. Full of excitement and anticipation of salvation from the barbarians threatening their land, they hardly noticed that their high priestess was unclothed, save for the few remaining shreds of her gown.

Rak'koth said something about Merelda and the other priestesses having had a "harrowing" experience, then allowed one of the guardsmen to wrap his mantle around her and take her away to a small chamber in the palace.

Whether it was the shock of all that had passed or a magical compulsion laid upon her, she found herself unable to speak aloud, to denounce this "hero" for the monster he had revealed himself to be. In her exhaustion, it was all she could do to allow the servants to bathe her, dress her in a silken nightgown, and coax some wine and a light meal into her before she collapsed onto the bed and escaped into the safety of sleep.

Her escape was short-lived. The next morning, she was shaken awake roughly by a brutish looking guardsman who informed her that the "Savior" had sent for her. Permitted to wear only her thin nightdress, she was led to the palace throne room and brought before the imposing, black-haired sorcerer with the graceful hands and crimson eyes.

Rak'koth exuded power and confidence as he sat back upon the royal seat, clad in a new black velvet robe, looking down upon her from the throne where the kings of Kal'Dathia had ruled for centuries. King Nek'krod was conspicuous by his absence, and she could only imagine what sad fate had befallen her broken monarch. The chamber was empty, save for the guard who had brought her here, and now stood at attention beside her.

"Ah, there you are, *High Priestess*. I trust you enjoyed your sleep?" Rak'koth asked, with what might have passed for genuine concern, had she not come to know him better.

She drew herself up with as much disdain as she could muster, refusing to be gulled by his deceptively kind manner. "What are you doing on the throne, *revenant*?" she asked. "And where is the rightful king?"

Rak'koth's eyes flared briefly. "Is it not the custom to kneel in the presence of your king, woman?" he asked, in the same quiet tone. Then his voice hardened as he pointed to the floor. "On your knees before me."

"You are not *my* king, abomination," she snarled, tossing her hair back as she shook her head, "and I certainly will not kneel to you!"

His eyes glowed more brightly, as if catching flame. "*I said, on your knees!*" He threw wide the fingers of one hand, releasing a bolt of red energy that leapt across the small distance between them and struck her chest like the crack of a whip, eliciting an anguished cry that drove her to the floor, helpless to resist further.

"Now, that is so much better, Merelda," he nodded with approval, resuming the voice that, even through her pain, caressed her ears as if he were stroking the fur of a cat. "I promised you that I would teach you to serve and obey me. I believe that we shall start your lessons this day."

Though breathless from the shock and the pain, she still managed to push her head up from the cold marble floor. She leaned forward on her hands as she gasped out her defiance.

"I am a high priestess of Shalloth. I have dedicated my life to serving him for his glory. He is my god and my sacred Lord. I will obey no one but him."

Rak`koth's laugh rumbled and echoed in the chamber. "Shalloth? Oh, my dear priestess, look around you," he invited, sweeping his hand in an arc before him. "Where is your mighty god now? Where was he when I drained the life force from his wizards? Where was Shalloth when I defiled his sacred virgins, your sister priestesses, for my pleasure?" He shook his head in mock sadness.

"No, my dear, I fear that your god has abandoned you as the weak being that he is, and that the only master you will serve henceforth sits before you now. And you *will* learn to serve me—and willingly," he finished, leaning forward and fixing her with his burning gaze.

"No!" she cried, though, in truth, she felt more than a little mesmerized by his crimson eyes and his deep, demanding voice, despite his cruelty and his black heart.

"Very well, priestess," he replied with indifference. "I have some business to attend to with our barbarian visitors at the border. I shall be gone for a short time. You may use that time to reflect on your decision. I have charged Captain Bek`kor here with the responsibility of watching over you in my absence. Alas, he does not share your reverence for Shalloth or for his priestesses. I am sure he will make your time in his care quite…memorable."

Rak`koth nodded slightly, and she felt herself jerked to her feet by Bek`kor's vise-like grip upon her arm. Then the brawny captain was hauling her from the chamber while she tried to keep pace with him, stumbling along behind as he pulled her down a long hallway and around a corner until they came to an iron door built of thick vertical rods welded to a heavy frame. The metal door creaked and squealed as Bek`kor pulled it open and entered the room, yanking her through the doorway.

"I trust you will enjoy my accommodations, priestess," he sneered. "This be the cell where prisoners are kept while awaiting justice from the Crown."

Merelda's confusion turned to dread as she glanced around the barren chamber where she was to be housed. It was little more than an empty stone box, measuring some twelve feet on each side with walls, floor and ceiling made of cold, dark marble. Already she could feel the chill from the gray stone that seemed to suck up any heat from a human body. The chamber was completely devoid of any furniture or other objects, with no privy but a hole in the floor over in one corner.

The captain chuckled as she shivered, then reached a paw-like hand to the neck of her gown. "You will not be needing this, my *Lady,*" he grinned maliciously, pulling down sharply and ripping the thin fabric from her body. He tossed the remnants to the floor, leaving her naked and exposed to his lusting eyes.

Shamed and humiliated, she tried to cover herself with her hands, but Bek`kor grabbed her small wrists in one callused fist and yanked them up above her head. "Oh, such a pretty body for a priestess, and what a shame to waste it on a eunuch like your weakling god," he whispered lewdly, his breath warm on her neck, rank and smelling of ale.

He groped her hard enough to make her moan in pain, running his rough hand down over her body and squeezing each rounded hip with his thick, callused fingers. Then he laughed as she cried out from the pain and tried to squirm away from his obscene invasion.

"I would wager you are nice and tight, you being a virgin and all. Mayhap you would like me to break you in some before the sorcerer gets back." Seeing the horror in her eyes, he laughed more loudly and released her, shoving her down to the floor as he stepped back through the doorway and slammed the heavy grating closed.

"I will be watching you, *priestess,*" he promised, taking up his post beside the door.

Her every movement visible through the iron bars, Merelda could not escape Bek`kor's predatory stare as she crawled to the far wall and sat with her legs drawn up, her arms encircling her knees. Afraid to change position without exposing herself further, she remained motionless, determined to stay awake and vigilant against the chance that the vile guard captain chose to follow through on his threat to defile her.

Feeling a desperate need for some comfort and strength, she turned to her god once more. She prayed to Shalloth most earnestly, chanting his name over and over again as she had during her ordeal of captivity in the Tomb—pleading with him, beseeching him to speak to her and offer some shred of hope and comfort, if not rescue, from this unbelievable nightmare. But he did not come to her now to offer any sign of his love or support, just as he had not come to her in the Tomb during the dark, terrible ordeal after Rak`koth arose from his long sleep.

She had been Shalloth's devoted, faithful servant for all of her life, and she had always been able to feel his loving presence inside her, comforting her, when she called upon him. But Rak῾koth spoke the frightening truth: Shalloth had done nothing when the Dark sorcerer drained the life from the king's wizards, and he had allowed his sacred priestesses—his virgin "brides"—to be brutally raped into unconsciousness, heedless of their cries for his aid in their moment of greatest need.

Now, it felt as if he had withdrawn from her completely, as though an unseen barrier had arisen to sever her from his beneficent warmth and strength. Feeling lost, she ceased her prayers and fell silent. Exhausted by the effort, her mind numbed and deadened, the high priestess struggled to fight off the hopelessness that threatened to engulf her once again, as it had done so many times since Rak῾koth had risen.

Nevertheless, as time passed, she grew listless and weary of resisting, feeling her body's need for rest wax stronger than her waning determination to remain alert. At last, her head dropped, her eyes closed, and, after a while longer, sleep stole over her.

She was awakened by the squeal of the iron door being opened. She saw fresh torches burning on the wall outside the cell door, which could only mean that she must have slept for some time. Hearing the heavy clomp of footsteps approaching, she looked up to see a guard—a different man this time—coming toward her, carrying a tray containing a cup of water and some bread and cheese.

She was dimly aware that he could have shoved the tray through the small slot in the bottom of the iron door. His reason for delivering it to her personally became obvious when he dropped the tray to the floor, then knelt down to maul her body, laughing as she tried to cover herself.

"Hold still!" he commanded, slapping her hard across her face. "I volunteered to take this duty, just to get an eyeful of the high priestess, and to get me a handful of these lovelies."

Her cheek stinging from the slap, she forced herself not to move as he continued to molest her with his coarse palms for several minutes. Soon, she heard his breathing change. Then came the sound of a belt being unbuckled, and she watched with growing alarm as he opened his breeches.

She waited with dread for him to throw her down and take her, as Rak῾koth had violated her sister priestesses, but instead, he remained kneeling. She closed her eyes and turned her head away, but she could not escape the sound of his breath coming faster and faster. Finally he uttered a series of low, rapid grunts, and she felt something on her skin as a musky scent filled her nostrils.

Recoiling in horror as she realized what he had done, she struggled free and crawled backward. He gave a satisfied chuckle as she grabbed a tattered strip of her shredded nightgown and tried frantically to wipe herself clean. He finished rearranging his clothing and reached down to grab her hair, yanking her face upward.

"There is more where that came from, *priestess.* Mayhap I will give you some again a little later." He grinned as he released her hair and left the cell, slamming the door behind him while she remained curled up on the cold stone floor, weeping with shame and disgust.

She slept again, though fitfully, dreaming of being attacked by vicious men or savage animals. After a time, she awoke to pangs of hunger in her stomach. The modest portion of food still lay on the tray where the guardsman had dropped it before he defiled her.

More disturbing than the need to eat, however, was the pressure building in her bladder. She closed her thighs tightly, struggling to hold her urine. She thought she would rather die than endure the humiliation of using the hole in the floor to relieve herself, if it meant doing so in full view of the loathsome man whose male scent still lingered on her body.

But, with the passage of another candlemark, she was faced with the ugly choice of using the privy hole or urinating in a puddle around her. Finally, cringing and flushed with embarrassment, she crawled to the corner and squatted over the opening, letting her bladder empty as hot tears of mortification streamed down her cheeks while the guardsman watched and taunted her.

The following days of her imprisonment in the barren stone cell were much like the first, one blending into another until Merelda lost count of how long she had been there. From time to time, Bek`kor or one of the other guards came to bring her more water, bread and cheese, and sometimes a bit of meat or fruit. Apparently, they had been ordered not to let her starve while in their care.

She came to dread the meal times because one or another of her keepers would often amuse himself by violating her with groping fingers. They seemed particularly pleased when their rough handling brought involuntary cries from her lips.

By the fourth—or perhaps the fifth—day, she felt utterly soiled and depraved. She had had to use the hole to relieve herself again and again, always under the eye of the guard who never missed the opportunity to make disgusting comments about her bodily functions. She had nothing with which to wipe herself clean, save for the remaining strips of her ruined gown, which she would throw down the hole afterwards.

She felt like a dirty, smelly animal. Her once beautiful, lustrous black hair had become a matted, filthy tangle. She had not been allowed to bathe, and the foul aroma of her own body odors assailed her senses. But most of all, as time passed, she felt less and less human.

She was reaching for the last scrap of food on her tray when she heard footsteps coming down the hall. Expecting the arrival of another guardsman to torment her, she did not bother to look up when the steps halted in front of the iron door, not caring which of the monsters had come to ogle and jeer at her.

Then a voice spoke her name in a deep, soft tone that was almost a caress, and she looked up to Rak'koth standing there—tall, dark, splendidly robed in deepest black velvet, gazing down at her with those crimson eyes that seemed to strip away all the layers that guarded access to her soul.

"Merelda?" he called again softly, waiting for her to respond.

Gods, the shame of *him* seeing her like this, the once-proud high priestess now filthy and degraded, reduced to living like a naked beast. It was worse than anything she had endured since being caged in this cold, stone prison, even the crude abuses by the men that had been guarding her. She could not bear his eyes on her, so profound were the feelings of humiliation and anger that she suffered for his twisted pleasure. Unable to escape those piercing orbs, she turned her head away.

"Are you not pleased to see me, Merelda?" he asked, as if genuinely wounded. "Do you not wish to hear of our glorious victory over the barbarian enemy?" Then his voice grew softer again. "Are you ready to come to me now, slave, to serve me?"

"I will not serve you like some common whore," she croaked, her voice hoarse from disuse as she continued to withhold her gaze from him.

Rak'koth chuckled maliciously. "You were *born* to serve, Merelda. It is part of who you are. Do you not yet see that? You willingly devoted your entire being to serving and pleasing your god. You surrendered your life, your love and your passions to him, willing to make any sacrifice, prostrating your body before him and begging to be used for his glory in any manner that he required of you. What was *that*, if not being his slave?"

"You twist everything to your evil purpose, usurper!" she spat, as much from despair as from anger. "My service to Shalloth was sacred, my devotion to him pure and chaste. He did not promise me your cruelty nor force me to wallow in the degrading lusts of the flesh."

Rak'koth laughed again. "He did not use your flesh, that is true—though, looking at your naked beauty, that he did not makes me wonder about his manhood, god or not. No, he did not possess your body, but he owned your *soul*. And that is the ultimate submission, the need to surrender fully that calls to your heart—even here, even now, with me."

"Never," she whispered, face to the wall.

"You will come to me in time, Merelda," he said knowingly. "You will beg to serve me." He began to turn away, then stopped and added, "And when you do, you will be no common whore. You will be *my* whore."

†††††

Well before the second eight-day had passed, Merelda was ready to die. She had tried praying to Shalloth again, though her futile efforts grew fewer and less fervent as time passed and despondency consumed her. Her imprisonment dragged on, and the guardsmen did not cease to torment and humiliate her. They mocked her as they used their hands on her, though even they approached her less often when the stink of her unwashed body grew stronger and her matted hair became thick with lice.

She began to believe the sorcerer's claim that her god had deserted her and left her to live or die on her own. Surely, the gods could intervene if they chose to—and clearly, they had not.

Then another frightening thought emerged from her morass of helplessness and despair, a thought that appalled and sickened her because she knew it to be true: She actually found herself hoping for Rak'koth to visit her again.

The gods knew that he was vile and wicked, a murderer and rapist, a desecrater of all she held Holy. She had no illusions about what lay in store for her if she begged audience with him again. And yet, could anything she would have to endure at his pernicious whim, even rape, be worse than the hell she awoke to in this cold, barren cell each time she opened her eyes?

She knew he would not seek her out this time. He was waiting for her to come to him. He did not lack for ready females to sate his evil carnal desires, of that she was certain. And he would not trouble himself to take her by force.

No, this was not merely about lust and pain, though that would surely be a part of her future with him. This was about making her suffer the humiliation of her own willing surrender. The knowledge of that, the most terrible assault on the last vestiges of her pride and dignity, was all that kept her from calling out his name.

Yet, by the end of the third eight-day, even that was not enough. She could not take her own life, did she have the means to do so. That would be the final sacrilege. But neither could she go on living like this. And so, loathing herself for her weakness, she choked down her humiliation and asked the guard if she might be allowed to see Rak`koth.

Chapter 18

Final Surrender

Three days later, when she had begun to lose hope of being summoned at all, Merelda was roused from what passed for sleep by a different guardsman, who announced that His Magnificence had deigned to give her audience. She was taken naked from her cell and prodded down the hallway to another room, where she was given over into the care of a female palace servant "to be made presentable for our Lord."

When she saw the simple amenity of a steaming bath and fresh linen awaiting her, she collapsed into tears. Soon, she was gratefully submerged in the gloriously hot, soapy water while the servant girl washed the filth from her body and the lice from her scalp. It required several changes of murky water to cleanse the vermin and the grime from her hair alone.

Later, she sat wrapped in soft white towels, eyes closed, luxuriating in the feeling of being clean for the first time in so long, and sighing contentedly as the girl carefully combed and brushed the tangles from her thick black hair. She was given a white, silky undershift to wear, seated on a sunlit balcony overlooking the palace courtyard, and offered a meal of rich broth with chunks of tender meat, biscuits, plover eggs and chilled fruit. She devoured every bit of it.

Just as she finished the last delicious morsels, a guardsman came to lead her to the throne room. When she arrived, Rak`koth was engaged in conversation with several generals and court advisors. She recognized some of them and tried to catch their eye, but they glanced at their former high priestess with curiously troubled expressions, and then ignored her completely.

Rak`koth was in good spirits, judging from his easy laughter. In that mood and setting, he looked handsome, almost noble, his dark, curly hair falling down over the gold embroidered collar of his robes. When he saw Merelda standing there, beautiful in her simple garment, his eyebrows raised and he inclined his head, dismissing those attending him with a wave of his hand.

As he turned the full gaze of his striking crimson eyes upon her, his first words dispelled any hope that his magnanimous mood would soften his manner with her. "Must I punish you again, slave, to remind you to kneel when you come into the presence of your master?" he asked ominously.

"No...No, my Lord," she hastened to reply, quickly falling to her knees as she recalled the painful lesson from her previous resistance. "I will remember, my Lord," she said, dropping her lovely, haunted violet eyes.

"Since I am your master, you will address me as such from this day forth. Is that understood?"

She hesitated briefly, offering a silent prayer for forgiveness to Shalloth, if he could still hear her—or if he even cared. Then, eating her pride, she whispered, "Yes...Master."

"Louder, slave."

"Yes, Master," she repeated in a stronger voice.

"That is better," he said, and she found herself feeling grateful for his approval, despite herself.

"You look quite lovely today, my dear. And you do appear better behaved. I trust that your stay with our captain was...instructive?"

She grimaced at the memory of her degradation at Bek`kor's hands. "They are depraved, cruel beasts, my Lo...Master," she answered, letting some of her bitterness surface in her voice.

"They did not take you, did they?" he asked, leaning forward to peer at her more closely, his voice sounding concerned.

It took her a moment to grasp what he was asking. "No, Master," she replied, her face burning with shame. "At least, they did not...They used their hands on me."

Rak`koth leaned back again with a satisfied nod. "Good. I made it clear that I have reserved the pleasure of having you for the first time myself." His wicked smile made her stomach clench as his meaning was made clear. "Now, I am told you asked to see me. Are you ready to serve me, slave?"

The high priestess had seen with her own eyes how her sister priestesses had "served" him, and had already resigned herself to their fate when she requested this audience. With a sinking heart, she nodded slowly.

"What would you have of me, Master?" she asked, her body trembling.

He crooked a finger. "Come and display yourself for me. I wish to look upon my property."

Fighting for a deep breath, she stepped up on the dais and stood before him. She could feel his burning eyes undressing her, even before he spoke.

"A slave does not come into my presence wearing clothing without my permission. Clothing is a privilege you have not earned. You will remove your shift."

Until this ordeal had begun, no man had ever seen her unclothed—not even Prince Mik`kel, all those years ago. But she had spent what seemed like days naked and bound before this man in the Tomb. Then she had been stripped bare in her cell and exposed to the licentious eyes and coarse hands of brutish men for endless days and nights. The thought of displaying her nudity before him now was less unbearable than it had been. Still, the intensity of her humiliation was enough to prevent her from meeting his eyes as she slowly pulled the shift over her head and let it fall to the floor.

"Now clasp your hands behind you," Rak`koth commanded coldly. "Do not move without permission."

The humiliation she had felt a moment ago was but a mere shadow to the shame that enveloped her now as she obeyed. She was most acutely conscious of the obscene way her body was displayed, as was clearly his intent.

Rak`koth stood and walked around her, leisurely inspecting every inch of her in a manner that made her feel as if she were a sleek mare being examined by its new owner. She shivered when she felt his fingers brush along the skin of her neck, though she remained as still as possible, recalling his threat. Then his hands were roaming freely over her body, sometimes softly, sometimes grasping her flesh roughly.

When she cried out, his eyes flared a brighter red. Then he relaxed his grip and began stroking her gently with his fingertips, exploring her with a feathery lightness so different than the way the guardsmen had touched her. To her dismay, she found her body betraying her, responding as he rubbed lightly over her most sensitive places. His expression of amusement only deepened her shame.

He continued his tender exploration until she gasped again—but this time, not in pain. His fingers seemed unnaturally warm on her skin, sending a wave of heat coursing throughout her being. Not hurtful, but another feeling instead, a tingling sensation new to her, one that frightened her even more than the pain because it felt...good.

"This is something your god denied you, slave," he said, stroking her, making her whimper softly. "He took you as his 'bride' to serve and please him, but he withheld the pleasure that even the lowliest woman may be allowed, if her husband so desires. Now, I will show you what you can earn from me, if you serve me well."

She felt his fingers grow hotter, pulsing against her flesh. It was a magical heat, unlike anything she had experienced, sending a quivering ripple of pleasure throughout her loins. She knew from the look in his burning eyes that he was using his Dark power to seduce her, enthrall her, even as he used pain to control and train her to his liking.

Against her will, she heard herself moan as the heat intensified and the quivering became a throbbing that made her heart race and her breath come in shallow, rapid gasps. It was growing, building, this lewd, wanton sensation that brought with it an unfamiliar and deeply unholy desire.

"Oh," she groaned, the small part of her mind that was still trying to resist this evil caress becoming horrified as she felt herself begin to press against his hand, striving...needing...on the verge of something she could not understand, but instinctively knew that she had been missing all her life.

Then, just as suddenly, he withdrew his hand from her, making her cry out as he left her needy and unfulfilled. "Not yet, Merelda," he whispered. "Only when you have earned it, and if it suits my whim.

Rak'koth withdrew his fingers and leaned closer to kiss her neck. Seeing her eyes widen, he smiled knowingly. "You respond well to a man's touch, my dear. Now it is time to begin serving me," he said, returning to his seat.

"How, Master?" she whispered, terrified by what he intended to do to her, yet fearful of displeasing him again.

"You will start by renouncing your pathetic god, Shalloth, and acknowledging me as the only master worthy of your worship from this day on," he said, grinning malevolently.

The blood drained from her face as she looked at Rak'koth in shock, beginning to understand what he truly wanted from her. To submit to his rape would be an abomination in itself, but to renounce Shalloth completely, to blaspheme against him and damn her soul...She could not deny that her god seemed to have forsaken her, leaving her to the mercy of this sadistic miscreant. But to be cut off from Shalloth's Holy love and grace forever, the only master she had ever served…Oh, gods, this she *would* not, *could* not, do!

"Slave!" he said, in a low, menacing voice.

Her fear momentarily overcome by revulsion, she shook her head. "Please, Master, I will…serve you. But I can not do *that*." And when he reached for her to inflict more pain, she twisted away and fell to the floor, sobbing.

Rak`koth stared at her, his eyes flaring. "It seems you did not learn your lesson well enough, priestess. I could force you, but it amuses me more to have you beg to serve me only. Perhaps you will benefit from a little more time with our guardsmen."

Then, as she watched in horror, he turned away and called out Bek`kor's name. Within moments, the captain appeared, coming to attention.

"Your orders, Magnificence?"

"My slave needs more time to think about the…finer points…of serving her master. Take her away," he said, turning his back.

"No, Master! Please," she cried out through her tears. "Please do not send me back there. I will do anything but…"

Her desperate plea was interrupted as Rak`koth spoke again to Bek`kor, ignoring her. "Captain, this time do not bring her to me until she begs for the privilege of serving me and me alone. Not until she says those very words." And, as suddenly as that, Merelda was pulled to her feet, dragged from the throne room and driven back to her stone cell.

"I see you could not stay away, priestess," Bek`kor snickered, twisting her flesh in his hands until he forced a groan from her, then shoving her to the hard marble floor. "You must prefer my gentle attentions."

The sounds of his revolting laughter and the heavy iron grating slamming behind him echoed in the small space, plunging her back down into a dark despair made all the more unbearable by the memory of her brief respite from the horror that had now begun again.

†††††

Ten days later, Merelda swallowed hard to keep the bile from rising in her throat and called out to the guardsman beyond her cell door. She no longer knew who she was, and she could hardly believe what she was about to do, to plead to be violated by that terrible man—and to commit the ultimate blasphemy.

All she did know was that, after having had the small luxury of feeling clean and well fed again, if only for a short time, she found herself unable to endure living in the cell and suffering the abuse of her keepers any longer. Not when the god she had prayed to so fervently, worshipped so devoutly with all her heart and soul, had abandoned her so completely, leaving her spiritually and physically destitute, alone for so long, in the grasp of this Dark sorcerer. Her strength to resist had simply disappeared.

Thus, when the guardsman came, she did not resist when he ordered her to move closer if she wished to speak to him, even knowing what he would do. She walked to the door deliberately, enduring his nauseating stare, and said, in a quiet voice, "Please tell Lord Rak'koth that I...I beg for the privilege of serving him and him alone." The last was uttered in a whisper, too shamed and revolted to hear herself say it aloud.

"Well, priestess," he answered with lewd delight, "mayhap you should be begging to please me first." She blinked but made no argument when he reached out and fondled her callously.

As he did so, she could not help but notice again the difference between this crude, clumsy mauling and the way that Rak'koth's long, graceful hands had felt on her body, making her respond to his touch even when he was enjoying inflicting pain. And the way his fingers had felt on her flesh when last he touched her, causing that unnaturally hot sensation that made her feel...She stopped herself from remembering and repeated her request to the guard, saying again the exact words she had been instructed to use.

It was yet another two days later before Rak'koth answered her request, two more days of listening for his step or waiting for the guardsman to announce that the summons had come. When it did, she gathered herself up and went willingly, heedless of her nudity and the stares of the men she passed in the hallway.

She was once again taken to the female servant, to be soaked and scrubbed in the steaming hot bath until her hair and skin were clean once more, then patted dry and clothed in a thin, satin undershift. She was led to the same balcony, this time to watch the red sun set into the horizon while she dined on roasted beef, rich gravy, warm bread dipped in an herb and butter sauce, and red wine from the palace cellars.

When the guardsman came for her again, she was surprised to find that she was not being taken to the throne room as she had expected, but to the sorcerer's private rooms. Her feet sank into the thick, dark green carpet as she was led into a large bedchamber, its walls lined with heavy brocaded curtains and richly-woven tapestries, with oil lamps burning in gold wall sconces bracketed into finely-polished oak panels. It was the old king's chamber, though Nek'krod was nowhere to be seen.

Instead, it was now Rak'koth who sat in the throne-like chair in the center of the room, placed midway between the door and the large, curtained and canopied bed that dominated the back half of the chamber. He was leisurely sipping wine from a jeweled goblet, his gem-studded rings sparkling in the lamplight. His crimson gaze ran up and down her barely clad body as the guardsman released his rough grip on her arm and silently bowed his way out the door.

Without hesitation, Merelda stripped the undershift from her body and fell to her knees in front of him, her soft skin glowing in the soft light from the oil lamps. She made no attempt to cover herself as she knelt there, hands by her sides, head down, waiting, while he examined her with his eyes.

"You learn well, Merelda," he said softly, nodding his approval.

"Thank you, Master," she replied in a whisper, relieved to have avoided his displeasure.

He took another sip of wine from his cup, then set it down on the small, oval table beside him. "You asked to see me, slave?"

"Yes, Master," she answered, speaking past the lump in her throat. "I...I beg for the privilege of serving you...and you alone."

"And your pitiful god? Do you renounce him and swear to worship me as your true master?" He stared at her with an intensity that made her flinch.

With tears running down her cheeks, she forced herself to breathe, then closed her eyes and nodded.

"Say it aloud, Merelda!"

"I...I renounce Shalloth and vow to worship you as my one true master," she gasped, terrified as she waited for the very ground to split open and swallow her, sucking her down to the oblivion of the Four Hells.

But nothing happened. It seemed that Shalloth did not even care enough about her to punish the sacrilege she had uttered.

A smile of triumph flickered across his lips as he motioned for her to rise and come closer to him. She felt a pink flush spread down her neck as she stood directly in front of him. Remembering his instructions from her last audience with him, she clasped her hands behind her.

Merelda shuddered from the touch of his hands upon her flesh again, stroking her until there came a tremble down across her belly. Accustomed to the rough hands of the guardsman on her body, she relaxed as Rak'koth caressed her almost lovingly. Even when he twisted sharply, she remained motionless, accepting the pain.

Seeing that she was learning to submit without complaint, he nodded his approval and rewarded her by touching her gently again, making her whimper softly as he traced the contours of her most sensitive female flesh. This time, there was no denying her response as the heat from his fingers sent tantalizing vibrations of his Dark power deep within her.

"Gods!" she cried, unable to stifle her moans any longer as her skin burned with pleasure, even as she fought back tears of abject shame. It was there again, even stronger than it had been the last time—that unholy desire, stronger than her loathing for it, deeper than her pride.

"Please," she moaned, though whether it was a plea that he stop or that he never stop, she knew not. Then, when he thought her needy enough, prideless enough, he took his hand away. She groaned in open frustration, thinking that he would leave her aching once more.

But, instead, he took her arm and pushed her down onto the bed. He leaned over her and she felt something pressing between her thighs. There was a sharp, stinging pain, then a feeling of fullness stretching her, invading her.

"No!" she cried, then "Oh!" as he withdrew, then thrust again. She threw her head back, her black hair covering her face and hiding her shame as she arched upward against him, striving to meet him through the pain, the heat growing more intense as he took her mercilessly.

"Please," she moaned, when she could catch a breath. "Please...Master...Let me..." She could not bring herself to say what she was begging for as she writhed under him.

"Good. Very good," he growled, delaying his pleasure long enough to teach her what would be expected. "You will always beg permission for release. Do you understand, slave?"

"Yes, Master. Yes. Only please..." she entreated.

He gripped her so cruelly that she screamed in shock and momentary agony. Then she felt his body stiffen as he groaned, while she hovered breathlessly on the edge of something powerful—a hunger that now threatened to overwhelm her. Yet, she knew she must somehow hold back until...if only he would let her...

"Now," was all he said, but that was enough.

Then, at last, it happened, a raging, aching fire that overcame the pain—or perhaps was fueled by it—a flame flaring to white heat and exploding deep inside her, sending wave after wave of scorching pleasure throughout every nerve in her body, consuming her until she knew that she must die from the sheer intensity.

For that terrible, ecstatic moment, there was nothing else in the world. She could not breathe. She could not move. Gods, she had not known it could feel like this...had never suspected...She heard a voice crying out, and recognized it as her own.

Then, finally, the all-consuming fire was receding, leaving her still alive somehow. She felt the weight of his solid male body upon her for a moment longer before he withdrew and stood up, leaving her...empty. She lay on her back atop the bed covers, sprawled open as he had left her, gazing wide-eyed at the man who was now, in truth, her master.

This evil tyrant, this adept of the Dark powers, had been right about that, too. This was the pleasure denied to her that men and women shared together so often, but that she had been missing in all her years of selfless service to her god. And, as she lay there, fully aware of being debauched beyond redemption, in the last private corner of her mind she bid farewell forever to her former god and to the life that she had known...

2385 (Present)

Merelda looked up, called back from her memories of ten years ago as Rak'koth entered the chamber. She watched with fascination as he walked past her, thinking that he had not changed in the decade since those first agonizing days when she had learned to surrender to his will. He was still the cold, ruthless man who had taught her to worship at his feet and serve his every need, a harsh, cruel master who did not hesitate to take what he wanted.

Yet, he was a visionary as well, with a determination that never faltered and a strength that never wavered. He was, perhaps, the only man alive who could have brought her to her knees and earned her fearful adoration.

And, though he used many women for his pleasure, she alone remained his constant slave while the others came and went at his whim. She prayed that he would never tire of her, and knew that she would do anything to see that he did not. And so, when he settled down into his chair and beckoned her to pleasure him, she went to him willingly, knowing that he had been right all those years ago. She was born to serve him, and would do so eagerly for as long as he allowed.

Interlude

Far to the west of Calderia lay the Duchy of Delgaria. There, in a small town, a man named Gorshal, sole proprietor, head barkeep and chief mug washer of the Lazy Strumpet, cleared away the empty bottle of Rillish wine and made a thoroughly perfunctory pass with a soiled rag at the crumbs of stale bread littering the table. Then he plunked down another bottle of the same cheap vintage in front of the customer, his only patron at this time of the morn.

Not that the burly man slumped over the table face down in a puddle of spilled wine was in any condition to notice a few stray crumbs of bread anyway. Gorshal didn't know the man's true name, but he frequented the ramshackle tavern quite often. Some of the other regulars had taken to calling him Scar, because of the jagged ridge of scar tissue running down the left side of his face from temple to jawline.

Of course, no one spoke the name Scar out loud in his hearing. He might reek of cheap swill, and too many days of living in the same dirty tunic and breeches without venturing within spitting distance of soap and water. His tangled black hair and ragged beard might be home to any number of small vermin, considering the filthy alleys and outbuildings where he laid his head on most nights after drinking until he was nearly unconscious. But the breadth of his shoulders, the power of his muscular arms, and the well-worn hilt of the sword on his hip would dissuade all but the most foolish or simple-minded from risking this man's ire.

Especially that sword. Gorshal was only the owner of a run-down tavern in a seedy alley, with girls available for the price of a room up the rickety stairs on the second floor. Yet, he had served his stint in Duke Robelin's army, and he would recognize the blade and scabbard of the Black Guard across a battlefield.

He had seen many of them when he had fought beside the duke's elite sword company, and had witnessed the swift death and terrible carnage dealt by the wielders of those legendary blades. Moreover, the silver trim on the hilt signified officer rank, perhaps a lieutenant or even a captain of the Guard, which marked the man as a doubly dangerous foe indeed.

Leaning forward to get a closer look, his arm inadvertently bumped the man's back. In an instant, the man was on his feet, the sword clear of its sheath, and its tip resting against the barkeep's neck. Gorshal flinched and gulped, terrified by the speed of response and the swiftness with which his survival beyond the next moment was suddenly in doubt, as he found himself staring into the violent, bloodshot eyes of a killer ready to strike.

"A mistake, good sir!" he cried, his voice quivering. "No offense meant! Just bringing a fresh one for you." He pointed with a tremulous hand to the full bottle on the table. "Please, take it. On the house, good sir," he pleaded.

Reagen remained frozen in position for a minute, his sword still extended, while his gaze took in the dingy tavern, the frightened, weaponless owner and the new bottle of wine. Gradually, the bloodlust in his eyes faded and he lowered his sword. Pointing it to the ground, he grabbed the bottle with the other hand, grunted something unintelligible, and strode out of the tavern.

Behind him, Gorshal groaned in relief. Then he stumbled to the bar, so unnerved that he grabbed the nearest mug and actually drank some of his own rotgut wine before he realized what he was doing.

Reagen walked to the nearby alley and turned the corner, then leaned against the crumbling plaster of the aging wall and slid down heavily, careless of the jolt to his spine when his hips slammed against the icy ground. That was close! he thought. Too close.

He had been so besotted with wine that he had almost killed the innocent tavern owner for nothing more than jostling a drunk. A foul smelling, unwashed, grimy, broken-down drunk with a deadly sword and a killer's instincts, who was no good to any one—not himself, not his old company, not even his...gods, his family.

He cringed as the memory of his beautiful, delicate Lindith and his little golden-haired girl, Merriah, brought back the dull ache of self-loathing and shame that he had spent every day and every night of the last two years trying desperately to escape, usually inside the bottom of a bottle. It never really worked, at least not for long.

He was lifting that bottle to his lips when the air before his eyes blurred. The vaguely defined face of a woman appeared, hovering transparently above the ground in the shadowed alleyway, the broken bricks on the opposite wall visible through her image. He blinked to banish the hallucination, no doubt the product of too many days of drinking himself into a stupor. Then her gleaming golden eyes in the vision met his, and her gentle words filled his mind.

No, Reagen, look not to the bottle for my origin.

He shook his head in disbelief. "Who or what in the Four Hells are you?" he challenged, with a voice made rough and hoarse by too many nights spent guzzling cheap drink in too many smoke-filled taverns.

Do you not know me? I am Doritha. You knew me better when you prayed to me before battle, before many battles. A smile seemed to play across her lips as she said this.

His mouth opened wide, but no words issued forth. Had he heard clearly? Doritha? Goddess of battle, reaper of souls who died bravely in war! She nodded silently to his unspoken question, her face somber and serious.

I have need of you, Reagen of the Black Guard. Your skills in fighting will be called upon to protect and train a prince who must become a mighty warrior.

Despite his sense of awe, his reply was bitter and full of shame. "I am of the Black Guard no longer. I am without honor. I could not even protect my..." His words ceased abruptly as he felt a spectral hand brush aside his long black hair and trace something on his skin that left a burning sensation behind his right ear.

I have marked you as my own, Reagen. As he reached up to touch the tingling spot, Doritha spoke again, her soft assurance surrounding him. *I know what you have been...and what you can become. Now, hear me well, for this is what you must do...*

Chapter 19

A Colloquy of Kings

They came to the edge of the border between Calderia and the Great Forest at the appointed time, a long procession moving across the iridescent layer of virgin snow that had fallen the night before despite the coming of Spring, and which now lay glistening under the early afternoon sun. A small troop of Royal Lancers preceded the king and his entourage of advisors and selected nobility, who were themselves surrounded by handpicked guards of the King's Elite, along with archers and foot soldiers.

Gavan would have preferred a smaller, less militarily imposing presence, arguing that this was, after all, a mission of peace, and less likely to provoke distrust if he did not appear to be leading an invading army. But, on this point, General Brurik had stood firm, arguing in return that, if he was to lend his support to a meeting with an enemy who had proven to be capable of perfidy and deceit, he would do so only if accompanied by sufficient force to deter any treacherous impulses that might arise.

For the same reason, the Royal Scouts had already inspected the open area where the meeting of the kings was to be held. Satisfied that no traps or other type of subterfuge had been employed, they returned to their side of the field, some hundred yards away from the tree line where their enemy counterparts, a patrol of Elfin fighters, kept a wary watch of their own.

Moving at a stately pace, the king's procession arrived at the northern end of the field and began to spread out. Contingents of archers, foot soldiers and King's Light flanked Gavan on either side, with the troop of lancers at his back.

On some silent signal, a group of Elfin skirmishers and fighters filed out from the Forest and formed a line along the southern end of the meadow, looking no less imposing—and no less inclined to bloodshed if the safety of their monarch was threatened.

Gavan sat astride his magnificent ebony destrier, dressed in a red leather tunic with the royal crest emblazoned on his left breast, black leather breeches and a red silk cape that flowed back across the flanks of his warhorse. He wore no helm, his flame red hair encircled by a crown of gold.

As he looked across the meadow, another group of Elves emerged from the trees, some dressed in familiar Elfin battle garb, while others wore flowing robes hued in lustrous shades of green and sable, brown and gold. Even to his human eyes, their carriage and demeanor set them apart from the other Elves, and marked them as people of particular power and influence.

Gavan's speculations were confirmed when the Elfin king appeared among them on foot, clad in a dark green tunic trimmed in gold, an emerald green cape lined with white fur, snow white leggings and fur-lined boots that nearly reached his knees. His long yellow hair moved freely in the chilly breeze, save for a plain silver circlet on his forehead that glinted when he moved beyond the shadows of the trees.

"Enemy or no, this is a man who looks like he is born to rule." Killian's voice carried an unmistakable tone of respect as he came to stand beside Gavan's right stirrup, his arms crossed. Wearing his father's colors and the golden circlet of a crown prince, he looked for all the world like a younger version of the king.

"Aye, that he does," replied Gavan. He swung his leg over the saddle and dismounted, intent on meeting Rillandariel on an equal footing in the most literal sense of the word. "And, by all accounts, he has governed his people well, for longer than I have been alive."

Killian stepped to his sire's side and laid a hand upon his arm. "Yes, Father, I know this. But remember also what he has done to our people." Killian's objections to the meeting had been strident and vociferous, dwelling on the murder of his uncle and the Scourge victims gone unaided by the Elves. That much Gavan had expected.

Yet his son had listened to his reasons—and his mother's quiet words—and he had not hinted, in word or expression, that he thought his father cowardly or weak. For that, Gavan had givens thanks to the gods. It was the least he could do to give ear to his son's counsel now.

Killian gripped the king's arm tightly, speaking fiercely. "Father, I beg you to be careful. This man's long leadership is no doubt partnered with cunning as well. If you must do this thing, unarmed, then carry caution as your shield."

Gavan acknowledged Killian's concern with a nod, and reached an arm around his son's shoulders. "I will that," he promised, his voice husky and low. Then he looked up, and a faint smile crossed his face as he gestured across the field. "It seems their king is the recipient of similar advice."

Killian followed his father's gaze. He saw a tall, slender warrior with closely cropped golden hair standing beside the Elfin king with a hand on the monarch's arm, engaging in some sort of heated discourse. Dressed in dark brown tunic and leggings, and wearing a breastplate and a belted sword, the warrior seemed to be remonstrating with the king about something of critical importance, perhaps entreating him not to go. He observed the Elfin king say something to the warrior, then grasp the hand holding his arm and firmly move it away, shaking his head as he stepped forward onto the field.

"I believe that it is time," said Gavan. "Pray the gods that we find a way to make this peace." Then he, too, squared his shoulders, lifted his head high and strode into the meadow.

They were of a height, these two kings, tall and strong and regal in bearing, though one was broad and muscular, the other lean and graceful. They came together in the center of the field, halting some five feet from each other in a small area that had been cleared of snowfall. The bright sun gleamed in the human king's fiery red hair even as it glinted off the Elfin king's long golden locks, while the wind caught their long capes that billowed out behind them.

Each looked past the other and saw their enemy's forces tensed and ready. Each felt the need to move slowly and greet each other carefully, to make no sudden movement that would incite the fears of those waiting with hands on spears or arrows nocked.

For several moments, both kings stood in silence, eyeing each other guardedly, like two proud male lions in their prime encountering one another at the boundary of the territories that each had marked out as his own. There was little in the way of established protocol to guide these kings, but Gavan, knowing he had requested the meeting, felt obliged to speak first.

"Welcome, my Lord King. I am honored to meet you," he began, offering a bow of his head in courtesy.

"Greetings, my Lord King," said Rillandariel, returning the gesture of respect of one monarch for another. "I am honored by your invitation a...not a little curious, I confess."

More silence that stretched into several minutes. Then a trace of wary expectancy as the Elfin ruler asked, "You wanted to discuss terms for peace?"

"Yes. Of course." Gavan straightened and fixed his gaze on Rillandariel. "But, if I may, I will begin by telling you what has prompted my request for this coming together now." When the other nodded his willingness to listen, Gavan resumed.

"Some time ago, I—that is, my lady queen and I—received a...visitation...from Morainen, the goddess we worship in Calderia. She spoke of a great evil across the sea, a puissant sorcerer who had conquered all of Surrikand and would be coming against us eventually..."

Watching the Elfin king's face as he described this visitation, Gavan noted that he did not seem surprised. Indeed, Rillandariel seemed to wrestle with himself for a moment before he spoke.

"I will tell you that I had a similar experience with Sallamarian, our Elfin deity," he revealed with some reluctance. "He told me much the same."

Gavan inclined his head. "Morainen told me something that I can scarcely credit still. She said that my son and heir, Crown Prince Killian, had been chosen at birth by the gods to lead the fight against this villain, that he had within him dormant powers that would be Awakened by a mage sent by the gods, bearing a blue sapphire given him as a guide and as proof.

"I will be frank with you, good king. I told Morainen that I had little care for some future threat from a foreign land, that I was fighting a war of my own at the moment. I told her that, if she wanted the help of my son, she could have answered our prayers and granted us victory." He saw anger flash in Rillandariel's eyes, though the other held his tongue.

"Then Morainen told me that there would be no victory for either side, that our two peoples must unite in peace against the greater enemy coming from across the Luminous Sea—and that Killian, my heir, must heal the rift with a marriage of state to an Elfin princess." Gavan shook his head unconsciously, reliving the moment in his mind.

"In truth, the idea seemed so preposterous, so outrageous, that I refused the goddess outright, even as I refused her mage when he came to me some months ago."

Rillandariel's eyes widened in surprise. "He came to you? This foreign mage is already here?"

"Yes. Even now, he is at my castle, awaiting the outcome of this meeting." Gavan watched a look of suspicion and distrust surface on the Elfin king's face, but elected to ignore it for the moment.

"And you refused him *and* the gods?" asked Rillandariel. "Why? Because you could not stomach a peace with the 'cursed Forest folk,' as you have named us?" The Elfin monarch's bitterness and anger came so swiftly that Gavan tensed, wondering if the other might lose control.

When he did not, Gavan sighed and nodded slightly. "To be candid, my Lord King, that is how I felt at the time. In truth, I had grown weary of a war that promises no end, a war where the fighting goes on and the death toll rises, but nothing is gained. And yet. And yet..." Here his voice matched the bitterness displayed by the other king a moment earlier. "I could not find it in my heart to seek a peace with an enemy guilty of such treachery and cruelty."

"*Treachery?*" Rillandariel cried out, with indignant outrage. "You humans dare speak of treachery, you who broke our treaty and sent your men to kill our trees and plunder our Thalesi grove?"

Gavan flinched inwardly as his enemy struck at his most vulnerable point, his shame that humans had been the first to betray the pact with the Elves. "I never sanctioned those violations," said Gavan sincerely, his voice full of remorse, "though the pressure from those merchants to give my consent was strong and unrelenting. Those who broke the pact were greedy men who acted against my decree. They were wrong to do so, and those we caught were punished."

Now Gavan's voice grew harder. "But there was no need for you to kill them outright and throw their mutilated bodies in my face! Did you think my people would allow that brutal bloodletting to go unanswered?"

"They were warned," growled Rillandariel in the Elves' defense—though, in truth, he had never personally approved such an extreme punishment against the intruders, and had been saddened and angered when he learned that one of his overly zealous Forest patrols had acted so ruthlessly.

"Yes, warned. And then slaughtered like cattle," Gavan retorted in disgust. Then his voice grew thick with anger and pain from a wound unhealed. "And when I sent Prince Orrin, my own brother, in good faith to settle the dispute before more lives were lost, he was murdered! Cut down in treachery under flag of truce!"

Now it was Rillandariel's turn to wince with shame and regret. "My Lord King, I did not order his death," he said earnestly. "We are an honorable people. I know not who was responsible. In the melee, in the heat of anger..." He shook his head. "Truly, I was sorry for his death."

Then his anger erupted again. "But you are not the only one who suffered the loss of family! You lost a brother, but I lost a *son*, struck down in his youth by one of your arrows." His voice broke a little as he gestured toward the Calderian lines. "Perhaps by one of the very bow men standing there, looking on now. Tell me, Lord King," he asked bitterly, "does he brag to his friends of killing an Elfin prince? Or does he even know whose life he stole away from me so callously on that black day?"

The Calderian king stood silent, buffeted by this onslaught of wrath and anguish. When he spoke, it was with sadness for all the lives stolen by the war.

"I heard of your son's death. And, though it shames me now to say, perhaps, at the time, I thought it fitting revenge for Orrin." He held up a hand to halt the other's eruption of fury at this honest confession. "But now...Now I grieve the loss of fallen sons and brothers and fathers on both sides. I am truly sorry for your loss."

Rillandariel heard the sincerity in the human's voice and felt his anger wane a bit as well. "As am I for your brother," he said quietly, after a time.

Gavan nodded, staring down at the ground. The two stood quietly for a moment, looking away, each feeling each other's grief, each trying to find a way around the anger and the pain that lingered, and would never truly leave his heart. But, as Gavan strove to let that pain go, the ugly specter of his people dying from the Scourge, wasting away in agony while he was forced to stand by helplessly, thrust its way back in his mind, and his anger surged anew.

He turned on the Elfin king, who was taken aback at the sight of the wrath suddenly returning to Gavan's face. "Tragic as their deaths were, those were casualties of war. But what of your unfeeling refusal to give us the Thalesi leaves when my people lay dying from the Scourge, that vile plague that killed so many? Was your bitterness for your son's loss so great that you exacted your revenge with the lives of the innocent, the women and little children and old men who never raised a hand against you?"

"What slander is this?" cried Rillandariel, lunging forward to stand so close to Gavan that the sudden creak of bowstrings being stretched taut could be heard from the

Calderian lines.   Quickly, Gavan turned and waved until his
archers lowered their weapons.   The Elfin king retreated a foot or
two but continued in a low, furious tone.

"What refusal?" he demanded.   "Even in the darkest
days of battle, when I wished you dead, I never withheld the
leaves we had promised!   Do you think us complete barbarians,
to let the innocent perish?"

Gavan snorted in disbelief.   "If that is so, then why were
there no baskets of leaves to be found at the appointed place
when I sent my healers to collect them?"

"I know not!" snarled Rillandariel, incensed by the
accusation that he would lie.   "But I will swear before the gods
that they were delivered in the usual fashion, at the usual time,
though many in my Council railed against it when I insisted that
the promise be kept!"

Gavan's mind reeled with bewilderment.   For all that
might be said about Rillandariel, for all the reasons to hate him,
he had never known the Elfin king to be dishonest; and the look
of outrage and indignation on his face was surely genuine, of that
Gavan felt certain.   But if the Elves had left the shipment, then
who?...

Gavan froze as the only other explanation assaulted him
like a blow to the head.   The merchants and traders!   They had
known of the location and the time of the delivery.   If they had
stolen the leaves to sell at great profit, feeding the cravings of
high paying buyers while knowingly allowing innocent people to
die from the Scourge...

Gavan knew the greed of those merchants, and knew just
as surely in his heart that they had stolen the leaves.   All those
needless deaths.   He found himself stumbling, nearly falling to
his knees from shock.

"My Lord King?" asked Rillandariel with surprise,
caught off guard by Gavan's near collapse.

Gavan slowly raised his head and looked at him with
shame.   "It seems that I may have done you a great injustice, my
Lord King.   All this time, I have hated you for what I thought
was a cruelty too terrible to bear, even from an enemy.   And now
I find that an abominable crime may be laid at the door of my
own people.   For this, I offer my humblest apologies."   He
bowed his head and looked away, prepared to hear the angry
accusations that must surely be his due.

Seeing his brother monarch laid so low, Rillandariel felt
a small softening of something rigid deep within him—a crack in

the wall of hatred he had built and fortified so assiduously throughout the long course of the war. The same hatred that now urged him to proclaim aloud a moral victory with this proof of the revolting depths of human avarice, to seize the chance to lash the human with harsh words of rancor and disdain.

Yet he found he could not form the words his hatred would have him speak, because he knew himself to be as guilty of blindness and a willingness to assume the very worst about the enemy as the shaken man who stood beside him now. Instead, the Elfin king reached out carefully and touched Gavan's arm.

"Why did you ask to meet me?" he asked quietly, without a hint of accusation or blame, as if he truly sought to understand. "Why now?"

Gavan was silent for so long that Rillandariel knew the next words uttered would be spoken from the heart. "I nearly lost my elder son." He pointed to the tall, red-haired youth that, even at this distance, could be seen to favor his father in all ways.

"An accident in training, as it happens. A foolish accident, in truth, but near to fatal, for all that. His horse slipped on some unseen ice and went down. His back was broken and his skull kicked open. My healers gave him up for dead."

Rillandariel could hear the residue of anguish and grief in his voice that remained even now as Gavan continued. "The foreign mage, Mik`kel, saved his life, with a skill and power only the gods could have granted. I believe that Killian stands there now only because the gods sent the mage to me."

He paused. "I tried to bargain with the mage for my son's life, promising to give him over to the fate the gods decreed if he would but save him. The mage refused my bargain, and left the choice to me. Yet, after my son had been healed, I saw no real choice left to me at all. Killian was training for war, this foolish war, when he almost died. And I knew that he would soon ride out to battle, eager to fight the enemy that he had learned to hate because I hated. And, if he died from that hatred, there would be no victory great enough to recompense his loss."

Gavan exhaled deeply, relieved to have it said, no matter how the Elf might use it to his advantage. But Rillandariel was gazing across the meadow and pointing to the slender, blond warrior who had been arguing with him before he took the field.

"My daughter, Ellianthia," he said, his pride and affection evident.

Gavan looked closer. "Your daughter?" he asked uncertainly, trying to reconcile his image of an Elfin princess with the armed fighter that stood on the edge of the field, staring back at him so boldly.

Rillandariel nodded. "I suppose she is the reason I am here with you today...or the most compelling reason, surely." He turned back to Gavan. "My daughter is a brave fighter who has hated humans, as have I, ever since they killed her brother. She was the leader of the patrol that caught your scouts deep in our Forest, looking for the Thalesi grove." His voice thickened.

"She was the only one who lived. They brought her back to me on a litter, covered with burns and blisters, her lovely golden hair—her mother's hair—scorched from her head by the Fire Spell that killed our people and our trees." He shook his head sadly. "You know, she told me she could hear the trees screaming their death throes in her head."

Gavan closed his eyes, imagining her pain. "It was not meant to be that way," he said quietly.

"No, I suppose not," said the Elfin king with weary resignation. "But it was. And it made her hate humans even more—so much so that now she begs me daily to return to the battle lines and let her take her revenge. But she came close to death again, in a raid upon your cattle, and I have not allowed her to fight again. I cannot, for I have seen her dead in my mind, even in my dreams, do I grant her plea."

His eyes met Gavan's directly. "That is why I agreed to meet you now. Before that happens, and I have lost all."

Gavan looked upon this leader of the Forest folk whom he had hated and reviled for so long, and saw now only another father like himself, afraid for his child and tired beyond measure of the fighting and the dying. Taking a deep breath, he looked into Rillandariel's eyes.

"Then let us make an end to the war, here and now, for ourselves and for our children."

"What do you propose?" asked Rillandariel cautiously, though he felt hope rising within him like the first warm ray of spring sunlight after a frigid, dark winter.

Gavan gestured at his people lining the northern edge of the meadow. "I have already ordered my army to fall back to permanent positions no closer than one half mile from your tree line. From this day forth, no one will be permitted to cross that line without my express consent. There will be no more raids against your timber or your Thalesi plants. Any men caught attempting to mount such a raid will be severely punished."

He looked at the Elfin king again. "I would ask only that, if you capture anyone trespassing in your Forest, you turn them over to me—alive—and let Calderia exact its own justice against them."

"Done!" said Rillandariel. He paused, then offered a concession of his own. "For my part, there will be no more attacks into human lands, and no more cattle raids. I, too, will forbid trespass beyond the border of the Forest. And, perhaps, after sufficient time has passed to begin to heal the wounds of war, we might discuss a resumption of trade according to our original agreement."

"My people and I will look forward to that day," said Gavan, smiling with satisfaction and deeply heartened by this unexpected offer.

One issue remained, an issue both were acutely aware of, and just as acutely reticent to broach. But both rulers had been warned that the peace, and perhaps the very survival of their peoples, hinged on yielding to the will of the gods in this matter. And, truth be told, both had known before they stepped a foot onto the meadow this day that the wyrd laid upon them by the gods could no longer be denied. Yet still they hesitated, until Gavan finally spoke the question neither could avoid.

"And what of the betrothal? Will you see my son and your daughter joined to seal the peace?"

Though visibly reluctant, Rillandariel assented with a nod. "I will accept this Handfasting of our children, though I would see the marriage itself take place—if it does take place—only after a proper interval, as is the custom of my people."

"Done!" said Gavan resolutely, and with great relief.

The decision made, Rillandariel gazed around the meadow at the humans and Elves gathered there. All seemed to be awaiting the outcome with what he knew must be growing impatience, judging by their shifting stances and the way their heads inclined together in whispered speculation.

"And what of your people, King Gavan?" he wondered aloud. "Will they accept this betrothal and this peace? If they are like mine, there are some who will never countenance this union of our races, some who would fain fight on, no matter the cost, than be denied their revenge."

"Then we must show them a better way, brother king," Gavan replied. Squaring his shoulders, he boldly extended his hand across the small space between them.

"Indeed. Then let it be peace," Rillandariel said; and, with the first true smile in longer than he could recall, he reached out and clasped Gavan's forearm tightly.

For a moment, there was no sound to be heard at all around the meadow. It was if that simple arm clasp had brought all life to a standstill. No distant hum of voices or rustle of shifting feet. No clank of metal against metal. No creak of leather or rattle of chain. No horses snorting, impatient to be moving. No birds calling to their mates. Every living creature within earshot seemed frozen in time, with even the animals seeming to mark the import of that simple gesture of two arms gripped in peace.

Then the silence ended. It began as a low murmuring noise arising on both sides of the field, punctuated by a few alarmed cries of "No! Never!" as the meaning of the kings' gesture of agreement sank in. Steadily, the sound grew louder and louder, rippling over the isolated cries of protest and drowning them out, gaining momentum and volume until it swelled into a deafening cheer from human and Elf alike that bounced around the meadow and echoed in the trees.

Both leaders grinned broadly, listening to the roar of affirmation and savoring the first precious moments of peace as they would a Holy Day feast laid before them. Then Gavan heard a wry chuckle escape Rillandariel's lips, and followed his gaze across the field to find the Elfin princess glaring back at them, offering no jubilant cheer, her arms crossed angrily on her chest.

Gavan turned and saw Killian posed in a strikingly similar stance. He leaned toward his brother king and asked, with some trepidation, "Have you told your daughter that the terms of peace include betrothal to my son?"

Rillandariel shook his head with a wry smile. "No, I saw no need to mention that small...detail...until I saw that peace was at hand, and it became necessary to do so. And you? Have you informed your son of this...arrangement?"

Gavan pinched the bridge of his nose and shook his head ruefully. "No, I fear that I neglected to mention it as well, for much the same reasons."

Rillandariel grinned ruefully "Then, my Lord King, I expect that the next few days will prove to be very interesting for both our houses. Interesting indeed."

Chapter 20

Bitter Concessions

"You want me to marry him???" Ellianthia's hazel eyes flashed dangerously as she wrenched herself free of the firm grip her father had on her shoulders and thrust her balled fists down on her hips, the sharp movement setting the golden bracelets on her wrists to jangling. "Did I hear you correctly, Father? You want to Handfast me to a gods-be-dammed *human?*"

One look at her father's face told her that he meant what he had just said, but she shook her head nonetheless, as if trying to clear a fog from her mind. "You can't be serious, Father! Me, wed to a man whose father killed my brother and your son?" Her faced flushed, her breasts rising and falling with rapid, shallow breaths, the Elfin maid stamped her boot.

"I don't give a gods-damn what peace terms you agreed to with that barbarian excuse for a king. I would not marry that murdering scum's bastard if Sallamarian himself came down and commanded it!"

"Actually, he did just that, as I already told you," replied Rillandariel mildly, crossing his arms and leaning back against the wooden wall of the now empty council chamber. He had learned over the years that indulging the impulse to yell back at his daughter during one of her rages gained him little, and only served to further stoke the fires of anger seething inside her. It was usually best to approach her as one approached a snarling tree panther—slowly and calmly, making no sudden moves. Thus, his voice was pitched low and smooth as he continued.

"I have told you, and all the others at the War Council, what Sallamarian told me, the warning about the coming invasion and the urgency of making peace between us."

"Yes, so I recall, *Father*," she growled sarcastically, as if to say her paternity was suddenly in question. "But you said nothing about me marrying some oafish, lumbering, hairy, foul-smelling *human!*"

She thought of Darillian, slender but strong, graceful and tender—and with a smooth, hairless chest, as was the way of all Elfin males, unlike the wooly humans she had met and killed in battle. She remembered the gentle, delicate caress of her lover's fingers on her body's tender places in the night. Then she imagined thick, clumsy human hands groping her crudely, tearing her clothing off and throwing her down on her back. The repulsive image made her stomach churn with disgust and her blood begin to boil anew.

"And just when is this travesty supposed to take place?" she snapped.

"Not for some little time yet. King Gavan told me that Prince Killian must undergo the Ritual of Awakening to his gods-given power before the Handfasting can occur."

"Gods-given power, my arse!" she snorted. She leaned forward and thrust her finger into her father's face, her voice spitting fire. "I will *not* be a fawn led to the slaughter. Gods-chosen or not, does that bastard lay but one hand on me, I will slit his throat and pull his tongue right out through the hole!"

Rillandariel sighed as he looked at his fuming daughter. All things considered, this was going about as well as could be expected.

✝✝✝✝✝

"You want me to marry her???" Killian shot to his feet and stood with feet planted apart, hands still resting on the sturdy arms of the dark mahogany chair in which he had been sitting until Gavan's outrageous announcement drove him upward in alarm. Eyes wide and mouth agape, he stared at his father, who nodded to confirm that his ears did not deceive him. Finding no relief there, he turned and sought reprieve from his mother.

Surely, she would not forfeit her own son's life to a marriage of state with the daughter of a king who had murdered so many humans...and Orrin! But there was no dissent forthcoming from the queen, who only looked upon him with regret and concern. Even Aisleen, sitting beside Briana at the dining board in the private family chambers, offered no objection, though he saw sympathy in her eyes.

The gods knew, he had tried to accept the abrupt change in his father's attitude toward the Elves. After their return from the meeting with the Elfin king, Killian had sat silently in his father's council room, listening with dismay while the king outlined the proposed terms of peace to the military commanders, nobles, and representatives of the merchants' and builders' guilds gathered there.

He had heard Gavan make mysterious reference to one "additional" peace proposal that would be revealed only after he had spoken privately to the "person concerned." But now, with this last term of the peace agreement revealed, the "person concerned" was no longer sitting, and he would no longer be silent.

"But, Father!" he protested. "It is one thing to make peace with the enemy, though you know my heart on that. But how can you ask me to *marry* one of them? Her father has the blood of our people on his hands!"

Gavan did not respond to his son's vehement tone in kind, but answered calmly and with some sadness. "Killian, many have died on both sides. Do you think I count the lives of our people, my own brother, any less dearly than you? Do you think I do not mourn Orrin still when I pass his bedchamber or take his young daughter on my knee?" He shook his head. "Yet, for all the reasons I have given, the peace must be made."

"But why must I wed this gods-be-damned Elfin princess?" Killian argued, desperate to bring his elders to their senses before this course was set and he was lost. "Did you not hear the people cheering, men and Elves alike? You do not need this marriage for the peace to go forward."

Gavan leaned forward in his chair and fixed Killian with his gaze. "They are cheering now, my son, full of relief and hope. But soon, the time will come when men and Elves must work together, fight together. Then the peace will be sorely tested. The old hatred and suspicion will not die easily, perhaps not even in this generation, when so many have lost loved ones and vowed retribution. It is my hope—our hope—that forging this kinship will serve as a symbol of unity between our peoples; and that it will help stay the hands of those who would otherwise strike out in anger and vengeance."

Killian knew a fluttering of dread in his stomach as he felt the jaws of the trap closing tighter and tighter. Then another image surfaced in his mind—the image of taking this Elfin maid to his bed. "But, it is not…natural! We are of different races," he insisted. "Do you expect me to…lie…with this Elf, to get a child on her?" he asked, feeling himself blush a little as he avoided looking at his mother and Aisleen.

When, after a lengthy silence, a response finally came, the prince was startled to hear his mother answering. "My son," she said quietly. "There have been other marriages between our two peoples, others who made such a choice. It is rare, to be sure, but not unheard of. Some of the couples lived in our land among humans, or in the Forest with Elfin kin, until the war made them unwelcome in either place. I am told that some of the pairings were...successful."

Killian began to protest again, but this time Aisleen intervened to finish the thought. "Besides, Your Highness, a betrothal is all that is required for the present. Rillandariel has requested a suitable waiting period before the marriage, and there may be some wisdom in that. The...consummation...need not be rushed."

Snap! went the trap jaws as they closed and locked upon him mercilessly, like cold iron teeth piercing the foot of a captive animal. Cornered on every side, Killian only barely resisted the urge to sweep his wine cup from the table and stomp from the room. It was all so incredible!

Then it became more unbelievable still when the king made a small gesture. A moment later, an auburn-haired man of middle years, garbed in a purple gown and gripping a thick staff, suddenly appeared in a corner of the chamber, as if he had just emerged from the wall itself.

"Killian," said the king, lifting his hand to calm his son's surprise. "You know Lord Mik`kel of Kal`Dathia, the mage who came to warn us about the coming invasion, and the healer who saved your life."

"Of course, Father." Relaxing, he turned and offered the mage a bow of respect and gratitude. Mik`kel had tended to him many times during his recovery, and he had come to like the man quite a lot.

"There is more you need to know, my son," continued Gavan, "much that Lord Mik`kel has to tell you..."

†††††

Killian lay on his back across the bed, fully clothed, with his arm covering his eyes to keep the world at bay. The fire in the hearth had crackled and blazed when he first entered his bedchamber and flung himself down. Now the dying embers glowed faintly, and still he lay motionless, lost in bemusement.

He trusted the Kal`Dathian mage, and Killian had heard the grim sincerity in his voice as he told his fantastic tale. But well-meaning and sincere people could be quite mad, like Nial, a distant cousin who had launched himself off the castle battlements one bright spring morning, fully believing he could fly.

At first, he had been repulsed by the thought of some alien power lurking within him, ready to be Awakened like some succubus waiting to occupy his body and devour his soul. But Mik`kel had sworn that this gods-sent power would not steal his soul or his mind. It would be a part of him, under his control and only employed for good.

Then there was this notion of being named by the gods to undertake an urgent mission to save his people and his land. The very thought sent fingers of fear and excitement walking down his back. To be sure, he wanted to make his royal father proud. An heir's duty to the kingdom had been deeply instilled at an early age. And he had to admit that the thought of doing something important, something vital, for his family and his people appealed to him—not to mention that it had all the trappings of a grand adventure, surpassing anything he and Gilly and Col had even dreamed of.

Yet, he had searched inside himself, and could find no trace, no hint of power there at all. Surely, Mik`kel could be mistaken, though the sapphire gem had blazed to dazzling brightness when Mik`kel held it before him, proof that his quest to find the Avatar had ended here, with the prince.

What would this Awakening entail, and how would he feel in its aftermath? Mik`kel had said that many things would be revealed to him, secrets that would guide him on a quest to seek the aid of unknown powers potent enough to battle the evil threatening his land.

As to the exact nature of these secrets, even Mik`kel claimed ignorance. But the mage had been exceedingly clear on one point. The Elfin maid must be with him on the journey, that she was to play a crucial role, though no one yet understood just what that might be.

Yet, for that to happen, he would have to become betrothed to this enemy, to stand beside her and speak the Holy words of bonding to someone he would have gladly slain in vengeance for his people. How could he simply banish the memories of what they had done to Orrin? And to Jenny. He felt a dull ache whenever he recalled his first encounter with the lord seneschal's daughter...

He had been just shy of his sixteenth name-day on that cool spring eve as he prepared to bathe away the day's sweat and grime from training with wooden sword and shield. He sat down in the large brass tub in his chamber, scrubbing his chest with soap while Erwan, his young page, anointed his tired body with steaming water heated in the kitchen below and brought up to his room in large kettles.

After sending Erwan for another round of hot water, Killian slipped lower into the warmth of the tub, trying to escape the spring chill that seemed to find its way into every room of the castle, no matter how tightly the glaziers sealed the casements and doors. Hearing a soft rapping on his chamber door, he called out permission to enter, thinking Erwan must have been fairly sprinting to return so quickly, and wondering why the lad would bother to knock at all.

But it was not his page coming through his door at that moment. He froze with embarrassment as Jenny, the lord seneschal's eldest daughter, entered, a stack of towels clutched in her hands. He sat speechless as she casually approached the tub, apparently indifferent to his nakedness only barely concealed beneath scant inches of soapy water.

"I thought my Lord might have need of these," she said in a low, silky voice, holding the folded cloths out as if that fully explained the presence of a young female, much less the seneschal's daughter, in his bath. She smiled. "I often help with the smaller duties of running the castle, to take some of the burden off my father. I will just put these over here, next to the tub."

He stared open-mouthed as she crossed in front of him. She was two years older, with dark curls spilling down over her neck that matched the brown of her twinkling eyes. She wore a snug-fitting dress, the tight bodice stretched taut over her high, firm breasts and the skirt outlining her hips in a way that evoked an answering tightness in his groin.

It was not a new sensation, since he had already discovered girls some time ago, and had begun to find his manhood coming to life on a regular basis, sometimes at the most inopportune times...like now. Sitting there naked and watching her walk produced a physical reaction swifter and more intense than he had thought possible. Killian did the only thing he could think to do. He quickly slid himself further down into the water.

Jenny giggled softly as she witnessed his strategic retreat. Then, to his surprise, she knelt down beside the tub. "Perhaps my Lord could use some help with scrubbing his back," she said soothingly, reaching over the side to trail her fingers lightly up and down his spine. "I know how hard it is...to reach behind here, I mean. Allow me to be of some small service."

Her touch sent a shudder through his body. He started to object, thoroughly stricken with self-consciousness. Yet, he only got as far as "But..." before falling silent, enthralled by the soft encouragement in her voice and the brush of one firm breast against his arm. With a knowing smile, Jenny scooped the soft, yellow soap out of the porcelain crock and began rubbing in ever-widening circles over his back and shoulders, eventually working her way down to his hips.

Killian felt her warm breath on his neck as she murmured, "Mayhap my Lord might need cleansing here as well." Then, abandoning all pretense of scrubbing him, she reached boldly around his waist and slipped her hand beneath the water, grazing the skin of his inner thighs. As his body responded, he held his breath, waiting for her to recoil or utter some offended condemnation before scrambling to her feet in hasty departure. Instead, she chuckled deep in her throat.

"There is no need for embarrassment, my Lord. You are a healthy young man, after all, and I am but your servant. And it appears that my Lord Prince could use some special...service," she breathed, beginning to reach further down. Then, before he could think of something—anything—to say, he heard a knock on the door. Erwan's knock.

"My page! Erwan!" he managed to whisper, completely flustered, trying desperately to think of some explanation beyond the obvious. But Jenny was not flustered at all. He marveled at how calmly she winked at him and leaned to kiss his lips, then rose to her feet with a satisfied smile, smoothing her dress down as she walked to the door. By the time Erwan had entered, carrying two steaming kettles in his hands, she was brushing by him with a nod of her head, leaving behind one confused page—and one very amazed princeling.

Sadly, that was Killian's only real encounter with her. They managed to be alone briefly on two occasions during the next eight-day, and Jenny was more than willing to make her sweet body available to his nervous exploration with hands and lips. Yet they were interrupted both times, forced to move apart while she hastily rearranged her clothing. She had promised to find a place and a time for them to be alone, "to finish what we started, my Lord," she said with a wicked grin.

But soon after that, she fell ill with The Scourge, along with so many others, and he never saw her again. She was sequestered away with all those afflicted while the court physicians forbade any contact with her. Later, he learned that she had succumbed, and had been laid to rest in a mass grave with the other victims of that terrible plague.

Since that black day, he had sought escape from the pain by losing himself in rigorous training, against the time that he might avenge her death upon the Elves who had taken her life by denying her the Thalesi leaves that might have saved her.

Killian shifted on his bed. According to his father, it now seemed that the Elves might not have held back the cure that she had needed after all. Yet, she had been his first love. And there was still Orrin, and all the others for whose deaths the Elves were clearly responsible. How was he expected to tolerate a betrothal to one of those same cursed Elves? Killian groaned as he rolled onto his stomach to stare blankly into the remains of the fire.

Chapter 21

The Awakening

All was in readiness in Brannock Castle, all preparations for the Ritual completed in precise accordance with the dictates of the gods. Mik`kel had long since memorized Shalloth's instructions for Awakening the Avatar's powers, and had made the necessary arrangements with the full cooperation of the king and queen. He had selected the first day of Spring as a symbol of rebirth, when the frozen streams began to melt and run again, and the trees won their victory over Winter and brought forth their new, brightly colored blossoms.

Mik`kel had chosen a windowless chamber deep within the bosom of the castle for its secluded location and the absence of unwanted light. He had cleansed the room with a Spell of Purification, then directed that a long altar stone be placed in the center. Narrow tapers measuring the height of a man and the thickness of a wrist were set at the corners of the smooth, rectangular stone, in exact alignment with the four corners of the world.

The bare, polished floor around the stone was filled with swirling sigils of divine power, awaiting only the mage's words of enchantment to release their potency. As for Mik`kel himself, he had fasted and meditated for two days to purify and focus his spirit in preparation for the coming ordeal.

After some discussion, Mik`kel had granted permission for the king and queen to observe the Ritual, acknowledging their right to bear witness to their son's Awakening. Aisleen and Niocal, as seeress and senior mage, were in attendance as well, sworn to remain silent and refrain from manifesting their own power under any circumstances.

All four observers now sat quietly in high-backed wooden chairs placed along the walls of the shadowy chamber. Gavan and Briana exchanged looks of parental concern. Niocal waited with great curiosity and some uncertainty. Aisleen appeared serene, confident in Mik`kel's skills and wisdom.

Thus, all was in readiness—save for the Avatar himself, who was notably absent from the chamber. The designated time grew near, and Mik`kel turned to Gavan asking the silent question.

"My son will be here," said Gavan simply, accenting his conviction with a nod. Mik`kel glanced at Aisleen, who smiled her reassurance. He returned the smile of the woman whom he had come to trust so highly, and allowed himself to relax a little.

A minute later, the chamber door opened and Killian walked in. As instructed, he came barefoot and clad in a long, silken robe. His fire-red hair fell to his shoulders, unadorned by circlet or headband. His clear blue eyes flickered around the room, taking in the stone altar, the candles, and the chalked swirls decorating the floor. Swallowing once, he wiped his moist palms against the sides of the robe, then turned to Mik`kel and forced a grin.

"I do not suppose you would consider delaying this a few years until Aaron comes of age?" he quipped nervously.

Despite the seriousness of the moment, the mage shook his head and released a low chuckle. *The boy has spirit and courage,* he thought, *and he will need that sense of humor to face what must be done.* Aloud, he said only, "Alas, I fear not, Your Highness. Your younger brother does not carry the seed. It must be you."

Killian echoed Mik`kel's thin laugh. "Well, it was a thought," he replied, with a shrug suggesting he was resigned to his fate, and a look of excitement in his eyes hinting that this fate was not entirely unwelcome. Then he grew sober. "I am ready, Lord Mage. What would you have me do?"

Mik`kel gestured to the stone pallet. "Take off the robe, step over the sigils carefully, and lie down on your back, if you would, Your Highness."

The prince shed his robe, revealing that he was naked, save for his small clothes. Self-conscious of his near nudity before his mother and Aisleen, he tiptoed over the arcane symbols and lay down on his back, assuming a prone position on the altar. A small hiss escaped his lips as his warm skin met the cool stone. His broad chest, slim waist and powerful thighs glistened with a light sheen of moisture, though the room itself was hardly warm.

"Now, close your eyes and cleanse your mind of all thought," said Mik`kel in a soft, hypnotic tone. "Breathe deeply and slowly, and prepare yourself to touch the gods-sent power within you." Then, beginning a barely audible chant, he grasped his staff and moved slowly about the altar, lighting each candle with a wave of his hand.

Another word of power uttered and the sigils drawn on the floor sparked to life in lambent hues of red and blue and silver. Within the chamber, a hum of power grew and coalesced around the mage. And when he drew the sapphire pendant from his robe and held it aloft, the gem flared to brilliance and the very air commenced to sing.

All gathered there, even Niocal, looked on in awe while slender rays of blue light radiated from the jewel and arced down to touch the burning sigils on the floor, then traveled back along the glowing web to feed and amplify the power of the gem. Suddenly, a shaft of pure white light erupted from the pulsing jewel and lanced down into the naked chest of the prince lying still upon the alter stone.

When the white beam pierced his body, Killian cried out and arched his back, as if straining to close the distance and take more into himself, until his skin grew luminescent. Then, as Briana gasped and Niocal stared in astonishment, Killian's body rose up into the air and began to float above the stone.

†††††

He was drifting weightlessly, suspended in the soft embrace of a billowing white vapor that felt light and ephemeral, yet buoyant enough to support him effortlessly, like a thousand tiny hands cupping his body and lifting him upward. He could not feel his arms and legs, though he sensed himself intact and whole.

The absence of sensation, of any anchor to his humanity, should have brought him to the edge of panic and alarm. Yet, somehow, he knew that he was safe, that he was…loved. And he knew, without knowing how he knew, that he was not alone in the diaphanous ether.

Though he saw no tangible shape or outline, and heard no sound in that quiet mist, he felt the presence of divinity drawing nigh. Then he was surrounded by several pairs of glowing golden eyes that bathed him in their ambient light, even as he began to hear their celestial whispers in his head.

Welcome, mortal child. Fear us not. We are your parents, as much as he who planted man's seed in woman's womb—and as much as she who bore you into the world in blood and pain. We have been watching you, waiting for you, since your soul took shape and substance.

Gradually, faces began to form around those glittering eyes, and he saw himself encompassed by beings of such unsurpassed beauty and splendor that he nearly cried. Another ethereal voice, a female by its dulcet tone, began to speak.

I am Morainen, goddess of your people. You are the first of the chosen Avatars who has ever been Awakened and called upon to serve the Weave in all the centuries since we first conceived this plan. And you are the first new mortal to be so chosen in two hundred of your years, after the peaceful passing of the one who went before you—a noble soul who never heard the clarion call to take up powers against the Dark, yet who served us faithfully in his own way.

Her golden eyes glanced to one side, and Killian saw the image of an aged man lying still in a leafy bower. Yet, as he looked closer, he saw that it was not the face of a man at all, but of an Elf, a Forest dweller, his long, silvery blue hair fanned out around his head like a halo, his gentle, wrinkled face serene in death's repose. An *Elf* had been the chosen one before him?

Yes, child, said another, deeper voice. *This was Fellinorian, one of my followers, a wise and loyal Elf. He lived a long and honorable life. You were chosen to succeed him on the day of his death.*

One of *his* followers? Then understanding came. This could be no other than Sallamarian, god of the Elves, whose melodious baritone reverberated in his mind.

Shalloth drifted closer and fastened his gleaming gaze upon the prince. *The time has come to unlock the powers that we seeded within you on the day of your birth, for the time when the Weave would have need of them. That need is now upon us. Look inside, child, and learn what we have granted you.*

Killian sank into himself, and saw layer upon layer of his being slowly peeled away to reveal a faintly glowing sphere encased in a thick translucent shell embedded deep within him. He knew, somehow, that this was his essence, his core, and that it was waiting for something—perhaps waiting to be loosed from the shell enclosing it.

He barely had time to wonder if other chosen ones had harbored similar spheres unbeknownst to them for all their lives. Then a burning wave of energy began to flow over him, through him, into him, building, intensifying until he thought he must surely explode in flames and be reduced to cinders.

Yet, his flesh did not sear and crack open, his blood did not boil and vaporize to crimson steam. Instead, he saw the shell around the sphere grow thinner and clearer, as spidery cracks appeared across its surface, small lines which deepened and widened into thick fissures that suddenly gave way and burst apart, unloosing an indescribable surge of power that engulfed him thoroughly.

Gods! It was as if he had been asleep for all his eighteen years and only now Awakened to vibrant, pulsing life. Glorious energy rippled up and down the length of his body, no longer searing hot but warm and bright now, as golden as the eyes of the gods encircling him. Then he heard their voices intertwining and echoing in his head as they gave name to their divine gifts:

I, Morainen, grant you greater strength and power than you have ever known.

I. Sallamarian, grant you endurance and longer life than the span of years meted out to others of your race.

I, Doritha, grant you increased prowess in battle. One will come to teach what you must know.

I, Lurendal, grant you vitality. Though you can die, wounds that do not kill will mend more quickly, and you will aid in the healing of other as well.

I, Ballor, grant you greater speed and agility.

And, finally: *I, Shalloth, grant you access to the paths of magic, though you must learn their ways. Seek ye the mage who will open these paths and heed his wisdom well.*

Speechless, Killian could do little but lie suspended in the comforting mist as their words faded to silence. He might have drifted for a moment—or an eternity—for time had little meaning here. Then, when he thought he might simply dissolve into the ether, Shalloth spoke again.

We will show you the first task that lies ahead for you and she who is to be your companion. What is to follow afterward must be discovered through your own endeavors. Look...and remember well.

A portion of the whirling mist parted before him and Killian looked out upon a forest scene. It seemed to be a grassy clearing sheltered in the midst of an ancient grove of regal trees. He sensed an abiding stillness in that secluded glade, a place of peace and sanctuary where no foot had trod within its bounds for long and long. The clearing was empty, save for a tall, broad, tangled mound of gnarled and twisted vines, their convoluted woody tendrils tightly interlaced in intricate design to form a brambled dome abloom with tiny purple flowers.

At first glance, he thought it to be one dense, impenetrable thicket through and through. Then he felt something urge him to take a closer look; and when he did, he saw that, beneath the mantle of interwoven vines and delicate blossoms, stood a massive granite monolith.

It was the height of two men and twice as wide, all but obscured by the thick, leafy vegetation clinging tightly to every visible inch of its dark stony surface, except for a small, palm-sized circle located on one side of the mound, the only spot that was oddly free of vine or flower. He had no inkling of the purpose for which this isolated glade and hidden menhir had been revealed to him, but the admonition to remember it well rang in his mind—as if he could do otherwise.

In the next instant, the image faded, and he was alone in the silence again. Then he was plummeting through the mist, spiraling down faster and faster until he thought he surely must be crushed on impact with the earth. But, at the last, he floated down and felt only a small jolt along his back as he encountered something hard and flat beneath him.

†††††

He lay there, unmoving, as corporeal sensation resumed throughout his body. He first began to feel his fingers and toes, then gradually his arms and legs returned to his control. Still, he did not shift or stir, content to let the world reclaim him slowly, while he struggled to understand all that had befallen him.

Then someone was calling his name aloud, bringing him back, pleading with him to speak or give some sign of life. Feeling apprehensive and unsteady, he settled for opening his eyes to narrow slits. After a brief, frightening moment of blurring, his vision cleared and he found himself looking up into his mother's beautiful, tear-stained face.

Briana shuddered with relief to see his eyelids flutter and gave silent thanks to Morainen. But her elation quickly turned to awe and fear, for Killian's eyes were lustrous golden ovals that blazed brightly in the darkened chamber, illuminating the features of his face in sharp relief. It was several heartbeats before the supernatural glow faded and his eyes were their natural blue again. Yet even that brief instant had been long enough for Mik'kel and the others to know beyond any doubt that they were, indeed, looking upon the gods' Avatar.

The spell was broken when Killian sat upright and shook himself as if throwing off the veil of sleep. He felt stronger and ravenously hungry, and announced to no one in particular that he could do with some wine. But when he tried to swing his legs over the stone to stand, he twisted faster than he had expected and nearly fell off the altar. What was *that* all about? he wondered, as the king moved quickly to steady him.

Briana brought a measure of wine that the prince gulped rapidly, clinging tightly to the cup as he relished the feel of the cool liquid in his mouth. He was as startled as any in the chamber when he felt something give in his hand, and looked down to see the heavy silver cup crushed and twisted in his grasp.

Later, as Killian ate his way through an entire platter of sliced roast beef, smoked white cheese and brown bread, he tried to tell them what had transpired during his heady sojourn with the divine. His voice full of wonder, he spoke of the rapture of being embraced by the gods and goddesses of legend, of their shining eyes and glorious faces, of being called their "child" and told of his importance in restoring harmony and balance to the Weave. He spoke of watching the golden seed that had been planted deep within him open to release his powers, and the naming of those powers by the deities who granted them.

"They told me that I had been gifted with greater strength, endurance, agility, and the ability to heal faster, though I am still mortal and can die. They granted me greater prowess in battle, and said someone would be coming to teach me greater skills. They did not say who that would be."

He turned to Mik'kel then. "They said as well that I was to seek a mage who would show me the paths of magic. Are you not that mage?"

Mik'kel shook his head. "I do not know, Your Highness. The gods said naught to me of teaching you magic. Perhaps another mage awaits you on your quest, to serve as guide and mentor in the ways of power."

Killian grunted and said nothing for a time. Then Gavan broke the silence. "My son, what of this quest? Was the nature of this task revealed to you?"

Killian described the image of the forest glade and the vine-encrusted monolith that rested there. "I know not what to say of it, Father, save that the stone seemed to call to me. I know not where it lies or what its purpose might be, only that I am to seek it out—and that I am to be joined by 'she who is to be my companion,' or so I was told." He turned to Mik`kel again. "I took that to mean the Elfin princess, to whom I am to be betrothed, as you foretold."

Mik`kel nodded thoughtfully. "So it would seem. But did they say nothing else of your journey or its destination?"

The prince shook his head and sighed. "Only that I must discover the rest through my own efforts, whatever that may mean. This mysterious quest confuses me, for all that it sounds a grand adventure."

"It confuses me too," said Briana, openly concerned. "And I, for one, would wish the gods had seen fit to be a little more forthcoming where my son's life hangs in the balance."

"As would I, Your Majesty," Mik`kel replied. "Much is left unspoken. I can only counsel that we must trust in the gods and have faith that all will be revealed in its own time."

Chapter 22

Unspoken Yearnings

"What do you think of our young prince, my Lord Mage?" Aisleen had offered to walk with him while he made his way back to his chambers to rest after the exhausting ritual. Her offer, and her interest in seeking his company more often lately, had pleased him greatly. In truth, he had come to look forward to their occasional encounters when attending the king, or at table when he took his meals with her.

Now he turned to her. "Please, my Lady, call me Mik`kel. I hope that we know each other well enough now to dispense with formal titles."

She smiled warmly, her lovely dark eyes twinkling in a way that left him staring a moment longer than politeness allowed. But she seemed not to mind, and only answered, "Of course, Mik`kel, if you will call me Aisleen."

The way she said his name, soft and low, felt like a gentle touch upon his skin. It had been so long since he had heard a woman speak his name like that. A little thing to some, perhaps; but to a man alone, in a foreign land and bereft of feminine companionship for longer than he cared to recall, it warmed him like a hearth fire on a chill winter's night.

"I would be honored…Aisleen," he replied, wondering if she could sense his pleasure. They walked together down a long corridor, catching glimpses of the red evening sky visible through the narrow casements spaced along the outer wall of the hallway.

"As for the prince, I am coming to believe that the gods knew what they were doing when they chose him. He is an impressive youth, strong in heart as well as body. Perhaps a bit impulsive and headstrong, yet who knows but that those very traits may serve him well in what he must do. It took courage to endure the ritual and the changes that must come of it. He has been tasked with shouldering a terrible burden for one so young, facing an unknown future, with the gods themselves to serve as judges of his success."

Aisleen nodded. "I feel as the queen does, that it would be better if we had at least some vision of what lies ahead for him. And, Mik`kel, what of this mage he is to seek? If it is wisdom that Killian is needing, surely he can turn to you," she said, with quiet conviction.

Hearing her words made him smile with pleasure, for it came to him that, of all the kings and lords he might impress, no one's trust and faith meant more to him than hers. He did not know why or how that had happened, but only that it was true.

They had reached the door to his chambers and, though weary to the bone, he was reluctant to part from her. Opening the door, he asked, "Perhaps I could make us some tea?"

Aisleen looked at his tired face and thought it best for him if she declined his offer, though she found herself drawn to remain. "No, My Lord...I mean, Mik`kel. You must needs rest, for your burden today was great. But I would see your chambers for a moment, to know if you are well settled."

He smiled and bade her enter with a wave of his hand, then followed in behind her, inhaling her sweet fragrance as she brushed past him. Just her scent alone was enough to make his heart quicken. More than once, he had imagined inviting her to his rooms. And now, here she was.

A man's chambers, she thought as she looked around. Simple and austere, suggesting one who gives more care to his arts than to his surroundings. Two rooms, one a spacious bedchamber, the other a smaller cove off to the side, filled with the familiar clutter transported from his apothecary shop—his many vials and jars, potions and powders, herbs and tinctures—and everywhere that offered space to store them, his books and scrolls.

The bed was wedged into a corner, sheets askew beneath a rumpled white goose down quilt still needed during the cool spring nights. She saw a closed cedar cabinet standing against a wall, likely housing his few garments and incidentals. The table and two chairs nearby were laden with more books.

A fire was burning in the hearth to keep the chill of nightfall at bay, and a black iron kettle and some cups rested on the mantle. Through a partially shuttered casement, she could see the crimson glow of the sunset.

The mage had dropped his satchel on the table and laid his staff against a wall by the time she finished her brief inspection of the chamber and returned her gaze to him. He was a very handsome man, she thought, not for the first time. Soft-spoken and kind, yet strong and masculine in his way, a way quite different than Gavan or the prince, whose size and force of personality seemed to dominate any room they occupied. But

Mik`kel's strength lay in his wisdom, the passion of his beliefs, and the power of his magic, a consummate skill and mastery that had left her awed this day.

"Not much to offer comfort to a Lady, I fear, though it serves my needs well enough," he said, acutely conscious of being alone in his bedchamber with this lovely woman, and having her full attention.

"I was thinking that tapestries and curtains might offer some warmth and cheer," she responded, though that was not at all what she had been thinking as she stared at his bed. "Perhaps something to brighten the room, there and there…" she said, pointing to a spot above his bed, and to the stone gray wall opposite the door.

As she spoke, Mik`kel's attention was drawn to her long black hair falling down across the green silken gown and resting on her bosom. He had been noticing her as a woman more and more lately, her eyes, her hair, her scent, and her breasts—the way they swayed gently when she moved, and the way their tips were visible against the thin fabric of her bodice. Even as he gazed at them, he thought he saw them harden and grow. He dared not let his eyes linger on them too long, for fear of being too obvious, but even a brief glance was enough to start a swelling in his groin.

He was imagining what it would be like to kiss that smooth pale neck when he suddenly realized she was saying something, and quickly raised his eyes to hers. He found her gazing at him with a pensive expression. When she blushed and looked away, he knew that she had seen where his eyes had lingered, and read his thoughts as if they had been written on an open page with large, bold strokes.

He wanted to tell her that it wasn't her hair and lips and body—well, not *only* that—which drew him to her, that it was not desire alone that made him want to take her in his arms and hold her close against him. But he hesitated to speak, for fear of embarrassing her if her heart belonged to another, as he suspected; and for fear that the awkwardness of unrequited feelings might raise a wall between them henceforth. So, he said nothing and let the moment pass.

Then she was begging his pardon for "chattering on so when you are exhausted," and taking her leave. She reached the door. "Mayhap we can discuss wall hangings another time, my Lord, when you are less fatigued."

So, it was "my Lord" again. Mik'kel winced inwardly at her return to that formality, but hid his disappointment and replied, "Forgive me, my Lady, for allowing my mind to...wander. Perhaps it would indeed be best if I rested now."

"Of course, my Lord." She started through the doorway, then turned back again and reached her hand out to squeeze his gently. "And Mik'kel, I would tell you once more that I thought you wonderful today."

With a soft smile, she was gone in a rustle of skirts. He stared at the door for several minutes after she had left, still smelling her in the air, and wondering what to make of her smile. Then he thought again of the touch of her hand and her parting words, and his lips turned upward in a grin as he staggered to his bed.

†††††

Aisleen closed her bedroom door behind her and leaned back against the heavy wooden panel, trying to let the fluttering in her chest and the warm quivering deep in her belly subside. She had left Mik'kel's chambers before embarrassing herself by letting him see the flush creeping up her neck to her face. She could still feel his eyes on her, caressing her body, almost as if he had been moving his hands over her flesh. Such strong, agile hands.

Her thoughts had aroused her, there and then, and she was certain that he had been aware of it. Men noticed things like that. She had seen that look in a man's eyes before, the way Gavan had gazed at her so many years ago. It had been a long time since she had truly welcomed that kind of interest from any other man but him.

Yet, tonight, she could not deny that she had responded to Mik'kel, to his voice, to his eyes upon her. She was not entirely surprised to find herself attracted to a man who commanded so much of her admiration and respect. She knew she was feeling a need to be with him more and more of late. She had told herself that it was only natural for her to be drawn to a mage of such wisdom and power, to seek him out as a friend, an advisor, and a confidante.

But this felt like no other friendship she had ever known. Not this nascent desire to be in his arms, not this unexpected tightness in her breasts nor this warmth deep in her loins—

feelings she had once thought reserved for Gavan alone, living on now only in her memories and dreams.

No, these stirrings for Mik`kel were no dream, no fantasy. Feeling vaguely guilty, as if she were somehow betraying her old love, she pushed herself away from the door and walked to one of the cedar wardrobes where she kept her gowns.

Where Mik`kel's chambers had been plain and utilitarian, hers were carefully furnished with cherished things accumulated over the years of her residence in the castle, things that made her feel at home and less alone. The large feather bed, covered with quilts and goose down pillows, was a treasured legacy from her parents.

She loved it for her memories of climbing into bed beside her mother on cold mornings when her father, the Earl of Devon-Baire, had left early to meet with his advisors. The wardrobes, and the chest of drawers for small clothes, hose and her few pieces of good jewelry, had also come to her when her parents died.

The polished oak table and finely carved chairs with brocaded cushions had been bequeathed to her by her mentor, Lady Leonora. It was she who had been the first to fully understand her gift of the Sight. It was she who had offered to take a nervous fifteen year-old girl under her wing to teach her that her visions were gods-sent, and not a sign of lunacy. And that was Leonora's own Scrying bowl, ornately carved and filled with purified water, that sat upon the table, a gift when Aisleen was named as her successor just before the old seeress passed the veil.

Closer to the fireplace sat the smaller, delicately carved redwood table for her powders and perfumes, a present from her sister, Maureen, delivered just before her eighteenth name-day. The richly-hued tapestries and curtains had been purchased in the village market, to match the thick magenta carpet brought all the way by trader ships from Gallardy to shield her feet from the cold stone floor.

Her other prized possession was the full-length mirror standing in an oak frame in a corner, adorned along the top and sides by brightly-colored ribbons, garlands and other mementos from solstice fairs and celebration days. There were two private treasures that she kept locked in a small drawer built into the base of the mirror: an emerald pendant and a dried garland of wildflowers, both gifts from Gavan almost twenty years ago, received in happier times and still preserved with care.

Yet, for all its warmth and color, her room felt lonely tonight. She had learned to live with loneliness since Gavan had married Baron Riordan's daughter the year before Killian's birth. She had her work and her friends to keep her occupied; and sometimes, when the loneliness receded during the press of her daily duties and activities, she almost forgot about it. Almost. She had had her share of suitors over the years, noble lords who praised her beauty, and wealthy merchants who valued her poise and breeding...and perhaps her noble bloodline.

Still, no man could compete with her memories of Gavan, and so she had declined their offers of marriage graciously—though, now and then, when her solitary life became too much for her to endure, she had shared her bed for a night or two, often as much for the company of another's warmth and closeness in those long, quiet times before dawn as for the physical pleasure given and taken in the dark.

But tonight, she felt a different kind of yearning. She pulled her gown over her head and lowered her silken undershift to the floor. Standing in front of her mirror, she looked upon the body that Mik'kel had all but undressed with his eyes when he thought she was not looking. Her raven hair was still thick and soft, her pale skin still smooth and supple. She traced her fingers down her body, imagining that it was Mik'kel's hands that caressed her.

She watched in the mirror as her hands traveled over the gentle swell of her belly and back along the curves of her full hips, imagining the feel of his stronger, rougher male hands on her tender flesh. Still dwelling on that image, Aisleen raised her hands and slipped a satin nightgown over her head, feeling the cool fabric slide over her sensitive skin as it fell down around her body.

After blowing the candles out, she slid beneath the covers of her bed and lay there in the darkened room, illumined only by the glowing embers in the hearth. Restless, she willed herself to rest, but sleep would not come easily. She could hear Mik'kel's voice, the way he spoke to her as they walked or sat at table of an evening. She remembered his strong, nurturing arms surrounding her in moments of distress. But it was not only comfort that she wanted from him now, for comfort alone would not ease the pleasurable ache in her belly.

Chapter 23

Blademaster

Killian sat sideways on the wide ledge of the stone window sill in his castle bedchamber, leaning his back against one side with his long legs drawn up and arms hugging his knees. Though dressed warmly enough in fawn-colored breeches and a white woolen tunic, the afternoon breeze coming through the open casement ruffled his hair and raised goose bumps on any exposed skin. Still, he wouldn't allow a gust of wind to drive him away from his favorite seat in the entire castle.

He had spent many afternoons of his boyhood sitting there quietly, hidden away from the general hubbub of castle life, looking out over the broad expanse of green valley to the east and imagining himself riding to battle on a brave and loyal warhorse. In his mind, he was holding the Gryphon banner aloft in one hand, with naked broadsword steel in the other, striking desperate fear into the hearts of Dunmorians or any other enemy foolish enough to come against the King's Champion in single combat.

If he leaned out of the window and craned his head far enough to the right, he could see the multi-colored roof tops of the village far below, where people shrunk to miniature in the distance went about their daily business—just as they had years ago, unaware that a prince just past his ninth name-day had once spent long afternoons contemplating what it would be like to be a baker's boy or a street urchin, free of tight-fitting, fancy clothes that made him itch at long formal dinners where he must sit up straight and look the part of the royal heir.

Those days were long gone now. They had given way to more mature pursuits and responsibilities, to sword practice and Parlan's arid tutoring, and tedious duties in the King's Court. And to more exciting pastimes, like getting into mischief with Col and Gilly, the three of them holing up somewhere with a pilfered bottle of his father's best wine, trading swigs and tales of dubious veracity about their respective successes with bedding chambermaids and burrowing under the skirts of willing village girls. As he had grown older, he had all but forsaken his private window perch, though his boyhood daydreams of glory and adventure had never entirely gone away.

Today, though, there was something comforting about returning here again, now when he was on the verge of an adventure greater than he had ever envisioned in his most embellished fantasies. He really was not sure why he had come here, except perhaps to escape the curious looks he was getting from everyone, even his mother and father, ever since Mik`kel's Ritual three days past.

In truth, he did not look any different, though he did *feel* different, stronger and less easily tired. The strange incident with the broken wine cup after he awoke on the alter stone, and the way that Col had shrank away from him in pain and surprise after he slapped him on the back with his usual greeting the following day, had confirmed that well enough.

Yet, for someone supposedly gifted with greater agility, he now found himself feeling, if anything, clumsier than he had before. It seemed as though, ever since the Ritual, he had been moving too fast or too slow, reaching for things and knocking them over, sometimes stumbling when he raced up and down stairs at his usual pace. Yesterday, during sword practice, he had found himself lunging past his opponent, tripping over his own feet as if he had suddenly lost all sense of grace. There was nothing particularly gifted about that, he would wager.

He was wondering whether there had been some horrible mistake about his future fate when Erwan knocked perfunctorily, then stuck his head in the door and said, "They want you in the small throne room, Yer Highness. Seems someone's come to see you."

Killian uttered a small groan, thinking that he had had quite enough surprises lately, thank you. "Who is it, Erwan?" he grumbled, swinging his feet down from the sill and nearly falling over himself in the process. Gods! Now I have forgotten how to walk! he thought, as he righted himself and strode to the doorway.

"No one as I would know, Yer Highness," replied Erwan with a shrug of his shoulders, diplomatically overlooking his prince's momentary stumble. "But I believe that foreign mage has him in tow." Killian grunted and pointed himself in the direction of the throne room.

When he arrived, he found the king and queen seated on their thrones, talking to Mik`kel while Aisleen hovered nearby. But Killian's attention was drawn to a tall, husky, stern-faced man with a livid scar running down the left side of his face, a small gold hoop in his right ear, and thick, black hair brushed back from his forehead and plaited in a braid that reached his shoulder blades.

Clad entirely in black leather, his creased, well-worn tunic and breeches of good quality but now shiny at elbow and knee, he reminded the prince of a pirate captain who had fallen on hard times—though the silver inlay in the hilt of his sword alone could have outfitted him in fine new leathers, had he chosen to strip the precious metal and sell it. The fact that he had not done so bespoke a special attachment to the blade hanging on his hip.

Mik`kel looked up as Killian approached. "Your Highness, allow me to introduce a man who has been called by the gods to play a role in your destiny. Prince Killian, this is Captain Reagen, come to us out of the Duchy of Delgaria."

As Killian nodded greeting, Gavan shifted on his throne and turned toward his son. "Mik`kel tells us that the good captain has come to offer you some special tutelage in weaponry. He is a former member of the Black Guard."

The Black Guard! Was this the man whom the god had foretold, the one who would come to teach him greater prowess in battle? Killian's pulse began to race. Though far to the west of Calderia, on the other side of Dunmoria, the fame of Delgaria's deadly fighting company had spread east across boundaries and frontiers.

The Black Guard was known to every callow youth who played at swords and dreamed of becoming a Blademaster. It was a name to conjure with, and Killian inclined his head gravely with respect, greatly relieved that this "pirate" had not been able to read his thoughts a few moments ago.

Reagan bowed from the waist, slapping his closed right fist against his chest smartly, then straightened his shoulders to a position of attention unmistakable to another trained in military discipline. "I am honored to meet you, Your Highness," he said in a deep, gravelly voice, as he turned an appraising eye on this broad-shouldered, fire-headed prince who gazed back at him with such obvious interest.

The king shifted on his throne and looked at Reagen. "And how fares Delgaria, sirrah? It has been years since my father, King Nicholas, went into battle with Duke Robelin and the famed Black Guard. He is a good man, though his efforts went awry, no fault to him." Gavan was referring to a valiant, though failed, attempt by the duke to broker a peace between

Calderia and Dunmoria some years ago, when Killian's grandfather sat the throne.

"The duke is well, as far as I am aware, Your Majesty," Reagen answered quietly, with no elaboration.

Gavan nodded. "His Black Guard is a most respected and feared force in battle. I would know why you are no longer with them, Captain."

Reagen hesitated. When he answered, his expression and tone were impassive. "I am no longer a captain in service to the duke, Your Majesty. The Guard and I...parted ways. I found I was no longer suited to be a member of the company." He stared straight ahead, remaining at full attention but offering no further explanation.

Gavan arched an eyebrow and leaned forward to regard the man in black with a flinty gaze. "Sirrah, if I am to trust my son and heir to your teachings, I would know more of this matter."

Another pause. Then Reagen lifted his chin resolutely and replied. "Your Majesty, I was told my past does not matter in this circumstance, that what matters now are the skills I can impart to your son, to aid him in his destiny."

"And just who was it that told you your past is of no consequence, sirrah?" asked Gavan, his irritation and suspicion palpable in the air.

When it came, Reagan's reply was steady and unyielding. "It was Doritha, Your Majesty, who convinced me to travel here to offer my humble aid. But, if that is not acceptable, Lord King..."

"Doritha, goddess of battle?" Gavan's other eyebrow arched as well, the mention of her name giving him pause.

"Your Majesty," interrupted Mik`kel quietly. "If I may explain. This man's coming was foretold to us, and he bears the mark of the goddess."

He moved to Reagen's side and asked a question of the man in black with his eyes. When the Delgarian nodded slightly, Mik`kel reached up slowly, and carefully lifted Reagen's braid aside to reveal a star-shaped sigil etched into the skin behind his ear. "I would beg you to accept what he offers, and to take the rest on faith."

Gavan said nothing for a moment, caught between his dislike of the mystery surrounding this stranger and his trust in Mik`kel's word. Finally, he consented. "Very well, mage. I will yield to your wisdom in this matter." He fixed his gaze back on Reagen. "I have no doubt of your skill with a sword. What is it that you plan to teach my son?"

Reagen relaxed his stiff expression as he peered thoughtfully at the prince, who had been watching this clash of wills with some interest, hoping that his father—who could be very obstinate indeed—would not dismiss the stranger's offer out of hand.

"I would first observe his manner and style of combat, Your Majesty, before I ventured an answer to your question."

"I see," said the king, thoughtfully. He respected a man who would first learn the lay of the land before choosing a course of action. "And when would you test his skills, Captain?" he asked, disregarding Reagen's disclaimer of his old rank.

"I am prepared to serve at your discretion, Your Majesty. Immediately, if you so desire." Reagen looked around at the limited space afforded by the small chamber. "But I would suggest that we repair to a more suitable venue."

"The practice yard, then," Gavan announced decisively, curious to see this drama play out. "And call Doughal. He will want to see this."

†††††

Killian crouched slightly, bending his knees and shifting his weight from one foot to the other as he faced the captain across the sparring circle. Raising the shield strapped to his left arm, he gripped the practice sword in his right hand, point to the ground, awaiting the signal to begin. Reagen had made no move as yet, except to test the blunted sword edge with his finger and whip the blade from side to side to gauge its weight and balance.

Movement in his peripheral vision alerted Killian that the crowd gathering to watch this unusual bout was growing larger as word spread. A moment earlier, he had seen Doughal emerge from the barracks, muttering at the news that his royal pupil was about to fight an unknown opponent "without so much as a by-your-leave to me!" Gavan himself had pulled the incensed Armsmaster aside to offer a few words of explanation, and to counsel him to watch and see what would transpire.

Now Doughal stood with arms crossed, staring intently at the stranger. He needed no explanation to understand what manner of fighter was about to take up arms against his prince. One look at the man—his aura of confidence and experience, the solid black uniform, the faint outline still visible on his tunic breast where a badge of rank had once been sewn, and the silver-trimmed sword hilt—told him all he needed to know in that regard. But why a past member of the renowned Black Guard had appeared at the castle to cross steel with Killian was a mystery, and one not to his liking.

Reagen raised his sword to vertical position. "If you are ready, Your Highness."

"What would you have of me, Captain?" Killian asked, feeling that same fusion of apprehension and excitement roiling in his belly that always preceded a contest of arms. He had never thought to face a member of the Black Guard in combat, mock battle though it might be, and the prospect left his palms sweaty and his heart racing.

"Just come at me, whenever you are ready, my Lord Prince," Reagen replied.

Killian nodded and began to circle the captain slowly. As his opponent turned with him, Killian silently recited Doughal's "essentials of close combat," as the stern Armsmaster called them: *Always watch your opponent's eyes, for they will tell you where he means to strike. Feint a bit and see how he jumps. Test his speed but conceal your own. Do not underestimate him; rather treat every opponent as dangerous. Never let him set the pace of combat. Choose your opening and strike. Parry and thrust, parry and thrust.* The lessons had been drummed into him ad nauseam, but now they echoed in his mind with a special urgency.

All right, then. Killian feinted to the left and watched to learn how Reagen jumped—which was not at all. He feinted to the right, then drove his sword forward, only to meet empty air, as the captain sidestepped gracefully, almost casually, then backed away. When Reagen eluded him easily twice more within the space of a minute, Killian needed no further confirmation that he was confronting a different level of expertise than he had ever faced before.

Embarrassed by the ease of Reagen's smooth evasions, Killian abandoned subtle feints and brought his blade across in a sweeping arc that would have surely cleaved his opponent in twain, were it not for the dulled edges—only to find his attack halted abruptly in mid-swing as his steel met Reagen's for the first time, with a clash that rang throughout the courtyard like a Temple bell at sunrise.

Reagen's eyes widened as he felt his arm go numb from the raw power in Killian's swing. Gods, a blow like that would have broken the wrist of a weaker man than himself. He had not encountered strength like that since his company had faced a clan of mountain Ogres in the Broken Hills and had to fight for their lives. Truly, the gods had gifted this one.

Reagen set himself with new respect for the prince, who was circling again, looking for an opening. Good, he thought, watching Killian close in. The lad was persistent, and did not look too ruffled. He seemed to have speed, and certainly enough strength. But he moved awkwardly, for all his quickness. Something was wrong.

The Blademaster gave a little ground and watched the prince step toward him. There! The lad's footwork was overly clumsy for a trained swordsman, and he overshot his mark when he thrust forward, as if his eye and hand were moving at different speeds.

Reagen considered what he had seen, then purposely dropped his guard a little, to see if the lad would take the bait. He did not, but came at Reagen with an overhand swing that would have knocked him senseless, had it connected. Reagen ducked, and drove at Killian's legs. Startled by the speed of his opponent's attack, Killian danced backward swiftly and nearly tripped over his feet. As he stumbled, Reagen thrust his blade forward and tapped the prince lightly on the chest.

"Point!" yelled Doughal, from somewhere off to the side, just as Killian felt the slight touch of what would surely have been a deathblow in real combat.

Seeing the prince's frustration and embarrassment, Reagen lowered his sword and stepped closer. "How long have you been having trouble keeping your feet and finding your mark?" he asked.

Killian felt his face flush from the clumsiness that had been witnessed by all gathered there. "Ever since the…for a few days, I guess," Killian replied, chagrined. "I am supposed to be more agile now, but I seem to be falling all over myself," he muttered, shaking his head with disgust.

Reagen pursed his lips in thought. He had heard Mik'kel's brief account of the Awakening rite, and something of the powers with which the lad had been endowed. Now the pieces fit together in his mind, in a way that was obvious to a seasoned veteran of more battles than this lad had years.

"Look here, my Lord Prince. You may have been gifted with greater agility and strength, but your body has not yet caught up with the changes. You will need to learn anew how to move, until your mind and body can work in unison again."

He walked to Killian's side and struck a pose, with one foot back and sword lifted at the ready. "Now, my Lord. Move along with me, and let your mind learn what your body can do."

Killian stared at the man who had bested him so easily, and knew instinctively that he was fated to place himself in this stranger's hands. He raised his blade and began to follow Reagan's steps in the dance of steel. Out of his line of vision, Doughal gave an appraising nod and began waving the crowd of onlookers back to their duties.

After half a candlemark of stepping through the pattern slowly, Killian had begun to stumble less and move with greater confidence. Reagen noted the change, and called a halt. "Now, face me again, and this time, use your speed as well as your strength." They touched swords lightly, then began to circle each other again. This time, Killian's thrust was more accurate and would have scored a point, had Reagen not deftly turned aside the blade with a flick of his wrist.

"Better, my Lord. But keep your feet closer together and balance on your toes. Like so," he said, demonstrating with a litheness unusual for such a burly warrior.

Killian nodded, determined to give a good account of himself, especially with Doughal looking on. Seeing an opening, he drove forward and thrust with his sword. Steel clanged as both fighters struck each other's blade again and again. Finally, Killian managed to drive Reagen back, and was pressing his advantage, extending his arm for a mighty "killing" thrust when the man in black suddenly twisted his wrist sharply, wrenching Killian's sword from his hand and sending it sailing across the yard.

Reagen waited impassively as the prince muttered a suggestion about an anatomically impossible act that the captain might care to engage in, then looked over at the blade lying on the ground and inclined his head. After a few more references to various body functions, Killian stomped over to retrieve his weapon, then returned to face his opponent. But as he raised his blade again, Reagen held up a hand.

"Do you notice anything about your sword? About the way it feels in your hand?"

Killian frowned. "You mean, besides the fact that I seem to be having trouble holding on to it?" When Reagen did not reply, he sliced the air with a few practice cuts and shrugged his shoulders, then stopped in mid-swing, with a thoughtful expression. "It seems to feel...lighter...than usual."

Reagen nodded his agreement. "And well it may. You are stronger now. Perhaps you need a blade that fits that strength." He turned and walked over to Doughal, having already marked him as a man with the aura of authority and leadership.

"By your leave," he said, gesturing toward the open door of the castle armory where swords, maces, pikes and other weapons of war could be seen stacked and shelved in neat rows. Doughal looked at him closely, curious about what this self-assured Blademaster had in mind, then shrugged his consent.

Killian exchanged puzzled glances with the Armsmaster as the stranger disappeared into the armory. The king, who had been observing all with great interest, kept his own counsel and waited quietly. After several minutes, Reagen returned, bearing a long, double-edged blade some three and a half feet in length. Though age and disuse had dulled its sheen, the quality of workmanship in steel and finely tooled leather hilt could not be mistaken.

"Old Crannog's sword!" Doughal exclaimed. "There has nae been a man to wield that blade with ease since Count Crannog took an arrow in his heart these forty years ago! That was the onliest way they could bring him down, you see, for he would cut a swathe through any who would face him fair. You would have that blade for him?" he asked, meeting Reagen's eyes.

"A good blade, it would appear, Lord Prince, for all its age," said Reagen, hefting the sword and placing the hilt in Killian's right hand. "A bastard sword, or so we called it in the Black...in the company I served. So named because it is somewhat longer than most swords, but still light enough to be wielded with one or both hands. The point is made for thrusting, but the real power lies in the edge. When swung with strength and skill, it will slice or crush a foe, man or beast."

Fascinated by the bastard sword's history, Killian began to raise the huge blade, expecting it to be overly heavy and cumbersome, but found, to his amazement, that he swung it up with ease. He stretched it out before him and felt it balance in his grip as if it had been made for him alone. A sense of rightness filled him, an excitement that needed some expression.

Looking around, he fixed his eyes on a nearby wooden post sunk into the ground, standing six feet high and measuring some four inches thick. He walked over to the post and eyed it carefully for a moment. Then, grabbing the hilt of old Crannog's bastard sword with both hands, he hunched his shoulders and unleashed a mighty swing that struck the post waist high and split the wood cleanly in two with a loud crack.

As the top half of the sundered post crashed to the ground, Killian laughed with pleasure and raised the heavy blade in salute to Reagen. The former captain nodded once, as if accepting the accolade, and replied simply, "A man's blade must suit him." Then he sent his eyes skyward, as if intent on measuring the sun's advance across the sky.

"Of course, yonder post made little effort to duck the blow," he remarked to no one in particular. "Perhaps, now, you might wish to try using the blade against an opponent with a bit more spring in his step." As Killian grinned broadly at the joke at his expense, Reagen raised his shield and closed the gap between them.

Chapter 24

Beneath the Armor

Doughal watched as the stranger in black brought the prince's first lesson to a close and made arrangements to meet again on the morrow. As Killian handed the bastard sword to Cullin, the smith, to be honed and polished, his father spoke briefly to Reagen, gripping the man's shoulder in an unmistakable sign of approval. Shortly thereafter, king and prince walked off together, Killian speaking with great animation and gesturing about him with an imaginary blade while Gavan listened and smiled benignly, in the way of a father taking pleasure in his son's accomplishments.

Reagen was left standing alone, his worn leather saddlebags lying at his feet where a servant had placed them. He bent over to retrieve them, then straightened up and looked around with some misgivings, unsure of his next move. Doughal eyed him thoughtfully, examining again the ugly scar slicing down his cheek, the well-worn clothing and the equally well-used look of the sword on his hip.

He had to admit that he had resented the notion of a foreign swordsman taking his place as the prince's instructor, even if it was the king himself who had asked him allow it. Still, in truth, it was not every day that a lad had a Delgarian Black Guardsman for a private tutor.

He also had to admit that the man had shown a keen eye for sizing up Killian's problems and making the necessary changes, changes that already seemed to be bearing fruit. And the choice of old Crannog's blade to fit the prince's hand bespoke a Blademaster's experience and wisdom. Nae, thought Doughal, the man has earned a fair chance, and I mean to give it to him, reservations or no. With that in mind, he stepped forward and faced Reagen squarely.

"I am Doughal, the Armsmaster. Welcome to Brannock Castle."

The Black Guardsman returned his gaze with a speculative look, as if sizing him up as well. After a moment, he offered an answering nod. "Reagan," he replied gruffly.

Hmm, thought Doughal, seems to be a wee bit of a chill in the air. Still, fair was fair. "You did a fine bit of work with the laddie. I will own that I was a mite disturbed when the king told me your purpose for coming, having had the training of the prince meself for some time now, you see. But, after watching how you worked with him, it seems he will be the better for it."

Reagen offered only a noncommittal grunt in response, but the hard look in his eyes seemed to soften somewhat. He raised his head and scratched the side of his cheek.

"Doughal, you say. Seems I know that name. There was a Doughal who fought for Calderia in the last great battle with Dunmoria some twenty years back. I recall it being said that it was he who had the courage to rally his men and fight through to the old King Nicholas when he was all but overwhelmed by an enemy charge. Are you that Doughal?"

The Armsmaster dropped his eyes, uncomfortable with the unexpected praise. "Aye, I was there all right, though hardly a hero, just a man fighting for his king. You were there, too?"

Reagen shifted the saddlebags on his shoulder and shrugged. "Just a green boy in his first big battle. But the men of the...my company...fought Dunmoria on that day as well, and your name was spoken with respect."

Surprised that the Black Guard held him in high esteem, Doughal felt some stirring of comradeship for another man who had stood against the enemy on that bloody day. Seeing Reagen start to glance around again with that uncertain look as the sun disappeared over the castle ramparts, Doughal came to a decision.

"Hae you a place to stay?" he asked.

Reagen shook his head, and Doughal thought he saw a touch of weariness, though it was hard to read the man's emotions. "No, I came straight to the castle when I arrived. I planned to find a place in the village."

Doughal grunted. "I can do better than that, friend. The prince's Blademaster rates a berth in the castle grounds. There is room aplenty in the barracks."

Something unreadable crossed Reagen's face. "No, I would as leave not live with the other men."

Thinking he grasped the reason for the man's reticence, Doughal scratched his neck. "Well, to be sure, an officer should rate his own room."

"Officer?" said Reagen warily.

Doughal pointed to the outline of the missing badge on Reagen's tunic breast. "Captain, I would judge, from the badge and, well, from other things." His voiced trailed off without further elaboration.

"I do not claim that rank or any other. My association with my former company is long over," Reagen said with an air of finality and a certain sharpness in his tone.

Doughal curbed the impulse to pursue the mystery of that declaration and rubbed his chin instead. He could be just as stubborn as any Black Guardsman, he decided, and it was best that the stranger know how things stood hereabouts.

"Look here, friend. If you are to be the prince's Blademaster, we can nae hardly treat you like a common soldier. Nae, that would look bad. Now, it is as plain as the...nose"—gods, he had nearly said scar—"on your face that you are a man who has commanded others; and besides which, the king himself calls you Captain. So, there it is, and nothing to be done."

Reagen stared at the courtyard gate with the look of a man caught in a trap. Doughal saw that look and wondered, but said only, "I can show you where to bed down, do you be willing."

After some hesitation, Reagen inclined his head in acceptance. Doughal led him across the courtyard and into a small stone building adjoining the common barracks. They entered an anteroom furnished with a scarred table and a few battered chairs, beyond which lay a short corridor with several doors visible. Away from the windows of the front room, the light in the corridor grew dimmer and the air more dank and cool.

Doughal gestured to a door on his left. "This is where I sleep. Two of the other rooms are used for storage, but there is another that you could have." He walked to the last door on the right and pushed it open. "It may need a wee bit of cleaning, but it is yours, do you care to use it."

Reagen entered the small room and glanced around, seeing the narrow bed, wooden table, high-backed chair and washbasin stand, all of which were covered in a thick layer of old dust. Not much, he thought, but better than the alleyways and vermin-infested holes that had been his lodgings for the past two years. Aloud, he said only, "This will do fine, and my appreciation to you."

"Good. You can leave your belongings here. I will show you where to eat," said Doughal, motioning for Reagen to follow him.

He waited as Reagen dropped his saddlebags on the bed, raising a small cloud of dust in the process, then led the way out the anteroom door to another narrow building with a stone foundation and a gabled roof. The windows in the outer walls were open to admit the waning afternoon light, while unlit torches set in sconces along the walls awaited the coming of dusk. The room inside was half-filled with men seated at long tables, wearing the uniforms of infantry, archers and pikemen, and a smattering of King's Elite. Doughal explained that the King's Knights, Royal Lancers and King's Light lived and ate in separate barracks on the other side of the courtyard.

The Armsmaster guided him to an empty table and signaled for the servants to bring the evening meal. Reagen had not eaten since early morning, and his stomach rumbled as he smelled the thick mutton stew served on trenchers of dark, crusty bread.

Plates of sliced apples, white onions and other fruits and vegetables preserved through the winter in root cellars arrived as well, along with flagons of cool ale. Soon, they were busily engaged in tucking away everything set before them, passing the meal in something resembling companionable silence.

"Hey, Doughal, me boy, leave something for the rest of us!" The Armsmaster looked up to see Torrey, a King's Elite lieutenant and an old friend, approaching the table, followed close behind by Wallace, his first sergeant, another longtime comrade. Both men were still wearing breastplate and helm, fresh from guard duty outside the doors of the throne room.

"Aye'" said Wallace, a short, stocky fellow with the neck of an ox and a merry twinkle in his eye, "Such a shame it be when a man must waste away to skin and bone while his companions grow fat on his dinner." The new arrivals doffed their helms and settled in at the table, eyeing the food hungrily.

"Horse turds, Wallace," retorted Doughal with a grin, picking up his dagger and skewering the last heel of bread just inches away from the hand that Wallace had sent creeping in that direction. "And mind you keep your hands to yourself, lest you wind up a few fingers shy."

"You wound me deeply, good sir," said Wallace, clutching his heart and shaking his head sorrowfully, then bursting out in laughter. The others joined in, all except Reagen, who stared down at his trencher and continued to eat.

"Who be your friend, Doughal?" Torrey asked amiably, nodding his head toward the black-clad stranger with the jagged scar.

"Gentlemen, and I use the term loosely, to be sure," Doughal replied, with a wry grin, "this be Captain Reagen, late of the Delgarian Black Guard and newly arrived to instruct the prince in some of the finer points of combat."

Two sets of eyebrows raised in surprise as Doughal finished his introduction and sat back to wait for the inevitable reaction. It was not long in coming from Wallace. "Instructing the prince? Are you truly from the Black Guard?" he asked, in a tone that managed to convey both respect and fascination.

Reagen stared down as he scooped up the remnants of the mutton stew. "I was. I am no longer," he said curtly, and resumed eating with a stony expression.

When it became apparent that the stranger had spoken his piece, Wallace and Torrey exchanged curious glances, then looked at Doughal, who shrugged, as if to say that they knew as much about it as he did.

After more silence, Doughal added, "Captain Reagen here was present at the Battle of Dunmoria some twenty years ago. Seems we fought on the same side, though ne'er did we meet."

Wallace nodded; then, with all the tact of a brown bear rooting around in a honey tree, he pointed to the man in black's cheek. "Is that where you got that?"

Reagen blinked at the mention of his scar, and the hand holding his spoon froze in mid-air. A fleeting expression of old pain was followed by a flash of anger in his eyes that took Wallace aback. "No," he answered tersely, in a husky voice that sounded like feet scraping on gravel.

Doughal, who had grimaced at Wallace's question, rolled his eyes to Torrey, who only shook his head. Reagen laid down his spoon, pushed himself up from the table and walked away.

"He is a strange one, Armsmaster," persisted Wallace, still oblivious to his brush with danger as he watched Reagen depart. "Why did he leave the Guard, and what is he really doing here?"

Doughal sighed. "I know naught, but that he was an officer in the Delgarian Black Guard, and that he is as skilled in weaponry as the legends about them claim. But it should be crystal clear, even to a dolt like you, that he does not wish to share his past, and I would advise that you abide by his wishes. 'Is that where you got that?' indeed," he mimicked with a sneer. "Look, you, I have seen him with a sword in his hand, and I would nae wish to cross blades with him in earnest. Now, close that gaping mouth and pass me them apples."

††††††

Reagen sat on the edge of the narrow, dusty bed, his feet planted apart, elbows resting on his knees with his head down. His neck and shoulders were still tight from the effort it had taken to restrain himself from smashing his fist into that bastard's face. What gave him the right to ask a total stranger about a battle scar? What gave any of them the right to ask him anything about his past? And Doughal, insisting on calling him Captain, when the thought of holding claim to that rank, after what he had done to dishonor it, made him cringe with shame.

The reason that he wore no captain's badge on his chest—not that it was anyone else's business—was because they had ripped it off his uniform, just before they drummed him out of the Guard in disgrace. He had stood outside the palisade gate as they slammed it closed behind him, leaving him alone, with no honor, no home, no friends. And no family.

Gods-be damned, he had spent two years swimming in the bottom of a wine bottle, trying to forget every moment of that dark time. And now these people wanted answers to their questions, answers that would rip the old wounds open again and make him bleed.

He suppressed the urge to get up and pace the room. He felt trapped, ensnared like some mountain cat caught in a cage, though there was neither lock on the door nor any bars on the windows. He was trapped because the gods wanted him here to nursemaid some lad playing at being a prince.

Why? Why him? Because Doritha herself had looked into his eyes and said that she had need of him. And because, maybe, for the first time since his descent into his wine-drenched stupor, he had some purpose for living, some reason to open his eyes of a morn.

"Oh, Hells. You knew it would be like this if you crawled out of the bottle and decided to live," he muttered aloud. "You knew damn well there would be questions and rumors, and people wanting to know why a Black Guardsman would leave his company and his home."

He shook his head in resignation. To be fair, the lad was not to be so easily dismissed. Killian looked to be much more than some callow lad playing at princehood. He had courage and will, and gods-be-damned strength enough to deal a deadly blow with his bastard sword. And the lad meant to do what was right, what was needed, which was all you could ask of any man. There was something else about him, too, something powerful that lurked behind those young eyes, waiting to be unleashed.

Ballor's balls, he needed a drink. Not that watered-down ale, but a cup of strong, dark wine. But that way lay his undoing, the loss of what little control he had taken back over his life, such as it was. And yet...and yet, oh gods, without the bottle, the memories haunted him. He had only to reach up and touch the scar, and it all came flooding back in bands of pain that gripped his chest like a claw ripping through his skin and closing on his heart.

He saw it all again: his lovely, gentle Lindith lying still and cold upon the rocky ground, her face bloodied and torn, holding the shattered body of their precious little girl to her breast...the glint of the sun on the Ogre's axe blade as it sliced into his cheek...then falling...darkness.

Gods, he groaned, as the memories overwhelmed him. All alone in his room, the fierce former Captain of the legendary Black Guard, veteran of a score of bloody battles, and brutal dealer of death to all who came against him, hid his ruined face in his callused hands and wept.

Chapter 25

Visions of Holocaust

She moved through the cool, darkened Forest with the grace and sureness that dwelling among the trees all of her young life had bequeathed to her. She was alone, as had been her intent when she had risen early from her bower bed, dressed herself quietly in tunic, leggings, quarter boots and hardened leather vest, then belted on her sword and climbed down the ladder to the clearing floor before the others in the Tree Palace began to stir. The crescent moon was still faintly visible in the western sky when she raised her hand in wordless greeting to the sentries posted on elevated platforms around the clearing, then slipped noiselessly away into the Woods.

Here among the thick groves of pine and birch and oak, where the sun's light would not penetrate the living barrier of leaves and branches for another candlemark or more, the gloomy shadows falling across the path matched her melancholic mood. Ellianthia walked listlessly along the dimly lit trail, her shoulders slumped and eyes downcast, so lost in angry helplessness that she barely saw the ground upon which she trod.

Had she been in the company of others, as when she led her patrol out on scouting duty, she would have borne herself upright, eyes ahead, striding forward with determination, looking every inch the confident, poised leader that she had honed herself to be—and which she took pains for others to see whenever they were in her presence. But, here, alone, she dropped her guard and allowed her forlorn posture to mirror her inner turmoil.

It was bad enough that her father—*her own father!*—had doomed her to this unspeakably vile marriage, without a care to her own feelings, her own private hopes and yearnings. But then he had to go and proclaim her coming Handfasting to this barbarian in open Council, in front of representatives of the whole Forest community.

Before two days had passed, the matrons of the clan, led by meddlesome Calliandra, had descended upon her. They had come like a swarm of industrious honey bees, abuzz with talk of arrangements to be made, people to be invited, and the "urgency" with which a Handfasting gown must be fitted and sewn, and a whole trousseau begun.

"I know it must be appalling to you, to be betrothed to this...human...my dear," Calliandra had gushed with a great show of sympathy and concern, though Ellianthia thought she detected an undertone of curiosity and fascination in the older female's appraisal of that very prospect. "But arranged marriages are never easy at first. I remember when Jerenellia had been promised to..."

She had broken off the tale with some regret when she saw Ellianthia begin to roll her eyes impatiently, and forced herself to return to the topic at hand. "What I meant to say, my dear," she continued in that syrupy consoling voice, "was that this is not the first marriage between our two races, and some have worked out reasonably well."

Then Calliandra had actually patted Ellianthia's head in a maternal, and slightly proprietary, gesture—she had always suspected that the woman would have gone eagerly to the widowed king's bed if he had but crooked a finger—and adopted a brisk, efficient tone.

"In any event, my dear, your father has given his word, and custom must be observed. No Elfin maid can go to her future husband without a proper Handfasting gown and other clothing...for her bower." The eyes of some of the younger matrons in attendance had positively twinkled at this delicate reference to intimate feminine apparel and the eager bedding it should inspire in a male, when properly displayed.

Ellianthia had taken one look at the bolts of soft, fine cloth held up for her approval—even some satin and sheer lace newly acquired from Calderia in the recently resumed trading—and had summarily banished the lot of them from her presence, going so far as to bar her door against Calliandra, who sputtered into silence and led her clutch of woodhens away, shaking her head dramatically and wondering aloud what she was to tell the king.

Handfasting gown indeed! She was a fighter, and fighters did not wear frilled gowns! Well, truth to tell, some of the other female warriors did. She had seen them at festive community gatherings or at home with lovers or family, sweetly scented with essence of lilac or wildflowers, wearing their flowing dresses and colorful skirts, their necks and wrists adorned with sparkling gems and delicate gold jewelry.

But she had not worn a gown since her brother's death, when she had taken his place in the fighting ranks and vowed to show her grieving father that he had not lost a warrior for an heir. And, on the few occasions when she had taken a lover to her bed, they had not seemed to mind her fighting garb nor the honest smell of earth and steel.

Gods, a trousseau! Sallamarian's testicles! She had already warned her father about what would happen if that murderous lummox tried to put his hands on her. She would let her breasts wither to empty dugs and her loins turn dry and shriveled before she would give *him* a glimpse of her in some lacy bower gown. The last thing she wanted was to wear something designed to incite this animal's crude lusts, thereby forcing her to cut him open on the spot.

No, if she had to go through with this gods-be-damned ceremony, she would do so outfitted in her battle gear, dressed as for combat with an enemy. And he was *still* the enemy in her mind, despite her father's treaty of peace.

Her anger and defiance buoyed her spirits for a moment, as did the deliciously gratifying thought of watching the human prince bleed to death in slow agony at her feet. But the pleasure faded as the dreary inevitability of her fate flowed through her again like a creeping poison, leaving her lethargic and despairing once more.

Ellianthia looked up to find herself arrived at the destination her feet had led her to while her mind had been elsewhere. She stood before a grand old redwood, its lofty height vanishing into the dawn mist above her. Strong and immutable, seemingly untouched by time and age, this sentient tree had been her friend, her sometimes confidant, her comfort in sorrow—her "Mother Tree"— since her real mother's death.

She had come to this ancient Lady of the Forest when she had grown reluctant to talk openly to her father of her grief and loss, for fear that it would only deepen his pain. She had come at other times over the years as well when she was troubled, seeking succor and relief in the Lady's quiet strength.

Now she stepped forward and threw her arms around the broad trunk, pressing her cheek down into the soft, corrugated bark and breathing deep the scent of "her" familiar scent. The tree did not "speak" in words, but she felt the sense of recognition emanating from the woody core, and saw projected into her mind an image of leafy branches curled gently down around her in welcoming embrace.

Hugging tightly with arms spread wide, she dropped her guard and opened her heart to the tree's tender probing, sharing her images of anger, fear and sadness. Speaking in her mind, and sometimes aloud, she talked again of her brother's loss, her father's betrayal by agreeing to this unthinkable peace and sacrificing her in the bargain, and her profound confusion about how she would face this destiny laid before her.

After a time of feeling enfolded and comforted in silent acceptance, Ellianthia began to get another kind of image from the tree. It was a vision of a sapling growing in the earth, pushing its way up through smothering brush and rocky soil, sending out roots in all direction, drinking in the heat and light from the sun and moisture from the rain. In her mind, she saw the young tree bending without breaking in the blustering winter winds, its sap slowing as it waited for the spring thaw to flow warm and freely again, then growing ever taller, ever stronger, until it took its rightful place among the giants of the Forest.

Ellianthia sighed, understanding what her friend was trying to show her: that, like a young tree, she must endure what lay in store for her ahead, must struggle and adapt...and survive. She nodded, though the tree had no eyes to see it, and turned to rest her back against the sturdy trunk for a time, eyes half opened as thoughts rolled over in her mind.

Around her, she heard the sounds of the Forest awaking, its inhabitants stirring and coming to life. White-throated sparrows and purple-feathered martins flitted from tree to tree, diligently gathering food or twigs. A murder of crows flew overhead, cawing and screeching in raucous discord.

Without conscious intent, she Sent her awareness out to the birds and got back sensations of hunger and the never-ending search to satisfy that gnawing emptiness; and images of sharp, blood-spattered beaks tearing into the soft furry underbellies of squirrels and hares that had the misfortune to catch the keen eye of the aerial predators. When she began to taste the hot coppery blood in their gullets, she quickly broke the bond and Sent her mind elsewhere.

Closer by, an old brown bear Sent back fragmented impressions of shiny scales flashing under water and a strong fishy flavor in his mouth, as he crouched over a Forest stream devouring a breakfast of speckled trout. She could sense the bear's pleasure at eating his meal, and the image of crawling back to his den to rest when his stomach was full.

Most Elves were born with some measure of ability to Link their minds with the flora and fauna of the Forest. The elders taught the children that this was their birthright, a reward for serving as Guardians of the Forest and all its inhabitants, and a boon to aid them in doing so. Some of her people were limited to receiving only the vaguest impressions from trees or animals, while others were able to "hear" simple thoughts or "see" fragments of images as they occurred inside an animal's brain.

But a few truly gifted ones, like Ellianthia, could actually communicate by sharing mental images with a tree or "speaking" inside the mind of a deer or bear or other beast of the Forest. With most animals, these Links were limited to very rudimentary thoughts and emotions, like "hungry" or "hurts" or "seeking mate-rut." Some, like wolves and Forest cats, offered more interesting and complicated exchanges, when they chose to communicate at all.

Ellianthia closed her mind to these impressions and touched her forehead to the tree again. She sensed herself beginning to accept that, like the sapling, she would have to endure and somehow survive. But she still didn't understand why this was all happening, why the gods-damned peace was so all-important anyway.

As if in response to her questions, the tree seemed to gather its awareness in a way that deepened the Link between them. Then, suddenly, terrifying images began to thrust their way into her head: the whole Great Forest on fire, trees and brush and grass ablaze in a horrific conflagration; white hot bolts of lightening and torrid streams of red flames sizzling as they roared through the air and struck the helpless trees; Elves bursting into flames and burning like torches as they ran in panic, trying to escape; the Tree Palace charred and smoldering, her father nowhere to be seen.

At first, she thought this to be a foretelling of the destruction that could be visited upon her homeland by the hated humans if the peace was broken and the war resumed, a warning that she must accept her father's decree Yet, when the image widened a bit, she could see that it was not the humans of Calderia unleashing this holocaust. She saw other magic users dressed in purple robes, and groups of strange little brown men clustered together. They were shooting out wave after wave of fiery destruction into her beloved Forest, turning all to flames and burning death as they danced with evil glee.

Then the scope of the vision expanded further. In the distance, she could see a fleet of great, black war ships floating at anchor while they disgorged boatload after boatload of heavily-armed enemy warriors: tall, blond humans carrying battle axes; short, swarthy swordsmen; lanky tribesmen dressed in animal skins and carrying long, deadly spears; hulking brutes wearing black armor and horned helms; strange men with lifeless eyes, clad all in gray; and many others in countless numbers.

Oh gods! she thought, rigid with dread. *That* was the threat that had driven her father to make the peace! Frightened and subdued, it came to her finally that she was fated to play some role that might prevent this devastating future, though her father could tell her little else. And, if the gods were truthful, the human prince had some role to play as well. In that case, she concluded angrily, she supposed that she would have to allow him to live, and even suffer his company, at least until the task was done—that is, unless he thought to take his pleasure with her, and found himself gutted like a fish.

"I understand now," Ellianthia said aloud to the tree, though what she said was true only in the most basic sense. But it was enough for now. It would have to be. She hugged "Mother" once more before pulling back from that precious communion and returning fully to the world around her. As she set her feet upon the path leading back to the palace, the early morning sun had begun to filter through the treetops, driving the gloom away for a time.

Chapter 26

The Bard's Surprise

After rigorous practice under Reagen's expert tutelage, Killian had begun to master his new gods-sent gifts of strength and speed, gifts that were proving to be formidable indeed. In truth, he had improved so much in his skill and prowess with the sword that no warrior under his father's command could best him now.

The strongest veteran knights, wielding their two-handed longswords, were no longer a match for him and his bastard blade. All who came to cross steel with him left the training circle beaten and awed by his astonishing power and agility as a warrior; and soon, word had spread beyond the castle walls of the fierce "Fighting Prince" who could not be defeated.

Even Reagen's own prodigious skills as a Blademaster were increasingly tested as they met for training day after day. The Captain pushed him hard, offering no quarter or respite, ever challenging him to do better. Privately, he marveled at the quickness with which Killian learned the most complicated attacks and killing moves that had earned the legendary Black Guard their renown as the deadliest swordsmen in all of Balleterria. Each practice session found him stronger, faster, more adept as a fighter, until, at last, the inevitable happened— the day when student surpassed mentor, as Killian finally defeated Reagen himself.

It was the first time in his life that the indomitable Delgarian warrior had ever yielded in a contest of arms and lowered his sword in surrender to another man. That he did so with no trace of regret or enmity, but only genuine pride and happiness for the victor, was a measure of the respect and esteem that had grown within him for the young prince whose heart and courage he had come to admire as much as his fighting skills. This was a prince whose cause he would be honored to serve henceforth, should he be granted the opportunity to do so.

For his part, Killian was thrilled to find that he had progressed to the point where Reagen would concede to him in sword combat. Yet, unbeknownst to him, his newfound agility was soon to be put to another kind of test, and in an entirely unexpected manner.

Several days after besting Reagen for the first time, he was at table with the royal family for the noonday meal. He was thoroughly enjoying tearing into a plump joint of steaming roast goose and savoring the hot juices running down his throat.

His father sat to his left, in whispered conversation with his mother. His brother, Aaron, was picking at his own joint of fowl more fastidiously, trying to discern how his mother managed to eat the greasy bird without acquiring the dark stains that seemed to find their way unerringly down onto his olive green tunic, despite his best efforts.

His sister, Rowena, snuck a fat morsel under the table to Sir Riffles, her fluffy brown and white spaniel. It was against the standing orders of the queen, who could hardly avoid being alerted to this surreptitious activity by the constant yipping of the frenetic canine as he attempted to wrest the meat away from the little girl's chubby fingers.

Killian was laughing at the dog's antics and sopping up the last drops of thick goose gravy with a heel of black bread when a royal page liveried in red and black entered from a side door and dropped to one knee beside Gavan's chair. After a quiet exchange, Gavan turned to his eldest son and arched an eyebrow. "It seems you have a visitor, my son. An Elf, if this lad's report is accurate."

"An Elf?" Killian asked with surprise, dropping the soggy heel back onto his plate. Ballor's balls! If this was one more messenger from the gods, with word of another task he must perform, he was going to ride to Father Venetius's abbey and petition the august cleric for leave to swear the vows and take the cowl. Well, all but the vow of chastity, he qualified with a private grin, thinking of his visit to Catty the evening before.

"Well," asked Gavan with some amusement, "Shall we have the visitor in and learn his business with you?"

Before Killian could respond, he heard an excited squeal from the general direction of his sister. "A real Elf! Oh, yes, please, Killy. Have him in," Rowena implored, her eyes dancing with delight and curiosity, even as she tried to look serious and well-behaved enough to receive a visitor. She had never seen an Elf up close, having been too young to meet the few Forest folk that had lived near the castle before the war had driven them away. Intrigued in spite of himself, and easy prey for his sister's earnest pleas, Killian shrugged and threw wide his hands.

"Show him in, by all means," he said, with an exaggerated look of pained resignation that only brought fresh squeals of laughter from the little girl.

The page returned a few minutes later, followed by a handsome, silver-haired Elf of indeterminate years. Tall and slender like most of his people, he was clothed in a shimmering satin blouse of azure blue, with billowing sleeves and open collar, snug black trousers with silver stripes running down each seam, and ankle-high doeskin boots. He wore a black velvet, broad-brimmed hat decorated with an amazing golden plume from some unknown exotic bird. He was armed only with a belt knife and an infectious smile.

When he neared the king and queen, the Elf doffed his hat and swept it down before him as he bowed low from the waist with a flourish that spoke of highborn breeding and courtly manners. At Gavan's bemused gesture, he straightened and tucked the hat under his arm.

"Permit me to introduce myself, Your Majesties. I am Palladarian, formerly of the Elfin Court, a visitor to your country for many years before the...conflict...that forced me to seek out other locales, and now a traveling minstrel."

As Killian stared in confusion, and Rowena's face lit with fascination at the words of this flamboyant stranger, Briana leaned forward to peer more closely at the Elf. After a moment of thought, a smile broke wide across her face.

"Good sir, I know that name and that fair countenance! Are you not the bard that abided in Gille-on-Green, and dazzled all in attendance at the Solstice Fair with your ballads some years ago?"

Palladarian grinned broadly and inclined his head. "The very same, Your Majesty, though your description of my performance is too kind. I am flattered that you would know my name and something of my modest talents."

Briana laughed, then quickly turned and whispered something to the page attending her. As he hastened away on her private errand, the king looked at her with a quizzical expression. She laughed again and touched her husband's arm.

"My Lord, our guest's talents are anything but modest, and he is hardly an itinerant minstrel—or leastways, he was not when last I saw him. You see before you Master Bard Palladarian, a musician and singer of the first rank. I watched him entertain when I traveled to Danilor to attend the birth of my cousin's son, and stopped to see the Fair that year. He enchanted all that heard him sing and play. He was much sought after, though it was rumored that he turned down every offer for a…private audience…from the noble ladies, for love of his own fair wife."

Gavan smiled at his queen in understanding, and gestured to Palladarian to come closer. "Tell us, if you would, good bard, how is it that you happened to leave the Forest and take up residence in Calderia?"

"Of course, my Lord King," the Elf replied in his lilting tenor. "Before the unfortunate war between our peoples—which I am so very happy to see put behind us, I might say—I had the pleasure of visiting your fair land several times. On one such occasion, I met and lost my heart to Catherine, a splendid Calderian lady who later honored me greatly by becoming my wife. Her family obligations made it difficult for her to leave Gille-on-Green for a period, so King Rillandariel graciously gave me leave of absence from his court, with the understanding that I would return with my bride when the time was more propitious."

As the Elf finished speaking, there came a small commotion at the door. The page entered with Kinnith, the king's bard, hurrying closely behind. When he saw Palladarian, he laughed aloud and hastened to cross the room, stopping only to bow briefly toward the royal table before seizing the somewhat startled Elf in a tight hug.

"Palladarian, old friend! It really is you!"

The Elf returned his laugh and his embrace warmly. "Yes, Kinnith. And it has been much too long since we both lifted our voices in song together. You are looking well, old friend."

"As are you, Palladarian," he replied in kind, grinning from ear to ear.

"I take it that you two know each other," observed Gavan dryly, having been all but forgotten for the moment.

Kinnith released his fellow bard from the crushing hug, but kept an arm around the Elf as he explained. "Yes, Your Majesty. I once had the pleasure of traveling to the Tree Palace and hearing Palladarian sing. Afterwards, he was kind enough to grant me audience, and we found that bards have much in common, no matter our race or place of birth. We met again some years ago at the Solstice Fair."

Gavan's interest in the Elf grew, the more he learned of him. "And where have you been keeping yourself, good bard, since last you played the Fair?" the king asked. "Would you choose to reside in Gille-on-Green once more?"

"Alas, no, Your Majesty," the Elf replied in a more serious tone. "When the war began, Catherine and I found ourselves no longer welcome in the homes and environs of those humans who had hitherto been counted as friends. It seems that several men from the surrounding area had been killed or wounded in the early fighting, and it was soon made clear to us that Elves—and those who would wed an Elf—would be better off living among their 'own kind,' as I recall the phrase.

"Unfortunately, after blood was shed on both sides, my 'own kind' had no greater love for my human wife than the Calderians had for me. Eventually, we found a home in a remote village where the war did not reach us, and there we settled in hopes of living in peace."

"And what of your lady wife, good bard?" Kinnith interjected. "Does she travel with you now? I would be most honored if you and she would guest with Jonetha and myself while you tarry here."

Palladarian grew somber, the sparkle disappearing from his eyes altogether. "I fear that will not be possible, old friend, for my dear Catherine passed the veil two years ago. She died giving me a son, a beautiful boy with his mother's gentle eyes and loving soul, who followed her in death three months ago."

"Oh, no!" Kinnith exclaimed, stricken with dismay. "Oh, my friend, I am grievously sorry. And the child as well..." He broke off speaking and shook his head sadly, as his arm tightened around the Elf.

The room grew very quiet for a time. Killian's curiosity about the Elfin bard's visit had been dampened by his obvious sorrow. Aaron wore a look of sympathy, and even Rowena stopped her constant fidgeting and yielded a rare moment of silence.

"I, too, am deeply sorry for your loss, good bard," said Briana softly. "I would have much liked to meet the lady who showed such courage and loyalty."

"Thank you, Your Majesty," he answered touched by the human queen's sincerity. "Would that she were here to meet you as well. I am certain that she would have been the richer for it."

After a brief lull, Briana continued. "We are told that you have come to see our son. I am most curious to know your reasons."

"As am I," said Killian, sitting forward, with an expression displaying equal parts of eagerness and apprehension.

"Why, the Dance, Your Highness!" the Elf replied directly to the prince, his smile returning. "I was traveling back to the Forest when I heard of your coming betrothal to Rillandariel's daughter. With your permission, I have come to offer you instruction in the Handfasting Dance."

"The Handfasting Dance?" repeated Killian blankly, having absolutely no clue as to the meaning of Palladarian's words. Nor was he the only one in the room who waited in ignorance for the forthcoming explanation, though Kinnith seemed less bemused.

"Allow me to explain, Your Highness," Palladarian responded, turning to face the prince squarely and offering another bow. "It is the custom among Elfkind for two people to plight their troth to each other both in word and dance. During the Handfasting feast, after the vows of commitment are spoken, the future husband and wife dance to signify the harmony and unity with which they hope to live their lives together. The Dance of Handfasting is a ritual pattern of steps and turns that all Elfin people learn in their youth, in preparation for the day when they will take the vows themselves."

"But I know nothing of this...Dance, good bard," complained the prince with evident discomfort. "I have heard naught said of it in the meetings held between your people and mine to prepare for the betrothal ceremony. Am I expected to perform this Dance as an Elf would?"

"My Lord Prince, you would not have been likely to hear of it before this," the Elf replied in a reassuring tone. "Being an Elfin custom, and one wholly unknown to humans, it seems most probable that neither the king nor his daughter will be expecting you to lead her in the Dance. Perhaps they intend to omit that part of the ceremony entirely." Palladarian smiled wistfully, remembering a deeply cherished moment.

"And yet, the Dance is a thing of joy and beauty. My Catherine had the good fortune to be instructed in the steps by an Elfin lady friend of mine, and performed it during our Handfasting rite with a grace and passion that stirs my heart even now."

He inclined his head solemnly. "If you will permit me, I would return the gift by imparting the ritual to you, for it may mean as much to your betrothed to share that moment as it meant to us when Catherine Danced with me."

Killian stifled a frustrated groan. Was it not enough that he had to stand up with this Elfin maid and vow to wed her, without having to prance and twirl for her as well? But he withheld a verbal retort out of respect for the venerable bard and the generosity of his offering, and because of the way his mother was smiling through the tears that had welled up in her eyes. Looking around the room, he sighed with resignation. Killian, my lad, he thought, you are as roped and hobbled as one of Glendannon's prize bulls. And, oh, how Col and Gilly would get a laugh out of this one.

†††††

His prediction on this count proved to be depressingly accurate. The very next afternoon found Colum and Gilmore in attendance for his first lesson in the smaller throne room, having insisted that wild Gryphons could not keep them from being on hand to offer their "loyal support." Glower as he might, they sat sipping wine with innocent smiles that threatened to erupt into laughter at any moment, as Palladarian motioned him to the center of the chamber.

At least his brother, Aaron, had had the good grace to be otherwise occupied, and his parents were mercifully absent, this being the time of day for their public audience. Rowena, on the other hand, had scampered in, holding her spaniel tightly in her chubby little hands, and planted herself firmly on the queen's throne, clearly intent on witnessing her older brother's humiliation.

She was now squirming impatiently and clapping for the entertainment to begin, while the dog circled the throne, yapping shrilly and trying mightily to find his way back up to her lap. Kinnith, another traitor to his cause, was perched on a stool in the corner, tuning his lute in preparation for providing what could only be the musical accompaniment.

"Now, Your Highness," said Palladarian, clad elegantly in a white silk shirt and rust-red breeches, "the essence of the Handfasting Dance is harmony and grace. Each partner's movements mirror the other's, although the male generally leads his female partner through the more rigorous twirls and leaps." Killian groaned audibly, while his erstwhile friends smirked behind their wine cups.

"Lacking an Elfin maid at present, I will assume the role of your betrothed. But Forest maids are not dainty damsels, so do not fear to be too forceful with me." He fluttered his eyebrows flirtatiously at Killian, which broke the dam on his friends' laughter, elicited a squeal from Rowena, and even won a grudging smile from Killian.

"We begin by touching fingertips thusly," said the bard, holding his hands up and apart in front of him. He waited expectantly until Killian slowly raised his hands in response. Although decidedly uncomfortable and leery of this whole undertaking, the prince felt naught but good will from Palladarian. Grateful to the Elf for his sincere desire to be of help, he allowed himself to relax and nodded his readiness.

Signaling Kinnith to begin a lively tune, the Elf proceeded. "Good. Now, the first move is a spin, followed by touching hands again. Then another spin and another touch."

He demonstrated these steps lithely, gesturing for the prince to do the same. Killian took a breathe, pirouetted a full turn, touched fingertips, spun again—and promptly tripped over Sir Riffles, who had picked that very moment to dash across the floor and run between his legs. The fall sent Killian crashing into Palladarian, and then all three—prince, bard, and canine—were tumbling to the floor in a knot of tangled limbs and paws.

Colum and Gilmore nearly choked on their wine from laughing so hard, doubling up and slapping the table as the red liquid spilled down the front of their finely-woven blouses. Rowena was holding her hands to her cheeks in surprise and giggling merrily, while Kinnith had taken to studiously inspecting a string on his instrument—though his shoulders were shaking most suspiciously.

Sitting on the floor, Killian cast a baleful glare at all present. Then, having lost any shred of dignity, he grinned ruefully and accepted a hand up from the Elf, who offered the diplomatic observation that "Your spins were really quite good, my Lord Prince. Now, with a little more care for the landings..."

At that point, Colum and Gilmore started spitting up their wine again. Killian glared over at them and shook his head, thinking that lifetime banishment to the Dunmoria border guard in his uncle's barony would be too good for those mirthful bastards, and sorely regretting that his father did not employ a cadre of royal torturers, as had other Calderian monarchs before him.

After a moment, Palladarian cleared his throat and motioned him back into position. "Perhaps it is best if we let that first sequence…sink in…a bit before trying it again. Let us move along to the next pattern." He stood next to Killian and grasped his hand with his own, pointedly ignoring the prince's muttered reference to equine excrement. "Now, in this next sequence, the betrothed stand side by side and take three rapid steps to the right, three to the left, stop, then three forward and three back again…"

Chapter 27

Handfasting

The dawn broke clear and bright on the day of the betrothal ceremony. Soon, the alizarin sun was rising quietly over Kings' Meet, the chosen site of the ceremony, so named for it being the very meadow on the Calderian-Great Forest border where Gavan and Rillandariel had first met to forge the peace. Human and Elfin advisors had agreed to hold the joining ritual on that spot, both because of its neutral location, and because it was now regarded as a place symbolic of good fortune and hope.

Since King's Meet was an overnight trip from Brannock Castle, everyone attending the ceremony had set out the day before and arrived this morning. Bethia, the head cook from the castle, had been up early, busily supervising the unloading of the wagons and carts containing the portable feast that her cooks had prepared in the castle kitchens, toiling under her meticulous and tyrannical eye, baking and roasting, chopping and boiling, then wrapping everything carefully to preserve it for transport.

She grumbled and muttered under her breath about "living like savages in the wild," and having to make do with a field kitchen where she would soon be putting the finishing touches on the more delicate culinary concoctions—the cream-filled pastries, rich custards and flavored gelatins that were too perishable to have endured the overnight journey. Only someone who knew her well would see the small smile of satisfaction beneath the litany of complaints.

Far removed from the kitchens, head seamstresses and their apprentices were bustling busily about the tents and pavilions of the noble-born ladies, making the final adjustments to colorful gowns and frocks fitted and sewn just for the occasion, while the ladies themselves were being powdered and rouged and combed by a small army of dressers and maids. A frazzled chambermaid struggled to button the little princess into her yellow satin gown while she held Sir Riffles in her arms, giggling and trying to tie a red bow around his neck. "He needs to be dressed up too, you know!" she explained to the harried servant who made no effort to conceal her eye roll.

Another, smaller army of man servants and valets were attending their lords, laying out the silken shirts, tunics, finely-tailored breeches, and elegant capes to be worn that day. Prince

Aaron offered dutiful cooperation to his dressers while he privately wondered if the rumors he had heard about what happened on the betrothal night were true—and why anyone would want to do *that* with a girl.

Meanwhile, the hero of the day's drama, Prince Killian, was enjoying a last moment of freedom in his tent, attended by his loyal companions, Colum and Gilmore. Killian had been up since dawn, too filled with apprehension and excitement to lie abed any longer.

Now, already dressed in his new red silk tunic with the fine gold braid at collar and cuff, black velvet breeches and dress boots, he paced the chamber restively. More than once, he wondered aloud whether the gods really meant him to go through with this Handfasting after all.

Aware with his prince's apprehension, Gilmore responded with his customary sensitivity by asking whether he could "inherit" Catty permanently, now that Killian would be betrothed and presumably otherwise occupied. Laughing, Gilmore ducked behind a nearby chair to avoid the heavy pillow that Killian launched in his general direction, while Colum posed a question of his own.

"Tell us, fuzz-face, do you know what this Elfin maid looks like?"

Killian paused in the midst of winging another pillow at the smirking Gilmore and shook his head. "My father told me that I saw her at Kings' Meet, standing beside Rillandariel on the day of the peace, but I have no recall of any Elfin maid there. I saw only warriors. And when I asked Palladarian, he gave me one of those mysterious smiles of his and said that she was 'tall and strong, with golden hair and a comely face.' Then he repeated that phrase about Elfin maids not being 'dainty damsels' and left it at that, with an odd look in his eye."

Col and Gilly looked at each other, then broke out in howls of laughter. "Tall and strong?" repeated Gilly. "Like our sweet, delicate Enid?"

Gilly puffed out his cheeks and squared his shoulders, then stomped heavily around the room, while Col clasped his hands together over his heart and squeaked in a high-pitched voice, "Oh, my Prince, we meet at last."

Killian groaned audibly at the thought of Enid, the broad-shouldered hostler's daughter who stood six feet tall, weighed at least fifteen stone and could lift the south end of a plow horse unassisted. To his discomfort, she seemed to have taken a fancy to the prince, managing to appear outside the village stable to smile and wave whenever he rode by.

Deciding that the only way to shut these clowns up was to ignore them completely, Killian walked away from the chortling pair and stepped over to the tent door. The truth was that he had not expended any great effort to learn more about the Elfin maid, other than that her name was Ellianthia—a melodious name, he allowed—and that she was much loved and respected by the Elfin advisors who had attended planning sessions for the betrothal ceremony.

Yet, when King Gavan had asked if the prince and the maid might arrange a brief meeting on some date before the ceremony "to get acquainted," the advisors had huddled in whispered debate, then emerged with somewhat strained expressions to say only that "The princess would prefer to wait, my Lord King."

That did not bode well, thought Killian, as he leaned his head out and stared out at some hills in the distance, now dotted with clusters of yellow daisies and wild roses. Still, it mattered not if the maid was comely or plain, slim or broad. This was only a betrothal, not a wedding, and what would occur between the former and the latter remained to be seen. It mattered only that this Forest maid held some importance to his task, his gods-sent task, and that the first step on that journey would be taken this very day. Still, he wondered if...

His thoughts were cut short by the clear, clean tone of the horn signaling that it was time to begin gathering for the ceremony. Killian glanced again at his friends as they prepared to go, wondering what the day held for them all.

††††††

Killian's family emerged from their spacious tents, one of two housing the royal families that had been arranged on opposite sides of the meadow. They were accompanied by court advisors, council members and other personages of high position—Mik`kel, Aisleen, Doughal, Brurik, Kinnith and Palladarian among them.

The rest of their entourage of courtiers, nobles and landed gentry trailed behind them, the ladies in their beautiful gowns, the lords in their finery. Military units commanded by General Brurik, including King's Knights, King's Light, Royal Lancers, archers and foot soldiers—all attired in ceremonial dress uniforms—were represented as well, although care had been taken to avoid the appearance of a large combat force descending upon the site.

As they walked across the meadow, Killian gazed out over what seemed to be acres of gaily-colored tents and awnings set up around the field, awash in splashes of deep crimson, bright orange, saffron, azure blue, emerald green and the like. Many of the tents were festooned with multi-hued ribbons and garlands, some flying pennants and flags that fluttered in the wind.

A huge, open-walled pavilion had been erected in the center of the field where the ceremony was to take place. It had been positioned there to offer some relief from the heat and the glare of the sun, allowing those standing beneath it to enjoy any cooling breeze that might happen by.

All around them, they could hear the sounds of lutes and harps and zithers being plucked and strummed, and the high, sweet notes of flutes and pipes swirling through the air, as musicians and minstrels of both races wandered through the crowd in bright, flamboyant costumes, strumming lively tunes and lifting their voices in celebration of the betrothal, the Peace, and the beauty of the day.

Jugglers and dancers and small acting troupes offered performances on temporary stages. Along the fringes of the meadow, merchants hawked trinkets and ribbons, minor charms and potions, and all manner of Betrothal Day souvenirs. And everywhere the atmosphere was as festive as a Solstice Fair.

Arriving outside the pavilion, King Gavan, Queen Briana and the other royal offspring were led away to their places of honor, leaving Killian alone with Colum and Gilmore. Palladarian beckoned Killian aside to wish him luck, then excused himself to pay his respects to King Rillandariel and take his place among the members of the Elfin contingent in attendance.

When the signal came, Killian stepped forward with his friends and found his path lined with two columns of King's Elite. The warriors stood at rigid attention with blades drawn and crossed to form an arch of swords as a show of respect and honor for their young prince. He knew many of them personally, and he felt their affection for him in their warm smiles and whispered wishes for good fortune as he passed by.

As he made his way up the center aisle, a hush settled over the gathered guests— Calderians seated on the left side and Elves on the right. For reasons of security, no man or Elf except the royal honor guards of each kingdom bore any weapons to the betrothal ceremony.

Killian marveled to see both races in such proximity to each other without open displays of belligerence or threat, though he doubted not that some of the two peoples present this day still harbored deeply rooted anger and hatred. He felt the same way, though some of his darker emotions had been tempered in the time since the Peace began.

He cast his eyes over the Elves gathered here, this tall, fair, slender people, with their long, flowing hair of gold or silver, clad in gowns or tunics of light pastels or rich Forest hues—in truth, an elegant and beautiful race, though a sworn and deadly enemy a short time ago. His visit with the gods, and the pleasant moments spent with Palladarian, had helped to soften his heart and dampen his anger toward them in some measure.

Yet, his memories of Orrin and all the others sent beyond the veil at their hands still stood as a formidable, and perhaps insurmountable, barrier to any true trust or faith, or any real desire to know them better. No, it was enough that he had come here to do his duty by his people and the gods, to join hands and swear a future union with this unseen and unknown Forest maid. Expecting anything more of him at this time would be asking too much.

He reached the center of the pavilion and stopped. Colum and Gilmore stepped away to stand with his family to the left of the low stage where Father Venutius and Mellisandria, the Elfin Wise One, waited to perform the ceremony. By mutual agreement, it had been decided that both of these august individuals would preside over the betrothal rites together, each in keeping with the custom of their own people.

Killian inclined his head in respect to them in turn— Venutius, large and round and jovial by nature, clothed in the voluminous gold and white robes of his office; and Mellisandria, her long, silvered hair falling down over her purple satin gown, slender and aged, but with a look of clarity and strength in her eyes that belied her fragile appearance. They bowed to the prince in return, then Mellisandria made a small gesture with her hand, and Killian saw Palladarian step forward and begin to strum the chords of a melodic Elfin tune.

There was a stirring at the back of the pavilion. A moment later, King Rillandariel appeared, tall and regal in flowing emerald cape and silver crown. All eyes turned toward the Elfin monarch, who, by tradition, would be escorting his daughter to her Handfasting. Despite his reluctance to do this thing, Killian felt a twinge of curiosity emerge. At last, he would lay eyes on this Forest princess chosen for him by the gods.

He peered forward, looking for the sweep of a gown or a flash of long, yellow hair, but saw nothing, save for the King and a tall warrior with short, golden curls, dressed in Elfin fighting clothes. From that distance, he thought he recognized that warrior as the same one who had tried to dissuade Rillandariel from going out to meet his father on the day when peace was made.

To his surprise, the king and the warrior started up the aisle, walking arm in arm. Rillandariel seemed to be whispering something to the warrior, who shook his head slightly and stared straight ahead. As they drew closer, Killian's eyes widened and his mouth nearly dropped open in astonishment. This warrior was a woman! By the gods, could this be Ellianthia walking on her father's arm?

From a distance, she looked every inch the Elfin fighter. She wore a dark brown, hardened leather vest over a long-sleeved white blouse, snug dark green leggings, and calf-high doeskin boots, with an empty scabbard and dagger sheath belted at her waist.

But up close, hers was the face of a woman, a beautiful woman, Elfin or no, with large hazel eyes, high cheekbones, tawny skin and full lips, all of it framed by hair the color of golden wheat just before harvest time. And though the leather vest concealed most of her chest, the deep cleavage visible where it laced across her open-necked blouse, and the curves outlined by her tight leggings, marked her as unmistakably female.

Morainen's tits! Was he supposed to swear betrothal to this woman or cross steel with her? If she was a warrior, then she was a killer of his people as well. Killian tore his eyes away from her and glanced at his father, expecting to see shock to match his own. Instead, King Gavan only raised his eyebrows and shrugged imperceptibly, as if to say, "Make the best of it."

He had known, gods-damn him! His father had known all along, but had "neglected" to mention this minor little detail! Even his mother, the soul of feminine decorum and propriety, did not appear surprised or disapproving, but seemed only to be appraising the warrior maid with curiosity. It was clear that she had known too, and had said nothing. Damn, was he the only one in the kingdom who had been kept completely in the dark?

While Killian was still gaping, Rillandariel delivered his charge to the front of the stage; then, keeping his hand on his daughter's arm, he turned his steely gaze directly upon the prince. Killian felt somewhat unnerved by the Elfin king's piercing stare, which seemed to be probing him, gauging his mettle then and there. But the Calderian prince had grown up under the watchful, and sometimes wrathful, eye of another powerful monarch, and he had learned to stand his ground with any man.

So, he bowed his head to show respect, then returned the Forest king's gaze with one of outward calm, though his emotions churned in his gut. Rillandariel must have been satisfied with what he saw, for he whispered some parting word to the maid, relinquished his hold on her arm and stepped away to the right.

Then Killian turned his eyes back upon the Elfin princess herself. So stiffly did she stand there, staring straight ahead, that he wondered if she intended to go through the entire ceremony without once looking in his direction. As if feeling his gaze upon her, she turned and let her hazel eyes flicker up at him for an instant, before turning away again. In that fleeting moment, Killian saw a look of unveiled hatred and disdain so intense that he felt the impulse to draw back and reach for his sword, had he been wearing one.

Indeed, so great was the anger smoldering inside her that he might have been looking into his own heart. It suddenly came to him that he had not given any thought to how *she* might be feeling about this betrothal. It was obvious that she was as reluctant to go through with the ritual as he, although "reluctant" might be a slight understatement. More like ready to drive a blade through his heart.

Then a strange and unexpected thing occurred. In the midst of feeling his own anger, he was surprised to find himself slightly amused as well. He could imagine how her father must have put the thumbscrews to her to get her to show up beside him this day, much the same way his own father had done with him.

The idea of her being as unhappy about Handfasting with an enemy—for she saw him as her blood enemy, of that there was no doubt—gave him a perverse sort of pleasure; and, in a twisted sort of way, also made him feel a little less hostile toward her, another victim of the gods' whim.

For her part, Ellianthia was entertaining an odd mixture of seething anger and grim satisfaction. She had seen the look of surprise in those striking blue eyes when he realized who she was. No doubt this prince had been expecting some soft, simpering maid like the human women he was used to, all dressed up in a pretty gown with a garland of flowers in her hair, blushing and stammering.

Such women were totally useless for anything, save mayhap for spreading their legs to make more human babies to infest the land, which they seemed to do with disgusting ease and regularity. But she was not useless or helpless. She felt the reassuring presence of the slim dagger concealed in her boot, in direct violation of the ban on weapons. She would be prepared for anything from this bastard.

Standing next to him in the flesh, she saw that he was as tall as her father, but broader and heavier. She supposed he was handsome enough for a human, in a brutish sort of way, with those penetrating icy blue eyes, aquiline nose and strong chin. The thick, fiery-red hair curling down his neck was unlike anything seen among the males of her people. His snug crimson tunic and tight black breeches were obviously cut to display the breadth of shoulder and muscular thighs that human females would likely find attractive, having never known a slender, graceful Elfin lover.

Her keen nose detected the scent of horses and leather and steel, and a faint odor of musk. They were honest enough smells, and not entirely unlike Elfin males, for that matter. But the comparison ended there. He was undoubtedly arrogant, probably clumsy and slow, and most likely given to drink. Still, he had a certain presence about him, and she sensed an aura of power that she could not identify, but found vaguely disturbing.

Any further thoughts about the man were interrupted as Palladarian's song came to an end, and an expectant silence fell upon the crowd. Then Father Venutius stepped forward and bowed to the royal families on both sides of the stage.

"Your Majesties, Lords and Ladies of the kingdoms of Calderia and the Great Forest, and all others in attendance this day. We have gathered here to witness a wondrous and historic event, the betrothal of the scions of two great Royal Houses. Before us stand Prince Killian of Calderia and Princess

Ellianthia of the Great Forest, who have come to plight their troth to each other in the presence of all.

"Let us pray the gods that the step they take this day, and the marriage that is to follow in the fullness of time, will place them on the path to mutual happiness and joy. And let us also pray that this betrothal will be a symbol of the joining of our two peoples, and will serve as a source of strength and unity in the days that lie ahead."

Then, as murmurs of approval were heard throughout the pavilion, Father Venutius unrolled a vellum scroll and directed his gaze to Killian and Ellianthia. "From the Book of Morainen," he began:

"And the gods created male and female, each with his or her own strengths, each with his or her own needs. Neither is whole, neither is complete, without the other, nor was it intended that they should be, for it is their fate that each must seek the other to be fulfilled. And the gods said that this is good, for it is in the seeking, the yearning for wholeness, that both discover the beauty of sharing and the joy of living, a joy that they would never know, were they solitary and isolated creatures, complete unto themselves, needing nothing, seeking nothing. Heart calls to heart, passion to passion, need to need. From that need grows the desire to please and to be pleased, to care and be cared for. And from that desire and caring grows love, deep and abiding, which is the greatest of all the gifts granted by the gods."

Laying the scroll aside, Venutius gestured for a page standing nearby to come forward. The small lad bore a red velvet pillow upon which rested two golden bracelets of Dwarven design, one slim and delicate, one thicker and wider, each exquisitely bejeweled with finely cut emeralds and diamonds set into the gold band. Venutius took the pillow and held it out before him.

"It is the custom of our people for the betrothed couple to place a bracelet on each other's wrist, as a symbol that their love for each other has no end, and as a visible sign to all who know them that they have pledged their hearts to one another." Looking at Killian, he nodded and said, "Your Highness, if you would seal this union, place the bracelet on the wrist of your betrothed and say, 'With this token, I pledge myself to you.'"

"Yes, Father," Killian replied, fighting back the uneasiness that threatened to make his hand tremble. He carefully took the slimmer bracelet in his fingers and turned to

Ellianthia, then waited for her to lift her wrist…and waited. Venutius waited. Their Majesties waited. The guests gathered there waited. And, after a space of some twenty heartbeats, he was still waiting. For her part, Ellianthia remained rigid and silent, her eyes locked on a spot beyond the stage, showing no inclination whatsoever to raise her hand and accept the token.

Then, just as the Elfin Wise One, Mellisandria, began to glare at Ellianthia and opened her mouth to speak, the Forest princess lifted her arm and presented her wrist in Killian's direction, still looking forward. Slowly, he slipped the bracelet over her outstretched hand, saying, "With this token, I pledge myself to you." When his fingers brushed against her skin momentarily, she flinched, but said nothing.

With an audible sigh of relief, Venutius turned his gaze to the princess. "Your Highness, if you would seal this union, place the bracelet on the wrist of your betrothed and say, 'With this token, I pledge myself to you.'"

Ellianthia gritted her teeth, still feeling the small shock of his fingers on her skin. His touch had been lighter and gentler than she had expected, but still she had only just resisted the impulse to jerk her hand away. She looked down at the slender band encircling her wrist. It was delicate and light and finely wrought, the gems reflecting the light like tiny flames burning within them. Beautiful enough, if one liked that sort of thing, she thought. No doubt human females would gush over a pretty trinket like this.

But Elves did not brand each other as property, even with golden shackles such as these bracelets. To her, it weighed as heavily upon her as if she were yoked to a stone, and she could not wait to be alone so she could strip it off and cast it away.

Mellisandria cleared her throat and looked at her through half-shut eyes with a wordless warning. Bowing to the inevitable, Ellianthia pursed her lips as though tasting something sour, reached for the wider bracelet and raised it to the prince's waiting hand. Gripping the circlet gingerly with her fingertips, she slipped it over his wrist, noting his long, powerful fingers and the fine red hair on the back of his hand as she did so.

"With this token, I pledge myself to you," she repeated, in a low voice that was almost a whisper. Quickly dropping her hand to her side, she resumed her preoccupation with the spot behind the Wise One's head.

Then it was Mellisandria's turn to speak. With an air of serenity, the ancient Elf stepped forward and bowed to the royalty, then to the audience before her.

"I, too, welcome Your Majesties and all those gathered here this day to celebrate the Handfasting of King Rillandariel's daughter and King Gavan's son. We of the Forest Kingdom wish to join with our Calderian neighbors to the north in wishing Prince Killian and Princess Ellianthia a happy and fruitful union. It is our hope that our two peoples will see in them a living example of the peace and harmony in which all of the creatures of the earth may dwell. And, as Guardians of the Forest, it is also our hope that our peoples will unite in preserving that harmony."

At Mellisandria's mention of preserving harmony, Ellianthia recalled the horrifying image shared by her Mother Tree of foreign invaders devastating her people and her beloved Forest. It was this image, seared into her mind and heart, that helped steel Ellianthia herself for the next part of the ceremony, as the aged Wise One reached down and clasped hands with them.

"This is the Elfin way of Handfasting, hand to hand, heart to heart." She brought their palms together, cupping her hands over theirs to seal the contract. Then the prince and princess, divided by a chasm of hate but united by the needs of their peoples, were joined flesh to flesh, as the Wise One spoke the Elfin Handfasting ritual:

Be as two roses on the same vine, reaching for sunlight, stems entwined;

Be as two eagles, learning to fly, wing touching wing, riding the sky;

Be as two streams that flow into one, becoming one river, mighty and strong;

Be as two embers bursting to flame, burning together, one in the same;

Be as two stars shining bright in the night, dispelling the darkness, sharing your light;

Nurture in illness, comfort in pain, shelter each other through thunder and rain;

Life is your journey, travel its ways, rejoice in each other for all of your days.

As the ancient ritual was intoned, Killian heard a sound that sent a shiver down his spine: the sound of scores of Elfin voices whispering in unison, solemnly reciting each word along with Mellisandria, many with tears in their eyes. Then he saw Ellianthia's lips moving as well, as her free hand darted up to her face and away again quickly. He could see that the warrior maid was struggling not to weep as well.

Their eyes met momentarily, his filled with uncertainty, hers with tears. Was that sadness he saw? Knowing he was privy to something not meant for him to see, he quickly averted his gaze.

Though shamed by letting the human see her cry, Ellianthia could not stop a tear from trickling down her cheek— shed, in part, for the beauty of the sacred ritual that every Elf knew by heart; and, in part, from the sadness of remembering how often she had stood and watched her friends share this rite, whispering those same words and dreaming that someday it would be her turn to hear them being said for her and the one she loved.

But that was not to be, not for her...not with *him*. She looked up at Killian again, half expecting to see him laughing at her tears, gloating over her weakness. But he was looking down and away, almost as if he were embarrassed.

Angry and confused, she felt immense relief when Mellisandria removed her hands and pronounced the Handfasting complete. Then she and Killian were separated as the crowd of humans and Elves began to cheer and throng toward them to wish them well. Her eyes still welling, she found herself in her father's arms, sheltered for the moment by his strength, hearing him whisper, "I love you, daughter." And, for that moment, it was almost enough.

Feeling rather dazed himself, Killian embraced his parents as well. The queen was crying, while the king gripped him in a tight hug and slapped his back. Aaron and Rowena were off to one side, looking a little lost among so many tall people. Colum and Gilmore had fought their way to him, and seemed to be shielding him from the worst of the press. Later on, he would tell his parents just what he thought of their little "surprise"; but for now, all he wanted was a very large goblet of some very strong wine.

As if reading his thoughts, King Rillandariel raised his voice and invited all present to share in the Handfasting feast. Then he led the betrothed couple and his royal guests to a long table reserved for them behind the stage, where Killian and Ellianthia were seated in the center, with her father to her left and his family to his right. Elfin music began to fill the air as large serving tables were brought forth and set up along the edges of the pavilion, then quickly laden with every kind of fare imaginable.

The kitchens of Brannock Castle and the surrounding countryside had yielded up great platters heaped with slices of tender spring lamb and honeyed hams, and sizzling haunches of roasted beef fresh from turning on the spit. There were plates of roast duck and goose, stuffed quail in wine sauce, grilled sea bass and eels, and shellfish resting on beds of steamed pilaf.

There were bowls of new potatoes swimming in butter and herbs; young cucumbers pickled in seasoned brine; boiled plover eggs in red vinegar; rounds of soft white cheese; oatmeal bannocks, yeasty breads and cakes of all descriptions; great barrels of beer and ale; and bottles of aged wine from the castle cellars to suit the most particular palette.

From the hearths, ovens and smokehouses of the Forest kingdom came an equally tempting array of Elfin favorites: trays of roasted venison, turkey and smoked wild boar; squirrel pie and rabbit stew; slow-cooked pheasant and spitted woodhens; and fresh-water speckled trout and smoked salmon from Forest streams.

Accompanying the meat and fish were cracked grain breads made from wild oats and wheat harvested near the southern expanses of the Forest; dandelion greens, leeks and tender shoots of bittersweet kalic; several varieties of mushrooms prepared in delicate sauces; plates of honeyed nuts; bowls of blueberries and raspberries sprinkled with brown sugar; tangleberry pies; and sliced apples cooked in wine and cinnamon.

These delicacies were accompanied by casks of dark, strong Elfin ale, hard ciders made from apples and pears, and fruity wines that tasted light and sweet, yet took the legs out from under anyone unfamiliar with their potency.

An unending stream of servants supplied those seated at the royal table with trays and platters of these delicacies, allowing them to sample each offering at their leisure. Killian found some of the Elfin dishes quite tasty, especially the smoked wild boar, trout and cinnamon apples. Two large flagons of the Elfin ale had soon warmed his insides, and almost had him forgetting why he was there and who was sitting beside him.

Ellianthia ate little of the Elfin food, and none of the Calderian dishes, seemingly content with sipping from a cup of berry wine and speaking in low tones with her father. She answered Killian's few abortive attempts at making conversation, obligatory as they were, with stony silence and looks of disdain or one word answers that offered no encouragement for further discourse at all.

Chapter 28

Dancing with the Enemy

The early afternoon passed thusly, as all feasted and drank their fill. Though many humans and Elves kept to their own kind, a number of brave souls of both races crossed the invisible line dividing them and found some matters of mutual interest to share. At some point, even the two kings stepped away from the table and bent their heads in private conversation.

When Killian heard them laughing together, he thought that passing strange, considering everything. He was wondering what they found so humorous when he heard an instrument being strummed with a distinctive flourish and looked up to see Palladarian approaching, resplendent as always, carrying his lute.

The Elfin master bard stopped in front of the table and bowed to each king in his graceful manner, then looked at Ellianthia with a broad grin and a twinkle in his eye. "Hello, my dear. You have grown even more beautiful since last I saw you."

At that, the first smile that Killian had seen all day from Ellianthia came to her lips, lighting up her face like sun breaking through the clouds on an overcast afternoon. "Uncle Palladarian," she laughed, and leaned across the table to embrace him. "I was so surprised to see you earlier. Surprised and happy. It has been too long."

"Uncle Palladarian?" Killian wondered if he had heard that correctly. "She is your niece?" he asked, shaking his head and glaring at the Elf, who nodded, grinning over Ellianthia's shoulder with the sly look of a cat caught in the creamery. Killian was not amused. All that time spent together, and nary a word about being related to his betrothed. Another "little detail" someone had neglected to tell him.

Needless to say, Killian was not in the mood for pleasant civilities when the Elfin bard released the maid, bowed in his direction and said, "My Lord Prince, I congratulate you on your betrothal. Forgive me for not being entirely…candid…with you earlier about my niece."

Then it was Ellianthia's turn to look askance at Palladarian. "Earlier? You *know* this man, Uncle?" she asked, turning to stare at Killian directly for the first time.

"I have had that honor, yes, my dear," he replied calmly, but with a sly expression. "A fine young man, from all that I have seen."

"Uncle!" she cried, not believing that her own mother's brother was admitting to being on friendly terms with this man, even speaking of him with approval. "And just when did this happen?" she turned and demanded of the prince, her hazel eyes flaring.

Killian frowned and spread his hands wide in confusion. "Just recently. But he never told me that you..."

"Ohh!" she exclaimed furiously, interrupting him and turning back to Palladarian, bent on skewering the truth out of him, if need be. But the Elfin bard chose that moment to wink at her, then turned to the crowd. He strummed his lute loudly in a way that got their attention, and effectively silenced the scathing remarks about to burst forth from her lips.

"Your Majesties, Lords and Ladies of Calderia and the Great Forest," he began. "It is our Elfin custom for a Handfasted couple to celebrate their joining with a Dance that symbolizes the harmony and unity they hope to share together. Have your appetites been sufficiently sated for the moment, we invite you to attend them."

At his signal, a group of Elfin musicians bearing lutes, tambour drums, pipes and timbrels emerged from the crowd and formed a ring around the stage. The Calderian guests watched with curiosity, while the Elves in the audience exchanged looks of surprise, for none of them had expected the human prince to even be aware of, much less perform, this thoroughly Elfin ritual. But no one was more surprised than Ellianthia, who stared at the musicians in astonishment, then stomped over to Palladarian, her right hand thrust down on her hip as if reaching for her absent blade, a dangerous look in her eyes.

"What is the meaning of this, Uncle?" she rasped, spitting out the words. "You expect me to Dance with him? What would this clumsy ox even know about *our* Dance of Handfasting?"

"Be at peace, Ellie," he replied softly, using the nickname he had called her as a child. "Your prince may surprise you," he added, with that same infuriating twinkle in his eye.

"He is not *my* prince!" she protested, but Palladarian had already turned to the musicians and nodded his head. With that, the piper's high, clear notes skirled in the air, rapidly joined by the drummer, whose rhythmic beating soon started feet tapping throughout the pavilion. Then the lute and timbrel melded with pipe and drum in the traditional Handfasting tune that had all the Elves smiling and clapping their hands.

Every Elf save one, that is. She growled in frustration and turned back to the prince, who looked only half as nervous as he felt, which was still a great deal calmer than she expected for someone who was about to make a total fool of himself—and her as well, in the bargain.

"Might as well get it over with, my Lady," he said with a tentative grin, rising from his seat and holding out his hand to her, polite as you please.

Hemmed in by the crowd from making any dignified escape, she set her jaw and nodded grimly. All right! If this idiot wanted to fall flat on his arrogant royal arse, she just might oblige him. Might be the best thing that had happened to her the whole gods-be-damned day. With that cheerful thought buoying her spirits a bit, she followed him up to the stage, amid cheers from the audience.

Just as she was about to face him, Palladarian slipped to her side and nodded pointedly to her breastplate. "The vest, Ellie," he whispered. "Do you plan to be the first Elfin maid to Dance in armor?"

Ellianthia looked down at the hardened leather breastplate and snorted. It mattered little whether she wore the vest or not, for this travesty would be over before it began. Still, *she* had no intention of looking the fool any more than she had to, and the armor was restricting, after all. With a shrug, she quickly unlaced the vest and let it fall to the ground at her feet, where willing hands whisked it off the stage floor.

Killian blinked as he got his first look at her full bosom and dark, prominent nipples clearly outlined against the thin white blouse that had been dampened with perspiration beneath the hot leather. Warrior or no, it was plain to see that this Elf was very definitely female.

As he gazed at her from the corner of his eye, trying not to appear too obvious, he felt his body begin to respond without his conscious will. Then he remembered where they were—and who she was—and his growing ardor cooled as quickly as it had arisen.

Focusing instead on running the steps of the Dance over and over in his mind, Killian struck the beginning pose, facing the maid with hands in the air. Looking surprised that he would know the opening position, she touched his hands briefly, and then whirled into the first turn, expecting to leave him standing there flat-footed.

Yet, he spun around as well and met her with his hands up to touch her fingertips briefly, then began to twirl again. She was so taken aback that she almost missed the turn herself, and only barely managed to tap his fingertips with hers the second time around before he was grasping her hand firmly and moving smoothly into the next pattern—three steps to the right, thrice again to the left, then forward, then backward.

Gods, she thought, where had he learned to do *that*? And whatever had made her think he would be clumsy? He moved with a grace and speed that she had never expected to see in any human, much less someone so broad and tall. Then she had no more time to think as he circled her waist with his arm, lifted her effortlessly and threw her into the air, twirling her body just enough to turn twice and land on her feet again facing him. So strong, she thought, somewhat breathless.

Recovering from her surprise, she felt her anger rising again. So! This arrogant human thought he knew their age-old Elfin Dance. Well, she would just see about that! Let him try to keep up with her, then, if he could. Calling on her years of practice, she let herself flow with the music, turning and stepping and spinning deftly through the pattern, prepared to Dance rings around this ignorant prince—only to find him always there where he should be, mirroring her steps perfectly, Dancing as if he had been Forest born.

Still stubbornly refusing to admit his amazing skill, and determined to best him at almost any cost, she purposely threw herself against him a little harder than necessary, waiting for him to stagger back and miss a step. But he caught her against him with strong, supple hands and then spun her away again so smoothly that it might have been planned that way. Gods-be-damned, where had he *learned* this?

Then the music and the clapping and the steps learned by heart seemed to take over, calling to her with the joy of the Dance itself. For a few minutes, she forgot about trying to best him, losing herself in the sheer thrill and pleasure of the rapid turns and intricate twirls, Dancing as the drum quickened and the lute strummed faster, driving them toward completion. She no longer wondered when he was going to drop her, for she was too busy just doing her own part as he flowed fluidly through his steps.

In truth, she hardly knew if her feet actually touched the ground before she was leaping or being lifted away again. He was not her lover, not even her friend. But, for an instant, it mattered not who they were, just two people sharing the Dance, and, for that brief time, it was glorious.

Then the Dance came to an end at last, the final pattern concluding when he lifted her by the waist and threw her straight up into the air. As she came down, his hands slid along her hips and up her waist to catch her. She came to rest in his arms, panting and flushed with a blend of exertion and excitement. She took a deep breath to calm herself, and only then became aware that the palm of his right hand had slid too far up her body and was pressed directly against one full, rounded breast.

He seemed to notice at the same instant, for he quickly moved his hand away and took a step back. "Your pardon, my Lady. I did not intend..."

Her head cleared and it all came back to her, the Handfasting to this disgusting, perverse human, his golden shackle on her wrist, and the unknown future beyond her control. "I am not your Lady!" she snapped, "and keep your hands to yourself unless you care to lose them!"

His eyes narrowed as she snarled the words at him. "*I said it was not intended!*" he growled, feeling both embarrassed at his mistake and incensed that she chose to think he had touched her there purposely. He had done her gods-be-damned Dance, done it to near perfection, save for one small slip. He had actually felt some measure of pride and pleasure, forgetting for a time whom his partner was.

But he would not forget again, he swore. Of that she could be sure, as he turned away in anger. And thus, with their momentary harmony shattered like shards of splintered glass, they stepped from the stage without any further exchange of words or glances.

The crowd was cheering at great volume and pressing in on them again as they made their way back to the table, forcing them to endure hugs, hearty slaps on the back, and words of praise from every quarter. Rowena was the first family member to reach Killian, jumping up into his arms and squealing. "Oh, Killy, you were wonderful!" she cried, squeezing him for all that she was worth.

Aaron came along behind her, grinning broadly, his usual reserve replaced by a look of brotherly pride. "Is that what you were doing with the Elf all those times?"

Killian laughed and nodded, ruffling the younger boy's hair as Gilmore appeared out of the crowd to slap his back. "That is no Enid you have there, fuzz-face. A girl like that could wear a fellow out," he announced with a grin, leering at the Elfin maid. Killian only grunted and headed for his seat.

Several feet away, Ellianthia was listening dutifully while her people heaped similar accolades upon her. Calliandra and her clutch of woodhens were positively effusive in their praise, all outrage at the princess' choice of wardrobe quite forgotten. She was beginning to make her way toward her father when Palladarian ambled by.

"Not half bad for a human, eh?" he chuckled, a look of sly triumph on his face.

"So it was *you* who taught him that!" she accused, remembering his surprising agility and skill in the Dance, as well as the feel of his large, strong hand pressing against her breast.

With no trace of shame whatsoever, her uncle offered a little bow. "And an apt pupil, I would say," he replied merrily, laughing as she turned on her heel and stomped away.

Chapter 29

The Secret Grove

The betrothed couple was still sitting side by side as dusk approached, enduring each other's company in frosty silence, when Killian saw Mik'kel and Aisleen walking toward them in the company of Mellisandria. Mik'kel bowed to both of them.

"Forgive us for interrupting your celebration, Your Highnesses, but we would beg a few minutes of your time to speak in private, if you would. I mentioned to the Lady Mellisandria that you had experienced some visions recently, visions that might hold some meaning for her. She has graciously agreed to meet with us and offer her wise counsel."

Ellianthia looked up with irritation and suspicion. "Visions? And whom might you be?" she asked in an imperious tone that bordered on rudeness.

Before he could reply, Mellisandria stepped forward with a reproving look that made Ellianthia blush and glance away. "This is Lord Mik'kel, a learned mage from Kal'Dathia, who has traveled here to aid us against the danger from across the sea," said the Wise One. Turning to his companion, she continued. "This is Lady Aisleen of Calderia, a gifted seeress known to our people, and one whose wisdom we value."

Feeling properly chastened, Ellianthia nodded respectfully and rose from her seat. "Very well, Wise One. I am at your disposal."

Killian agreed and rose as well, following Mellisandria and the others to her private tent set apart from the pavilion on the Elfin side of the meadow. They entered to find the interior adorned with beautifully woven tapestries of intricate design suspended from the overhead supports; and large, feather stuffed pillows dyed in Forest hues of green and brown and goldenrod that were spread around upon the earthen floor.

After inviting her guests to be seated, the aged Wise One lowered herself carefully down upon a soft doeskin pillow and turned her gaze expectantly toward Mik'kel. Ellianthia, who had managed to sit somewhat apart from the Calderians, waited with guarded curiosity. Taking his cue from Mellisandria, the mage began.

"As you know, Prince Killian has been chosen by the gods to play a special role in the coming battle against Rak`koth and his armies, a battle for which this fell sorcerer prepares even as we speak. We know not when he will come to these shores, but that he will come is certain."

Inclining his head toward Killian, Mik`kel continued. "We do not know just what will be expected of the prince in the coming days, only that he must search out a lost mage, a sacred task for which the gods have prepared by granting him certain powers to aid him in his quest. I was sent here to perform the Ritual that would Awaken the prince to these powers.

"When I did so, some information was revealed to him that may be of great value. Unfortunately, the meaning of that information was not made entirely clear. From what Prince Killian has told us, it is my belief that some of what he learned during the Awakening may have meaning for our Elfin allies. It is with that hope that I seek your counsel, Wise One."

Mellisandria nodded, but it was the Elfin princess who spoke first. Mindful of the Wise One's watchful gaze, she adopted a respectful tone. "I would ask why the gods chose a human for this task, when there are other races who inhabit Balleterria and have an equal stake in her defense?"

Mik`kel offered an equally respectful reply. "An excellent question, Your Highness. The gods have informed us that they have been selecting potential Avatars for the past eight centuries, against the threat of this very danger. It seems that Prince Killian is not the first to be chosen, nor have those in earlier times been only of the human race. Indeed, I believe the prince learned something of interest to the Elves in that regard."

The princess cocked an eyebrow but said nothing, content to await further explanation of this revelation. Mik`kel turned to Killian. "If you would proceed, Your Highness."

And so Killian began to speak, telling them what he could remember of his incredible visit with the gods, describing his Awakening to his powers, the naming of those powers, and the words that echoed in his head as the gods charged him with the task to be accomplished. Mellisandria listened with close attention, nodding silently from time to time, keeping her own counsel for the moment.

Ellianthia remained quiet as well, though her expression revealed the ebb and flow of several emotions upon her face. When he reached the part of the tale concerning the Avatar that had gone before him, Killian turned his head to the princess and addressed her directly.

"My Lady, I was shown the face of the last person chosen by the gods before me. I was told that he had lived a long, honorable life, and that I was selected to follow him only on the day of his death. It was not the face of a human that I saw. As it happens, my predecessor was one of your people."

Ellianthia's eyes widened in surprise, but now it was Mellisandria who responded first, leaning forward with intense interest. "An Elf? Can you describe the face you saw, Your Highness?"

Killian nodded, closing his eyes for a moment to fix the image he had seen clearly in his mind. "I will try, Wise One. He lay as if asleep. His face showed the lines of great age, but his expression was calm and peaceful. I remember that his hair was silvery blue, of a color I have not seen often among your race."

Mellisandria inhaled sharply. "You say his hair was silvery blue? Did you learn his name?"

Killian thought carefully for a moment. "I believe they told me his name was...Fellinorian."

Mellisandria let out the breath she had been holding and Killian saw tears begin to glisten in the ancient Elf's eyes. "Fellinorian," she repeated in a low, wistful voice.

"You knew him, my Lady?" asked the prince, seeing that this name clearly had some special meaning to her.

"I knew him very well," Mellisandria murmured softly. "He and I were very...close...for many years. Longer than the lifetime of anyone here. He was gentle and loving, and wiser than any other person I have ever known." She shook her head slightly, as if still in disbelief.

"If any Elf was worthy of being chosen to carry the powers of the gods, it would have been he. But he never spoke a word of this to me...and I thought we shared everything." The aged Elf relaxed her shoulders and let the tears stream freely down her face.

Killian spoke in a quiet, comforting tone. "My Lady, I do not believe he knew of it himself. Rather, I believe he was like me, fully unaware of the powers seeded within him, until the gods called them to life."

The tent grew silent, all there wishing not to intrude on the memories of the venerable Elf who held such deep feelings for this old friend now passed beyond the veil. Ellianthia had never known Fellinorian, but she knew it would take much to make the Wise One weep openly. Killian saw her sympathetic expression and felt some lessening of his anger toward her.

After a few minutes, Mellisandria finally looked up, wiping the tears away with a small, delicate hand. Then Ellianthia broke the silence.

"Prince Killian," she said, using his name for the first time since they had known each other. "You have told us of your role in this quest to be undertaken at the gods' behest. But what part am I to play in your task?" A hint of bitterness crept into her voice. "Is it not enough that I consented to this sham of a Handfasting to seal the Peace, and thus promote the unity needed for the coming battle? What more would the gods have of me?"

Killian shrugged, striving to quiet the hackles that were rising as he heard her tone. "My Lady, I can not tell you that. I know only that the gods spoke of you as 'she who is to be your companion,' and told of your joining me on this journey—and that the future would be further revealed through our own efforts. I know not the true meaning of this, but it was clear that you were to play some part of great importance."

The Elfin maid pursed her lips as if considering further questions. Then she seemed to take him at his word that he knew nothing further, and lapsed into silence again to ponder what little she had been told.

Killian turned to Mellisandria. "Wise One, I am at a loss to know which path to take from here. I was told to seek out a great mage who would guide me in the paths of magic. Lord Mik`kel believes that this refers to someone other than himself, but where or whom this other mage might be remains a mystery for the present. The visions given me while in the presence of the gods offered me but one clue only, if it is a clue, in truth. A vision of a place. Perhaps you know something of it. It seemed to be in the Forest, a clearing in a grove of tall trees…a place that seemed sacred and untouched, as if no one entered there."

Mellisandria put aside her bittersweet grief and now sat erect, staring at him with intense scrutiny. "Describe this clearing," she insisted, her voice quickening.

Killian looked up and away, as if working to recapture the scene in his mind. After a moment, he spoke in a quiet, distant voice. "There was a large, tangled mound of twisted vines bedecked in flowers…purple flowers. At first, I thought it only a single, overgrown thicket of vines; but looking beneath, I saw a massive stone, granite perhaps, standing as high as two grown men."

He looked back to Mellisandria, and was startled to see suspicion and a glint of anger in her eyes. When she spoke, her voice was laced with powerful emotions.

"What else did you see when you looked at the stone, Your Highness?" she demanded, in a tone that made him hesitate to answer.

He searched his mind again. "Naught else...save for a small circle the size of a hand, placed on one side of the stone, in a place free of vines."

Then Mellisandria was on her feet with a speed and strength unexpected for one so aged, her voice as sharp as a whetted blade. "You speak of a sacred place, a place known only to the Elves for centuries past! How come the gods to reveal this place to you, who are not of our people?"

Taken aback by her intensity, the prince could only spread his hands in confusion. "I know not, Wise One, only that it was revealed to me as a place of importance to my destiny. Tell me, please, do you have knowledge of this place?"

Mollified by the look of sincere and genuine confusion playing across Killian's countenance, Mellisandria felt her suspicion recede a little. Whatever he might know, she sensed that he meant no harm. She considered for a moment, glancing around at the upturned faces of those respectfully awaiting her reply. Finally, satisfied that this next step must be taken, she lowered herself to the ground again and composed herself.

"I am the Keeper of the Secret Grove, a sacred duty passed down by one who held it before me, and others before her. This is a duty I have maintained for these past one hundred years. I was charged to watch over it and guard it, against the day when, according to an ancient prophecy, 'One will come to split the stone.' The Grove is a place secluded deep in the heart of our Great Forest, unknown to any but myself, the king, and a few other elders, all of whom are sworn to keep the secret with their lives."

She sighed, reticent to say the next words. "Though I can scarcely believe it, the Grove may well be the place revealed to you in your vision."

Killian sat back, feeling a blend of relief and dread at learning something more about the next step he was destined to take. His relief appeared to be matched by Mik`kel's excitement at Mellisandria's reluctant revelation, as the mage leaned forward.

"Can you take us there, Wise One?" Mik`kel asked.

Mellisandria peered back at the mage. "Only Elves have been allowed to enter this scared place," she said firmly. "Only Elves and, now, perhaps this human, for the gods have made it manifest that the Grove awaits his coming, though for what purpose I know not. You may accompany us there, but I do not know if the Grove will allow you to enter the clearing where the Sacred Stone stands. If not, you must remain outside.

"I suspect that only the prince, his 'chosen companion'—here she turned to Ellianthia, who frowned, then shrugged slightly and nodded—"and the Keeper of the Grove may be permitted to approach the Stone."

Mik`kel acquiesced to her decision with a small bow, pleased to be granted even this much. "And when might this be accomplished?"

"On the morrow," Mellisandria replied decisively. "I will inform the king and the others of the need for some haste in this matter. It is nearly a day's journey to the Grove, so be prepared to leave at first light." She hesitated, looking back and forth between Killian and Ellianthia and smiled slyly.

"On second thought, be prepared to leave at mid-morning." Then she stood up, signaling that the meeting had come to an end.

Chapter 30

Bowers and Beddings

Killian and the rest of the party walked back to the pavilion following the meeting, each lost in thought, considering the import of what had just transpired. Night had fallen while they had been with Mellisandria, and campfires were now ablaze around the meadow and in front of the tents, lighting up the darkness and casting long shadows as people passed in front of the flames. Given the distance to travel back to the castle or the Tree Palace at night, it had been agreed that the royal families and their respective parties would spend the night in their tents, before setting out in the morn for home.

Killian was cautiously excited about the prospect of journeying to the Secret Grove to solve the mystery of his vision. He was also hoping that the festivities were now over, so he could return to his tent and be free of this dress tunic that was chafing his neck, and the new boots that were pinching his insteps.

Ellianthia, uncomfortable enough with being in the company of the Calderians, was much less sanguine about the coming of the night—knowing that one particular Elfin Handfasting custom remained, and girding herself for what lay ahead.

The party arrived back at the pavilion to find many of the lords and ladies still dancing and singing to the merry sounds of a lively quintet comprised of both Calderian and Elfin musicians, who had somehow managed to find common ground in the language of music. As they reached the table, Killian saw his father and mother engaged in amiable conversation with Rillandariel and Palladarian. The two groups came together, Mik`kel giving a brief account of the meeting and their plans for a journey to the Secret Grove at mid-morn.

King Gavan was in the midst of asking for further details when a large contingent of Elfin guests converged on the royal table, laughing and talking excitedly. Ellianthia looked at her approaching Elfkin and gave a disgusted sigh, knowing all too well what they had in mind. Calliandra and a male Elf named Cassallirian called for attention by raising their hands.

"Your Highnesses, the Handfasting bower is in readiness and we are here to escort you," the garrulous Elfin matron loudly announced. Her statement brought cheers and whistles from the "escort" party, along with some exaggerated winking and leering.

Killian did not like the sound of this, though what a "Handfasting bower" might be was beyond him. But he soon found out, as Calliandra went on to explain about yet *another* Elfin custom that anyone had neglected to mention to him—one that involved leading the newly Handfasted couple to a special tent where they would spend their first night together, in order to "come to know each other better."

A deep frown crossed his face. It did not require a great deal of imagination to ken what "coming to know" each other better meant, and he was having no part of it. The last thing he wanted to do was to spend the night in the company of this haughty, angry princess.

"This is not a Calderian custom!" he protested to any that would listen, looking at Ellianthia as he did. He fully expected her to be as vocal as he in her protestations, considering her behavior toward him all day and her threats about any unsolicited contact. But she was curiously silent on the subject, though the angry scowl on her face spoke volumes.

Then Palladarian stepped over to Killian's side and said quietly, "Your Highness, this is an Elfin tradition that celebrates the consummation of the Handfasting ritual. It is always done, and no Handfasting ceremony is considered complete without it."

The prince's frown darkened even more as he replied with a furious whisper, "I have no intention of 'consummating' anything with her! I prefer to sleep in my own tent tonight."

The Elfin bard gave a placating nod, then continued. "I understand fully, Your Highness, and it is not necessary to actually...do...anything with the princess. But it would be seen as a bad omen for the Handfasting—and for the peace between our peoples that it signifies—for the betrothed couple to spend their first night apart."

Killian glared at Ellianthia, who snorted and turned away. Just add this to the growing list of details they had kept from him, he thought, slapping his hand to his thigh in frustration. Still, Palladarian's appeal to the sealing of the peace was hard to ignore, as the cagey Elf undoubtedly knew.

"Let us get this over with, if we must needs do it at all," he muttered, scowling in angry resignation.

Palladarian nodded to Calliandra, who squealed with laughter. Killian hardly had a chance to glance over his shoulder to nod good night to his parents before he and the princess were being led away into the night by this raucous, celebratory crowd of Elves, who obviously thought it the height of cleverness to offer ribald comments and bawdy suggestions all along the way.

He even overheard the one called Calliandra giggle as she said something to Ellianthia about having heard that human males were known to be particularly "well endowed" in certain parts of their anatomy. The lewd comment brought a round of laughter from all within earshot, save for Killian and his betrothed, who managed to blush and recoil in disgust at the same time.

Soon, they were standing in front of a colorfully decorated tent, while being showered with congratulations and crude remarks undoubtedly intended to "stimulate" their ardor. Then the Handfasted couple was literally shoved inside by several pairs of hands that quickly tied the tent flap closed. The prince scarcely had time to note that the large tent was divided into several smaller chambers before he felt a surprisingly muscular arm encircle his neck tightly and the cold edge of a blade press against his throat.

"Now hear me, *human!*" Ellianthia growled, her hot breath blowing against his ear. "I am here because the traditions of my people must be upheld tonight. But do you think to sate your repulsive rutting urges with me, you had best think again." She emphasized this last by pressing the edge of the dagger even harder against his skin, until it seemed she would draw blood.

Well, that was just about enough! Feeling his pent-up rage about to explode, he calmed himself and nodded ever so slightly, then relaxed his body, as if to show her that he had taken her "point."

Then, when she relaxed a little as well, convinced she had made herself clear, he suddenly shot his hand up to her wrist and clamped down hard, pulling the blade from his throat and twisting her arm in the process. Completely caught off guard by the speed and strength of his reaction, Ellianthia groaned loudly, having no choice but to drop the dagger and spin away from him, holding her wrist in pain.

Killian stomped closer to the Elfin maid, his nostrils flared with anger, his finger pointing in her face. "Now *you* listen to *me*! I could not care less about 'rutting' with you, as you so delicately put it, in any way, shape or manner. So you can hie yourself into the next chamber and curl up and die, for all it matters to me!" He started to spin on his heel, and then turned back with a dire tone in his voice.

"And do not *ever* pull a blade on me again or I will surely skin you with it!" With that, he picked up the dagger and slammed it into the central tent pole with a force that left the blade quivering three inches deep into solid wood, then turned his back in contempt.

Ellianthia stared after him in shock. Then she warily approached the pole and struggled to pull her dagger from the wood. After repeated tugging and twisting, the blade finally slipped free, leaving her arm sore from the effort.

She momentarily considered burying the steel squarely in the middle of that broad, arrogant back of his, but remembered his speed and strength, and thought better of it. Instead, she reached to her wrist and ripped the betrothal bracelet off, throwing it at his feet. It bounced and rolled into a corner of the tent.

With a grunt of frustration and rage, she stalked away into the next chamber and threw herself down upon the bower bed. She sprawled there, holding the dagger against her chest and thinking murderous thoughts, while she inhaled the heady aroma of wild rose and lilac petals that had been sprinkled all over the covers, undoubtedly by Calliandra and her woodhens, in anticipation of the use for which the bower bed had been intended. She lay there for some time before turning on her side and falling asleep, the blade still gripped tightly in her palm.

†††††

Aisleen was standing in the late evening shadows on the edge of the meadow, looking out over the camp and watching the fires burn low, when she heard footsteps approaching. She turned to see Mik`kel looming out of the darkness, bearing two goblets in his hands.

"My Lady," he said, with a small bow, "I trust I am not intruding."

"Not at all, Mik`kel...and remember, it is Aisleen." She took the proffered wine and gave a small curtsey in return. "Thank you, kind sir."

Mik`kel smiled and bowed with a flourish, almost spilling his wine as he did. They laughed together, then stood quietly, sipping the smooth, aged wine and watching the camp prepare for sleep.

"Quite an eventful day," Aisleen offered, after a comfortable silence. "I thought Killian and Ellianthia were going to wring each others' necks several times, but they seem to have survived relatively intact—though one can only imagine the two of them penned up together in the betrothal bedchamber for an entire night." She gave a sparkling laugh that sounded to him like delicate chimes being caressed by a gentle wind.

"Indeed," chuckled Mik`kel. "I do hope that they will both emerge whole and unscathed in the morning, or at least well enough to endure the ride to the Secret Grove." At the thought of the morrow's adventure, he grew more solemn, though no less intrigued with the possibilities. The seeress nodded, shivering slightly in the cool night air.

"Oh, Aisleen," he said, with some concern. "It grows later and you are cold. Perhaps I might accompany you to your tent."

"I would like that, Mik`kel," she said softly, inclining her head in the direction of the place where her tent had been erected. They walked along through the night, carrying their wine and speaking of the day's events. When they arrived at the front of her tent, Mik`kel attempted to relieve her of the goblet before he departed; but, to his surprise, she reached out to touch his hand.

"Perhaps we might finish our wine before you go. Would you care to come in for a moment?"

"Of course, I would be honored," he said somewhat formally, though feeling decidedly less formal as his pulse quickened at her invitation.

She led him inside the tent, where a lantern glowed on a small table against one wall. Like his own, her tent was divided into two smaller rooms, an anteroom and a sleeping chamber beyond. She offered him a seat in one of the two small camp chairs, saying, "If you will excuse me for a moment, I will change into something else. I have been in this gown all day, and it grows heavy from the dust and the mud."

Mik`kel watched her slip away behind the other wall, leaving her delicate scent behind. It was warmer inside the tent, out of the night breeze. He looked around the darkened interior, his thoughts on the woman in the other room. It felt more intimate being alone with her in the tent than it would in the castle, knowing that she was disrobing but a few feet away.

Aisleen returned shortly, wearing a long, thick white robe, her undershift tantalizingly visible at her neck. She sat beside him in the other chair, taking her goblet from his hand and sipping again.

The smooth skin of her pale neck caught his eye and held it. Though she was fully clothed, the curves of her body could not be entirely concealed by the robe, especially with her back gently arched and her chin tilted back to catch the last drops of the cool liquid. She finished the wine and lowered her cup, smiling directly at him, saying nothing.

He gazed at her soft, full lips, glistening wet with the wine, and his firm resolve to behave in a gentlemanly fashion finally crumbled. Setting his cup down, he leaned forward suddenly, took her in his arms and kissed her mouth. As he pressed against her, he felt her relax into the kiss. Her arm crept up around his neck and began to pull him closer.

Then, as he reached to touch her lustrous black hair, he felt her stiffen slightly and push herself away gently. He released her immediately, embarrassed and angry with himself for falling into those beautiful lips.

"Please forgive me," he stammered. "I had no call to be so forward. It is only that...that you are so beautiful, Aisleen and...and I have been wanting to do that for so long. Your pardon, please, my Lady."

She looked at him with those lovely eyes and he saw no anger there, only distress, before she lowered her head. Of course, you idiot! he thought, she still loves *him*. What did you expect, that she would forget her love for a king for the likes of you? Yet, even as he scourged himself mentally, he felt the burning need to know once and for all, to hear it from her directly, no matter the cost. Gathering his courage, he spoke the question he had resolved never to put to her.

"It is the king, is it not?" he said quietly. "You love him."

Aisleen raised her head up sharply, her eyes wide with surprise. "Has it been so obvious as that?" she asked tremulously.

"It...It is none of my business. It was only that..." He stopped, unable to bring himself to say what he wanted to say, that he wished she loved him instead of Gavan. His courage faltered and he rose to go. But as he did, he felt her hand holding him back.

"Wait," she said, gripping his hand firmly. "Please, let me explain."

"You...owe me no explanation, my Lady. I should never have presumed..." He stumbled through his words and started to pull away again.

"But I *want* to tell you, so you will understand fully," she pleaded, her hand still holding his tightly. "Please sit down, Mik`kel, and listen to me. Please."

He sank down to the chair again, unsure that he could really bear hearing her confess her love for the king after all. She took his hand in both of hers and leaned forward, looking into his eyes as she began to speak.

"I was born in Devon-Baire, a small earldom on the northern coast of Calderia. My father was the earl, and a close advisor to King Nicholas, Gavan's father. My mother was a countess who attended the queen when at court. My parents and I lived on a large estate close to the sea. We were very happy. But, at the time of my first moon flow, just past my thirteenth name-day, I began to have these...visions...small, brief visions at first, an image of a face or a place or some event. I knew not what they meant. They frightened me a little, but I did not know that I was any different from other children."

A faraway look came into Aisleen's eyes as she hearkened back to her childhood memories. "When I grew a little older, I began to be able to Find things—an earring my mother had lost that I Saw in the pocket of a discarded dress, a missing puppy trapped in the wine cellar, things like that. When I told my parents about it, they looked at each other, then told me that I had the gift of Sight. I later discovered that my father's mother had been a seeress of sorts, though she never left her village."

Mik`kel listened, though his thoughts were on the taste of her lips on his, and the great sense of loss he had felt when she pulled away. Aisleen's expression changed to remembered fear as she continued.

"One day, when I had just passed my fifteenth name-day, I woke up with a terrifying vision of my home and all the land around it destroyed by a great wave that came from the ocean and washed everything away. I Saw corpses floating everywhere, the bodies of my parents and others. I Saw buildings destroyed, trees felled, cattle drowned, and everywhere, water."

She shuddered at the memory, and Mik`kel instinctively put his hand on her shoulder to comfort her. She leaned her face against his hand for a moment, then lifted her head.

"I ran to my parents screaming, telling them what I had Seen. They believed me, perhaps because of my granmer's Sight. My father ordered all the family and the servants to go inland, up to the hills due west of our estate. He gathered all the livestock as well. We stayed in the hills for two days and nothing happened."

"A false vision?" asked Mik`kel, thinking of how young the seeress looked at that moment as she told her tale.

"Well, so I thought," said Aisleen. "Then, on the third night, there was a terrible earthquake. A great wave came from the ocean and swallowed up the estate and everything for miles around. Our home was sorely damaged, but no one was killed, no bodies floating like in my vision."

Mik`kel squeezed her shoulder gently. "So, your Sight saved your family."

Aisleen nodded, relieved to be past speaking of that memory. "After that, my father said that I had a real gift of the Sight, and that I must go to see Lady Leonora, the king's seeress who lived at the castle. When he took me there, she was very kind to me. She questioned me and reassured me that the gods had given me a special power. She told me it was a thing to be valued and developed, not feared. She took me on as an apprentice and taught me how to control my gift, to use it for good."

Aisleen's look had softened as she spoke of Leonora's kindness and support. Then her face grew serious again. After a moment, she stood up and began to pace a little, a sign of her inner turmoil.

"It was at the castle that I first met Gavan. He was the prince and heir to the throne then, just past his nineteenth name-day. He had heard of my gift of Finding, and first came to me in a state of agitation. It seemed he had lost his signet ring, a gift from his father, an heirloom passed down from every king to his first-born. He was desperate to find it before his father took note of its absence."

Aisleen hesitated, her robe swishing lightly as she moved. "Gavan was young and strong and vibrant, with that fiery red hair and laughing blue eyes. I was smitten with him from the first. I agreed to use my gift to Find the ring. When I Saw it, the ring was lying under a table in the bedchamber of a

young   noblewoman   whom   he   obviously   knew
rather...intimately."   Aisleen shook her head with a wry
expression.

"As taken as I was with him, I might have been jealous
of his...attentions...to the lady. But I knew he was a young
man, with a man's appetites, and all I could think at the time was
that I wished it had been me in his bed."

The seeress looked down, embarrassed by her
admission. Mik'kel listened in silence, watching the way the
glow from the lantern glistened on her shiny dark hair as she
paced, holding one hand in the other. He was still conscious of
her soft curves beneath the thick robe, but the way she was
talking about the king made his stomach tighten. Had she not
already pleaded for him to listen, he might have excused himself
to avoid hearing any more.

When she looked up again, Mik'kel could see old pain
reflected in her eyes. "Even at that first meeting, I knew there
was something between us. We began to spend time together,
and we grew very close. We were lovers for nearly a year. We
even spoke of asking his father for permission to become
betrothed." Aisleen paused. "But it was not to be."

"The king did not approve of the betrothal?" asked
Mik'kel with some surprise. Surely, this beautiful and gifted
lady would have been worthy of a prince's love, he thought,
even worthy to be a queen.

Aisleen stopped pacing and sat down again beside him,
her hands folded in her lap. He could hear the sentries calling
out to each other as they walked the guard line around the
perimeter of the Calderian royal encampment. It was late in the
evening, but he would hear her story through to its conclusion
before he bade her good night and left her to her memories.

"I do not think King Nicholas disapproved of me," she
said, after some delay. "He valued my gift, and he was a friend
to my father, the earl. But there were other, more political,
considerations. At that time, Calderia was still actively fighting
the war with Dunmoria. Duke Kendrick of Glashan and Baron
Riordan of Murrough, both vassals of King Nicholas, held the
lands bordering on Dunmoria, and often took the brunt of the
fighting.

"There were rumblings from these border states that the
war was taking too great a toll on their lands. There were also
rumors that Baron Riordan was losing his stomach for war, and
might withdraw his forces from the fighting—thus leaving the

Dunmorians with an open route to invading deeper into Calderia. So, to ensure his continued loyalty, King Nicholas agreed to a marriage of state between his son, Crown Prince Gavan and Briana, Riordan's eldest daughter."

"Ah," said Mik`kel quietly, beginning to see how this unhappy tale would end, and feeling sympathy for the ill-fated lovers, despite the dying of his own hopes. "And Nicholas knew naught of your plans to marry when he swore the pact with Riordan?"

Aisleen shrugged, her eyes downcast. "He may have suspected. But he was fighting a bitter war, and he prevailed upon Gavan to do his duty for the good of the kingdom. When Gavan came to tell me that he was to marry Briana, he raged against the king and threatened to defy him, to gather me up and leave Brannock Castle forever.

"I would fain have thrown myself from a tower, rather than send him to the arms of another woman. But Leonora made me see what I must do, if I truly loved him. I could not let Gavan destroy his life for me by refusing his father, nor could I rob the land of a future king. So I told him that he must marry her and take the throne one day. It was the hardest thing I have ever done in my life."

There was silence in the darkened tent, broken only by the sounds of crickets chirping outside in the night. Mik`kel looked upon this lovely lady, her head bowed, seeming to grieve even now, after nearly twenty years.

"And you and he never again...?" He left the question unfinished, knowing the answer without hearing it from her lips.

"No. He was much too honorable a man to be unfaithful once he married, though I confess I might have been persuaded to take him to my bed again anyway. But he asked me to stay on as seeress when Leonora was gone, if I was able to endure, and I could not refuse him. In time, he grew to love Briana, and I was content enough to serve him and the kingdom. I harbor no anger toward Briana. She has been a good queen. She has loved him well, and borne him three fine children. And I have had my work and my memories."

"And you never married," said Mik`kel, trying to accept the finality of her decision to forever keep Gavan in her heart, if not in her arms.

She shook her head slowly. "I could not. I have...known...other men over the years, but..."

He held up one hand to stop her from saying any more. "But no man could replace him in your heart," he said, completing her thought. "I understand now. Please forgive me, my Lady. I will respect your wishes. I only hope that we can remain friends." Resigned to her choice, he placed his hand upon her cheek, cupping it gently as if touching her for the last time as he stood up to go.

"No! Wait!" she cried, surprising him by the strength of her grip on his arm. "You do not understand, Mik`kel. I thought no man could replace him—*until I met you*." She stood to face him, fixing her lovely eyes on his, her words tumbling out rapidly, anxious to forestall his leaving.

"Since I have known you, I have felt things that I never thought to feel for any other man again. I have watched you often, and thought of you even more. I have admired your strength, your wisdom, your healing skills and your gentleness. I have felt the need to be near you." Then her words slowed, and her voice dropped to a whisper. "I have...wanted...you, as a woman wants a man," she confessed softly.

Mik`kel thought the earth would surely quake as he heard her words, so strongly did his heart begin to pound. Unable to believe his ears and desperate to do so all the same, he took a step toward her and suddenly found her in his arms again, hugging him and pressing her head into his shoulder. He held her tightly, breathing in her fragrance as he felt her heart beating next to his. He was drawn to her full lips and began to seek her mouth with his own, then hesitated.

"What is it, Mik`kel?" she asked breathlessly, sensing his reticence as she leaned back to look at him.

He relaxed his hold on her and dropped one hand away. "Earlier, when I kissed you, you pulled away. Perhaps you are not ready for..."

She smiled and hushed him with a finger to his lips. Then she stepped back and lowered her hands to the belt of her robe. Keeping her gaze fixed on his, she slowly untied the belt and shrugged out of the garment, letting it drop to the ground where it lay like a white cloud around her feet. She stood there before him without a hint of shame, wearing only the thin white undershift that molded to her breasts and hips, her hardened nipples and the dark triangle of hair beneath her belly clearly visible through the all-but-transparent fabric.

"Undress me, Mik`kel. Please," she asked quietly.

Transfixed by the sight of her nearly naked body, and her throaty invitation to disrobe her fully, he found himself unable to move or speak for a moment. He felt an ache in his groin as his desire and need for her mounted. Mistaking his hesitation for some lingering concern about her readiness, even now, Aisleen lifted her hand to her throat and stroked the smooth skin lightly with her fingertips.

"Mik`kel, it was only that I have not kissed a man...I mean, *really* kissed a man like that since...well, in a long time, nor have I had the desire to do so. When you embraced me, I but needed a moment to catch my breath. But I am ready now."

And when he still did not move toward her, enthralled by the sight of her beauty after so long without a woman to love, she ran her hands sensuously down over her body, holding his gaze as she asked, "Must a lady beg to be bedded, Mik`kel? For I will beg, if that is what you desire."

He groaned and crossed the space between them in an instant, gathering her into his arms and kissing her hungrily. This time, she did not pull away, but threw her arms around his neck and strained to draw him even closer, her lips wet and sweet as she opened her mouth to his tongue.

He felt her breasts brushing across him as she swayed slightly in the kiss, his powerful arms crushing her to him. She felt the unmistakable proof of his arousal as he pressed against her belly, and she ground herself against him to show her eagerness to be taken.

Then his hands were slipping down her back, sliding lightly over the smooth material of her thin garment until he reached her rounded hips and cupped them tightly. As she moaned, he began to gather the fabric up in his hands until it rose above her waist.

Grasping the hem, he continued to lift the undershift up and over her head, letting it fall behind her. And when he stepped back to drink in her in with his eyes, she arched her back proudly, offering herself to him, wanting to show him everything.

Mik`kel felt his need grow as he reached out to trace gentle circles around her breasts, making her whimper with pleasure as he bent his head to kiss each delicate tip. Then, while she was still gasping from the touch of his lips, he leaned down further and gathered her up in his arms, carrying her into the bedchamber while she clung to him tightly and sought his mouth with hers again.

Laying her gently on the covers of the bed, he quickly shed his robe and loosed the ties of his small clothes, then climbed into the bed beside her and buried his face in her bosom. "Oh, my Lady," he groaned hoarsely, as his tongue flicked out and laved her while his teeth nipped lightly at her tender flesh until she cried aloud with pleasure.

"Mik`kel," she breathed huskily, her voice thickened with desire. She brought her lips closer to his ear, feeling the need to confess all while his hands explored her body freely, moving over her gently rounded belly.

"Today," she whispered, gasping as his fingers touched and stroked her satin skin, "when Mellisandria was speaking the Handfasting, I thought of standing up there with you. I imagined that those beautiful words were being spoken for us. And later, I could not help but think of being led to the bower bed to lay with you like this."

"Oh, my beautiful Aisleen," he whispered back, needing to tell her everything as well as he caressed her lovingly. "I have lain awake in my bed when the castle was asleep, lonely, yearning for you. I barely kept myself from stealing to your door late at night, to beg entry into your arms and into your bed."

Her heart leapt to hear of his burning need for her during those long nights when she, too, had been alone in the dark, restless and thinking of him. Then his fingers were touching the silkiness of her inner thighs, brushing over the soft curls nestled between them. She groaned loudly and opened herself to him as he teased her lovingly.

"Oh, Mik`kel," she pleaded, squirming and twisting helplessly under his knowing hands. "Come into me. I need to feel you."

He knelt over her as she moaned again and rose up to meet him. Unable to wait an instant longer, he fell forward into her liquid heat, inhaling sharply as she received him, caressing the length of him. She cried out his name and wrapped herself around him, drawing him deeper still.

He lay on top of her, moving slowly, gently for a time, then more urgently, driven by the long nights of need and desire he had endured without her. Losing all control, he took her harder, faster, making her gasp, her breathless sounds blending with his groans.

"Yes! Oh, yes!" she cried, matching his desperate need with her own. They hovered on the precipice of agonizing pleasure until neither could endure another moment of the sweet torture. Then, surrendering everything to each other, they hurtled down together into the inferno, consumed by its flames.

After a time, as the exquisite throbbing finally ebbed and their breathing slowed, he kissed her tenderly, then cradled her head in the hollow of his shoulder and stroked her hair. They lay there together in silence, each marveling at the pleasure they had shared. Finally, she turned her head into his chest and quietly sobbed her happiness as they drifted into slumber.

And thus it was that, on the night of the royal betrothal, while prince and princess slept apart in cold and solitary beds, one of them clutching a knife to her breast, two others joined together to celebrate the union of man and woman in the way the gods had intended—and found their future in each other's arms.

Chapter 31

An Emperor Displeased

Emperor Rak`koth, ruler of all Surrikand, was furious. His generals and advisors knew his mood and did their best to melt back into the shadows, out of his deadly line of vision. He sat forward in his seat, crimson eyes flashing, fingernails raking the armrests of his throne as he glared down at the object of his rage standing before him now.

Master Shipwright Suk`kar, a proud man, was trying very hard not to tremble visibly under the emperor's baleful stare. He knew better than anyone else present why Rak`koth was incensed. It was his report on the current status of the fleet, a report he had dreaded sending, even as he had handed it to the Imperial courier to be delivered. Soon after, he had been hastily summoned from his many duties in the shipyards of Mertania to appear "immediately!" at the palace.

"Are you purposely trying to undermine my plans to sail for Balleterria this year, shipwright, or are you simply incompetent?" growled Rak`koth. "You know the fleet must launch before the coming of the storm season, and you gave me your assurances that this could be accomplished by the date I required. Now I receive word from you of yet another delay before the last ships are delivered. What is your excuse this time?"

Suk`kar, a barrel-chested, middle-aged man whose dark brown beard was peppered with gray, wrung his thick, callused fingers and tried again to explain. "Your Magnificence, the last ships are almost ready. But, as you know, my Emperor, the shipments of lumber from the mills in Paressia have been slow to reach our shipyards. And, when the lumber did arrive, it had to be shaped and cured, especially the wood for the hulls. That took time and it could not be hurried, not if you want ships that are seaworthy enough to make the long voyage."

"If I want? If I want?" Rak`koth repeated angrily, his eyes narrowing to burning slits as his voice rose to fill the chamber like thunder in a summer storm. "What I *want* is someone who knows how to practice their trade and complete their work on time! When you told me of the delays in receiving the necessary lumber, I gave orders for the shipments to be increased two-fold, did I not?"

He swung around and fixed his baleful stare on his chamberlain, who swallowed nervously as he came under his emperor's piercing scrutiny. "Belk`eth, were my orders for more lumber from Paressia not issued and obeyed?"

"Yes, Magnificence, of a certainty!" the chamberlain replied, nodding his head vigorously. "I personally saw to it that your orders were delivered to the Paressian mills, with the warning of the consequences if they failed to do so."

Rak`koth then returned his wrathful gaze to Suk`kar. "Are you telling me the shipments were not adequate?"

"No, Magnificence, they were. But with the previous delay and the sheer number of ships to be built, the last ones have taken longer than expected. My yards have been busy day and night, but we have had only so many dry docks available to build the ships, especially the larger vessels needed to carry the horses and some of the siege equipment. They required a special hull design and oversized bays."

The emperor leaned further forward, scowling darkly. "Excuses, man! Endless excuses! All of your requests for resources to build my ships have been granted, have they not, shipwright? Have I not placed sufficient supplies and men at your disposal?"

"Yes, Magnificence, you have indeed provided me with men," Suk`kar hastened to reply, his fear mounting as he saw that this was going even worse than he had feared. He strove desperately to find a way to explain the realities of his trade to a ruler who could see only that his wishes had been thwarted. "But not all the men available have the special skills to do the work needed. I only have so many skilled workers to crew each shift, and I can not work them any faster or they will collapse."

"Then let them collapse!" roared Rak`koth, slamming his fist down. "Work them until they drop, then drag their bodies away to make room for new men, if that is what it takes!"

Blood drained from Suk`kar's face as the thought of the Death Roads churned in his mind. His crews were loyal, hard-working men who had already been laboring so hard for months, hardly seeing their families. There had been dark rumblings among them, and angry looks directed at him when he berated them to work harder and faster. More than one man had already provided graphic suggestions about exactly which anatomical orifice Suk`kar could stuff with the extra gold he offered.

All this was clearly lost on Rak`koth, who turned to a guardsman standing to the left of him. "Bring them in now," he ordered.

The shipwright stared straight ahead, wondering what was to come next, as he heard footsteps approaching behind him. "Are these your men?" the emperor asked quietly, like a deadly Thracyllian viper poised to strike.

Suk`kar turned, surprised to see Pal`kur, his first assistant, and Ken`ket, his chief foreman, being brought to stand beside him. Both men were perplexed and frightened, and the sight of their master looking so cowed and nervous did little to calm their fears. "Yes, Magnificence, these are my men," he replied, naming them and their positions in turn.

Rak`koth nodded slowly, then spoke directly to Ken`ket. "Tell me, foreman. Was something to happen to first assistant Pal`kur, would you be able to take his place? Would you have the knowledge to do his work?"

"Ye...Yes, Magnificence," Ken`ket stuttered, glancing uncomfortably at Pal`kur, then at Suk`kar, confusion evident in his expression. "I have studied under Master Suk`kar and Pal`kur for many years."

"I see," replied Rak`koth, in a deceptively quiet tone. Then, without warning, he raised his right hand and pointed his long fingers at Pal`kur. As Suk`kar and Ken`ket looked on in horror, the first assistant suddenly clutched his chest and bent over double, emitting a series of grunting sounds as he slowly fell to his knees. He writhed in pain as he fought to breathe, his face turning purple, his eyes wide with terror. After a final futile struggle, he exhaled once and pitched forward on his face. The emperor lowered his hand, ignoring the twitching body on the floor.

"Ken`ket, I have...promoted...you to Pal`kur's place," he said with a menacing smile. "I expect you to work the crews harder, no matter how many collapse, until my ships are finished. If you do not, you will suffer his fate. Is that clear?"

Ken`ket, stunned by the callous murder of a close friend before his eyes, could only croak out "Yes, Magnificence." Suk`kar was still staring in disbelief at the lifeless body of the man who had worked by his side for a score of years, and who had once saved his life by pushing him from the path of a falling spar that had hurtled down from the rigging to crash to the deck—the same man who now left behind a widow and three fatherless boys, his own godsons.

Rak`koth beckoned for Ken`ket to come closer. "Tell me, first assistant. How many of your men are too tired or too weak to work today?"

"There are perhaps fifty or sixty men resting in the barracks today, Magnificence."

"Fifty or sixty? Hmm." The emperor motioned to a Legionnaire officer standing at attention some ten feet away. "Captain Tev`vor."

"Yes, Magnificence!" The officer marched forward and snapped back to attention, his back ramrod straight, black helm cradled in the crook of his arm.

"Captain, I want you to accompany our new first assistant, Ken`ket, back to the shipyards. When you get there, go to the barracks and round up every man who says he is not able to return to work immediately. Then take all of those slackers out and crucify them. I want them nailed to crosses where all the other ship workers can see them. When they are dead, leave their corpses hanging there to rot or feed the crows. Perhaps that will be sufficient to convince the men that I will tolerate no excuses for any further delays."

"At once!" said Tev`vor, slapping his fist on his chest in salute. "Come with me," he growled, dragging the stunned and speechless Ken`ket out of the room by the arm.

"Now, Suk`kar," said Rak`koth, fixing his gaze upon the shipwright who was staring at him with horror and barely disguised hatred. "I warned you that I would not be denied my fleet on time. You would be joining your men on the cross, did I not think that your skills are still needed. But lest you think that my need for your abilities makes you immune from punishment for failure—and make no mistake, you have failed me thus far— I have arranged for a way to express my displeasure, and offer you some…inspiration…to improve, at the same time."

With an ominous laugh, Rak`koth raised his hand and beckoned to someone at the back of the chamber. Again, Suk`kar heard the sound of footsteps coming closer, but this time accompanied by the soft swish of fabric brushing the floor.

"I believe you know these people as well, shipwright," said the emperor, inclining his head to the left. Suk`kar turned and gasped aloud, his face stricken with alarm as he recognized the two females being escorted by hard-eyed guardsmen, their large hands like bear paws encircling the smaller feminine wrists of his wife and daughter.

The older of the two was a pretty woman, perhaps ten years his junior, with brown eyes and straight, honey-colored hair that fell down over her ample breasts. Though her waist and hips showed some signs of thickening with maturity, she carried it well, with the look of a woman in the prime of her life.

"Shilela!" he cried out, starting forward toward her, only to be restrained roughly by the heavy grip of a guardsman's hand on his shoulder.

The woman's frightened, questioning look at her husband sought an explanation that he was at a loss to provide, for he knew no more than she about why the Imperial soldiers had wrested her from her home and brought her to the palace under guard. When no reason was forthcoming from him, she dared to glance at the throne.

Her eyes filled with awe and dread as she beheld for the first time the dark, striking man who was her emperor, sensing his strength and power—and capacity for cruelty—in the way that women always could in his presence. His crimson eyes roamed over her body with frank interest that brought a blush to her face. Emperor or no, she knew when a man was disrobing her with a look, and she quickly averted her gaze in fear and embarrassment. She found herself surprised that he would look at her with *that* kind of interest, with so many beautiful young slaves available at his whim.

The other female standing beside her was a comely young girl, perhaps not past her nineteenth name-day, round of breast and hip as well, though more slender in the waist than Shilela—but with the same coloring and facial features that clearly marked her as kin to the older woman.

"Thalia! My daughter!" cried the shipwright again, once more halted in his attempt to reach her and his wife when the guard grabbed his arm and twisted it roughly up behind his back.

"Father?" the girl cried out in return. "Why have we been brought here?" Her bewildered expression wrenched his belly as agonizingly as the brutal hand threatening to snap his arm.

"What is the meaning of this, Magnificence?" he demanded, speaking through pain that made him wince with each word. "My family is innocent of any wrongdoing. Surely, they have no part in this! Punish me if you must, but let them go, I beg of you."

Rak`koth chuckled briefly, then his face grew darker. "It is *I* who will decide a fitting punishment for your failure," he replied, his tone stern and unyielding. Then he turned to the guardsmen holding the women. "Strip them!"

Before Shilela and Thalia could even grasp what was about to happen, the grinning guardsmen grabbed each of them by the hair with one hand and swiftly ripped their dresses open from bodice to hem in one violent motion. Shrieks erupted from their throats as their ruined dresses fell away.

Then the sound of rending fabric was heard again as their undershifts were torn from their bodies as well, leaving mother and daughter completely naked, exposed to all the men present in the throne chamber.

The sight of his wife and daughter being manhandled and publicly disgraced was too much for Suk`kar. He managed to wrest himself free from the guard holding him, and lurched toward his family—only to be halted abruptly by a stream of crimson light that flashed from the sorcerer's hand and slammed into him, driving him to his knees. The women screamed as he slumped forward, dazed by the magical blow.

"Now, ladies," said Rak`koth calmly, indifferent to their tears as he let his eyes roam over their bared flesh. "I do not wish to kill him, at least not while I have need of his skills. But I can make him suffer the agonies of the Four Hells without spilling a single drop of blood...and I will, unless you listen carefully and do exactly as you are told. Do you understand?"

Both women nodded fearfully, unable to speak through throats suddenly gone dry. They stood together, their hands covering breasts and groin in a futile attempt to preserve some small modesty.

"Very well," he said. "Now, Master Suk`kar has displeased me by failing to finish my fleet in the appointed time. Among other things, he has been too lenient with his men, putting his concern for them ahead of the empire's needs." His eyes flared to a brighter red and his voice grew hard.

"But *I* am not lenient, as he will soon see! Both of you will remain here in the palace with me as my 'guests.' As punishment, one of you—I will decide which—will become my pleasure slave. That one will serve my needs, as he did not, for as long as it takes him to complete his task."

Rak`koth watched as Thalia wrinkled her brow in confusion, then raised her hands to her mouth, so shocked by his words as their meaning became clear that she forgot about covering her body. How amusing, he thought to himself. The girl is still a virgin, judging by her horrified reaction. Shilela, the wife, remained motionless, though the consternation on her face made her own inner tumult evident. This one is stronger, he mused, not quite so shocked by his intent.

"I imagine that this arrangement will encourage our shipwright to fulfill his obligations all the more quickly, knowing that every day that he delays means yet another day that I will be enjoying the use of his wife or daughter in my bed."

While Thalia shook her head in wordless disbelief, her mother looked fearfully at her beautiful daughter, imagining the cruel perversions of the flesh that this evil satyr would inflict upon her youthful innocence. With great effort, Shilela gathered her strength, somehow finding sufficient breath to ask a most important question.

"And the other one, Magnificence, the one who is not chosen to...serve you. What is to become of her?"

Interesting, he thought. The mother seemed already resigned to the fate he had imposed, and was something less than horrified. Aloud he replied, "She will be put to work in the kitchen, doing the most menial tasks as penance for Master Suk'kar's transgressions. But if he does not show me sufficient progress within a very short time, then she, too, will learn to serve me as a woman serves a man."

Shuddering at the thought of her daughter subjected to his depravity, Shilela raised her head, lowered her hands to her sides and squared her shoulders. In doing so, she was quite mindful of the way her bare bosom lifted and caught his eye.

"Then I beg you to choose me to serve your pleasure, Magnificence. I know how to...please...a man," she said, swallowing her dignity and shifting her stance to spread her legs slightly apart in silent invitation. "My daughter is young and inexperienced. She knows little of what a man desires, and would not please you as could I."

"Mother!" Thalia cried. "I can not bear to think of you like...that. It would break Father's heart—and mine." Her eyes brimming with tears at the terrible choice being forced upon them, she faced Rak'koth, her desperation lending her strength.

"Please, Magnificence," she begged, unable to believe that she was saying the words that came from her lips. "Please let me serve you. I can learn to please you, if you will only choose me and allow my mother to go."

Shilela knew what Thalia was attempting to do, for her sake. But she could not let her young, innocent daughter outdo her in this degrading competition, not if she wished to see the girl spared. Better that she, a mature woman who had welcomed her man between her thighs many times over the years, and knew a great deal more about the pleasing of a male, should sacrifice herself for Thalia's sake—and the sake of her husband, who had already felt the agony of the emperor's wrath.

Yet, disturbingly, she was also vaguely aware of something more than just the desire to save her husband and daughter. Despite her outrage and abhorrence for the man sitting on the throne, she found his aura of power and absolute control both frightening and fascinating, something that she had never experienced with the gentle man she had married. Indeed, she even felt some perverse satisfaction in knowing that her naked body could capture his interest, though she immediately rebuked herself for entertaining such depraved thoughts.

And, to her further dismay, she found that being examined by Rak'koth's burning eyes while she was so wantonly displayed had actually caused a quickening of her pulse and an unexpected trace of heat. She did not cower or look away, determined to let him see how a mature woman responded to his demands, if that was his desire.

Rak'koth's eyebrows rose slightly as her eyes met his. Few women dared to meet his gaze so boldly, and he inclined his head toward her with a mocking smile, as if he knew exactly what she intended and was interested to see how she measured up.

He laughed, turning to one of his officers, who had been examining the naked females with undisguised lust. "An intriguing choice, is it not, Colonel? Youth or experience. Innocence or maturity. And both so eager to please me. Which would you choose?"

"Why not have them both, Magnificence? " the officer asked with a malicious grin. "They both belong to you now, though I think I would enjoy breaking the young filly more, putting the crop to her flanks...and other tender places."

"True enough, Colonel," Rak'koth agreed, enjoying the thought of whipping the girl into submission with his own hands, as he had done so often to other young slaves. "But, I think our shipwright will perform best for me if he has the incentive to save at least one of his women folk from serving me so...intimately. So, for now, I will make a choice." He turned back to the guards holding mother and daughter. "Bring them closer to me," he ordered. "Oh, and send for Merelda."

†††††

Within minutes after his summons, the sound of bare feet hurrying across the floor marked the arrival of the black-haired, violet-eyed slave, who stepped up onto the dais and fell to her knees at her master's feet. Since she had not incurred his displeasure recently, he had allowed her some clothing this day, a thin strip of emerald green silk tied across her chest and another narrow slip of silk hanging down between her thighs from a gold chain circling her waist.

"How may I serve you, Master?" she asked, looking up at him, hoping that he found his property pleasing to his gaze this day as he had last night when he had used her so well. After sating himself, he had even allowed her the privilege of taking pleasure for the first time in an eight-day, a certain sign that she was in his favor. She would do everything possible to remain that way.

Rak`koth reached to stroke her hair gently, feeling a stirring in his groin as he looked upon her. He had many slaves that he used at his whim, but few could endure the gift of his pain so willingly or be needy as she. He decided against using her then and there, content to wait for a brief time while she served him in another way.

"My pet, this is Master Suk`kar." He pointed to the man who still lay crumpled on the floor, his senses addled by the magical attack.

"And these are his wife and daughter," he said, indicating the two naked females waiting with trepidation to learn the outcome of his decision. "One of them will have the honor of serving me as a personal slave until Master Suk`kar earns her freedom."

"Yes, Master," Merelda replied, knowing what he expected of her because he often commanded her to be present when new slaves were presented to him, such as the young females who were required to come to the palace to receive permission to marry. He made her attend him then because he knew it was difficult for her to witness his selection of a new plaything, well aware that any one of these more youthful women might replace her as his pet slave, taking her coveted place at his feet. And, to add to her humiliation and distress, he would sometimes amuse himself by requiring her to help teach the other women how to serve him.

Merelda looked at the mother and daughter with appraising eyes. She felt some sympathy for their initial fear, but she knew that one of them—the fortunate one—would soon be given the privilege of serving her master. She had quickly discovered that he would not tolerate jealousy from her when it came to other slaves; and she had long ago learned to obey without any hesitation, knowing that his punishment would be very swift and very painful.

In truth, she had come to love and need him so much that she wanted only that he be pleased, even if it was sometimes between the thighs of another. She would never wish to deny him the pleasure that he deserved. If she truly loved her master, she thought, how could she want anything but his happiness?

Mother and daughter stared at the beautiful slave with awful fascination as she approached them. Shilela was old enough to recall who and what this raven-haired, nearly nude beauty had been before Rak`koth's Awakening.

Oddly, the former high priestess did not appear to be unhappy in his service, though Shilela had seen for herself this day that he was an exceedingly cruel and demanding master. The woman looked at her with warm, gentle eyes, the eyes of a person who seemed surprisingly content and satisfied.

"Very well," he said, having made his decision. "Take the mother away to await my pleasure, Merelda. I have business elsewhere for a few days, but I will expect her to be well instructed in the ways of a bed slave when I call for her. As for the daughter, have the girl given something to wear and sent to the kitchens."

"Yes, Master. I will prepare her for you." Merelda bowed and took the shipwright's wife by the hand.

Shilela's sigh of relief was audible, even as her daughter struggled against the guardsman gripping her, sobbing, "No, Mother! Let him take me, please!"

The older woman reached out a hand to comfort her, drawing her into a tight embrace. "It is for the best, my dear," she whispered. "Be strong and do as they say. I will come to you when I can." Then, with a worried look toward her husband, who still had not moved, she turned to Merelda and said quietly, "I am ready."

Rak`koth watched his pet slave lead the other woman away, one naked and the other nearly so. He regretted that he had other pressing matters to attend to for the next few days that would keep him occupied elsewhere. But he smiled with anticipation, thinking that he would enjoy learning what lay behind Shilela's curiously bold stare when he took his pleasure with her.

He looked over at Suk`kar, whose eyes were still glazed over, then motioned to another of his officers. "Captain, when our shipwright remembers who he is, arrange to have him taken back to his yards and show him the men hanging on the crosses. Give him a good look at the consequences of his leniency, then put him back to work. And do remind him that his wife will be my 'guest' until his task is finished."

Chapter 32

Into the Forest

After spending a long and fitful night in the Handfasting bower, Killian was awakened by someone calling the names of the prince and princess. In a few moments, Ellianthia emerged from the rear chamber of the tent, combing through her hair with her fingers. "They are here to take us to the Handfasting breakfast," she said flatly, rubbing sleep from her eyes. "They will not give up until we go with them."

Without meeting his gaze, she walked quietly over to the corner, picked up the betrothal bracelet and slipped it back on her wrist in silence. Killian made no remark, but simply followed her out through the tent flap to where a group of Elves, led by the irrepressible Calliandra, were waiting for them. Surrounded by their escort, they endured the knowing smiles and suggestive comments of the well-wishers in polite silence as they walked to the pavilion.

Fortunately, the Handfasting breakfast was a brief, informal affair, hastened to a speedier conclusion by Mellisandria's pronouncement that it was time to start on their journey. After a visit to separate privies to relieve themselves, and a few minutes to take leave of family and friends—with promises to inform them of all that transpired in the Grove—the betrothed couple was led to the edge of the meadow where the rest of the traveling party had gathered. Mounting their horses, they soon left the noise and the people behind as they began the pilgrimage to the Grove.

The soft, loamy soil muffled the sound of the horses' hooves as the riders made their way into the Great Forest, along a narrow, little-used path winding through the tall pines. Filtering down through their trunks and branches, the late morning sun painted irregular splashes of golden light across the dark, moist earth.

Mellisandria led the way, riding astride her small brown mare, her ceremonial gown exchanged for more practical tunic and leggings in soft earth colors. Ellianthia rode close enough to share a quiet conversation with the Wise One.

Killian followed some paces behind, riding a chestnut stallion from the castle stables, having left his own Sutherland back at the pavilion because the massive warhorse would have been less nimble in the dense Forest. He wore the bastard sword strapped across his back in a leather shoulder sheath made especially for him under Reagen's direction. Beside him rode Palladarian, who, as a master bard, had knowledge of much sacred Elfin lore, including the legends of the Secret Grove.

Behind him, Mik`kel and Aisleen rode together, trading mysterious smiles and managing to touch knees or hands more than was absolutely necessary, even given the limited width of the path. General Trillafarien, still professing suspicions and distrust about the humans despite the Handfasting ceremony, had insisted on joining the party, and now brought up the rear.

Riding in and out of the patches of sunlight, surrounded by the trees and underbrush, Killian was increasingly conscious of how different the Great Forest was from the flatlands and hills of Calderia. The Woods were like a living presence enclosing them, the further they traveled into its depths. He knew the Elves regarded all life therein as sentient; and, though his human eyes and ears were blind and deaf to much of that experience, he could almost imagine that the lofty pines and broad, sturdy oaks watched him as he passed by.

What might they be thinking? he wondered, these ancient beings that stood quiet and strong throughout the cycle of the seasons, enduring summer heat and frigid cold, lightning storms and autumn rains. Some of them had already been here when his people came to this land, their noble lives spanning countless generations of humans. What wisdom they might share, what lessons might be learned, could he only reach out to them somehow.

Mellisandria guided the riders through a small clearing stirrup-high in wild yellow daisies and purple crocus, alive with hundreds of butterflies fluttering and darting by, their brilliant variegated hues—orange and brown, black and gold, purple and blue—shimmering in the bright sun. Aisleen laughed with delight like a little girl at their glittering beauty, while Mik`kel watched her face and her sparkling eyes.

Then the seeress "oohed" with delight and directed his attention to Ellianthia, whose outstretched arm was covered with a dozen of these delicate creatures. Killian looked on as well, amazed by the sight of the Elfin maid smiling and talking in a low, soothing tone, as if these ephemeral creatures were friends alighting to visit for a moment. He was also struck by the genuine pleasure she seemed to take in her communion with them, and by the gentleness of her smile.

Killian thought that she looked more relaxed and at peace than he had yet seen her during their brief, angry acquaintance. Here in her own element, among the trees and denizens of the Forest she called home, she seemed a very different person. Palladarian must have seen his expression because he leaned forward and grinned.

"The maid is not all fire and steel, though she would have you think otherwise." And Killian, who had finally decided to forgive his erstwhile Dance instructor for neglecting to mention that the maid was his niece, nodded thoughtfully.

After a few minutes, Mellisandria led them out of the clearing and down a shaded slope into a gully lined with delicate fronds of maidenhair and celesta ferns. A shallow stream some twenty feet wide ran along the bottom of the small ravine, rippling over rounded stones worn smooth and flat by ages of water racing over them. Small eddies and sheltered pools near the banks were filled with tiny fish and other water life, while black and green winged dragonflies hovered and flitted about, intent on the pursuit of food or mates or whatever other activities dragonflies engaged in during their brief lives.

The water was only a few inches deep in some places, barely covering the fetlocks of the horses, and shallow enough for the clopping sound of iron striking rock to be heard. As he rode across, something caught Killian's eye.

He turned his head, astonished to see a large brown bear and her small furry cub standing upstream about twenty-five feet away, calmly fishing for trout, apparently quite unconcerned about the presence of people traveling by. A little further up the stream on the far bank, a fox and her kits walked in single file along the bank, also seemingly oblivious to the potential danger from the riding party.

Killian was confused by the indifference of these wild animals to his passage, since no animal he had ever hunted had lingered after catching even a whiff, much less a glimpse, of a human predator. But when he saw Mellisandria and the Elfin princess smiling at the animals and discussing their size and coloring, it came to him that there was an explanation for why the wild life did not fear him or the others: they recognized the Elves as Guardians of the Forest and trusted them.

Killian pondered this as the day wore on and the miles slipped by. In mid-afternoon, Mellisandria called a brief halt to allow them to stretch their legs and partake of a small repast of trail bread, smoked salmon, dried fruits and nuts. It was during this respite that Killian sought out Mellisandria and Palladarian for the answer to a question that had been puzzling him since their encounter with the animals at the stream.

They smiled as he approached and gestured for him to join them in a drink of cool water from a leather flask. Ellianthia sat on the ground close by, her legs crossed and eyes closed as if resting, though he was sure she could hear every word. Trillafarien stood a little apart from the rest of the Elves, saying nothing, but with a frown of disapproval on his face for unnecessary courtesy given the prince.

"Wise One," Killian began, when he had swallowed a mouthful of the refreshing liquid and passed the pouch back, "there is something that confuses me about what I have seen today."

"I would be happy to enlighten you if I can. What puzzles you, Your Highness?"

"The animals by the stream. They seemed to have no fear of you at all. I assume it was because they knew you as friends, and even as protectors."

"That is true, Prince Killian," said the ancient Elf. "We Elves have been their Guardians for the centuries we have lived among them, at the behest of our god. It is our duty, and our honor."

Hesitant to give offense, Killian chose his words carefully. "So I thought. And yet, at the betrothal feast, your people cooked and ate all manner of beast and fowl—venison, boar, squirrel, pheasant and more. How is it that your people can serve as Guardians to the Forest animals, and yet hunt them for food?"

Mellisandria looked at him thoughtfully, though with no sign that she had been affronted by his question. "This is a fair question, one that all Elves must confront at some time, most often when they are young and can not abide the thought of killing animals that they regard as friends, especially those that come so easily to their hand. It is true that we serve the Forest and all the life that dwells within its boundaries. We watch over and protect our trees and animals from outside predators, and from those who would kill them for sport or profit."

Palladarian nodded as the Wise One continued. "Yet, our people could not live without harvesting some plants to feed ourselves or to weave the cloth that shields our bodies from the elements. Nor could we all survive for long without meat for our campfires or hides for our protection. Even so, some of our own people refuse to eat the flesh of Forest animals and prefer to live solely on grains, fruits and vegetables found in the wild or cultivated in small gardens."

"We need not justify our ways to humans," interrupted Trillafarien with a growl, glaring at Killian as if defying him to answer the unspoken challenge.

Before Killian could respond, Mellisandria intervened. "Like it or not, General," she replied caustically, returning his glare with her own, "we have reason to believe that the prince is the Avatar of the gods, and that he has business here in our Forest. And His Highness has offered no offense, but simply seeks to understand our people better. You would do well, General, to make the same effort concerning his folk."

Trillafarien looked at her for a moment, surprised to see the Wise One come to this human's defense and take his side against her own kind. But, seeing that he would get no support for his hostility from the Wise One, the Elfin general snorted, then turned on his heel and walked away.

"If I may add something to this," said Palladarian, "We Elves strive to live in balance and harmony with the Forest. All living things are sacred to us. We harvest no plant and take no animal's life unless it is necessary to sustain our own. We kill only what we need and waste nothing. We do not hunt for amusement or pride or sport.

"When we must kill, we offer our thanks to our god, and to the spirit of the plant or animal for sharing that life with us. And, in return, we pledge to continue serving and protecting all others of their kind who dwell in the Forest."

Killian said nothing for a moment while he considered Palladarian's words, trying to fathom the paradox of being both Guardian and hunter. But any other questions he may have posed were forgotten an instant later, when Ellianthia suddenly cried out "No!" and stood up, her head turning back and forth as if trying to catch sight of something that could not be seen. Soon, her eyes riveted on some point to the east of where the party had halted.

"Danger! Fear! And a young one," she explained hurriedly. Then she was off, sprinting in that direction with a haste that bespoke great urgency.

Killian blinked, uncertain about what was occurring. In an instant, Palladarian was at his side. "Follow her, Your Highness," said the Elf, placing a hand on his shoulder and gripping it tightly. "Follow her and learn."

On his urging, Killian set out after Ellianthia, racing through the Woods, calling on his gods-given speed to keep pace with her before she vanished into the distance. Looking to his left, he saw the bard in pursuit as well.

After a few moments, he outdistanced Palladarian and began to draw closer to the Elfin maid. Despite his feelings toward her, he watched with admiration as she sped through the trees, making hardly a sound, placing her feet deftly for all her haste and dodging obstacles with the grace and agility of a leaping stag.

She topped a small rise and halted abruptly, then disappeared down the other side. Following close behind her, Killian barely stopped himself in time to avoid tumbling down the steep bramble-filled slope of a ravine to a streambed some fifteen feet below. There, his eyes took in an alarming scene.

Halfway down the thicketed decline, Ellianthia knelt near the body of a fallen doe lying on its side. By the twisted angle of its spine, he could see that its thrashing attempts to stand were futile. The deer had broken her back somehow, though it was hard to imagine such a fleet-footed animal tripping and falling so severely.

Then he saw something wiggling about in the Elfin maid's arms. A closer look revealed a young fawn, opening its mouth in a silent squeal as it struggled frantically to reach its crippled mother. Ellianthia held the fawn tightly to her breast, but her eyes were fixed on the bottom of the ravine.

A moment later, Killian saw what had broken the doe's spine. A huge black panther crouched below her, staring up at the maid. Its powerful shoulders were hunched to spring again, its four-inch fangs extended and dripping hot saliva as the great Forest cat opened its mouth in a menacing growl that rumbled from deep in its throat.

To his astonishment, instead of turning to flee, the Elfin maid was looking at the panther with a calm expression on her face, slowly shaking her head back and forth, as if willing the deadly killer to leave. And, incredibly, the cat seemed to hesitate, frozen in place as it gazed up at her, even as its needle-sharp claws gripped the sandy bottom of the streambed preparing to pounce.

Though conscious of Killian's presence behind her, Ellianthia could spare no attention to tell him to back away and leave this to her. She had heard the mental cries of fear and panic of two terrified animals coming from this direction the moment she had opened her mind to do a routine scan of the Forest.

All during the race to come to their aid, the images of shiny black fur and slashing claws, and the smell of hot, fetid breath from close behind, had filled her head, along with frenzied thoughts of danger and fear. Then the sensations of a sudden, crushing weight and a sharp, agonizing pain had assaulted her mind, just as she reached the ravine.

Now, she knelt, cradling the panicked fawn while she Sent the silent command *No!* along the mind Link to the crouching feline. *No,* she Sent again, this time more gently, more calmly, as she stared into the panther's large yellow eyes and shook her head slowly. *Big one yours, small one mine,* she Sent, followed by the image of her rolling on her back and exposing her throat in submission to him, then crawling away with the smaller prey in her "paws."

The images flowing though her Link seemed to be working, judging by the great cat's hesitation in the midst of springing. Gradually, the panther relaxed his stance and Sent an image of himself standing over the dying doe and roaring his ownership, while he allowed the Elf to slink away with the fawn, tail between her legs. Ellianthia relaxed a little as well, sensing that the "bargain" had been made.

Then, suddenly, the young animal squirmed out of her arms, its movement distracting the panther's attention and weakening the Link. The cat's head came up, a mighty roar erupting from his throat as he tensed to spring again.

Seeing the Elfin maid in danger, Killian acted without thinking, drawing the bastard sword from its sheath and leaping down the slope to stand between her and the panther. He held the blade before him in both hands, balancing on his toes, preparing to meet the enraged predator when it leapt at him.

"No!" cried Ellianthia aloud, struggling to strengthen the Link and regain control before any blood was shed.

Then someone was singing, filling the ravine with strong, sweet tones that reverberated and echoed as they blended into an aching melody, a song that seemed to embrace every living thing within hearing, soothing all anger and calming all fears, leaving peace and serenity in their place. For that moment, there was nothing in the world but the sound of that golden voice.

Glancing to his left, Killian saw Palladarian standing serenely at the top of the ravine, crooning to the panther, singing a parent's love for a child, a friend's love for a friend, as he fixed it with a steady, gentle gaze. Then Killian watched in amazement as this great ferocious beast closed its jaws and slowly sank down on its belly, stretching its paws out before it as if ensorcelled by the song.

Even as the Elfin Bard kept singing, he gestured for Killian and Ellianthia to back up the slope slowly and join him above. Grasping the now docile fawn in her arms, the Elfin maid stood and carefully made her way up the incline, the prince following her, his blade still in hand as he eyed the panther warily.

When they reached the top, Palladarian ended his song and smiled with relief, then motioned for them to leave the panther to its kill. As they hurried away, they could hear the sound of powerful jaws ripping and tearing into flesh and bone.

They walked in silence for a short time, Ellianthia in the lead carrying the fawn, Killian and Palladarian a few paces behind. Unable to contain his curiosity any longer, Killian turned to the bard.

"What were the two of you doing with the panther?" he asked, the sense of wonder strong in his voice. "It was as if you and she were casting a spell, you with song and she...talking without words or suchlike. I have never seen a wild animal tamed like that."

Before Palladarian could answer, Ellianthia spun around with an exasperated expression. "What were *you* trying to do back there, get us both killed?" she snapped. "I could have handled it without you waving your big sword around."

Killian stopped in mid-stride and stared at her in amazement. "Why, you ungrateful little..." he began, shaking his head in disbelief. Then he reached up over his back and sheathed his blade with an angry shove before jamming his fists down on his hips.

"As I had nothing better to do for the moment, I thought I might try to save your life, since the little pussycat you had under 'control' looked like he was about to take your head off. But I can see I was wasting my time!" Snorting with disgust, he turned and walked away, his boot heels digging deep holes in the soft earth.

"You have no idea what I was doing or what I can do! I did not need your clumsy interference!" she called out after him angrily, though he gave no sign of hearing her.

"He was only trying to help you, Niece," said Palladarian quietly, who had observed the whole exchange with a mix of amusement and concern. "He knows nothing about your gift for Linking. He thought you were in danger—as did I, by the by—and acted without thought to his own safety. I believe you owe your betrothed an apology."

Betrothed indeed! she fumed, resuming the trek back to the place where she had left the others waiting. Truth be told, however, she was feeling more than a little confused about this human. He was the son of a great enemy, and therefore her enemy.

Yet, he was not entirely what she had expected. He was not clumsy or awkward or brutish, despite her continuing determination to cast him in these terms. His performance of the Handfasting Dance yesterday had shown that; and, minutes ago, she had been startled at the speed with which he had followed her during her dash to save the fawn.

Moreover, he had moved through the Forest almost as quietly and gracefully as an Elf, though she shuddered to think she would ever admit that to his face. He was arrogant and stupid about Elfin ways, to be sure; but he was passably well spoken, when he was not yelling. And, despite his hand groping her breast during the Dance, she was not entirely certain that he would have forced himself on her last eve, even had she not held the knife to his throat.

Of course, he might be biding his time, waiting until she had dropped her guard. But she could almost believe his disdainful denial of any desire to "rut" with her. And he had acted to save her this day, if Palladarian was right—not that she had needed saving, she insisted to herself, her anger returning at the thought of being treated like some helpless human female.

Her uncle had said she owed him an apology, but the idea of humiliating herself by actually seeking forgiveness for her anger at his unwelcomed rescue attempt made her stomach clench. Still, all in all, he seemed a most confusing person.

By the time she reached the others, the afternoon was waning, and the rays of the sun sinking toward the horizon had begun to cast a reddish glow where it was visible through the trees. Mellisandria smiled as she saw the fawn in Ellianthia's arms and came over to stroke its head, offering gentle assurance that it would be well cared for.

"We will have to take it with us, I suppose, and hope that we can find another doe to nurse it," she said. Then, looking at the setting sun, the Wise One announced that they would be making camp for the night in a small clearing nearby, for it had grown too late to continue on to the Secret Grove this day.

After attending to the horses, Mik`kel and Mellisandria sat apart in conversation, while Trillafarien relaxed his grim demeanor long enough to let the fawn lap water from his cupped hand.   Palladarian and Killian volunteered to gather fallen branches for a fire, and soon returned with armloads of deadfall.

While they ignited the wood and set the water to boiling, Ellianthia busied herself with unpacking the ingredients for stew from the provisions they had brought in their saddlebags, laying out small pieces of dried rabbit meat, carrots, potatoes, leeks and wild barley, along with salt and rosemary for seasoning.

When Aisleen approached with a quiet offer to help, the Elfin maid initially refused. Then, recalling her earlier reaction to Killian, Ellianthia relented and handed the woman her belt knife to cut the vegetables into smaller chunks. She had hardly spoken a word to this rather striking human female, but Mellisandria's testimonial to Aisleen's gift made her seem a little less useless than Ellianthia might have otherwise thought her. After a while, she found herself exchanging brief comments about various ways to prepare meals on the trail as they waited for the meal to cook.

Soon, the thick stew was bubbling, its rich aroma wafting over the camp and whetting appetites.   Ellianthia produced hard trail biscuits, placing one in each bowl and ladling the steaming stew over them.   For a time, there was little conversation as the party sat around the fire, enjoying the savory fare. Sliced apples and soft white cheese rounded out the meal, washed down by stream-chilled wine from a leather pouch that was passed around the circle.

Feeling pleasantly full, Killian rose and walked a distance into the Woods to relieve himself. When he emerged from the trees, he was surprised to find Ellianthia waiting at the edge of the clearing.

Thinking that she was on her way to answer nature's call as well, he stepped aside to let her pass, but she lingered, gazing down at the ground, her foot tracing patterns in the dirt. Finally, after some hesitation, she looked up at him.

"I guess you meant well enough today, back at the ravine," she admitted, in a low voice almost devoid of inflection. "I know you thought you were helping, even though I could have dealt with it myself, " she finished brusquely, unable to completely curb her frustration over his interference, even in the middle of offering what passed for an apology.

Wary of this unexpected act of contrition—if that was what this was supposed to be—and still resentful of her earlier accusations, Killian frowned.

"It looked like you were in danger," he insisted, unwilling to apologize for coming to her aid. "And I thought it best that I fight it, rather than take the risk that it would attack."

Ellianthia grunted in frustration. "But look you, it was not just the fawn that I was trying to spare from bloodshed, it was the panther as well. As a Guardian, I am called upon to watch over all the animals, including the hunters. I do not blame the panther for taking the doe down. It is part of what he is, part of what he must do to survive. I tried to save the fawn because it was too young to die. We protect the young most of all. But killing the panther without need would have been wrong, too. And the risk was to me, not you."

The prince crossed his arms and bit his lower lip as he thought about her words. Finally, he spoke. "Now look *you,* Princess. A Guardian I may not be, but I would spill the blood of a cat to save a person on any day. We are supposed to be companions of this quest, and companions help each other, though why the gods would yoke us together..." He shook his head, leaving the rest of his thought unspoken and started back to the campfire, then halted.

"Just what *were* you doing with the cat? How did you stop it from attacking you?" he asked, determined to take this opportunity to learn more, since she had deigned to approach him.

Ellianthia shrugged slightly, deciding that it would do no harm to tell him. "Many of our people can Link with trees and animals of the Forest. That means we can sense impressions and feelings from them, images of what they are seeing or thinking, although most animals and trees do not really 'think' in the same way we do. Often, it is just vague impressions or primitive emotions. A few of us—and I am one of those with the gift—are able to share our thoughts with the trees and animals. It is part of our legacy as Guardians of the Forest."

Killian cocked his head to one side, his blue eyes peering at her intently as he tried to grasp her meaning. "Can you actually control them that way...with your thoughts, I mean?"

The Elfin maid shook her head. "Not 'control' exactly, at least not the more clever, stronger-willed animals who can think for themselves. With them, it is more like 'suggest.' I was 'suggesting' to the panther that I was no threat to a big, fierce male hunter like him, and that I would yield the larger kill to him if I could take the smaller prey—hardly a mouthful to him, after all—and leave."

Ellianthia shrugged again, pursing her lips. "He probably thought it was not worth the effort to fight me for the little one, or at least that is what I was Sending to him."

"And Palladarian? I have never heard anyone sing like that before. Morainen's tits! Um...I mean, the cat lay down in front of him like he was a pet," said Killian, still feeling a sense of wonder at what the bard had done.

"My uncle's gift is Song," she replied, with some pride. "That is why he is a master bard. I have heard it said that he could charm the birds down from the trees. There is magic in his voice, enough to cast a spell as much as any mage. When I was a child, my mother used to say that he..."

She broke off abruptly, catching herself before revealing any thing so personal as a cherished childhood memory. Still, Killian thought he saw a look of wistfulness cross her face as she recalled some time of long ago.

Sensing that she had revealed all she intended to, Killian inclined his head. "Thank you for telling me." When she said nothing further, he began walking back to the fire, hearing her following some little distance behind.

That night, everyone slept on blankets and cloaks under the stars, rather than trouble themselves with raising tents. The summer night was warm enough, and the trees sheltered them from cooler breezes. Mik`kel and Aisleen had placed their blankets close together and lay facing each other, though without touching.

With no need to pretend a closeness they did not feel when away from the crowds of well wishers, the betrothed couple slept apart from each other—Killian between the bard and the general, Ellianthia and the Wise One curled up next to the fawn. As the fire crackled one last time before it collapsed into embers and sleep descended over the camp, their last thoughts were of the morrow and what discoveries it might bring.

Chapter 33

Splitting the Stone

The morrow came soon enough, for Mellisandria had the camp up and stirring shortly after dawn. They each took time to relieve themselves, splash water on their faces, and munch on a cold breakfast of bread, cheese and slices of a blood-red fruit called balesca that Killian had never seen before. There was a palpable feeling of anticipation in the air, and all seemed ready to pack up and be on their way without further delay.

Then, just as they were about to leave the camp, Killian witnessed another scene involving Ellianthia that filled him with wonder. He saw her kneeling beside the fawn at the edge of the clearing, gently stroking the young animal's neck and murmuring reassurances while she peered out into the Woods, as if waiting for something to happen. Curious, Killian paused in the midst of cinching his saddle to watch, again surprised by this unexpected display of tenderness so different from the cold, unforgiving side she had shown to him thus far.

His interest was rewarded when, a few minutes later, he heard a quiet rustling in the trees and turned to see a beautiful golden doe step slowly out of the Woods. As with the bear and the fox he had seen yesterday, the deer seemed unafraid of the camp and its inhabitants as she walked forward to nuzzle the Elfin maid's hand.

Killian knew that Ellianthia must be using her gift of Linking, judging by the way that she held the doe's gaze without speaking aloud. Whatever she was "saying" must have been persuasive because the animal lowered her head to sniff the fawn, then bent her neck to nudge the young one closer, directing it toward the row of teats hanging down from a rounded udder that was clearly swollen with milk. For its part, the fawn let out a squeal of joy and began sucking greedily, its small body trembling with contentment and relief.

Killian shook his head, wondering if he had ever seen anything in nature more beautiful than this frightened and hungry little creature being nurtured and comforted like that, so soon after losing its mother to the panther. Not only had the Elfin maid called the deer to her, but she had also managed to find one with a full supply of milk to give succor to the fawn in its time of great need.

As he watched the doe lead the little one away, the fawn following eagerly in search of more milk as they both disappeared into the trees, he saw the look of true happiness on Ellianthia's face and could not help but smile himself. This warrior princess was full of surprises, he thought.

Then the members of the party were mounted and traveling again, wending their way toward the destination that, according to the Wise One, lay some two candlemarks away. Killian watched Ellianthia, who rode ahead of him, sitting her horse like a warrior, back held straight, thighs gripping the mare's girth—though no warrior he had ever known had such shapely hips and comely legs.

The air grew warmer as the sun climbed higher in the sky, until shafts of bright yellow light began to filter through the canopy of leaves and branches arching over them so far above. After a time, they came to an area of dense brambles and thickets, impassable save for a narrow trail that wound through the wall of thorns, requiring them to ride single file.

Mik'kel, who was not the most enthusiastic of riders, had been feeling the return of yesterday's aches since mounting up this morn. He was also less than thrilled by the way the sharp points of the thorns announced themselves in painful fashion whenever he swayed too far in either direction.

The mage was wondering how much longer his arms and legs could withstand this silent assault when he began to sense a powerful magic, even while they were still some distance from the Grove. It started as a faint tingling sensation in his fingers and toes, but was soon spreading throughout his body. Something waited for them up ahead, something ancient and undisturbed for long and long. And it knew they were coming.

Then they were through the thorn wall and riding into a grove of tall pines that seemed completely surrounded by the thickets, as if designed to form a protective circle around the trees. In the midst of the Grove lay a small clearing, perhaps the very one that Killian had described in his vision.

It was there that the feel of the magic was strongest. With his mage sense, Mik'kel could see the aura of power enveloping the open area like an invisible dome that began at ground level and rose some fifty feet above at its apex.

As they drew closer, he encountered a growing resistance that made proceeding forward more and more difficult with each step, as if the very air around him was becoming thicker and more impenetrable. He might have tried to fight it with his own power, but there was little point in doing so—and perhaps little wisdom as well, if the magic was gods-made. Old magic indeed, he thought, content to let events happen as the gods intended without invoking his own considerable arts.

Just when he thought they could advance no further though the aura, Mellisandria raised her hand to signal a halt and slid down gracefully from her mare's back. Spreading her arms wide and turning from side to side, she spoke in a voice filled with respect and reverence.

"Behold the Secret Grove. Our people have been the Keepers of the Grove for centuries, the only ones trusted with the knowledge of its existence and location. The power that you sense around you has guarded this Holy place from intrusion or defilement over the ages, waiting for the prophecy to be fulfilled one day by the 'One who will come to split the stone.' I believe that day is now at hand."

The ancient Wise One's words only added to the sense of awe each person felt as they dismounted to stand in this sacred place, a place that had waited in silence, undisturbed for ages untold, to play its part in the destiny that was now about to be made manifest. Even Palladarian and Trillafarien, who had known of its existence, had never traveled here, had only heard of it in legend.

Ellianthia, though mystified—and more than a little nervous—about what possible role she might have in this unfolding drama, felt privileged and deeply honored to be in the presence of something that was so wondrously wrought. Surely, Sallamarian himself had had some hand in this.

All eyes turned to Killian, who, unlike most of those present, had felt no resistance, no difficulty in passing through the hidden barrier. It seemed to part before him as if it "knew" him and was welcoming him, accepting him into its bosom. He stood looking around him, feeling an eeriness that sprang from having been here already in his vision.

He recognized the same grassy clearing, the same tall mound of tangled vines adorned with purple flowers, and the same granite monolith hidden beneath. Save that, here, now, the mound seemed taller and broader than in his vision, the flowers with crimson centers more vibrantly purple, and the aged Stone more massive and imposing.

He might have gone on staring for some time, but Mellisandria brought him out of his reverie. "It is time, Prince Killian. You must take the hand of your chosen companion and lead her through the aura, so that she may join you before the Stone."

Accepting the inevitable, Killian moved forward to the edge of the clearing, then turned and looked at Ellianthia, holding out his hand. After some hesitation, she inhaled deeply and walked over to his side, raising her hand tentatively to press her palm to his. For the second time in two days, she felt his long, powerful fingers touching her skin gently, and was amazed to feel all traces of resistance to passing through the aura immediately disappear.

She looked up at him, his flame-red hair gleaming in the sun, his blue eyes clear and bright with excitement. What kind of power did this human possess, that he could so easily enter this sacred place, this Elfin sanctuary where even Mellisandria trod lightly? She gripped his hand more tightly, wondering what might happen if she let go. Then, with a nod to her, he stepped out into the clearing.

They walked directly to the mound, hearing no sound save that of their own footsteps, the pounding of their hearts, and the rustle of the grass as they brushed against it in their passing. When they reached the mass of tangled vines and stood before the Stone, he felt humbled by its megalithic size and grandeur. The surface visible beneath the branches and the blossoms appeared smooth and flawless, with no sign of weathering, as if time had stood still for ages here in this place of power.

Killian did not know what he was meant to do next, but he felt drawn to walk around the Stone while it waited for him to unlock its mystery. Still leading Ellianthia by the hand, he had paced perhaps a quarter of the way around its base before he found that same palm-sized circle that he had seen in the vision, positioned partway up the side of the monolith. Knowing instinctively that this was what he had been seeking, he raised his hand toward the circle and looked at Mellisandria for final confirmation that he should proceed.

"It is your destiny," she said, nodding once. With that, he stepped forward and placed his palm flat upon the circle.

At the instant of his touch, a brilliant flash of golden light erupted from the circle, encasing the Calderian prince and the Elfin princess. It lasted for the space of several heartbeats before fading away, or so it seemed to Killian until he turned to look back at the others.

Then several gasps arose from the observers, Ellianthia's loudest and nearest of all, for Killian's eyes were two luminous orbs glowing with divine presence, as if the gods themselves had entered his body and now looked out through their Avatar upon the awestruck mortals gathered there. In that moment, any lingering doubts that he was indeed the chosen vessel of the deities vanished from the minds of those who had witnessed it.

Almost immediately thereafter came a deep rumbling that shook the ground and rattled the lofty branches of the trees around them. A strong gale sprang up from nowhere, whipping hair and clothing about, and making them blink from the force blowing against their faces. The deep vibration seemed to be emanating from within the Stone itself as, before their wind-stung eyes, a vertical crack appeared in that flawless gray surface.

Soon, the crack became a narrow crevice running down from top to bottom, then widened steadily into a rift that grumbled and creaked with every inch of movement, cleaving the granite and snapping the vines that covered it. Then two stone doors, each some five feet in width, pivoted as if on hinges and swung outward, revealing a dark, mysterious opening into the monolith.

Killian glanced at Ellianthia, who was staring back at him with the same expression of shock written on the faces of the other Elves and humans waiting behind them on the edge of the clearing. Though the glow in his eyes had dimmed, he was undeniably the prophecy fulfilled, for all could see that the "One who will come to split the stone" stood before them. She tried to pull her hand away, but he shook his head slightly and pointed toward the opened doors, knowing that their presence was required there. Gathering his courage, he led her inside.

The moment he stepped over the threshold, another golden light flared up, illuminating the interior and evoking cries of amazement from all who bore witness. While the outside of the monolith had a smooth, plain granite surface, the radiance suffusing the interior revealed a beautifully constructed chamber, perhaps ten feet in diameter, with ornately-carved stone arches curving up high above Killian's head to meet in a vaulted ceiling.

Beneath the arch to his left were several small niches and a shallow alcove. But what caught his eye immediately were the four stone tablets mounted to the wall at eye level directly before him. Some three feet high and two feet wide, the tablets were covered with engraved symbols, each different from the others. It appeared to be writing of some sort, but none that

Killian recognized. Below the tablets sat a rectangular stone box with a circular symbol carved into its lid.

The prince and princess stood unmoving for a time, their eyes flickering everywhere around the chamber, taking in the elegant arches, the finely detailed carvings and other fixtures that spoke of a master artist's work.

"Who *made* this place?" Killian wondered out loud. "And what strange language is this?" He finally released Ellianthia's hand and stepped forward to run his fingers over the etched symbols of the closest tablet, then turned to her with a bemused expression.

She peered intently at each of the plaques before pointing to the one on the top left. "I think I recognize some of the writing on this one. The words seem to be in the Elfin tongue, though they are...different."

"That one is written in High Elvish, an older form of our language spoken centuries ago," said a melodious voice from over their shoulders. Killian and Ellianthia turned to find Palladarian standing in the doorway, with the other companions gathered close behind. Apparently, the protective aura preventing the others from entering the clearing had dissipated with the splitting of the Stone. "The tablet next to it on the right seems to be some form of Olden Dwarvish, though my knowledge of that tongue is more limited."

The bard waved his hand at the other two tablets, one of which was covered in spirals and swirls of uneven size that looked more like random scribbling than a formal language. The other showed a collection of crude pictures and symbols of some kind, such as a circle with radiating lines that might stand for the sun, along with images depicting crouching figures with elongated limbs engaged in some unidentified activity.

"Of these other two tablets, I know nothing at all. Perhaps they are written in the language of races who walked this land long ago, but have now vanished."

As the rest of the party crowded in to examine the amazing chamber, Killian examined each of the tablets more closely, considering how Palladarian had described them. It occurred to him that something was missing, though he could not quite...Suddenly, it came to him. He turned to the bard with a puzzled expression. "Why is there no tablet inscribed in the human tongue, the language of my people?"

Palladarian arched his brow, taking a moment to consider the prince's query. But it was Mik'kel, himself a newcomer to the land, who offered the most likely explanation. "Your Highness, it seems likely that the gods created this Stone and the tablets inscribed herein some eight centuries ago, when Rak`koth was last defeated. But that would have been long before your people first came to Balleterria, according to what Aisleen has told me. I suspect that there is no tablet in your language because these ancient messages were placed here to be found by one of the races living here at that time.

"In other words," Mik`kel added with a grin, "it appears that the gods were not expecting you."

"So it would seem," said Killian, smiling wryly. "Perhaps the gods do not foresee everything." Then he pointed to the tablet Palladarian had identified as the one written in High Elvish. "Can you tell us what this one says, Master Bard?"

"I will certainly try, Your Highness, if you will give me but a moment to confer with the Wise One." Palladarian looked at Mellisandria, who edged her way past the others and came to stand next to him in the crowded space. The two Elves bent their heads together for a time, reading through the words inscribed there in their lilting Elvish tongue.

They whispered between themselves as they compared possible meanings, gesturing to one symbol or another, sometimes expressing agreement, other times indicating differences of opinion with a shake of the head or a wave of the hand.

Finally, they reached a consensus and turned back to Killian. Palladarian spoke for both of them.

"The form is a little archaic, but Mellisandria and I have agreed that the best translation reads as follows":

> *In cavern deep, red stone to delve*
> *to serve as compass faire;*
> *Above the clouds, seek ye the door*
> *that waits beyond the stair;*
> *On distant isle, where dwells a mage*
> *who mourns his Ladye rare.*

All listened as the bard recited the inscription, then repeated it again. Killian attended very closely, knowing that it must have some meaning for him, but finding himself completely baffled. "I fear the meaning of this riddle escapes me," he confessed. "A red stone, a door above the clouds, a mourning ma...a puzzle to be deciphered, but where to begin?"

"Indeed, it does appear rather cryptic, Your Highness," agreed Mellisandria thoughtfully. "An odd conundrum to carry within its mysterious phrases a guide to the quest that lies before you. It speaks of something you must do. Perhaps this is the journey you must take, a journey that begins with finding a red stone in a deep cave." She pondered a moment longer, then her eyes lit up with understanding.

"I believe the red stone must be a ruby! I have heard that rubies can store great magical power, though never have I possessed one of my own."

"That is true!" exclaimed Mik`kel, sharing her excitement as he drew closer. "In my native land, rubies have ever been used as talismans and channels of power."

Trillafarien spoke up then, his surly attitude of yesterday now replaced by an obvious interest in the enigma. "If there is a ruby to be found deep in a cavern, the most likely location would be the Dwarven gem mines hidden beneath the Misted Mountains, for that is the only source of rubies known to our people."

"I believe you may be right, General," said Palladarian, with a smile of approval for Trillafarien's contribution. "The mountain folk mine nearly all the precious stones, the diamonds, emeralds—and rubies—that are produced in Balleterria."

"Then," Aisleen suggested, "it would seem that the first step on the journey would be to travel to the Misted Mountains and seek the aid of the Dwarves in finding such a gem."

"Yes," replied Mellisandria, "though whether the Dwarves would be willing to offer any help at all, much less allow you access to their hidden mines, is another question indeed. They are a secretive people who guard their mountains, and their cache of gems, with the fierce protectiveness of a lioness guarding her cubs."

"Still, it would seem we have no choice but to travel there and petition for their aid in this," said Killian, returning to the conversation with the air of someone who has accepted that something must be done and was now determined to do it. "Though to what purpose such a gem might be put remains a puzzle to me. What is this 'compass faire' the riddle mentions?"

"I think I can be of some help in that regard," offered Mik`kel. "The sailors on the ship I boarded to reach your land used a device to stay their course across the trackless sea when the stars were hidden by clouds and storms. They called this device a 'compass.' The ruby must be such a compass—a talisman to guide you in the direction you are to travel."

There was silence as Killian and the others considered this possibility. Then Ellianthia, who had been staring around the chamber as she listened to the others, spoke up.

"So, mayhap the ruby will guide us on our way, assuming for the moment that the Dwarves would be willing to part with such a treasure. But what of this door above the clouds? How could such a door exist, and where? And what of this distant isle where dwells a forlorn mage?"

Killian listened to the Elfin maid's questions, noticing that she had spoken of the ruby guiding "us on our way," a sign that she seemed to be accepting her part in the quest that lay before them. "I know not where or how a door could exist above the clouds," he replied, shaking his head. "But I am wondering if this 'mourning mage' is the same one that the gods spoke of to me. Perhaps he is the one I am destined to find, the one who will teach me the paths of power." He looked to Mik`kel as he finished.

"That may be, Your Highness, though I have no knowledge of where such a mage is to be found."

As he finished speaking, Aisleen made a small noise and pointed to the stone box resting on the bench below the tablets. "What of this?" she wondered aloud. "Perhaps this contains something of meaning."

Ellianthia, who was closer to the container, reached forward to lift the lid, but it did not move. She tried again, pulling harder, but nothing happened.

Recognizing the circle set in the lid as similar to the one on the outside of the monolith, Killian acted on impulse and pressed down on it with his hand. Once again, a flash of bright light appeared and a click could be heard, as if a latch had been sprung. Then the top of the box swung open, readily revealing the contents within, as if it had been waiting only for the person meant to unlock its secrets.

The sides and bottom of the container were lined with a rich purple velvet cloth that looked to be as well preserved as if it had been placed there yesterday. And there, resting on the cloth, were several objects of various shapes and sizes.

Mellisandria gazed down at the array, then looked back up at the others and spoke in a hushed tone. "I would hazard a guess that these objects were placed here by the gods to be found and used by the Avatar and his companions in undertaking the quest. If I may, Your Highness?" she asked, looking to Killian for his approval.

When he gestured for her to proceed, she reached into the box and held up the first artifact, a long silver chain on which was suspended a large silver pendant with a hollowed space in the middle, about the size of a child's fist. As she lifted it to the light, Mik'kel peered closely at the shiny object. With a flash of inspiration, he reached into his robe and pulled out the silver pendant with the blue sapphire set in the middle, a sapphire about the size of...a child's fist!

"Look!" he exclaimed, holding it up for all to see. "This is the pendant given to me by the gods as a talisman to locate Prince Killian. It has the same silver design and an opening for a gem in the middle. If the prince is meant to seek a ruby to serve as a 'compass,' then mayhap this pendant is meant to fit that very gem when it is found."

"You may have the right of it, Lord Mage," Mellisandria said. "In which case, I believe this pendant was meant for you, Prince Killian." She turned and passed the object to him. He took it from her hand and began to examine it closely, noting its fine engraving and expert craftsmanship. Then, abruptly, his vision wavered and grew dim, and everything else around him seemed to fade from view, leaving him alone and confused, as if the world he knew had suddenly ceased to exist.

†††††

He stood in a dark cave, immersed in a blackness devoid of any hint of light, unable to see or hear anything but the beating of his heart. Where was he? What had happened to the others? He was reaching around him anxiously, trying to feel something, anything, when an image of the silver pendant appeared, floating silently in the air in front of him, looking exactly like the object from the box—except that now, the center of the pendant was no longer empty. It encased a brilliant red jewel with myriad facets that sparkled brightly, pulsing and glowing as it spun slowly before him, around and around, suspended on its chain from somewhere above in the darkness.

The sheer beauty of the glittering stone so enthralled him that he could not look away from it, feeling captivated by the light emanating from deep within its core. Only a master jeweler with great skill could have cut it so expertly, in just the right way to reflect the light so splendidly, and to fit the silver circle so perfectly.

He knew then that the pendant and stone were meant to be joined together, a perfect match, one with the other. There was divine power in that union, of that he was certain. It looked so real that he found himself reaching out to grasp it, but his hand passed through the spectral image and into the blackness beyond, although the luminous gem continued to glow.

No, it would not be that easy. Nothing about this task was likely to be easy. Not uncovering the full meaning of the riddle. Not undertaking the quest that was about to begin. Not gaining permission from the Dwarves to search their hidden mines.

His mind raced with thoughts of what he must do, what it now seemed that he had been born to do. He saw his destiny before him, a future that called to him to seek out the stone in a dark place deep in the earth, to retrieve it from the location where it rested, awaiting him, and to hold it in his hand at last. He felt a sense of rightness, a sign that they were following the path intended for them, and that the journey would only truly begin when the gem had been found.

††††††

The vision lingered for another moment, then disappeared, and the world around him gradually returned. He heard voices saying his name, and felt a hand on his shoulder, shaking him gently to get his attention.

"You were glowing again, Lord Prince," said Mellisandria, a question in her eyes.

"The pendant and the stone!" he exclaimed, still somewhat disoriented. "I saw the red jewel set in the pendant, floating before me in a dark place, like a cave! They fit together as if made for each other. I believe you have the right of it, Mik'kel. We seek this talisman to guide us on our way."

"A vision of the gem, you say? This is, indeed, very promising," said the Kal'Dathian mage, the excitement plain in his voice. The news pleased the rest of the party as well, each one heartened by their success in divining the meaning of the first part of the riddle. Ellianthia gazed at Killian thoughtfully, appraising him with new eyes after all that had transpired since first he glowed with heavenly light and split the Stone.

Unaware of her pensive expression, he inspected the pendant once more, then placed the chain around his neck inside his shirt, letting the piece come to rest on his chest. The metal felt warm, almost comfortable, against his skin, like it was meant to be there.

Meanwhile, the Wise One had lifted the next object from the drawer. It appeared to be another pendant, though the center of this one was not hollow. It was made of solid quartz or some other translucent crystalline material, about the size of a woman's palm and suspended on a braided leather thong. The pendant itself was in the shape of a five-pointed star, each point radiating out from the hub.

Mellisandria handed it around among the others, hoping that one of them might have some inspiration as to its purpose. Each examined it in turn, even General Trillafarien, who held it gingerly in his roughly calloused fingers and turned it from side to side. But nothing happened, not even when Killian took it from Mik`kel and closed his hand around it for a moment, before passing it on to Ellianthia.

Yet, when she took it from him, the quartz began to glow softly, as if coming alive in her grasp. She stared at it in confusion, turning it over and over while shaking her head, as if to say that she had no idea why it had responded to her alone. Now it was Killian's turn to look at her with new eyes as he saw the crystal pendant respond to her touch. And when the Elfin maid started to pass it to Mellisandria, the elder Elf pressed it back into her palm.

"No, my dear. I believe this was meant for *you* to carry."

"For me? But why?" Ellianthia questioned, feeling apprehensive—and perhaps a little excited—to be singled out thusly.

"I know not, except that you are the chosen one's companion," replied the Wise One. "I cannot say what purpose this will serve, or why it answers to your touch, but you alone made it glow. Let us hope its purpose will be more forthcoming along the way. For now, I believe it best for you to take it into your custody."

Ellianthia looked around and saw the others signaling their agreement, even Killian, who encouraged her with a little smile. "Very well," she replied, accepting their consensus, albeit still with some misgivings, as she placed the leather thong around her neck so that the crystal star hung down under her tunic between her breasts. Like Killian's pendant, hers seemed meant to rest there.

With that settled, Mellisandria then reached inside the box again and took out the last remaining artifact, a black iron object about a foot or so long, cast in the shape of what appeared to be a small hammer or axe. Although the fine workmanship on the edges and surfaces suggested that the casting had been done by someone with great skill, the piece itself was rather plain, and could have been dismissed as an ordinary tool of some sort—save for an exquisitely cut emerald the size of a robin's egg that was embedded in the spot where the handle joined the blade.

She passed it around to the rest of the party, but there came no glow of light or other sign of any kind to indicate what its purpose might be, or for whom it might have been intended. When it came to Aisleen, the seeress lifted it and peered at it more closely, wondering if she could use her gift of Finding to locate its true owner or perhaps its place of origin. She sensed that her attention was drawn to somewhere in a westerly direction, but could not be certain. She said as much to the others in the party as she passed it on.

When it came to Palladarian, he remarked that there was something familiar about the iron object as he gripped it in his hand, as if he had seen its like before, though he could not recall where or when. When he told this to the others, Mellisandria suggested that the bard keep it in his possession for the time being, in the hope that something might occur to him later. Palladarian agreed to do so, pleased to have his Wise One's trust.

The box now empty, Mellisandria requested that the others look around the chamber for any other small treasure that might be of some use. The alcove set into the wall contained a small pedestal that looked as though it may have housed a statue or some religious relic at one time, but it was empty now. There seemed little else to be found in the room, until Aisleen spied a small velvet pouch lying in the back of a niche higher up on the wall.

"Look here," she said, reaching into the shadowy recess and drawing the bag forth into the light.

She handed it to the Elfin Wise One, who opened the drawstring and looked inside, then gave a startled little cry as she drew out four flat oval stones, each about four inches in length and two inches in width, all of them the color of light jade with thin veins of gold spiraling into a helix.

The stones were smooth and highly polished, and their identical shape and color clearly marked them as part of a matched set. The others looked at them with curious uncertainty, but Mellisandria needed no explanation to know what she held in her hands.

"Why, these are Speaking Stones! I have never seen one, but I have heard them described by clan elders when I was but a girl."

"Speaking Stones?" asked Ellianthia, with a blank look. "You mean stones that talk?"

The Wise One chuckled softly. "No, my dear, not exactly. These Stones are imbued with a magic that allows the bearer to speak across great distances to another person who carries a similar Stone. They are very rare, almost forgotten in our time. Surely the gods meant them to be used in your quest. I will need some time to learn more about their use, but I believe they will be a great boon on your journey. If you will allow me, I will keep them for the moment to study them further." When Killian and Ellianthia agreed, she placed them carefully back into the pouch and tied the drawstring securely to her belt.

Then, with a final look around the chamber, they walked back out of the Stone into the afternoon sunlight. With the magical aura that had surrounded the Grove now gone, the place appeared much as any other clearing in the Forest, save for the granite monolith that remained, open and empty, its treasured contents removed, its purpose seemingly fulfilled at last after ages of solitary waiting.

There was sound and movement all around them in the clearing now, as birds, butterflies and other small animals began to appear, already intent on reclaiming the place where no living thing had entered for so long. Mellisandria glanced back at the opened stone once more, pleased by the thought that it would soon become a home for her beloved creatures of the Forest. Then, with a satisfied smile, she turned her eyes ahead to the future.

And so, the long era of the Secret Grove as a place of power came to an end that morn. Still, it was a measure of the deep respect and reverence that this ancient site had commanded for centuries that the travelers remained silent as they mounted their horses and rode away.

Chapter 34

Conundrums and Plans

When Killian and the others emerged from the Forest at Kings' Meet that evening, they were met by a messenger who informed them that the monarchs of both royal houses were gathered in the Elfin king's tent, awaiting their arrival. After a brief delay to relieve themselves and wash up a bit, Mellisandria led them to the king's tent.

There, they were all greeted warmly and ushered to seats around a long table, where they were offered wine and a light repast. Gavan and Rillandariel sat side by side, with Ellianthia seated to her father's left and Killian to his father's right, next to Queen Briana.

Killian noted that, in addition to the monarchs, a number of other humans and Elves were in attendance as well. He saw Brurik, Doughal, Kinnith and even Reagen sitting at one end of the table. Several unfamiliar Elves were seated at the other end.

His friends, Colum and Gilmore, were also there, standing behind the king, apparently acting as his aides. He caught Col's eye and gave a questioning look. Col grinned and inclined his head toward Gavan, as if to say that his father would explain. And, indeed, following a brief whispered conference with the Elfin king, Gavan rose to speak.

"Thank you all for coming. King Rillandariel, my Lady Queen and I give you welcome. We are gathered here for two reasons. The first is to welcome back Prince Killian and Princess Ellianthia from their journey to the Secret Grove. We wait with great interest and curiosity to learn what they have discovered." He smiled at the betrothed couple before continuing.

"The second reason for asking you here is less propitious, but necessary all the same—to seek your assistance in the formation of a Joint Council of War, a melding of the leaders of our peoples, whose task it will be to begin planning for the black day that the forces of the foreign Empire invade our lands.

"Not long ago, our two peoples were at war. Now we gather in peace to make common cause against a fierce and ruthless enemy who threatens us all." He gazed around the table at the expectant faces, some appearing more pleased than others about this coming together of two former enemies under one roof.

"Such an undertaking will require the combined resources of both our kingdoms and the unconditional cooperation of their leaders. It is our mutual hope"—here he included the Elfin king with a slight bow—"that this first meeting will lay the groundwork for such cooperation. Allow me to formally introduce the Calderians present here to our new allies, though I suspect we have all had occasion to learn of each other under less fortunate...circumstances."

He turned to look down the table as he gestured to the Calderians in attendance. "You know my Lady, Queen Briana, who shares my rule and my heart. This is General Brurik, Commander of our Army. Next to him is Doughal, our Armsmaster; Reagen, a Blademaster and warrior of great skill who has instructed my son; and Kinnith, our King's Bard. Some of you already know Mik`kel, the Kal`Dathian mage, who was sent by the gods to aid us against the peril that comes to our shores. And Seeress Aisleen." As he announced their names, each person stood in turn and nodded before returning to their seat.

Then King Rillandariel rose to join his brother king. "I, too, welcome you all on behalf of the Elfin people. I would re-introduce Mellisandria, our Wise One; Master Bard Palladarian; and General Trillafarien, Commander of the Elfin forces. Beside him is Amarillia, our chief strategist. And these are Corandillian, Bowmen Captain; and Horse Captain Berollien," continued the king, pointing to the two muscular Elfin males sitting beside Amarillia, similarly dressed in Forest hues of greens and browns, each with the bearing of someone accustomed to command.

After the introductions had been completed, the people on both sides sat quietly, studying one another. Any good commander made it his business to know his enemy as thoroughly as possible, to know his strengths and vulnerabilities, character and proclivities. Thus, while the military leaders of both races had not met their counterparts face to face, in a sense, they already knew each other well from years of meeting as enemies across the battlefield.

What they had learned about their enemies had brought a grudging respect, for each side had fought with courage, and as much honor as war allowed. Now they would see if respect won in time of war could beget trust in time of peace—trust, and perhaps, a kind of friendship.

Rillandariel resumed his seat and raised the question that was uppermost on the minds of those seated around the table. "Now that we have been introduced, I would know just what occurred at the Secret Grove this day." He looked at the members of Killian's party expectantly.

Mellisandria began with a brief account of their journey to the ancient site and a description of the aura of power that had surrounded it like a protective wall. Amarillia, Corandillian and Berollien had heard of the Grove in legend, but had never had occasion to see it. When the Wise One described how the aura had yielded to Killian's presence, thereby confirming his right to enter the Grove and approach the Stone, all gathered there turned their attention to him.

Taking their cue, Killian offered his description of his first sight of the clearing and the monolith resting at its center. "I knew not what to do when I stood in front of the Stone with Ellianthia, but I felt drawn to touch it. I had the odd sense that it had been waiting for me—or for us." He glanced over at the Elfin maid, who was thinking that it was the first time she had heard him speak her name.

Then everyone present, monarchs and members of the newly-formed Council of War alike, listened with rapt attention as Mik`kel spoke of the bright light that had erupted from the monolith at the prince's touch, of the golden glow shining forth from his eyes, and of the mighty rumbling and the sudden wind that had heralded the splitting of the Stone while they looked on. Those who had not seen the spirit of the gods glowing in Killian's eyes looked at him across the table with new respect, while those who had witnessed his transformation during the Awakening Ritual, or in the Grove itself, nodded their agreement.

A most dramatic testimonial to the wonder of these events came from a wholly unexpected quarter, when Trillafarien rose to confirm the miracle that had occurred that very morn. "It happened just as the mage described. It was as if the gods themselves were there with us, looking through the prince's eyes," said the Elfin general, bowing toward Killian in an open gesture of humility and esteem.

"Your Highness, I would ask your pardon for doubting you and the divine nature of your quest; and I will swear before all here this eve that, henceforth, you will have my full support."

Killian stared at Trillafarien in surprise, then graciously inclined his head in acceptance of the general's sworn pledge of loyalty, feeling greatly moved—and not a little relieved—to have won so staunch an opponent to his cause. Watching this amazing exchange, Amarillia and Corandillian looked at each other with raised eyebrows, and then to Berollien. To see so adamant and openly bitter a foe of the humans as General Trillafarien himself bow his head in respect to the human prince did as much as anything else they would hear that day to convince the other Elfin military leaders that their full allegiance to this human prince was warranted.

After a pause, Palladarian told of entering the monolith and discovering the amazing chamber that awaited them therein. He described the four tablets found upon the wall, each with a message inscribed in a different tongue. Then, in a lyrical voice, the bard repeated the riddle for all to hear:

> *In cavern deep, red stone to delve*
> *to serve as compass faire;*
> *Above the clouds, seek ye the door*
> *that waits beyond the stair;*
> *On distant isle, where dwells a mage*
> *who mourns his Ladye rare.*

A buzz of conversation around the table followed Palladarian's recitation. There could be little doubt that the riddle must indeed be intended as a guide to undertaking the quest, and that recovering the red jewel from the Dwarven mines must be the next step to be taken—though Amarillia echoed Mellisandria's earlier reservations that the Dwarves would not take kindly to the notion of their hidden mines being entered by outsiders, based on what she had heard of the mountain folk.

"I agree, Lady Amarillia," said King Gavan. "However, I fear that we must endeavor to seek their help in this, and find some way to prevail upon them to grant it. Unfortunately, they are not due to come out of their mountain hold to trade with us again for another two months or some such, and I doubt that we can afford to delay the quest's beginning for that long. So it would seem that Prince Killian and Princess Ellianthia must travel to them, if we can determine where they might be found, that is. They have an uncanny way of making themselves scarce when they choose to."

Queen Briana leaned forward with a look of inspiration. "Mayhap we might ask one of our own traders, one who has had contact with the Dwarves before, if he knows how such a meeting might be arranged."

"The very thing to do," her husband agreed, smiling at her and beckoning over his shoulder. "Lord Gilmore, pray discover if such a trader remains in our camp and bring him to us."

"At once, Sire," replied Gilmore with a short bow, and left the tent with some haste, as he was anxious to return and hear more of what transpired in the meeting.

While they awaited the arrival of the trader, Ellianthia continued their tale of the day's events at the Sacred Grove, describing how the rectangular box had opened only to the prince's touch. Rillandariel then asked to see the artifacts they had recovered.

Killian and Ellianthia took the pendants from around their necks and passed them around the table, while Palladarian also displayed the small iron object he was carrying. Everyone examined the objects closely, but could offer no further insight into their purpose.

They listened closely as Killian told of his vision of the pendant floating before his eyes, joined with a sparkling red gem. They learned how the star pendant the Elfin maid carried appeared to be intended for her, especially when they witnessed it glow briefly as it was returned to her hand. Of the iron artifact they could say little, and passed it back to Palladarian for safekeeping.

Then Mellisandria produced the Speaking Stones and explained their use. No one there except the Wise One and Palladarian had ever heard of the existence of magical objects such as these, and all expressed great interest. King Rillandariel asked for a demonstration, whereupon the ancient Elf handed one of the jade-colored ovals to her king and asked him to wait for a moment, then left the tent.

Several minutes later, the Stone in the king's hand began to hum quietly. Soon after, Mellisandria's voice could be heard issuing from the Stone, asking, in a clear though somewhat distant voice, "Can you hear me, Your Majesty?"

As the others there looked on with surprise, Rillandariel laughed with delight. "Indeed I can, Wise One!" he exclaimed. "I can hear you quite well! What a wondrous gift from the gods. And can you hear me?"

"Yes, Your Majesty, quite clearly," came her reply, more loudly now.

"Excellent!" said the Elfin king. "Please return to us now."

Within minutes, she was seated once again at the table, answering questions about the origins of the Stones, the distance over which voice communication might take place, and the like. Briana seemed particularly taken by the idea that they might be used to maintain contact with her son and his betrothed on their journey.

The Elfin Wise One nodded her approval. "My thoughts exactly, Your Majesty. If you will allow a suggestion, I would give one Speaking Stone each into the keeping of the prince and princess, so that if one is lost along the way, the other may still be used. I would further propose that we select one person from each of our peoples to be the bearer of the two remaining Stones, so that both Calderia and we of the Forest kingdom can make contact as needed."

King Rillandariel looked at his daughter, who nodded slightly, then back at Mellisandria. "Wise One, since you are most knowledgeable about the Stones, I would ask that you serve as our bearer."

"Of course, Your Majesty. I would be happy to do so," she responded with evident pleasure.

Gavan and Briana held a whispered conversation, then the queen nodded and turned to Aisleen. "Seeress, my Lord King and I are agreed that you should be the bearer for our people. It was already our hope that you could use your gift of Scrying to inform us of their progress along the way, and it would seem fitting that your gift be used for this purpose as well." Feeling proud to be thusly honored and trusted, Aisleen immediately acquiesced, while Mik`kel smiled at her approvingly.

Just then, Gilmore returned with a thin, balding, hawk-nosed man clad in the brown leather tunic and breeches which traders often favored during their travels over great distances. The man bowed to the monarchs, and to the others present around the table, looking thoroughly intimidated and not a little confused as to the reason for being suddenly invited to attend this august body. Gilmore offered a brief introduction.

"Your Majesties, this is Errol of Camdin, a trader with experience in commerce with the Dwarves—or so I was told by his peers."

"Your Majesties," said Errol, bowing again. "Please forgive my humble travel attire. I was just packing up to leave at dawn." He looked around the tent, noting the obvious interest with which he was being regarded. "How may I be of help?" he asked respectfully.

Gavan explained the need to make contact with the Dwarves and the purpose thereof. When the king had finished, Errol took a moment to think on what he had been told.

"Sire," he said finally, "as it happens, I have had some dealing with our Dwarven friends. They are an elusive lot and most difficult—nay, impossible—to find, save when they emerge from their mountains to trade. I know not the hidden location of their hold; and, in truth, I doubt it much that they would be willing to invite the 'outlanders' as they call us into their home." He scratched his beard thoughtfully.

"However, I do know of a certain place just into the Misted Mountains where we have conducted business a time or two, though I can offer no surety that they would be inclined to meet with anyone."

"I understand," said Gavan. "Would you be willing to lead a party, including Prince Killian and Princess Ellianthia, to this location? The Crown would look favorably upon you in any future matters of commerce; and, of course, you would be compensated for any loss of business you might incur while serving as their guide."

The trader regarded the king's offer with a look of shrewd understanding. He was sorely anxious to regain the good graces of the Crown after his guild had suffered grievous damage to its reputation from the theft of the Thalesi leaves by some of his more unscrupulous brethren. Too, the promise of special consideration from the king in future business held no little appeal for him.

In less time than it would take to bite into a coin to verify its gold content, Errol was bowing deeply and proclaiming, "I am at your disposal, Sire. How soon should I be ready to leave?"

Gavan chuckled to himself, amused by the trader's quick appraisal of the situation and his immediate grasp of the practical benefits accruing from pleasing the Crown. "We will let you know anon, do you remain in camp."

Already counting his good fortune, Errol bowed once more and was turning to leave the tent when he was brought to a halt by another regal voice calling to him.

"Good sir," said Briana, "I would have you tarry a moment longer while I discuss another matter with the king."

"Of course, Your Majesty," said Errol, wondering what the queen might have in mind. He waited respectfully as she bent her head toward her husband in quiet conversation. After a brief discussion, Gavan nodded his head in agreement and Briana turned to address her eldest son.

"Killian, since you will be traveling west and passing near enough to Murrough, I would have you take the time to meet with your grandfather, Baron Riordan. As you know, his health has been declining, and he has not been fit to visit us for some time. It may be the last chance for any of us to..." She paused, a look of sadness crossing her face briefly.

"Well, who knows what the future holds. But, as I can not go to him right now, I want you to carry a personal letter to him from me, and another missive explaining the situation we are confronting. I realize it may delay your journey to the Dwarven mines for a bit, but..."

"Of course, Mother," Killian interrupted, stricken by the thought that his grandfather could be so close to passing the veil. "I will be glad to do so. I have missed him as well."

"Good," she replied. "That is settled." She turned back to the waiting trader. "Good sir. I trust you can accompany my son and the others to my father's barony and still make good time to the mines in the west?"

"Yes, Your Majesty. It will mean a small delay, but I know a path through the mountains near Murrough that will speed us on our way." With that, he bowed his way out of the tent and hastened to make his preparations.

Chapter 35

A Quest Begun

After a brief hiatus for refreshing their wine goblets, Rillandariel rose again and cleared his throat to speak. "Now that the arrangements for a guide have been made, it would behoove us to consider who else might accompany Prince Killian and his chosen companion on the journey. We can not know what lies ahead beyond acquiring the talisman, nor how long or arduous their path might be, ere they reach their final destination. They will have need of support," he observed, glancing around the table for opinions.

General Brurik was the first to speak. "We might send an armed company of men with them for protection—men and Elves, that is," he added, in deference to his allies.

"True, General Brurik," replied Amarillia, after some consideration. "That would offer greater safety. Yet a large armored company might slow their travel and require more frequent re-provisioning of supplies and feed for the horses. And such a host of warriors might be seen as a threat if they must needs pass through lands beyond our own. There is something to be said for a small party traveling fast and light," she concluded.

Having had reason enough to learn respect for the former battle captain's skills as an opponent and a most capable strategist during the war, Brurik nodded graciously. "There is wisdom in your words, my Lady. Indeed, it may be that a smaller group would be more advisable."

"Your Majesty," said Mik`kel, rising, "if I might be of service on such a journey, I am yours to command." The mage's offer sent a sinking feeling burrowing into the pit of Aisleen's stomach at the thought of a long separation from him, now that they had come together at last, though she strove to keep her expression from betraying her.

Gavan held up his hand. "I doubt not that you would be a great help, Lord Mage. But I fear I will have greater need of you here. You are the only Kal`Dathian among us, and hence the only one who can speak with first hand knowledge of the enemy we are likely to face, and what measures we may take to counter him when he comes."

"As much as I regret saying it, my father speaks true, Mik`kel," Killian added, unashamed to allow his feeling of loss for being without the mage's company to be known. "You are needed here, though dearly would I love to have you with us—as much for your wisdom as for your skills in the ways of magic." The fondness and respect he had come to feel for his first mentor in the paths of power was not lost on those gathered there, least of all Mik`kel, who returned his gaze warmly. Sitting by his side, Aisleen breathed a small, silent sigh of relief.

"Then, Your Highness, I might suggest another mage, perhaps Niocal, to go in my place," offered Mik`kel. "From what I know of him, he is strong in the power. I am given to understand that he will be arriving from Brannock Castle on the morrow. Perhaps he would be willing, do you and your sire agree."

King Gavan had given his approval when Mellisandria addressed the group with a wistful inflection in her voice. "Would that these old bones could stand the long stretches in the saddle and cold nights on the ground, for I would gladly propose myself for the journey. And I am afraid that our captains here"—nodding at Corandillian and Berollien—"would be best used lending their experience and skills to leading our warriors against the enemy when the time comes."

Gavan's glance at their faces revealed expressions of rueful resignation, for neither was so old that his blood was not stirred by the thought of undertaking such an enterprise as a mysterious quest. Yet, even as the Wise One spread her hands in a gesture of regret, another lilting Elfin voice was heard.

"If I may, I will go," Palladarian announced, rising to speak. "I have some knowledge of spells and a facility with languages. I am familiar with the Dwarven tongue, which will be of some use. And," he added, glancing at Ellianthia with a twinkle in his eyes, "it would allow me to keep an eye on my niece."

"Uncle! I am no longer a child," exclaimed the Elfin maid, shaking her head with exasperation and some embarrassment. Secretly, however, she found herself instantly heartened by the idea of his presence on the journey, knowing that she would be glad for his company, especially when traveling with the humans.

"Besides," continued the bard in a more somber tone as he turned to Rillandariel, "I would rather keep busy these days, if you will give me leave to go, Sire."

Mellisandria and Amarillia looked upon their old, dear friend with sympathy, as did all those who were aware of his loss and the pain that still dwelled in his heart. The Elfin king, who knew much about loss himself, looked at his daughter. Seeing her expression, he did not hesitate further.

"You have my leave, brother of my Lady wife, though I confess I am loath to see you go again so soon after returning to us. We will miss you, and pray that you will come back to us ere too long."

Even as Palladarian bowed and resumed his seat, another voice, this one deep and gruff, rumbled through the tent, drawing all eyes to the tall, husky man in black with the scarred cheek. "Your Highness," said Reagen, standing at attention facing Killian, "I offer my sword and my life to you and your betrothed." He slapped a closed fist to his heart sharply and bowed his head, in the manner of a Delgarian officer addressing his commander.

"You are volunteering to go with us, Captain?" asked the prince, taken a bit aback by this unexpected turn. He had imagined that the Blademaster would be more than eager to be free of the uninvited wyrd laid upon him by the goddess, Doritha, now that his training was nigh unto completed.

"I am, Your Highness. I was sent to offer my skills to you, such as they are. You have proved to be a more than apt learner. Indeed, no other man but you has bested me in twenty years. It seems I have little left to teach you. Still, I believe I can be of some aid to you, Lord Prince. I have no other...obligations...at this time, and I would fight at your side, if you will have me."

Then, to Killian's surprise, the Delgarian dropped to one knee and bowed his head. "I...I ask that you take me into your service as your liegeman, Your Highness. I will serve you faithfully and well, to the death."

Killian looked to his father with some uncertainty. He had never had a man swear allegiance directly to him, rather than to his sire—though Col and Gilly behaved as if they had—and he wondered that a man of Reagen's experience and ability would want to bind himself in service to a lad half his age.

Moreover, it seemed a daunting responsibility to accept, particularly because, in swearing to him, Reagen formally and publicly renounced all loyalties and ties to his former liege lord, Duke Robelin of Delgaria, and to the Black Guard as well. To a man with a long history of service to that illustrious band of warriors, such a step was momentous indeed.

Still, Killian had grown to respect and admire this gruff, taciturn Blademaster who spoke most eloquently with his sword. And Gavan seemed content to have the captain oath-bound to his son, judging by the king's smile of approval. So, feeling both nervous and proud, Killian squared his shoulders and spoke the ritual words he had heard so often when men pledged themselves to the king.

"Captain Reagen, I accept you into my service as my liegeman, with all the rights and duties thereof. I would consider myself most fortunate if you would join us, good sir," Killian added with sincerity, pleased at the prospect of having such a formidable fighter at his back. "And despite your kind words, Captain, I suspect you still have much to teach me."

As Reagen rose and slapped his fist to his chest again, the prince caught the looks of doubt and uncertainty on the faces of Ellianthia and the other Elves present, and hastened to explain. "My father told you that Captain Reagen had been endeavoring to further my skill in combat arms. Perhaps I should add that the man who stands before you is a former officer of the Delgarian Black Guard, and that Doritha, goddess of battle, marked him personally and sent him to me."

Killian's words brought looks of speedy reappraisal from the Elfin side of the table. Amarillia, Corandillian and Berollien exchanged whispers, with Ellianthia leaning forward to join in as well. Whether it was the mention of the fabled Black Guard, of whom even the Elves had heard, or Doritha's taking a direct hand in his choosing, it was clear that their esteem for Reagen had risen quickly. Their hasty conference at an end, Amarillia turned back to Killian and spoke for all of them.

"Even among our people, the name of the Black Guard is held in high regard. We are pleased to welcome such a redoubtable warrior in support of our cause."

Reagen was returning to his seat when Gavan heard the sound of throats being cleared discreetly behind him, and turned to see Colum and Gilmore practically foaming like rabid dogs, their nostrils flaring with barely restrained impatience to speak. The king laughed, remembering well the ardor and enthusiasm with which young knights sought adventure and glory.

"Yes, yes, young Lords, I know the fire that burns in your bellies, and I am concerned for the safety of the prince and the princess as well. I might allow *one* of you to accompany

Prince Killian and the others, at least part of the way, keeping in mind Lady Amarillia's well-taken point about the drawbacks of sending an overly large group."

He then turned to the Elves, seeking their agreement. "If our Elfin allies would like to propose another of their people to serve as added protection, that would bring the total number to seven, which would seem a prudent size."

"I am sure we can find another among our people who would be eager to join, Your Majesty," ventured Corandillian with a wry smile, recalling the drives of his own youth as he gazed at the two young Calderian lords—who, no doubt, were already hatching plots in their heads about how each might maneuver himself into being chosen to go.

"Indeed," said Mellisandria, "I have in mind a most skillful healer who would be of great benefit to the party in the event of illness or injury. He is quite talented, and a likable fellow as well."

"Very well, then, if all are agreed," concluded Gavan, "the only remaining questions for the nonce would seem to be how much time we have before the enemy arrives on our shores, and how quickly the prince and princess must embark on their journey." He turned to Mik`kel. "Lord Mage, can you tell us anything more about when this sorcerer might come against us?"

Mik`kel stroked his auburn beard as he pondered the king's inquiry. "My Lord King, when I sailed from the Isle of Serenity to Calderia, there were seamen aboard who had crewed ships that docked in various ports along Surrikand's coast, including Mertania, the biggest port on the continent. The sailors reported that Rak`koth is building a great fleet of ships, and has been doing so for some time now."

The mage rubbed his palms together pensively. "I know not how close he is to launching his fleet. But is he to arrive this year, he must do so before the storm season comes, for the Luminous Sea is said to be too turbulent to navigate safely after that, especially for ships carrying the large numbers of men needed for a full-scale invasion."

General Brurik rose as Mik`kel finished. "My King, I also have information that Rak`koth's fleet is near to launching. I can provide a more detailed account, based on what I have heard from those I dispatched to learn of his invasion preparations. But there seems little doubt that he will be upon us before the summer storms."

Alarmed by these revelations, Ellianthia rose, placing her palms squarely on the table and leaning forward intently. "My Lords, do you say that we have two months at most before he comes...and possibly less than that?"

Mik`kel glanced over at Aisleen, their eyes meeting as they both shared the thought that time would not be so short now if both kings had heeded his warning months ago, and made efforts to bring their foolish war to an end sooner. But there was little to be gained at this point by castigating both races for their blindness to the greater evil, so Mik`kel merely nodded to confirm the Elfin maid's conclusion.

"Then it would seem we have little time to lose," said Killian, facing all gathered. "How soon before we can all be ready to leave?"

††††

Two days. That was the answer to Killian's question. It took two days for the necessary supplies to be gathered, plans to be made, travel routes to be discussed in more detail with Errol the trader, and farewells to be tendered to families and loved ones.

Killian spent a good part of both days with Mik`kel, practicing the "focusing" exercises that the mage had begun teaching him sometime after the Awakening Ritual. The exercises were meant to help him improve his ability to concentrate inwardly, to touch the magic that now lay within his reach, only awaiting his mastery of the power.

As before, Killian sat with legs crossed and eyes closed for long periods, working to become more adept at sinking down inside himself to find the core of power buried deep, the power that been released from its shell. "Find the power and call it to you, and the magic will come, little by little," Mik`kel promised. "Use the exercises to prepare yourself for the day when you will call great magic, mayhap even greater than we can imagine."

Killian followed each instruction religiously, impressing his mentor with his diligence and determination. By the end of the second day, Mik`kel pronounced him much improved and congratulated him on the strides he had made, while impressing upon him the need for continued practice. Then he walked the prince to the door of his tent and kissed both cheeks, in the traditional Kal`Dathian manner of parting.

Killian passed his last evening before leaving in the company of Colum and Gilmore, sharing a bottle of wine while they offered lurid speculations—in his hearing, of course—about what might have happened with the Elfin princess on his betrothal night. When he grunted and shook his head, Gilmore had nudged Colum in the ribs and made a comment about the warrior maid "wearing our lad out." But the familiar attempts at ribald humor fell rather flat that eve, perhaps because each knew that their lives would be changed forever in the coming days, what with Killian's journey and the coming invasion; and because each knew that their years of youthful innocence were coming to an end.

It turned out that Colum had won the right to be included on the quest, and Gilmore spent an inordinate amount of time bemoaning how he had been "cheated," though neither of them would tell Killian exactly how the matter had been decided. So, with two leaving and one staying behind, the three boyhood friends sat and drank, trading stories about the past and voicing speculations about the future, sharing their affection in the unspoken way that young men grown as close as brothers often do.

The next morning, the queen wept and bade Killian to be careful, while the king clasped him tightly to his chest and spoke quietly of how proud he was of his son and heir—and then, with moistened eyes, bade him be careful as well, "for your mother's sake."

Aaron, who seemed to be growing taller every day, confided that he wished he were going with his older brother, and made Killian promise to remember every detail of the journey and share it with him when he returned. Rowena, too young to understand the seriousness of what lay ahead for her brother, kissed him with her sweet little lips and made him promise to "Bring something back for me, Killy. Something nice."

Ellianthia had spent the time collecting her equipment, walking alone in the Wood and saying goodbye to her Mother Tree, when she was not talking with her father and Mellisandria of what might lie ahead. When it was time to go, she hugged them both and spoke of her love for them, with a catch in her voice and an errant tear that she quickly wiped from her eyes, before mounting and riding to meet Palladarian, who had already taken leave of his king.

Reagen had not been expecting anyone to see him off, but Doughal came to him and gripped his arm in a soldier's farewell, offering his best wishes and godspeed, while urging him to guard his prince closely. The Black Guardsman clasped the veteran Armsmaster in return, strangely moved by the sentiment offered from the first warrior with whom he had shared any real feeling of comradeship since the day when he had left his company in disgrace.

The only notable—and potentially disastrous—disruption to a smooth departure came when Niocal joined the small band shortly before they were to leave. Ellianthia peered at the battle mage with some intensity as he approached the group, trying to place this human who looked vaguely familiar. Then recognition came, followed closely by an explosion of anger.

"I know you!" she exclaimed, racing over to stand directly in front of him, pointing her finger in rage, her other hand going to the hilt of the blade on her hip. "You are the human mage who murdered my people and my trees with your gods-be-damned fire!"

Niocal, looking greatly stricken and deeply ashamed, spread his hands in supplication. "Please, my Lady, I did not mean to cause so much destruction. I yet have terrible dreams about that day." He shuddered as the image of the killing and the holocaust he had unleashed came vividly to his mind once more.

"But, in truth, when your fighters ambushed my patrol, all I could see was my friends dying around me, with no way to escape."

As he spoke, he peered more closely at her, and another wrenching image came to his mind as well, an Elfin archer with golden hair crouching in the trees and loosing the shaft that put an end to Farris. This vision called up some of his own wrath from its hiding place beneath the layers of guilt and remorse.

"And *you* were the one who killed my captain, with no warning, a cowardly deed!" he retorted angrily. "You put an arrow in his chest and left him to bleed to death. You never gave him or any of us a chance!"

The Elfin maid bristled at that, her hand beginning to draw the blade from its sheath. "You were trespassing on our land, slinking in like common thieves," she accused. "We had every right to protect our Forest, and you had been warned, human dog!"

She might have continued baring steel against him, with dangerous consequences for one or both of them, had not Palladarian stepped in to stay her hand with his own and drag her apart from the others to speak privately to her. "Listen, Niece," the bard declared in a quiet, no-nonsense voice. "We were at war. Many, too many, died on both sides. Did you not expect this mage to use his power when his companions were dying before his eyes? Had you not just killed all of his men?"

"But Uncle," she protested vehemently, "he used his horrible magic to burn our people alive!"

"Yes," Palladarian replied, wincing inside at the terrible image her words elicited. "I know. It was a fell thing to do. But that strong magic is the very reason King Gavan asked him to go with us. Besides, he was chosen by their king, and we must honor his wishes. You do not have to like him, but we must all work together."

She glared at the Calderian mage, galled all the more by the knowledge that Palladarian spoke truly. She also recalled Niocal's act to free her from being trapped under the tree, and the odd expression of regret and confusion just before he had used a spell to disappear that day, as if he had wished things could have gone differently. Still, she could hardly stand to see his face, much less travel with him, without feeling the pain anew, as if the wounds had been freshly inflicted.

"Very well, Uncle," she replied, her voice ominously cold. "But you had better keep him away from me, for I would just as soon kill him as look at him."

Killian and the others in the party, which now included an Elfin healer named Dellendrien, had discreetly remained aloof from this caustic exchange between the Elfin princess and the human mage. When Ellianthia finally mounted her mare and followed Errol out of the camp, Killian let her go ahead of him, so that she could ride up front with Palladarian and the trader.

He remained a few paces back, with a thoughtful, and unusually quiet, Colum at his side. Niocal had wisely decided to stay well away from the seething maid for the present, and rode behind with Dellendrien, making light conversation as two people who have just met are wont to do. Having appointed himself as rear guard, Reagen took up his solitary post behind the mage and the healer.

As Errol had already explained, the journey would take them west across Calderia for some days before turning north. They would pass through the Duchy of Glashan and, per the queen's request, up into the Barony of Murrough, where Riordan, Briana's father, still ruled in vassalage to Gavan.

There, Killian would visit with his grandfather and deliver the letters sent by his mother and father.

With this done, they would head through the mountains below Dunmoria, cross the West River and continue past the Duchy of Delgaria and through the Westlands until they reached the Misted Mountains. Errol estimated that they would be travelling for as long as two eight-days, depending on the horses and the weather, before they arrived at the place where he hoped to meet with the Dwarven traders and help them gain access to the mines.

And so, on a warm morn, this small band of old friends, new acquaintances and enemies turned uneasy allies—all brought together by circumstance and need—cast their eyes to the west and rode away from Kings' Meet, carrying with them the hopes of two races who must remain behind to stand against the coming of an enemy more dangerous and evil than they had ever known before.

†††††

Two of those remaining behind, the Kal`Dathian mage and the Calderian seeress, stood on a small hill in the heat of the morning and watched until the riders vanished over the horizon. Afterward, they walked hand in hand along the edge of the Forest, savoring the coolness offered them by the early afternoon shade from the great trees.

"Will you be able to Scry them all the way to the Misted Mountains?" asked Mik`kel, enjoying the feel of her delicate hand in his as they ambled side by side.

Her eyes sparkled as she looked at him, then grew reflective. "I believe I can. I asked both Killian and Ellianthia for a lock of hair to strengthen my ability to find them, so that will aid me. And," she added, with a hint of promise in her soft, lovely eyes, "if we work together and join our power, I expect that we can track their progress over some great distances indeed."

Mik`kel considered the possible ramifications of her offer to "work together," and felt his arousal for her stirring, recalling the wonder of her body as he had caressed her with his hands and lips. She saw that unmistakable look in his eyes and felt an answering heat in her belly, thinking that mayhap it was cool enough now to invite him back to her tent, where she could change from her outer gown to something lighter—or nothing at all. With an unspoken agreement, they began to stroll in that direction.

Chapter 36

Princes of the Empire

They entered the Imperial throne room as a group, seven Princes of the Empire, clad in black tunics decorated with silver epaulettes, breeches with silver trim running down the side, gleaming black riding boots, and flowing crimson capes that swirled around their legs as they strode across the floor. Each carried a silver helm in the crook of his left arm, and wore a razor-edged saber belted on his waist.

All of them favored their sire in size and form, tall and broad shouldered, slender of waist and hips. Four of them— Bek`tol, Sti`vak, Mal`kite, and Rek`kah—had their father's black ringlets curling down their neck. Two others, Pav`vel and Sak`kith, had inherited their mothers' dark brown locks, while the last, Jek`kar, had hair the color of coppery gold.

Rak`koth watched with satisfaction as his sons approached, their bodies held erect and proud, a look of arrogance and confidence in their eyes. That all seven of the young princes had grown tall and strong was a stroke of good fortune for which any father would have given thanks to the gods, had he been inclined to acknowledge those pathetic divine powers in the least. That these princes had grown so tall and strong in so short a time was nothing short of miraculous, considering that none of them had yet reached his eleventh name-day, as measured in true years.

Yet each son had achieved the size and physical maturity of a young man less than a decade after his birth, due to Rak`koth's magical enhancement on the night of their conception in the Tomb—magic which had spurred their growth beyond anything expected, especially by their mothers, who paid the ultimate price of this unnatural development.

Indeed, all but one of the priestesses had perished giving birth, so great was the damage done to their bodies by the enormous size of the unborn children. Each mother had been cut open less than five months after impregnation, when the pain and the damage to internal organs became too great for the women to bear. Only Saleria, Jek`kar's mother, had managed to survive the forced delivery.

For that reason, Jek`kar—the Golden Prince, as some called him for his coppery gold hair—had been the only one of the seven boys to have known his own natural mother. While the other sons had been put to the breast of wet nurses, then weaned and given over into the hands of male tutors and instructors under their father's watchful eye, Jek`kar's mother had been granted the privilege of occasional visits with her son over the years. Thus, he was the only son who had even the slightest cause or inclination to see women as serving any purpose other than being used as palace servants, pleasure slaves or brood mares.

Rak`koth's reasons for allowing Saleria to visit with her son had little to do with sentiment. He had felt nothing for her, or any of the priestesses, as he forcefully injected his seed into their unwilling bodies; and he had felt no sense of loss when they died in childbed. Nor did he believe that maternal influence was of any benefit whatsoever to young men being groomed to rule. In his eyes, females were for giving pleasure and bearing children, and he encouraged his sons to learn that lesson early in life.

However, Rak`koth did have some small respect for strength and the determination to survive—as long, of course, as that strength and determination did not conflict with his own needs. And Saleria was, indeed, a survivor, though the painful ordeal of the highly abnormal pregnancy and child bearing had left her permanently weakened and fragile, capable only of light duties such as sewing and mending.

So, because she alone survived, he allowed her to live out her days and earn her bread as a seamstress' helper in a small shop in Palace City, half a mile from the palace gates. And, if she found a way to share a few moments with Jek`kar during visits to the palace to pick up clothing in need of repair, his father gave no word forbidding it.

"Greetings, my sons," said Rak`koth, as the seven heirs to his Imperial Throne reached the dais, then fell to one knee and bowed their heads.

"Hello, Sire," they answered as one, raising their heads up but continuing to kneel before him.

"Get up," he gestured with impatience. "Get up and let me look at you. It has been some time since I laid eyes on all of you together, and I would hear how you have fared in your assignments." His voice grew stern, though a hint of amusement remained in his eyes. "Mind you, I have had reports from the governors, so I caution you to be truthful."

Most of his sons had spent the last year scattered throughout the lands of his empire, charged with becoming familiar with the cultures and the peoples that his vassal lords ruled in his name. He knew that their magically induced rapid physical growth did not necessarily go hand in hand with developing the wisdom and judgment required to govern others—and their own natures—wisely and well.

Those abilities could only come with time and experience gained from observing how other seasoned leaders exercised power and control. That was the reason he had fostered his sons out to the courts of his vassals, knowing that when they had gained that necessary experience and skill, they would take over the reins of leadership themselves, as governors of his provinces or generals of his Armies. Then his dream of having loyal, trustworthy "strong right arms" in positions of power would be realized.

Rak`koth listened as each of his scions described the state of affairs in the lands to which they had been sent. He interrupted their accounts from time to time to ask probing questions about the loyalty of his vassal lords or the lessons imparted under their tutelage.

Bek`tol and Sak`kith reported that Paressia and Brukkesh were "well under control now." There had been minor uprisings in both lands by some of the workers forced to labor under grueling conditions to meet the additional demands for milled lumber and harvested crops imposed on them, in preparation for the coming campaign against Balleterria.

"I rode with the Black Legion when they caught the Paressian rebels, Sire," Bek`tol announced proudly, grinning from the vivid memory of cutting down the hopelessly outnumbered and ill-equipped men and women as they fled the terrifying charge of the ebony-helmed and armored Legionnaires. He particularly enjoyed the memory of slicing his saber into human flesh like a butcher carves raw meat, then watching the blood gush from their wounds as they died.

Rak`koth saw the bloodlust in his son's eyes and nodded approvingly. Still, as he listened, he hoped that Bek`tol had learned as much about leadership as he obviously had about the joys of crushing resistance to authority.

Mal`kite reported that the shipyards of Mertania were bustling with activity, and that there hardly seemed to be enough room to house all of the men pressed into service building the mighty armada ordered by his sire. He had developed a fascination with the sea, and spoke with some excitement about the scores of finished ships anchored along the Mertanian coast in sheltered bays and inlets, awaiting the time when the loading of soldiers, horses, supplies and equipment earmarked for the Balleterrian invasion would begin.

"But, Sire," Mal`kite added with some petulance, "though I have insisted—in your name, of course—that the crews work harder to finish by the date you have commanded, Master Shipwright Suk`kar all but dismissed me with weak claims that the delays are the fault of a shortage of skilled men and the number of ships demanded. I would have his head for his impertinence!"

The emperor held up his hand to restrain Mal`kite's exuberant appetite for retribution. "And who then would build the ships, my son? When an underling is necessary to achieve your goals, you must be sure that he has outlived his usefulness before visiting true justice upon him. But fear not. That problem has already been resolved. I have reached an understanding with Master Suk`kar that should expedite completion of the fleet. Then you may have his head on a pike if you wish."

Rak`koth smiled to himself as the mention of Suk`kar's name brought to mind the man's buxom wife who, even now, awaited him naked and at his disposal when he had time for her. He had seen a certain look in her eyes that belied her expressions of horror and shame, and he relished the idea of sampling that ripened fruit soon.

He turned next to Sti`vak, who had been summoned back from his visit to Jarlond. "And how fares Olev, our vassal in the north, my son? I have heard naught of any problems from that quarter. Still, inheriting his position by beheading his father might have left a sour taste in his mouth, even after all these years," he observed with some amusement.

Then he leaned forward, all traces of humor gone. "How do you judge his loyalty?"

Sti`vak met his father's eyes with confidence, proud that his opinion would be sought in the matter. "Sire, Olev continues to provide a ready supply of the coal and other ores needed by our armorers to make weapons of steel, with no delays and no excuses," he added, looking pointedly at his brother, Mal`kite, with smug satisfaction. Placing his hand on the hilt of his sword, he continued.

"The blade I carry was crafted from a special shipment of the finest ores, and presented to me as a personal gift from the Jarlonder leader himself. If he harbors any ill will toward you for the manner of his father's death, he keeps his own counsel. Indeed, I have taken his eldest sister into my service as one of my personal bodyguards. She is a fierce fighter in battle and," he added slyly, "no less ferocious in bed."

"Just take care that your tigress does not slip a blade between your ribs one night when you are 'testing her mettle' between her thighs," warned his father, chuckling softly as a chastened expression replaced the proud look on Sti`vak's face.

"And now, to Sudenor," said Rak`koth, fixing his gaze intently on Rek`kah. "I have had word of certain large sums of gold being wagered on arena fights between war hounds and armed slaves. Was this charming spectacle your idea, my son?"

Rek`kah shrank from his sire's burning eyes, then squared his shoulders and struck as defiant a pose as he dared in the presence of his emperor. "Father, there is nothing else to *do* in Sudenor! The emerald and diamond mines yield their treasures with disgusting regularity, hardly requiring oversight from a Prince of the Empire. I have had no decent rebellions to put down nor even any fierce warrior women to bed," he grumbled, looking at Bek`tol and Sti`vak with undisguised envy.

"The females in that backward land are short and ugly, like their men, and they hardly ever bathe. They stink as if they sleep with the hounds. I might as well try mounting a sheep. Were it not for the slaves I took with me from the palace, I would have no women to use at all."

Rak`koth's eyebrows rose. "So, you force slaves to fight war hounds for your amusement?"

"It is *boring* there, Father. And I allow the slaves to be well armed. Sometimes, one of them actually manages to draw blood from a hound before he dies. We wager on the length of time that a slave can survive. It does help to pass the time."

Now it was Rak`koth's turn to display a sly expression as he listened to Rek`kah complain. "I see. Well, perhaps you would prefer to join your brother, Pav`vel, in Dul`Char. I am sure the shamans there can find something to help amuse you."

The corners of Rek`kah's mouth quirked in disgust at the thought of living among those savages. As bad as Sudenorian females smelled, they did not reek of fresh blood and gore from the daily human sacrifices.

"Um...no, Father," he replied hastily. "That will not be necessary. I will find some other...diversion. I have been training with the war hound handlers, learning to command the beasts. They are magnificent. Soon, I will have their loyalty, and they will obey me well enough to take them into battle. And, in the meantime, I hear that some of the Sudenorian females in the western hills actually bathe on occasion. I could..." The rest of his words were drowned out by laughter from his brothers as they watched him squirm uncomfortably.

When Rak`koth had finished joining in the laughter, he turned to Pav`vel. "What of our barbarian horde, my son, and the foul little creature that oversees them in my name? Does Chu`tek still mumble about avenging his dead brethren some day?"

Pav`vel ran his fingers through his thick brown curls as he considered the question. "No, Father, the head shaman does not speak openly of killing you any longer. But I doubt it not that his little prick would stiffen—if he even has one—from the pleasure of gutting you and wallowing in your blood, if he thought he could do so and live. Still, he keeps his savages in check and follows your orders, though he complains that his men grow soft and weak without an enemy to fight. It seems the empire has grown too peaceful for his tastes."

The emperor looked thoughtful. "Yes, I know well that he would gloat to see me stretched out on his bloody altar. But he serves my purpose for the time being. That is why I have placed you there, my son. Not only to keep a watchful eye upon the repulsive little man, but to gain the respect of his barbarians, so that someday you will command them, after I cage their magic users in my dungeons and keep them as pets. Yet, I will have need of their blood magic in the coming battle for Balleterria. So, for the present, I allow them some illusion of power."

"Of course, Father." Pav`vel felt very pleased with the responsibility of such an important role being entrusted to him. "I will continue to watch and learn, at your command."

Now he had heard from each of his sons, except Jek`kar, from whom he did not need a report, since this son had remained at the palace these past months, learning the ways of the Imperial Court at his father's side. Rak`koth sat back on his throne and laced his fingers together across his chest.

"It seems that all of you are doing reasonably well," he said, with a deliberate glance toward Rek`kah to remind him that his behavior would be noted carefully in the future. "I will expect all of you to meet with my advisors and provide a more detailed account of what you have observed thus far. I will also expect you to continue to 'watch and learn,' as Pav'vel says, against the time when you will assume power in those lands."

After hearing their assurances that they would do as he directed, he continued. "There is another reason for calling you away from those duties, in addition to providing me with your personal reports. The time for the conquest of Balleterria draws closer, and I have decided that some of you will accompany me when the Imperial fleet sails."

The emperor's announcement sent a murmur of excitement rippling through the young men gathered before him, each of them captivated by the thought of a great adventure, each of them hoping to be among those chosen. Those who had incurred their father's displeasure at one time or another immediately regretted having done so, if it lessened the chances that they would be granted the honor of going with him. Some whispered among themselves as they waited nervously for him to continue.

Rak'koth held up his hand for silence. "For reasons that should be obvious, I can not take all of you with me. Some of you will be needed where you are. It is important for the Imperial family to maintain a presence here at home, so that certain of my vassals do not feel emboldened to take advantage of our absence. I will need the eyes and ears of those who remain behind to alert me to any problems that might arise while I am gone. Is that understood?"

When all of his sons had nodded sharply and slapped their wrists to their chests, he continued. "Now, the campaign for Balleterria will take some time...time enough perhaps for me to send for more of you later, while others here return to take your place."

He leaned forward and met the eyes of every son. "In the meantime, I will expect those of you who abide here to put aside your disappointment and serve me faithfully. Is that clear?"

"Yes, Sire," they swore in unison.

"Good. I have not yet decided who will be leaving with me when we sail. Much will depend on the needs of the empire, and on your behavior during the time before I depart. I will inform you at the appropriate time." His stern mood vanished, replaced by something that might resemble paternalistic indulgence.

"Now, you may enjoy the comforts of the palace tonight, before giving your detailed reports on the morrow. Dinner has been prepared for you. For those of you who did not bring your slaves along, feel free to use any here that take your fancy.

"But do try to leave at least some of them in good enough condition to serve me after you are gone," he added with a wry smile, mindful that more than one of his slaves had suffered grievous injury when one son or another grew too exuberant in taking his pleasure. Then, amid the sounds of their laughter, he dismissed them to their evening of reunion and pleasure.

As he left the throne room for his private chambers, he gave some thought to his son, Jek`kar. Keeping him at the palace had given Rak`koth the opportunity to observe him closely. In doing so, he had found that Jek`kar had much in common with his brothers, yet seemed different from the others in some unexpected ways.

Jek`kar was as tall and strong as any of his six brothers—perhaps stronger, since he had bested them all with sword and lance at one time or another, and was absolutely ruthless in a fight when angered. He carried himself with the same pride and self-assurance that had been bred into all of the young princes, and he was equally as vocal in expressing his displeasure when his desires were thwarted.

Nor was he any less inclined to partake of the pleasures afforded him by the female slaves, who actually appeared to welcome being summoned to his bed, unlike those who often returned bruised and battered from serving his brothers. Not that Rak`koth gave any care to the way that his sons treated the slaves when enjoying their bed sport.

Yet, while Jek`kar had shown himself to be as tough and lusty as any of the others, Rak`koth had seen another side to this son as well, a quieter, reflective side that seemed more inclined to reason things through than to act impulsively or rashly. He threw himself into weapons practice and studies of military strategy with fervor enough; but he could also be found in the palace library from time to time, engrossed in books about ancient history or talking to the old royal scholars.

These learned men were surprised to find one of his youth interested in musty old topics. Indeed, they reported to the emperor privately that the young man had a thirst for knowledge and the mind to make good use of it.

In some ways, Rak`koth realized, Jek`kar reminded him of himself, when he was first drawn to the ways of power and sought out those who might instruct him. Perhaps the time was approaching when he might begin to test his sons for the gift. He had refrained from doing so to this point, due to their immaturity in true years. Mastering the art of sorcery required wisdom and self-control. But, when he did test them for the gift, he suspected that he would find Jek`kar had inherited some measure of his powers.

If so, the young man might have the potential for following his sire down the paths of magic. He certainly seemed intelligent enough. The question was whether he was sufficiently ruthless and dedicated to using such powers to shape and control others in the manner necessary to sustain and expand his empire.

Rak`koth prided himself on his ability to see beyond the petty sentimentalities and concerns that plagued most men and held them back from taking what they wanted; and on his capacity to foresee what must be done to keep what he had taken. He knew that, after he had conquered Balleterria, the complexities of ruling an empire that straddled two continents would weigh heavily upon the shoulders of one man, even a man as powerful and tireless as he.

It would be to his benefit to place someone in charge of the newly vanquished lands. That man would be an overlord of sorts, someone strong and merciless when need be, capable of ruling in his name with a firm, guiding hand. Perhaps Jek`kar might come to fill that need, with the proper tutelage; and, if he also had the gift of sorcery…

Rak`koth ceased his musings as he reached the entrance to his private chambers, deciding to let the matter of his son's future rest for now. Time would reveal how Jek`kar might best be exploited for his purposes, and whether the young man would prove to be worthy of his trust. For now, he would enjoy some wine and the attentions of two of his many slaves, the red-haired twins sent to him as a gift from the Brukkeshan governor in hopes of currying his emperor's favor. His lust had already begun to show in his burning eyes as he opened the door.

Chapter 37

Council of War

The mid-morning sun streamed into the second-story council chamber through the long, narrow windows built into the northeast wall of the castle, windows designed to prevent any attacking force from gaining entry through the slits that measured six feet in height but less than a foot in width. Thin fingers of sunlight penetrated these narrow apertures and sliced across the room from one side to the other, falling upon the large, oval oak table and the people seated there, then continuing on to the opposite wall where the Royal Crest of black Gryphons rampant on a red field was mounted directly behind King Gavan's chair.

Gavan watched as Mellisandria and several other Elfin members of the Joint Council of War entered the chamber, then made their way to their places next to King Rillandariel and Amarillia. After the first gathering of the Council held at Kings' Meet, Gavan had volunteered to host the next meeting at Brannock Castle, as a way of welcoming the Elves back to Calderian soil as friends and allies.

For their part, the Elves, at Rillandariel's urging, had accepted the invitation as a show of good faith, by traveling into the heart of their former enemy's fortress—thereby demonstrating their trust in Gavan's honor and sincere commitment to the union of the two peoples born of necessity and mutual need.

Save for the absence of Killian's party, all of the Calderians who had attended the first Joint Council meeting were present now, including Mik'kel and Aisleen—who were, at that moment, engaged in an animated discussion with two senior Calderian mages: Alistair, a stocky, robust man with dark, intense eyes; and Elspeth, a petite, white-haired matron with kind eyes and a reputation for being far stronger in the power than her diminutive form would suggest.

There were, however, some notable additions to the Council. Father Venutius was on hand to lend moral and spiritual guidance. Lord Janneth, Knight Commander, Captain Rodric of the Kings' Light, and Colonel Regis of the Royal Lancers had each been invited, since they would play a vital role on the field of battle when the invasion forces reached their shores. So, too, would Captain Innis, leader of the Royal Scouts, and Lord Latharn, Colum's father, who served as an army subcommander under Brurik.

Baron Glendannon was there as well, representing a cartel of landowners who would be providing the majority of the livestock, grain and other supplies that would feed the Alliance Army, with compensation from the Crown. Last to arrive was Lord Quillan, Admiral of the small Royal Navy currently anchored in Breckon Bay, who would be called upon to offer whatever support he could muster against the vast fleet of enemy ships preparing to set sail for Balleterria.

Gavan recognized most of the Elfin Council members from their initial gathering, though he found a few of the Forest folk unfamiliar. He assumed that Rillandariel had selected them for the special contributions they would be making in defense of their homeland.

Seeing that all were seated, Gavan squeezed Briana's hand, returned her smile of encouragement, then rose and faced the Council. "As your host, it is both my duty and my pleasure to convene this meeting, and to give welcome to all of you gathered here this day. I will say at the outset that my heart is gladdened to see so many friends and allies come together in our cause. The path that lies before us will be difficult indeed, and will test our strength and courage mightily in the days to come. I am heartened that we will be facing that test together."

As those around the long table nodded in agreement, the Calderian monarch continued, this time in a more somber tone. "The business at hand is to prepare for the enemy's invasion, an invasion which, according to various sources, may be coming quite soon. It is a formidable threat indeed. I would ask General Brurik to share what we have learned thus far."

The gruff commander of the Calderian forces acknowledged his sire's request with a crisp bow as he stood to report, his posture rigid, his red and black uniform impeccably neat. The veteran general's graying hair was cropped close to his head in a manner that emphasized the sharp, angular lines of his cheeks and jaw. And when he spoke, he did so in a voice that would have commanded attention anywhere, even had he been dressed in farmer's homespun or a smithy's apron.

"As you know, the first rule of any military campaign is to know as much about the enemy as possible. After the Peace was made, we sent informants and observers to the Empire of Surrikand, to learn what we might about the strength of the emperor's forces and the fleet of ships that he will be deploying to carry those forces to our lands.

"This Rak`koth is a shrewd leader, with watchful eyes placed everywhere throughout his realm. A number of our informers were never heard from again after their arrival in his lands." Brurik's grim tone reflected his regret for the loss of men he had sent to their deaths in the service of their country.

"However, some of our men managed to make their way safely to the coastal towns of Mertania, the region where the enemy's shipyards are located, and from where the invasion will be launched. Those men have sent back information gleaned from watching the shipyards, observing movements of soldiers, and listening in taverns and other establishments where useful knowledge might be overheard. We have also spoken with merchants and sailors whose ships ply their trade in the ports up and down the enemy's coast. Getting them to talk to us was no small task, for they fear their emperor greatly."

Brurik lowered his hands to the table and leaned slightly forward, as if to emphasize the import of what he was about to say. "Though I could scarcely credit the reports at first, it seems that this sorcerous emperor has a fleet of some four score or more ships, perhaps as many as one hundred vessels waiting to transport his forces across the sea. This is in addition to various barges and vessels designated for carrying food, supplies, animals, military equipment and the like. The true number of ships is unknown; but it is, to my knowledge, the largest armada of war ships ever assembled in any age or time."

Amid whispers of "One hundred ships!" heard around the table as the Council reacted to this dire news, General Trillafarien stood to put forward the question that was most critical to a commander facing an assault of this magnitude. "What estimate of the number of soldiers that the enemy might field against us, General Brurik?"

Seeing that his Elfin counterpart had gone straight to the heart of the matter, Brurik straightened up again and faced him. "General, though I fear the answer contains some speculation, the information gathered from our people puts the possible number of enemy forces at between forty-five and fifty thousand."

Cries of astonishment and dismay echoed throughout the council chamber. Many of the members could be heard clamoring for more information. Finally, Amarillia's stern tone prevailed in getting Brurik's attention.

"Is that possible, General? And what kind of forces do you speak of?" she asked, tugging unconsciously on the tightly woven platinum braid falling across her left shoulder.

Brurik waited until the tumult had subsided before replying to the stern, slender Elfin strategist whom, he reminded himself, he had faced across a battlefield scant months ago. "Well, my Lady, Rak`koth is rumored to be sending thousands of his Imperial Black Legion, an elite mounted cavalry, who are said to be the most brutal and ruthless fighters in his empire.

"There was also word of several thousand Dread Riders, a mysterious force spoken of in awe and fear, even among the emperor's own people. Little is known of these fighters, save that they are unlike normal men, and rumored to be possessed by the Dark and nearly invincible in battle." Brurik shook his head. "These two groups alone represent a serious threat to us in open battle."

"You spoke of 'these two groups alone,' General," said Lord Janneth in a deep, somber voice. "What other forces we can expect to face?"

The Calderian general's expression grew most grave as he answered his knight commander. "Unfortunately, Rak`koth has the advantage of drawing upon all the conquered lands of his empire for his armies. Not all of these other peoples are known to me as yet, but there are said to be large forces from regions such as Paressia, Brukkesh, Mertania, and Sudenor. I have also had reports of Jarlonders, a fierce clan of hill people said to be berserkers in battle. The emperor is even known to employ beasts in battle, war hounds or the like, though this last seems too bizarre for me to credit."

"Perhaps I can be of some aid in this matter," said Mik`kel, breaking off his conversation with the senior mages to rise and address the assembled members. "My father, King Nek`krod ruled Kal`Dathia until Rak`koth usurped his throne and slew him. I am familiar with these other nations, or former nations, of Surrikand that the sorcerer has enthralled and absorbed into his empire.

"Each of these conquered nations can easily provide many thousands of men at arms to serve as human fodder for his conquest. In addition to the peoples already mentioned, there are a host of Dul`Charian barbarians whose shamans, I am told, practice a kind of foul blood magic that may present the greatest threat of all, when combined with Rak`koth's own fell powers.

Mik`kel started to sit down, then added, with disgust in his voice, "And I would not be too quick to dismiss the notion of the emperor using beasts and animals in war. We have learned of monsters called Gruks, similar in some respects to your Ogres, that have been captured and trained to do his malignant bidding."

Daunted by the overwhelming size of the enemy threat, Amarillia fought down the churning in her stomach and strove to remain outwardly calm. "General Brurik," she asked, in as matter-of-fact a voice as she could manage, "How many Calderian warriors can take the field against this enemy?"

The general thought it ironic that he would never have dreamed of revealing that critical information to this formidable Elfin commander as recently as six months ago. He hesitated briefly, looking at Gavan.

"Proceed, General," said the king. "We can have no secrets between our peoples now."

"Very well, Sire." He turned back to Amarillia. "Calderia can field some six thousand foot, pike and bow within the month, if needed...more, have we time to train others, though I doubt that we will." Brurik then turned a questioning eye to his knight commander.

Lord Janneth raised his tall, brawny frame from his seat and stroked the bushy brown mustache that covered his upper lips and curved down around his lantern jaw. "I have four thousand knights in full plate, brave men and true, sworn to king and country, each with his squire and a destrier caparisoned for war. I have nearly a thousand knights-in-training, though they are young and untried in battle."

Captain Rodric did not wait to be called upon, but stood and offered his salute to the general. "The Kings' Light are now two thousand strong, sir, and ready for the call," he volunteered, his earnestness and pride winning a nod from Gavan and a warm smile from Briana, though she shuddered at the memory of the near loss of her son in practice with that unit.

"I have twenty-two hundred Royal Lancers prepared to fight," reported Colonel Regis, equally proud of the men under his command.

General Brurik nodded and faced Trillafarien and Amarillia. "All told, some fifteen thousand men, not counting Royal Scouts and the King's Elite who guard the castle and the persons of the royal family," he concluded, returning to his seat.

"I can add my own personal household knights, numbering nearly two hundred," said Lord Latharn, rising briefly.

"A force to be reckoned with, to be sure, good General," said King Rillandariel, as he turned to his own commanders. "And what of our strength, Trillafarien?"

The Elfin general spoke aside to Amarillia for a moment, then faced his sire again. "I believe we can also promise seven thousand warriors at the ready, Sire, skilled with bow and blade. Is that about right, Corandillian?" he asked, turning to the Elfin Bow captain.

"Yes, General," replied the sinewy Elf clad in Forest greens, "though sending to the western Forest villages to recruit our cousin Elves will swell our numbers." He turned to the slim, dark-haired Elf sitting beside him, one of those that Gavan had not recognized. "Allow me to introduce Captain Gillardian of the western Forest."

The western Elf, dressed in Forest browns and tans, rose and met the eyes of those around the table. He was one of the shorter, smaller Elves that Gavan had seen enter the chamber, and he wondered idly if his people were descended from different stock than their eastern kinfolk.

"I am honored to be called here to this gathering, to join in defense of our lands," said Gallardian, with a graceful bow. "Though the people of our villages number far fewer than those of our eastern cousins, I believe I can promise perhaps some eighteen hundred warriors to join with yours, General."

"They will be welcome and much needed, of that I am certain," Trillafarien asserted, turning his attention now to Berollien.

The Captain of the Elfin Horse rose to answer the question spoken by his general's eyes. "I command just over thirty-two hundred mounted Skirmishers, sir. My riders and I are at your disposal."

Trillafarien nodded to his old friend, then addressed his king. "Sire, I estimate that we have some twelve thousand warriors to join with our human allies," he reported with some pride, though the sober expression he bore in the telling was anything but optimistic.

It then fell to Queen Briana to voice the grave doubts that all were thinking. "A goodly number, General, and we know well the fierceness of the Elves in battle," she affirmed respectfully. "But, by my tally, we are twenty-seven thousand against more than forty-five thousand or more of the enemy! How can we hope to prevail against invaders that outnumber our brave warriors nearly two to one?"

No one answered immediately, as all attending the Council pondered the enormity of the challenge. Then Aisleen broke the silence with a question of her own.

"Forgive my ignorance of battle tactics and war, my Lords, but can the enemy truly conquer the whole of Balleterria with even fifty thousand men? This is, after all, a vast continent. Surely, it would require many more than even that large number to take and hold all the lands from Calderia in the east to the Misted Mountains in the west, and from the northern mountains to the Great Forest in the south."

"It might, indeed, my Lady," replied General Brurik, "were the enemy to try to conquer all of Balleterria at once. But this Rak'koth and his armies will almost certainly seek to first take and occupy a port and the surrounding lands." He pointed at the easternmost area of Calderia on the map spread before him.

"Perhaps he intends to drive inland to Brannock Castle, here. Once the invader has secured the port and established a defensible foothold, he can send his fleet back to Surrikand to gather more forces and land them unopposed on our shore as well. In truth, it would take some time to build up his armies sufficiently to win control of the entire continent, but I fear there would be little to stop him from doing so, should he defeat our main forces early on."

"And," Mik'kel added grimly, "hold in mind that Rak'koth vanquished the nations of Surrikand one by one, employing the strategy of forcing the warriors of each conquered people to join his armies and fight for him in turn or risk the slaughter of their women and children. A despicable and ruthless practice, but effective enough, for who among us here would continue to resist him if he held our loved ones captive and began to torture or kill them before our eyes?"

"Then my question remains," said Queen Briana. "How can we prevail against an invading army large enough to overwhelm any defense we can muster?"

Seeing those in attendance continuing to lose heart, Gavan placed his hand over his queen's, then spoke loudly enough for all present to hear. "In view of this problem, we—King Rillandariel and I—have just been discussing the need to request aid from the Dwarves, making the case for the mutual benefit of joining forces against a foe that threatens all the races of our continent. Being content to remain within the safety of their stronghold is a luxury they can no longer afford."

Gavan looked around the table. "Does the Council agree, we will contact the prince and princess through those amazing Speaking Stones and ask them to put the case to the Dwarven leaders when they arrive at the Misted Mountains."

Though doubtful of receiving aid from the reclusive Dwarves, the other members readily signaled their assent. Gavan then continued. "Moreover, we might also look for aid from another quarter. Duke Robelin of Delgaria has been a strong friend in years past, in the last open warfare against the Dunmorians. I think it would behoove us to send an emissary to Robelin as well, to invite him and his Black Guard to join our cause."

The mention of Delgaria—and the legendary Black Guard—as a possible ally sent a ripple of whispers around the table, offering some glimmer of hope to the otherwise dispirited gathering. It had the effect that Gavan had intended in that dismal atmosphere, since he knew that the possibility of enlisting the duke's aid would help to rally the Alliance to undertake the fearful task that lay before them, whether or not Robelin actually joined with them in time.

Wanting to end the morning session on this promising note, Gavan was about to lean over to Rillandariel and suggest that they adjourn for the noon meal when Briana spoke again. "My Lord King," she said, employing the formal title that she rarely used when they were nestled beneath their bedcovers, "I am certain that Duke Kendrick of Glashan in the west and the young Earl of Devon-Baire in the north will also join our fight," she added, glancing at Aisleen, who nodded in agreement, knowing that her brother would see the wisdom of doing so.

"However, I would suggest that there is one other potential ally dwelling in the west, one that we have not yet considered."

Caught in the midst of conferring with the Elfin king, Gavan straightened up and looked at his wife with a puzzled expression. "Do you speak of your father, the baron, my Lady wife? We are aware of his failing health. Perhaps he will be able to guard the border against Dunmoria and still provide us with some forces, but…"

"No, my Lord King, I speak not of the baron, but of Dunmoria itself!"

Gavan's blue eyes grew wide with surprise, an expression that was mirrored by the other Calderians around the table, given the bitter enmity and warfare that had been the legacy of the two countries for long and long.

"*Dunmoria?*" he asked. "But they have ever been our enemy since the separation. Do you mean to ask *them* to join with *us*? Even could we trust King MacRae—and we can not— what makes you think he would agree to…?"

"A truce?" Briana replied, finishing his question. "My Lord King, we have agreed that this foreign invasion threatens the lives of *all* the peoples of Balleterria. Would we not be willing to try to set aside our enmity for the Dunmorians, at least for the nonce, did it mean the salvation of our land? And, if we would, might they not as well, once they learn of the danger to themselves?"

Almost as an afterthought, she added, "And who knows? Perhaps what began as a temporary truce could become a more permanent peace when the danger from over the sea is passed."

Realizing that he had never even considered that possibility, Gavan closed his mouth on another protest and gazed at his wife with a bemused expression. The awkward silence was broken by the sound of a throat being cleared. Gavan turned to see Baron Glendannon rising to his feet.

"Sire," said the Baron. "Perhaps we might give some thought to the queen's suggestion. I, too, know well the history of our two countries, two lands joined by blood but divided by hatred and the pain of wounds unhealed. Yet, I have seen signs indicating that not all Dunmorians bear us ill wishes, nor may they all wish to persist in living as sworn enemies forever."

Seeing that the king appeared very skeptical, the baron pursued his point. "Sire, some merchants of my acquaintance have spoken to me of…overtures…from Dunmorian merchants to open discussions of trade with Calderia. There have been rumors that some of the younger Dunmorian nobles—those who were scarcely born during the times of bitter warfare, and who harbor no personal hatred of their own toward us—have quietly suggested that it is time to seek an end to the feud between blood kin and find a way to lessen hostilities."

Gavan looked at his wife, who nodded almost imperceptibly; then at General Brurik, who was frowning, but with a thoughtful expression on his face; then at Rillandariel, whose neutral expression made it clear that he did not wish to intrude in Calderian affairs on this point. Unprepared to make any immediate decision about this unexpected proposal, he said finally, "We will take the matter under consideration. Now, if my brother king is of like mind, I would suggest we adjourn this gathering to eat." With the Elfin monarch in agreement, Gavan set a time to reconvene in the late afternoon and brought the meeting to a close.

†††††

Shed of his crown and formal attire until meeting with the others again later that day, Gavan leaned his elbows against the sill of the open window and gazed out of the royal bedchamber at the green hills in the distance, breathing in the sweet scents of grass and wildflowers. After making an appearance at the noon day meal, he and Briana had encouraged all present to enjoy a brief respite from the serious matters at hand, and had then excused themselves and retired to their private rooms.

Now, comfortably clad in a loose cotton tunic and breeches, he was trying to banish those dire matters from his mind long enough to digest his meal in peace. Briana had announced that she intended to nap. She lay on the bed breathing softly, eyes closed and bodice unlaced, her amber hair arrayed around the face that seemed to grow more beautiful to him with every passing season. He counted himself the luckiest man in the kingdom, noble or commoner, just to wake up beside this strong, lovely woman each day of his life.

At this moment, Gavan envied the tranquil expression on her face as she dozed, for, try as he might, he could not suppress the ominous image of a horizon filled with enemy vessels of war bearing down on his coastline, filled to the bows with ruthless, black-hearted killers who cared little for the lives of the innocent people they had come to destroy. They had to be stopped at all costs, which led him back to the matter that his wife had broached just as the meeting was ending this morn.

Yes, he thought, beginning to pace a bit, it was the question of the Dunmorians that was weighing most heavily upon his mind at this moment. The thought of making a peace— any kind of peace—with those sworn enemies of many decades made the recent success with ending the hostilities between humans and Elves seem like patching up a lover's quarrel.

His audible snort of disbelief at the prospect of treating with Dunmoria did not go unnoticed, though perhaps it was his pacing as well that brought a soft question from across the room. "What troubles you, my husband?" asked Briana quietly, opening her eyes and raising her head from the silk-encased pillow to look at him. "Is it the matter I proposed this morn?"

Gavan smiled. Ever could his lady read his thoughts, sometimes in the most uncanny fashion. When he nodded, she patted the bedspread beside her.

"Come sit with me, my love," she coaxed with a fetching smile that he could not have resisted, even had he wished to. When he had crossed the chamber and settled down beside her, she reached to take his large, callused hand in her small, delicate fingers and fixed her green eyes upon his.

"Husband, I know that seeking a truce seems a most unlikely notion, particularly when put forth by me. After all, my father has spent his entire life guarding the borders against the incursions of those very Dunmorians, when he was not at war with them outright. And indeed," she added with a wry smile, "had it not been for your father's need of my father's continued commitment to that defense, there might never have been cause for a marriage of state; and I might not be the woman lying beside you now."

"Heart of mine, I have never regretted..." Gavan replied earnestly, only to be silenced as she raised her hand and pressed her fingertips gently to his lips.

"Hush, my love," she whispered. "I do not doubt your caring for me. I meant only to say that I have reason enough to know the sad and violent history that has divided us from our cousins to the west. And still, I would hope for some chance to enlist them to our side in the dangerous days that lie ahead."

Gavan nodded, gazing at his lovely lady. He wished fervently that he could escape the madness of this coming war altogether and lose himself in her enchanting eyes. Then his gaze travelled lower, drawn to her open bodice and the rounded flesh revealed behind the undone laces. Not for the first time, it came to him that the last war, and threats of yet another one now impending, had kept him far too preoccupied of late to enjoy the pleasure of her embraces as often as he might.

Acting on a sudden impulse, he bent to kiss her red lips, then buried his head between her breasts, kissing the side of each soft mound while his hand strayed down the side of her leg and reached up under the hem of her gown.

"Oh!" she breathed, startled by his unexpected but very welcome advance as his fingers won past the formidable barrier of feminine undergarments and found their way to the edges of her silken smallclothes, then slipped inside. She, too, had missed the passion they had shared before the war intervened and took him away from her so often.

"But the Council…" she breathed, even as she eagerly raised her hips, her skin burning from the intimacy of his touch.

"The Council will have to wait, my love. Just for this moment, let us pretend we are but two commoners in a little cottage by a lake, with no matters of state or governance to trouble us. I have just come home from the fields after thinking of you all day, and…" The rest of his words were muffled as he lifted her gown and undershift up to her waist and lowered his head past her belly to kiss the delicate flesh.

"Oh!" she moaned again, curling her fingers in his fiery hair and pulling his head down against her. "Oh, my Lord King!"

†††††

Those who knew the king and queen well could not help but notice a change in their mood and demeanor when Gavan reconvened the Council later that afternoon. He seemed more relaxed and at ease after the noon hiatus, as did the queen, who had apparently elected to rearrange her hair and change her gown. The royal couple grinned at each other, as if sharing a private joke, before seating themselves and calling the meeting to order.

Gavan began by announcing that he had reached a decision regarding the proposals to seek aid from the west. "Lord Latharn," he said, addressing the older noble who had served his father, King Nicholas, before him. "We have decided to send you to Delgaria as our emissary. You came to know Duke Robelin personally when Delgaria and Calderia were allies in the war with Dunmoria. Perhaps that old friendship will be of help to us now in convincing him to join us. I will send a letter explaining our situation, which you will deliver to him by your own hand, and wait upon him for his reply."

"Yes, Sire." Latharn rose to his feet and bowed deeply in acceptance of the mission. "I will do my best to be persuasive."

"I trust you will," Gavan responded. "Now, as to the matter of Dunmoria. Despite my serious doubts about the prospects of effecting a truce with our deeply estranged cousins,

I am prepared to make an attempt to do so, given the gravity of our situation. Baron Glendannon has made mention of certain signs that a lessening of hostilities may be acceptable to some in their court, and has expressed an interest in pursuing that goal.

"To that end, I have decided to send the baron to Dunmoria as our personal representative to treat with King MacRae. Are you prepared to do so?" he asked, turning to the landowner.

"I am indeed, Sire," answered the baron, allowing a small smile to cross his face. "I, too, would know if these signs have any meaning."

"Very well, then," said Gavan. "Lord Gilmore will accompany you on your journey to Dunmoria. I believe his youth may offer some additional advantage in gauging the mood of the younger nobles," he added, amused as he watched the young lord's expression change from surprise to obvious excitement.

Gavan leaned over to whisper something to Rillandariel, who inclined his head to listen, his golden hair gleaming in the light from the torches lit to dispel the shadows in the darkening chamber. Then the handsome Elfin king turned his keen eyes on those gathered there.

"Let us hope that the emissaries traveling to the west will win the support we need. But, in the meantime, we must prepare to defend our lands with the resources we can count on now. We will entertain any thoughts or counsel about how this might best be done. Perhaps we might begin with your thoughts, Admiral Quillan," he suggested, looking at the senior naval officer, "since the enemy will come to us from the sea."

The admiral, a broad-shouldered, solidly built man with a dense, black beard trimmed close to his face and weathered skin darkened by a life spent upon the deck of his ship, stood to answer the Elfin monarch. "Your Majesty, the best time to strike against Rak`koth's forces would be while he is still at sea, where he would be most vulnerable. Had I a large enough fleet, I would counsel sailing to meet him long before he reaches our shores."

Quillan spread his large, sinewed hands. "Alas, Calderia has had little need for a strong navy, save to guard our merchant ships from the occasional pirates that lurk along the trade lanes. I have less than a half a score of fighting ships, far too few to engage the enemy's vast fleet in an open sea battle."

"Can you do nothing to halt their advance, Admiral?" asked Rillandariel.

Quillan rubbed his beard thoughtfully. "Well, Your Majesty, we do have one advantage, that of speed. I think it likely that our smaller, faster ships might be able to outmaneuver their larger, slower vessels and strike against those running on the edges of their fleet. That would be a way of whittling them down some and delaying them, if nothing else."

Rillandariel was thanking Quillan for his frank appraisal of the situation when he saw Mik`kel finishing a hushed conversation with the other two mages. The Kal`Dathian rose to speak.

"Your Majesty, I must point out that, in addition to Rak`koth's armies, there is the matter of his battle magic. It is certain that he will bring his own formidable sorcerous arts against us. He will also employ his Imperial wizards, and the Dul`Charian shamans with their fell blood magic. Together, they pose a grave danger to us, above and beyond his military might alone. We have not yet discussed that threat, but we must be prepared and plan for it."

"What hope is there that we can prevail against these evil magics, be they so powerful as you suspect?" asked Mellisandria, desiring candor, though uncertain if she truly cared to hear the answer.

"Wise One," replied the mage, with equal frankness, "Much depends on whether Killian and his companions can fulfill the task set for them by the gods. It may be that we cannot prevail against Rak`koth's Dark powers without the aid of the lost mage and his knowledge. But, if my unhappy years spent toiling in the Wizard's Academy in Kal`Dathia did naught else, they did instill in me the knowledge of potent battle spells— knowledge that I neither sought nor valued at the time, but which may come to serve some purpose after all."

Mik`kel then turned to address both kings. "With your Majesties' approval, my Calderian colleagues and I will send out the call for other mages and magic users who are strong in the paths of power to join with us, so that we may share our arcane knowledge and learn to stand together, even as human and Elfin warriors must surely do."

He paused for a moment, as if reluctant to continue. Then he straightened his shoulders, determined to commit all he had in support of the course set forth for him by the gods.

"There is one more magical art that I can offer, though I confess that I am loathe to employ it for destructive purposes. In addition to the battle spells I was trained to wield as a Kal'Dathian wizard, there were other skills I learned on the Isle of Serenity—skills only ever intended for peaceful uses by the gentle brethren of the Isle, but which may be adapted to our needs in time of war."

Seeing that he had everyone's attention, he resumed. "I speak of Unity magic, a method by which small groups of mages could be taught to work in concert, to combine their powers, thereby increasing the strength of both offensive and defensive spells beyond those cast by individuals alone. Such magic may take a greater toll against Rak'koth's forces than he foresees, beginning with his fleet, ere he makes landfall."

Gavan and Rillandariel hardly needed to glance at each other to confirm their mutual agreement with the mage's request. "Let it be done, good mage," responded Gavan decisively. "I can scarce believe that we omitted our magic users from the estimates of our strengths. We will offer what support we can, under Royal Writ, if need be."

"Thank you, Your Majesties," Mik'kel replied, as the other mages present began to debate in earnest whispers concerning whom they might first seek out.

"Now, let us turn to the question of where this enemy invasion is most likely to occur," said Gavan, glancing at the two Generals present.

Trillafarien looked at Brurik, then rose to speak first. "The coastline that borders the eastern side of the Great Forest is lined with cliffs, rocky overhangs or boulder-strewn shores that would offer a most inhospitable terrain for landing a large army. So, too, would the dense Forest itself, through which they would need to pass afterwards—and through which they must labor mightily to move great numbers of men, animals and equipment, while falling prey to a hail of war arrows launched by hidden bowmen all about them. Were I the enemy commanders, I would look elsewhere to land."

Brurik bowed to his Elfin counterpart, then gestured once more to the large map. "Here is the coast of Calderia," he began, tracing his finger down along the jagged line on the eastern side of the continent. "Like our neighbors to the south, much of Calderia's shoreline is bounded by high cliffs or rocky crags, and so affords us a natural defense against invasion. Indeed, there are but two places where such a massive landing could be done successfully. One is here, in the harbor of our main port, Breckon Bay, as I mentioned earlier. The other is here at Devon-Baire, some miles up the coast to the north. Now, were we to position a means of early warning in both likely locations..."

Chapter 38

Armada

Jek'kar, the Golden Prince, stood on the seaward balcony of the Mertanian Palace, gazing out over a sight that swelled his heart with pride and quickened his pulse with excitement. Before him lay scores of ships of his father's Imperial Fleet anchored in the harbor, sleek and tall and smartly trimmed, smelling of fresh paint and varnish. These mighty vessels rolled gently on the incoming tide, awaiting only the arrival of a few more ships before setting sail across the Luminous Sea for the distant shores of Balleterria to fulfill his father's destiny of conquest and rule.

Though he always strove to maintain a calm, mature demeanor in front of others, especially his father, Jek'kar had nearly lost all restraint and danced with elation when Rak'koth announced that he would be one of three sons sailing with the fleet when it left port. Bek'tol and Rek'kah would be going as well, while his other four brothers would remain behind to continue their apprenticeships with the trusted leaders who would be governing the vassal states of Surrikand in the emperor's absence.

But *he* would not be left behind, mired down in the day-to-day affairs of these conquered provinces. He would be standing on the deck of his father's Imperial flagship, feeling the brisk sea breezes whipping through his coppery gold hair as the powerful, newly-built vessel sliced through the ocean swells, taking him to new lands and great adventures.

His only regret about his departure was the thought of leaving his mother, Saleria, behind. He alone of all his brothers had known his true mother. She was soft, gentle and loving, so unlike most of the other women his father kept around the palace.

Though she was often ill, and always easily tired, she had somehow found the time and strength to visit him over the years. She was generous with her affection, and would speak to him of her youth, of her memories and dreams—dreams from another time he did not recognize, but which he knew she held dear all the same.

From time to time, they would walk together in the palace garden or meet briefly to share a cup of tea and some honeyed scones that she had baked for him in her tiny room behind the seamstress' shop where she worked. When she was able to work, that is, for her weakened condition sometimes kept her abed for days on end.

His father never spoke of her or even asked about her, though Jek`kar was sure that his sire was aware of his mother's periodic contacts with him when she came to the palace. He was less certain that his father knew of his occasional visits to her humble home on days when he had business outside the palace walls, and could make his way there discreetly. She was always pleased to see him, and never missed a chance to greet him with a kiss or to bid him farewell with a hug and a prayer for Shalloth's grace upon him.

Though he accepted her blessings in silence, it made him somewhat uncomfortable to hear her speak of the "old gods." After all, he had been taught for all of his short life that men like his father were born to reign and shape their own destiny, with no help or interference from some "eunuch gods"—as his father described the old deities—who wished to keep men as weak and powerless as they.

His mother had never spoken against his father or his actions directly, saying only that his father was a man possessed by the desire for power and glory who would "reap the harvest of his deeds someday, for better or ill." But, on the day that he went to tell her his exciting news of being chosen to sail with the emperor, she had done something quite unusual. Her face filled with concern and sadness, she had criticized his father's decision to invade Balleterria.

"My son," she began, holding to his arm for support as she lowered herself down carefully into the chair placed next to the only window in her one-room dwelling. "You were just a small child when your father conquered all the nations of Surrikand, too young to remember what it was like before he became emperor and took away their right to control their own lands and make their own choices. You know only one way, your father's way."

She leaned toward him and took his hand in hers, speaking more earnestly than he could ever recall. "You have never known what it is like to live among people who still enjoy their freedom, who cling tightly to their dreams and their faith in their gods."

Saleria's voice took on a tone of old regret. "I confess that it was our lack of faith in the gods that drove the old king to seek help from other powers, ancient powers we did not understand—and which, once Awakened, birthed the terrible empire under whose iron yoke we labor even now."

When Jek'kar opened his mouth to protest this treasonous description of his sire, his mother hushed him with a look and a gesture. "I have never said a word against your father in your presence because...well, because he *is* your father, and I know you love him. I only speak now because I love you, too, and because I fear greatly for your life if you do this thing."

Her voice grew firmer. "I must warn you that the peoples in these foreign lands across the Luminous Sea will not willingly surrender and meekly submit to Imperial domination. They will fight for their freedom, with the help of their gods...and I believe that they will have the power of right on their side."

For some time after bidding her farewell and leaving her tiny home that day, Jek'kar had been troubled by his mother's words. Raised to know no other truth but that the strong were made to take dominion over the weak, and to fulfill the vision of a world united under a powerful leader, he could not understand why she would say such things, things for which others had been put to death after merely uttering such thoughts aloud.

In truth, he could not fathom why any people or nation would resist the magnanimous offer of the emperor's protection and leadership. His father granted all that and more, in return for surrendering some false sense of pride and the mistaken desire to govern themselves without the benefit of his power and wisdom.

No, they were like children, needing a firm hand—perhaps, at times, even a brutal hand—to remind them of the need to trust in his father's vision and join in the grand destiny that he offered them. Surely, his mother could see that, could she not? This question was still nagging at the back of his mind when a deep male voice spoke behind him, almost in his ear.

"Pleasing news, my son," said the emperor, coming to stand beside him and share his view of the fleet below. "The last ships under construction will be here shortly. Master Shipwright Suk'kar has done his work well. It seems he only needed the right incentive, after all," Rak'koth chuckled.

"Yes, Father," replied Jek'kar obediently. He knew the "incentive" of which his sire spoke, for he had heard the tale of the shipwright's wife and daughter whom his father was keeping as his "guests." Though he might have wished such a stern measure had not been necessary, he thought it foolish of the shipwright to fail his emperor on a matter of such great importance.

Had the man worked as quickly in the beginning as he had in recent days, his family need not have become involved at all. Nor would the men whose corpses hung rotting on the crosses erected in the harbor have been crucified in this grim fashion, had the shipwright not allowed his crews to slack off.

But Jek`kar was too excited by his sire's words to dwell on the matter for long. "We leave soon then, Father?" he asked hopefully, his mother's odd warning buried beneath the exciting images of adventure streaming through his mind.

Rak`koth nodded approvingly, seeing his son's impatience to begin the conquest. "I believe you may be nearly as eager as I to set sail. Rest assured that it will not be long now. In truth, it will take some days after the last ships are delivered before we can transfer all of our forces, animals and supplies onto the vessels and be ready to depart. But, even as we speak, the men from my Black Legion and the armies of our vassal states are approaching. They will set up camps here in the surrounding hills, awaiting the orders to board when all is ready."

He smiled wryly. "As for my Dread Riders...It is better to keep them separated from the other men because they make them nervous. They will be arriving just before our departure, and will have their own ships, along with their shamans. But you and your brothers will be aboard my flagship with me. Does that please you, my son?"

"Yes, Father," Jek`kar replied, grinning broadly.

"Good. I will be meeting with you and your brothers soon to discuss the roles that you will play in the coming campaign. I expect you all to perform as sons of the Emperor and to make me proud."

For a moment, his eyes burned more intensely and his voice took on a warning tone that made Jek`kar shiver. Then he relaxed and smiled, clapping his son on the back with what, for Rak`koth, passed for fatherly affection.

"In the meantime, take some time to look around the port and familiarize yourself further with our fleet. Sample the local wine and women, and enjoy yourself." And with that, he turned and strode away, leaving Jek`kar to gaze out over the ships once again, his thoughts already leaping forward to the time when the order to weigh anchor would at last be given.

†††††

Later that day, Rak`koth returned to his chambers in the Mertanian Palace after meeting with the harbor master to ensure that he had a full understanding of the number of men and animals to be accommodated on the ships, and the type of equipment and supplies to be loaded aboard the barges when all the vessels had arrived. The harbor master, all too aware of the sad fate of his old friend, Suk`kar, had offered earnest assurances that he would spare no effort in seeing that the emperor's demands would be met on time, and in precisely the manner he desired. No doubt, the bodies hanging in his harbor served as an equally compelling reason to keep Rak`koth satisfied with his work.

The emperor glanced at the Mertanian pleasure slaves awaiting him in his bedchamber. For the past few days, he had been fully occupied with overseeing the many preparations for the coming launch of the fleet. Now that he had assured himself that matters were well in hand, he could give some thought to other, more pleasurable, pursuits.

Perhaps it was time to send for Shilela and begin teaching her what it meant to serve and please an emperor, rather than that pathetic excuse for a husband whom she had chosen to protect by submitting herself—a man who had no inkling of how a woman like her really needed to be treated and used. He had seen her anguish and fear, but perhaps something else as well deep inside her, something waiting to be revealed that she had not yet admitted to herself.

He walked out onto the balcony and gazed down upon the ships in the harbor again. Everything was going according to plan since the problem with the wayward shipwright had been addressed. Even now, warriors levied from all the vassal states of Surrikand were converging on the port city, the greatest invading force ever gathered under the sun of Tiaran.

More than forty-five thousand men were coming at his command, led by his terrible Black Legion and his invincible Dread Riders. All of them would be committed to but one goal: to fulfill his destiny by invading and crushing the weak and foolish nations of Balleterria, thus bringing her peoples and her riches into his great empire, under his sole dominion.

He stood on the brink of a grand and historic conquest, with forces massed to do his bidding even mightier than the Dark armies he had gathered centuries ago when he had challenged the old gods and the "good" wizards like Shaldassamer, most puissant of his wretched ilk. Just the thought of his old enemy was enough to make him grip the windowsill so hard that the wooden frame cracked and shattered in his powerful fingers.

He looked down at the broken wood, then laughed and tossed the fragments to the floor. No need for the old rage now. He had Awakened to a time when the old gods were impotent, and those who had opposed him once had long since crumbled to dust. He alone had the power to bring the nations of Tiaran to their knees. He alone had the knowledge to bring order to their useless and chaotic lives. Now, in this new time, nothing would prevent him from seizing that which was rightfully his.

His crimson eyes flashing with exhilaration, Rak`koth spread his arms wide and called up but a small fraction of his power. He gathered the Dark magic to him, savoring it, seducing it, caressing it like a woman's flesh. Then he thrust his hands forward and, with a thunderous crack, hurled a lightning Bolt from his fingertips that arced across the open sky and crashed into a grove of elm trees half a mile away, ripping them up from the ground and scattering them like sticks in a hurricane, igniting flames that would burn until all was consumed. And *that*, he swore as he gazed with pleasant satisfaction upon the destruction he had wrought, would be the fate of any fool, peasant or king, who dared to oppose the Emperor of Surrikand!

End of Book One

Coming Soon

The Shining Stone: Book Two of The Avatar of Calderia Trilogy

If you would like to comment about the book, please contact me at:

www.facebook.com/AvatarOfCalderia

* 9 7 8 0 9 8 9 5 9 6 2 1 3 *